NOT EXACTLY STEALIN'

Not Exactly Stealin'

Copyright © 2010

Cover image copyright © Oyster Point Press

Paperback
ISBN-10: 0991042514
ISBN-13: 9780991042517
Ebook
ISBN-10: 0991042557

Typography by Torborg Davern

NOT EXACTLY STEALIN'

BRUCE SINCLAIR

OYSTER POINT PRESS

PREFACE

WHO REMEMBERS THE '90S? THE CLINTONS WERE IN THE WHITE HOUSE. The SUV was the new thing. Martha Stewart was a household name. Cell phones were clunky things a few people carried in cars.

More important to our story Charleston, South Carolina was still Charleston. Big patches of the city were shabby and ungentrified. The old families lived in the old houses and maintained the old rituals in their kingdom by the sea.

And there was and is an underbelly of the city of organized and disorganized crime that the visitors never see.

1

DALE RALSTON, SAT IN THE OFFICE OF A LOW-LEVEL FEDERAL PROSECUTOR named Dubiel. She wore jeans with a multi-colored silk jacket, t-shirt and linen shoes, a bright spot of color in a beige room.

Dubiel was pouring Dairy-dream into his coffee and stirring it with a little stick acting all phony polite as if he were genuinely concerned. He shot her a sly look, said, "I know this comes as a mighty big shock to you, Missus Ralston."

All the while he was running the videotape on a home movie screen showing her husband Collier nearly life-sized having sexual intercourse with a lobbyist to the South Carolina legislature. The film was right vivid with Collier often changing positions, which Dale assumed was to impress the woman who had to be forty years old if she was a day. Dark roots showing in the brass blond hair. An enthusiastic face that said she was a go-cup girl with season tickets to see the Gamecocks play and party hard into the night afterwards.

The Fed Dubiel had styled hair and a broken nose. His blue blazer hooked behind a small gun on his hip, which was weird for a prosecutor, like maybe he thought his life was in danger, or maybe just liked to swank about armed. She noted his cowboy boots and thought yeah, it's a hayseed tough guy act. Twangy mountain accent said way upstate. Oconee County maybe.

He worked out of the state capital in Columbia but was down in Charleston for this special event of shocking the hell out of Dale. He had been acting real pleased with himself ever since she came through the door and got situated in front of the movie screen to see her state legislator husband get busted for bribery on film. When she had refused coffee, he'd made a big show of leaving the room to get some himself to stall around and heighten the tension before he ran the feature film.

"This? Why should it shock me?" said Dale. She waved at the screen with a nice hand. She had always had nice hands. "Men tend to move around a lot when they're trying to impress a girl."

Dubiel gave her his aw-shucks grin. "Now I know we're all modern and big grownup boys and girls and all that. But I mean that there's your husband up there on the X-rated screen. See? Nice close up, huh? Whups, there he goes again. Full face. Bigger'n all get-out."

Dale was thinking she'd like to take two aspirin with a cold Coca-cola and lie down. Or maybe have a stiff gin and tonic.

Dubiel said, "Well now I guess it ain't no secret that we got a whole mess'a legislators under indictment right now. They's all fambly men and church elders and such. And a lot of wives aren't even thinking through to the problem of paying for legal defense. They just decide in their own minds it's not him and kind of shut out the reality of the situation. Kind of a psychological effect thing. Denial or something. Trying to keep their lives from unraveling"

"Why should I want to deny it?" She listened to her own voice. A trace of the years she spent in New York still came through, although she had basically regained the southern accent of her childhood.

Dubiel didn't seem to catch that, having too good a time humiliating her. He turned up the audio. "OHHH Gaad!" went Collier's voice. "All this nookie and cash mun-ee too. This is better'n ordinary stealing."

4

"There," said Dubiel. "That's the best bit. Where he flat-out admits he's taking a bribe as well. Towards the end of the film you'll see him pick up the envelope of cash. Want me to fast-forward it?"

Dale twisted her mouth, disgusted. "Whatever."

He sped the film forward, Dale watching the two naked bodies flailing and jumping like a jerky old silent movie if they had had x-rated back then. They must have had the camera hidden in the room. Was the woman in on it? Was she that shameless?

Collier had never been much in the sack. Over anxious to please at first and then increasingly bored. Mostly he liked dewy-eyed admiration from the college girls he got to work for free on his campaigns or in the legislative office in Columbia. Calling them aides or interns. Pumping them full of how great it would look on their résumés. Dale checked her thoughts. Pumping them full. The sorry bastard would hump a snake if somebody would hold the head. Their honeymoon had been a dress rehearsal for infidelity.

She had been married to Collier for four years. At thirty-one, he was three years older than she, a legislator from the ritzy downtown district of Charleston with a pretend law practice on the side that was really run by his bitch sister.

When Dale left New York to come south and marry him, she had studied the other legislative wives to see if there was a special "look" she had to imitate. She found a lot of unnatural blond hair tortured into space helmets. Avon eye makeup. Heavy perfume. Rejecting that, she had decided to keep her dark hair long for a few more years and dress like she had been doing in New York. Now that she was twenty-eight, she had started to wonder if maybe it was time to cut it but still look a bit wild, maybe curl it like Marisa Berenson. She had those kind of slim, dark good looks.

In the video, Collier was sitting on the edge of the bed counting hundred dollar bills in an envelope. His calves had been losing their hair for some time now. He said his trousers rubbed it off and worried about it a lot.

"Two thousand dollars," commented Dubiel. "He done sold himself down the river for two G's."

The dyed blond woman got up and sashayed across the motel room, buck-naked, pear-butt waggling. Some cellulite dimples in those hips. She undid the chain and opened the door.

Dale thought, there it is. Yeah, she was in on it. Maybe they had something on her.

Brief moment of Collier startled at her action, holding the cash fanned out like a poker hand he was holding close to his chest. Then the look of sheer, disfigured horror at the FBI standing in the door like Easter Island stone faces. Holding out flip-open wallets with badges, the agents informed him he was under arrest in voices out of the old Dragnet. They must teach them those baritones at FBI school.

Dubiel froze the action with Collier holding the cash over his privates. The audio stopped with Collier jabbering about there being some kind of a mistake.

"Yes, indeed some kinda mistake all right. Ol' Collier just got up on the wrong side of the bed." Dubiel couldn't help but laugh at his own humor.

The image of her husband, slightly blurred with the stop-action, just hung there on the screen like free-floating anxiety. He looked like he was having a mix of a hangover, mild stroke and a collapsed lung. Dale was supposed to fall apart and cry now. Let Dubiel hand her a Kleenex and ask if she could go on or wanted to take a break. Could he get her a Diet Pepsi or something?

Instead, Dale looked at her watch. "So just what do you expect out of me?"

Dubiel walked to the window and looked out the blinds of the new annex on the Federal courthouse. It had been built over loud objections from the preservation crowd because it chopped up a little park with a bronze egret fountain spewing water. He was taking his time, wondering why she wasn't blubbering. Figuring she was a hard-ass Yankee broad, slow to break, but she'd get there soon.

Wrong on both counts. Dale was from South Carolina but midstate, a little suburb of the capital called Irmo. Same town as Donna Rice who annihilated the presidential career of Gary Hart. That, and she wasn't likely to break down. She had known her idiot husband would be in the net the day the first arrests in Operation Chump Change hit the newspapers. Some of his asshole buddies were in the first bunch. Waylon and Skeeter and Marvin gaping at the cameras, doing the perp walk. Since then, there had been fifteen more indictments spread out, three a week, to maintain the statewide suspense.

She couldn't figure how Collier had been arrested but not made the news. She guessed the feds had their ways. Maybe this was his week and she'd see it on TV tonight.

"Now Miz Ralston, you got to unnerstand that we may be in the employ of the federal government, but we're from this state—all of us got roots here—and we got its best interests at heart. These organized dog track gambling interests are hell-bent on corrupting the ordinary folks of this state and could do it just as easily as they done bent our finest public servants."

Dale rolled her eyes. God, she hated his voice.

"Looking after the best interest of the state as he is, the U.S. Attorney figures we need some quick and quiet guilty pleas. Some light sentences, and we get this whole thing put behind us so the governor can go forward with his agendas."

After he's milked it for maximum media potential, thought Dale. And after he's terrorized the legislature—all of whom are on the take in some shape or form—into playing ball with him. Which really means giving him a second term to do nothing, but plan a run for the U.S. Senate.

"So what's the problem?" she said.

"Well it's just that some of these ol' boys been putting up a defense. Crying entrapment and all that."

"Asking for jury trials?" Dale smiled. Her husband didn't really practice law, and Dale knew little about trials, except that it was awfully hard to get unanimous verdicts and a lot of ordinary folks were in favor of being corrupted by dog track gambling.

Dubiel probed at a back molar with his tongue, then gave his grin. "At least until they get a look at the videos. Then they become right docile and play along. Point the finger at their best pals and help us spread the net wider and get this over with once and for always."

"Is Collier going to do that?"

"Collier is . . . Collier is right confused at the moment. That's a natural reaction, of course, so much is happening now in his life. So many choices for the future."

"What you mean is he'll get his savage sister Rannie to defend him. And she'll find about fifteen evidence violations and not really be warmed up."

Dubiel drank coffee, sucked his front teeth and looked a little more fortified. "Let's just say we want a clean sweep. And Collier is currently standing in the way of that objective. So why don't you just set down with the boy and have a good old heart-to-heart with him. Apply the voice of sweet reason. Tell him to not cost the government a pile of money in these tight budget times in having to convict him. That way nobody but you and me need ever see that video. Say now, you want a copy of it? Like for your home entertainment center or something?" He gave her a slow, leering smile.

"My divorce lawyer might be interested in it," Dale said off-hand.

That agitated him. She was off the rails and he had to get her back on. "Well, now, now I know how you must feel. Believe you me. The shock of it and ever'thang. But there ain't no reason to rush to divorce. Men will get up to tricks now and again. It's time to stand by him in his hour of need."

"I don't think you understand," she said in a level voice. "My odious husband's been fucking other women since the first year of our marriage. I've known about it for the past two years. We separated a month ago. We don't talk anymore except with our teeth clenched. He can get a slap on the wrist or life-plus-ninety-nine in the Black Hole of Calcutta. I'm indifferent."

Dubiel did a confused routine. "Say what now? You cain't wish that on him. You're the power couple of Charleston."

She stood up. At six feet in height plus two inches of heels, she towered over the man.

"What are you doing?" he said.

"You showed me a movie. Now I'm going to beat the crowds to the exit."

She went out leaving the bewildered image of her husband on the screen.

Shit, she thought. There goes the alimony.

2

"YOU KNOW I FELT I WAS LIKE MAYBE A MARSH HEN SITTING ON A NEST OF eggs or something," said Lenny in his drug burnout voice.

Rannie, which was short for Randolph Ralston, sat in the smelly little interrogation room with her client Lenny "the meltdown" Womble. He was locked up busted in the Charleston County jail for an ungodly amount of cocaine. Drove his Camaro straight into the marsh, jacked-up on dope. The cops fished him out and, along with his private arsenal of automatic weapons including a goddam TEC-9, they found enough coke in the trunk to fill a cement bag.

Lenny looked around the dingy walls covered in graffiti. "I guess I could have checked my identification. Seen I wasn't a marsh hen. But there was a lot of water in the car."

He was wearing the prison costume. Shower shoes. Orange jumpsuit with his skinny wrists and ankles sticking out. He was twenty-five, maybe twenty-six years old with a straw pile of hair and the eyes of an ancient zombie. He actually had a coke hole burned through his nose like you hear about but never see. Air would sometimes make a faint, almost musical note through it. He'd touch it with his finger like he was playing a tin whistle.

Rannie said, "Lenny, you're in big trouble. Now straighten up and focus."

"There's an auto shop up on Remount Road. They put the rear spoilers on my Camaro up there. They know who I am. They'll verify I'm not a marsh hen." He touched the hole in his nose.

Rannie rolled her eyes disgusted. "Lenny, we can talk now or I'll come back when the drugs are out of your system. It's a straight up-or-down choice. But in whatever part of your brain is still functioning, I want you to register this. The Solicitor is going to give you thirty years for the coke."

"What? The cops think my car wreck is drug-related?"

"Yes. The contents of the trunk. It gave them that distinct impression."

He acted amazed. "I'm starting to feel abandoned . . . maybe even abused by the system. Isn't it here to protect me?"

Rannie lowered her voice. "Lenny, where have you got your money buried?"

Despite his appearance, Lenny was Charleston society's dope dealer—the recreational drug connection for doctors, lawyers, and other professionals. He had made a pile of money over the years. A lot had gone through his hands, but a lot had been stashed. Lenny didn't have the brains to use offshore banking facilities. He was a bury-it-in-plastic-pipes type of guy. He nodded lazily with his mouth open. "Ohhh, yeaaah. Riiiight. Mister Spainhour is wanting his cut."

Spainhour was Lenny's wholesaler, a local Dixie Mafia hood.

The jailer outside the door rapped on the metal and asked was Rannie about ready to leave. She snapped at him she'd tell him when she was damn good and ready. And in the meantime get way back from the door. She wasn't in any danger.

Rannie said to Lenny, "The money. Where is it?"

"They took my wallet when I came in here."

It took Rannie half an hour to worm it out of him, but he finally told her. His loot was buried under an azalea bush at his house on Kiawah Island.

Shit, Rannie thought. The cops had already seized his property down there. Probably had a picnic, parade, and fireworks to celebrate. Rannie stood up to leave. She told Lenny to toss beanbags, learn the Macarena, whatever was allowed in this colorful educational setting.

Lenny said he knew Mister Spainhour was worried about him. "Tell him I'm devoting my life to God while I'm in here. It's turned me around completely."

As Rannie walked past some trusties mopping the floor. The prisoners hooted, whistled, and yelled "ooo-bebby come get down on this thang." With her flame red hair and lush body, she was more tits and ass than they had seen for days. It didn't bother her a bit.

Rannie was thirty-two years old and had nine years of civil and criminal practice under her belt. Most people thought she was the meanest lawyer in Charleston, and it was a pretty fair assessment. She had inherited her daddy's practice and built on his knowledge and reputation in a fearsome way. Her brother was in practice with her, but he spent most of his time in Columbia as a legislator in charge of chasing page girls.

Back at the entrance desk, Rannie flipped her clip-on prison I.D. back to the clerk. He said don't be a stranger. Just drop by any time the notion strikes you. She said she'd be back at least once a week to this wonderful child development center. And next time warn her when they had served pinto beans for lunch.

Calvin Whitesides the beer gut slob bail bondsman who ran accident cases for her was waiting right there at the desk. Chain smoking and watching the TV with the sound off. Wearing jeans, tennis shoes, and a high-school letter jacket in the summer heat. Stinking like a pig.

"Y'all took a dam' sight long enough," he muttered. "You having a conjugal visit or something?"

"It was a real *pas de deux,*" said Rannie. "But tell me something. Serious question. You ever consider breath mints?"

He blinked at her, lost somewhere between the French ballet step and the insult. Got angry. "You know . . . you're . . . you're pretty commonplace. You know that?"

"I got what we came for. Okay? We can go do a summer clearance on Lenny's assets."

The news didn't brighten Calvin's mood. He was still pissed at the insult. "Well, I want a cut. I've had enough of being jerked around by you, little Miss Rambo."

Rannie gave him a sour look. "Sure, you figure, she's a girl. Take advantage of her. I'm quick with a hug. Soft touch when it comes to helping out vagrants. Always ready with guidance for the misguided. But getting pushy with me is strictly taboo. Got it?" She jabbed his chest with a long nail, and he jerked back.

It was only by chance that Rannie glanced at the TV behind the reception desk. On the screen her brother, Collier Ralston, the state legislator was being taken out of a motel room in handcuffs.

Rannie was furious. "What has that idiot done now?"

3

RANNIE RALSTON FOUGHT HER FEROCIOUS TEMPER AND DROVE HER
Cadillac Seville at a conservative speed to avoid attracting attention
on Kiawah Island. The tightly patrolled private resort had homes that
hit the multi-million dollar range all sited artistically around a series
of golf courses and ponds where real wildlife made occasional guest
appearances. You got to it by driving over the Stono River, then twenty
miles south of Charleston past tomato farms and finally over a long
causeway through the marshes. The car dashboard clock said midnight. Few lights were on in the houses.

Bail bondsman Calvin Whitesides who brought her clients – "ran
her cases" in the vernacular – sat beside her smoking, smelling like he
hadn't changed his underwear in months. Per usual, he wore a high
school letter jacket, this time over a Grateful Dead t-shirt. In this heat,
no wonder he stank.

Rannie was in her work clothes, seersucker suit, navy blue spectator
pumps. She had had a long day and now she had to spend her night
coming down to Kiawah with a shovel in the trunk and Calvin riding
shotgun. She let loose with a raft of complaints.

"Got to drive twenty miles out of town in the dark to dig up a fee
from Lenny. Says his liquid assets are buried a yard due south of an
azalea bush. Like Lenny knows which direction south is. Or an azalea

from his adenoids."

"Lighten up," said Calvin. "Lenny's got half a million bucks buried down here in a hefty bag. And he's so fucked-up he won't even remember telling you about it."

"Low grade moron," said Rannie, pushing her thick red hair back off her neck. "Wondering if he's a marsh hen. Don't use my ashtray. Throw it out of the goddam car."

"Don't bust a gut," Calvin pouted, flipping his cigarette butt out the window. It shattered into little sparks on the asphalt behind them as they cruised real slow looking for mailboxes.

"Don't light another one."

"Okay okay."

Rannie was double-pissed. Her stupid-ass brother getting caught with a whore lobbyist who set him up for the FBI. Their Daddy had always said Collier was a complete no-brain and couldn't cut it as a lawyer. That's why he had turned the firm over to Rannie. Or really she had just taken it over. Collier would go limp on every case that came in. Wanted to run off to Columbia and play grab-ass with the little page girls and interns.

It was important that Rannie get this half million if it really was a half million. Lenny couldn't count beyond nineteen. She needed the money because she was the sole support of the Ralston family now, the only one who actually worked. Mother living in the plantation culture past. Vacuous sister Moira daydreaming and feeling colors with her fingertips or whatever it is she did all day. Wimp of a brother headed for prison and his leech of a fashion model wife sitting on her duff being exquisite.

They found Lenny's weekend house in an area labeled Seabird Cottages. Rustic wood up on stilts. Pelicans and gulls and terns painted on the mailboxes. View of the golf course but cunningly separated by a clump of palmetto jungle from the really serious mansions.

Rannie pulled into the drive and turned off the engine. Sat listening to the night. Surf boomed in the distance. The Cadillac looked appropriate for the neighborhood. Calvin the mouth-breather had expected to drive down here in his rusted-out 1969 red Barracuda. That would have gotten security force cops on them like flies on shit. Can we he'p you folks with something? How's about getting out of the car while we check with the owner of this here propity about your identity? Nah, Rannie needed to be on-hand for this. That and she didn't trust Calvin with spare change, let alone half a mil.

They got out and stepped over yellow tape that marked the house as being closed by the narcs. Feds got all hyped up about seizing dope property. Porsches and forty-foot boats and luxury houses all up and down the sea islands. Couldn't wait to auction off this one. Calvin found the spot a yard from the shrubbery and the shovel chuffed in. The soil was sandy, thank God. Bermuda grass.

"What is there about these dope dealer imbeciles," said Rannie, "that they feel compelled to buy resort real estate? Walk into a closing with a suitcase full of cash. It's like hanging out a big sign that says 'arrest me.'"

Cops had kept Lenny under surveillance ever since he'd bought this house. When he cruised straight into the marsh thinking it was the "Stairway to Heaven" it was a narc's dream come true.

"Have you ever considered keeping your voice down?" said Calvin.

He was right, but Rannie didn't like being corrected. Fat sack of guano. He was always giving her little sly jibes. Trying to inch his fees up. Saying he wondered what the cops would think about the work he did for her if they just happened to hear a rumor about it. Maybe they'd come around and ask him questions straight on where he'd have trouble not telling the truth. He might have to cut the right deal with them, and she'd be disbarred, do jail time.

Rannie sucked in the salty sea breeze while Calvin dug, piling the dirt up in a little rampart. Houses all around to max out the use of the land. Camouflage them with elaborate landscaping.

"It won't be deep," said Calvin hopefully. He was gasping now with the effort, probably needing a cigarette. "Lenny's too lazy to dig it too far down."

"Bastard's more trouble than he's worth," said Rannie. "Thinking he's serving the carriage trade. Coke hole in his nose you could stick a pinky through."

"You sure got it rough," said Calvin. "Having to drive forty-five minutes and watch me dig a hole to score big money."

"Hurry it up will you?"

"You nervous about the patrols?"

"No, I want to get back to town and do some work on the house. I'm stripping the old wallpaper in the upstairs hall."

"Jezus. We're gone walk off with half a million in bills and you want to work on your house. Whyn't you hire somebuddy."

Rannie said, "It's a hobby. Reduces tension. You ought to take up a hobby."

Calvin gasping even more. "I got one. I drink to excess."

"Drinking's bad for you. Interrupts your normal sleep cycles. Makes you even more tense."

"I can handle it. Besides, I'm fixin' to be brain dead some day soon."

She said, "You're already there."

Calvin kept digging, trying to think up a comeback and at last gave up and just dug. He took off his letter jacket unleashing the stink of his sweat. Dug some more. He was down four and a half, five feet.

Rannie said, "Is that the plastic bag. Dig carefully. Use your hands or you'll tear it."

Calvin was getting real peevish. He said, "What am I? A re-tard? Anyhow, you get down and dig with your hands. You want your ten percent you just get down in the dirt and help."

"I can't. I'm a girl. It would ruin my nails." She paused a beat. "And what's this ten percent business?"

Calvin was down there now digging with his hands in the dirt. Scooping around the plastic. He said it was time they reversed their fees. The reason bondsmen got no respect—got treated like dog shit— was they didn't demand a big enough cut. Lawyers got rich off of cases run to them. Bondsmen doing the real work. Ten percent was plenty for her. Ten percent of half a million was a big bunch of bucks for pleading Lenny guilty. Lying to him. Telling him she'd got him a real deal. It was enough for Rannie and all he was going to give her.

Rannie was thinking fast. "So this is the big muscle play. I object, you go whining to the cops about how you're trying to run an honest business and I come along and corrupt you."

"Yeah, something like that," Calvin said. He kept scooping with his hands and flinging dirt. It was a huge hefty bag like you'd put leaf and lawn clippings in. He was tugging the bag out now.

She said, "It's not just this deal is it? You find it easy to push me around on this one, you jump your fees up on everything. Make it stick and I'm working for you."

"Sounds like a natural arrangement."

"And then I become like an insurance policy. You do something stupid, get busted, you cut a deal with the cops. Offer to roll over on me for leniency. I been working nine years for this lawyer gal. Running her cases for a percentage. That ain't legal is it? Wire me up and I'll do a deal with her so you can bust her ass good."

"You took the words right outten my mouth."

Rannie watched Calvin's big toad-like body hunched down in the dark. Spoke cautiously. "You've been knowing me for quite some time. Why do you think I'll cave in right here tonight?"

He was digging with his hands, scooping and throwing it. "'Cause if you give me shit, I got the gun."

"You're carrying a gun?"

"Right."

"And it's loaded?"

"Of course. We're going to walk out of here with a assload of money and I'd bring an unloaded gun? Mebbe say 'bang' and scare evahbuddy off?"

He was digging around the bag some more. Rannie's mind was racing. One of the last pieces of advice her daddy had given her was get into tax law. Stay out of criminal. You try to make a living in a sewer, you come up smelling like it.

Chunk. A little funny noise. Different from the digging.

"Dang," Calvin fumed.

"What's wrong?"

"Nothing."

Rannie had heard it. The fat slob had dropped his gun. He was feeling for it in the dark. It had been in the waist of his jeans the whole time. Then finally been squeezed out by his exertion. In the dark he couldn't see it.

She said to not move. She'd get it. Sat on the edge of the hole, reached down and put her hand right on it.

"Gimmie that," said Calvin, grabbing at her, taking hold of her shoulders and dragging the top of her body down into the hole. "Gimmie it. It's mine." He was pushing her down now, looming over her, taking a grip on her throat. Shit, he was trying to kill her. Both hands on her throat. Thumbs digging in. Her feet kicked violently in the air. The night was starting to go fuzzy.

Rannie didn't know if it was a single or double action so she cocked the hammer just to be sure. Jammed it against his chest. Pulled the trigger and the shot flared in the dark, driving Calvin back against the side of the hole.

Rannie scrambled up. Christ what a loud noise! Would anyone hear? She listened to the dark. Surf booming. Wind rustling the palmettos. No lights coming on in any of the houses. Lazy rental cops were probably asleep back at the guard post at the front gate. Do their rounds on the hour.

Calvin lay there twitching, making little gasping noises. Then he was quiet. Not breathing.

Rannie rubbed her throat. Strangulation left nasty marks. She knew this from viewing corpses. She'd have to wear a scarf for several days.

The bag was green. A double-thick Hefty bag as advertised on TV. Rannie dragged it across the grass to the car, heaved it up, and dumped it in the trunk. A half million was surprisingly heavy. Threw in the shovel. Fool Lenny didn't have brains enough to bury it in plastic pipe. Weather would have gotten to it in no time.

Leaving Calvin's body in the open hole, Rannie drove the causeway off the island past big patches of marsh and little creeks. Up an old road lined with live oaks and Spanish moss the way the whole of the Lowcountry had been before the population explosion and everything had turned to crud. It had been nice when she was a girl, her daddy bringing her down to Kiawah to sit shivering in a duck blind. Back then you had to go over by boat and there was nothing on the island but a palmetto jungle and the abandoned Vanderhorst plantation house. She treasured those moments when she was Daddy's girl. No loud-mouthed drunk of a mother dominating things. No stuffed shirt brother. No manipulative little whiny sister. Moira was too scared of bugs and dirt to go hunting.

Rannie fought like a mad dog to hang onto her own small fragments of the old landscape. She was restoring a house on narrow little Rantowles Lane just off Legendre Street. She wanted to get back and work on it. Get that old wallpaper off and everything ready for the plasterers. That would be relaxing. Tire her out so she could sleep a few hours for once.

She stopped at a bridge that spanned the narrow Stono River. Looked at the gun. Smith & Wesson .38. Maybe a four-inch barrel. Calvin probably bought it in a pawnshop in North Charleston. She could toss the gun out of the car window and hear it splash as it sunk. On second thought she'd keep it. She might want to plant it on some asshole later on. She put the car in gear and drove on towards the pink glow of Charleston's lights above the magnolia trees of the county golf course.

4

"IF RANNIE RALSTON HADN'T SENT YOU, I'D THINK YOU WAS SOME KINDA asshole," drawled Bubba Spainhour. "Just wandering in here talking big dog. I mean why don't you go back out in the bar and bang some pots and pans together? Tell the whole unruly world you're in contention for the vice-presidency."

The word 'asshole' frequently got applied to Hunter "Hootch" Gibson, but he never took notice. He figured his boyish charm and good looks snowed everybody. He was over six feet with sandy hair, a solid build, and a distant resemblance to the movie star Brad Pitt, which he never denied when anyone pointed it out. Besides, he would come into the corpus of his trust fund when he was thirty-five, so he didn't have to give much of a big goddam. What made him decide it was time for a more adult lifestyle was when nobody around the KA house seemed to know him anymore. He was twenty-six years old and still trying to get his undergrad degree from the College of Charleston. His frat membership had been sacrificed for non-payment of dues four years earlier, and with a new draft of brothers *in situ,* he had become odd man out.

Hootch had his entries in the asset column. Old Charleston family with parents who had conveniently died young and left him money. Along with the trust fund and being handsome, he was a crack shot.

Over the years, he had won pistol and skeet shooting championships throughout the Southeast. This made him a man of note at deer hunts, birddog field trials, and other gentry type events.

Unfortunately, the cops had confiscated all his guns four months back during the involuntary commitment proceeding. He had been drinking a lot more heavily then, and peer pressure from Lenny Womble had led him to mixing dope with it. Things had gotten a bit out of hand which led to shooting out streetlights thus necessitating an unpleasant thirty-day observation at a county mental institution.

Since then, he was smoothed out on a maintenance level of alcohol. He'd start drinking around noon each day, go into the night. Besides, he wasn't as fucked up as his old buddy Lenny. Nobody could be that fucked up. No, next to Lenny, Hootch was playing at the top of his game.

Lenny and Hootch had been real rounders at the College of Charleston where they were fraternity brothers. Lenny lacked the advantages of a trust fund though, and when he flunked out, he was forced to find gainful employment. Which he did by expanding a minor marijuana distributorship into a connection with the local Dixie Mafia for cocaine, just as it got going as the drug of choice for the upscale. As a former frat boy, Lenny made downtown contacts and soon had a lock on the carriage trade.

What Hootch had decided to do was take over Lenny's book of business. Lenny was in jail, probably forever. He had a hole in his nose and no grip on reality. Fuck the nostalgic brotherhood of the past. Hootch figured if he stuck with juice like his parents' generation and kept the white dust out of his nose, he could have a limitless profit margin.

That's what he told William T. "Bubba" Spainhour and Randy

Travis in the back office of *Juleps*, a trendy restaurant and bar down in the old market. Bubba ran it as a laundry for his numbers, dope and other miscellaneous racketeering. As a result the drinks were big and the meal portions hefty, and that along with honey waitresses kept the place filled.

The back office was pine paneled with a big swordfish mounted on the wall and ashtrays from hotels in Houston and Dallas. Pretty tasteless, Hootch noted, but that's the Dixie Mafia for you. It might have been a den in a low-rent subdivision across the Ashley River on the south side of the Charleston peninsula.

Bubba smoked menthol cigarettes and wore silk body-tapered shirts with long pointed collars. No necktie. The sleeve cuffs turned back under to get them off his wrists. He looked like he belonged at a blackjack table in Las Vegas.

"You need somebody stable, Mister Spainhour," said Hootch confidently. He smiled that handsome smile and dangled his Ray-bans casually. "Somebody with social connections." He had had a couple belts of vodka at another bar, so he was feeling pretty smooth.

Bubba gave Randy Travis a look. Randy gave him one back. Randy was Bubba's chief muscle. He had a flattop hair cut with a ducktail in back like a hot-rodder from the 1950s. The two had grown up together "on the same dirt road."

"I thought you was just out of the loony bin," said Bubba.

Hootch flashed an aw-shucks boyish grin. "That was a misunderstanding. They apologized and everything. It's in litigation now. False imprisonment. My attorney—you know my cousin, Rannie Ralston—says I can expect a substantial settlement."

In fact, it was Rannie who had pushed Hootch to seek employment with Bubba. What with one expense and another, his trust fund income was all used up before the monthly check even arrived. Hootch was real behind on his legal bill, and she figured Bubba always needed a mule to carry dope. No-brainer kid to take the dive if something went wrong. Hootch, not being aware of this, saw himself in more of a management position.

Bubba said there was no rush on replacing Lenny. Most of his customers were right tense about him being in the can. They were professional people and more nervous about their business licenses than their recreational drug needs. Lenny was awful spacey there at the end prior to his incarceration, and there was widespread fear that he was rolling over on his clients.

"That sounds grim," said Hootch, seeing an opening.

"Alls it mean," said Bubba, "is Lenny's contribution to the business gone be slow 'til round the end of the physical year. We just need to stay focused and not look too far beyond the next game."

Hootch frowned, then raised an eyebrow sternly. It was his let's-talk-turkey look he practiced in the mirrors behind the bars where he drank. "You're being awful acquiescent about that prospect of Lenny running off at the mouth. We're talking a Beavis and Butt-head routine here. Incoherent and cognitively impaired on weed, coke, downers, you name it. Even with his limited recall, you don't know what names he's liable to spill out."

Bubba gave Randy the look again. "I got layers of protection."

Hootch was always impatient with a man of limited vision. Hootch was taking one course a semester, limping towards his degree in Business Administration. Typically he'd sign up for three and drop two of them before the halfway-point. This kept his trust fund money flowing and gave him an educated perspective on things that Bubba lacked. He was currently hanging with Entrepreneurship 415. They had just finished the new business start-up chapter. He told Bubba that he ought to diversify, get into a more sophisticated line of business. Bubba said, such as? Hootch hesitated, not wanting to just throw out his best ideas for anyone to take and run with.

Bubba looked at his watch impatiently.

Hootch twisted his mouth, then decided what the heck. "Stolen Civil War archives," he said. "Letters, maps, rare books. That kind of thing."

"Do tell," said Bubba. He was understandably skeptical.

"Sure," Hootch enthused. "I got a toehold in the business already. When I was a legislative aide one summer—you know, up in Columbia—I'd steal stuff for Collier Ralston." Hootch shot him the raised eyebrow again. "Collier Ralston the *state legislator.*"

"Ain't he the one just went down for bribery?"

Hootch laughed, checked himself in a big Budweiser mirror, flicked his hair. "The same."

"He don't seem too reliable as a buyer, gettin' picked off as easy as he did."

Hootch waved that objection away. "He's just one of a legion. Your fanatic collector is crazy as hell. Pay big bucks for a diary or a letter he can't even show his pals. Just sit there of an evening with a brandy and splash and enjoy the sucker. Maybe wear a rebel army uniform as he does it."

Bubba rubbed his jaw thoughtfully. "Don't get me wrong. I respect tradition. Keep the Confed'rit flag flying. Heritage not hate. All'a that. But I pretty much know where I stand with a dope addict. All these collector folks . . . well . . ."

"I provide that source," Hootch said confidently. "I know a hundred of them. Old man Huston down near Jacksonboro . . . well, I'm giving away trade secrets. But the College of Charleston library has a rare books room stuffed full of Civil War archives. No problem to loot the entire collection." He leaned forward, lowered his voice. "You see, they don't put tattle-tape into the stuff or a catalogue number on it because it would mess up its authenticity. Go in looking like a college kid. Everything's cool. Got a backpack and all. Once you're out the door with it, you're the owner. You act innocent, maybe a little teary-eyed. Say your granddad gave it to you on his deathbed."

Bubba sighed. "You had your daily medication yet?"

Hootch reared back, surprised that his charm wasn't working its magic. Bubba was such a dirt-bag. "It's a sure bet," he insisted. "And it's just one of my many creative brainstorm-type notions. Which is why you need me as Lenny's replacement."

"You just gonna walk in and steal it," mused Bubba.

Hootch argued, "It's not really stealing. Anybody who'd lay out bucks for a Beauregard letter – dear Maude, the weather's fine up here, lost half my army yesterday – shit, he deserves to get parted from his money."

"I was talking 'bout the liberry," said Bubba.

Hootch looked confused. "That don't count. Everybody steals from a library."

"Sure he's an asshole," Rannie said over the phone to Bubba Spainhour. "I can't pick my cousins."

Bubba had called to tell her he couldn't figure a place for Hootch Gibson on the roster. Talking around the fact he was a career criminal as he always did. He said being in the restaurant, laundromat, and video game business as he was, he always had pressure on him to win at the next level.

"You're not just trying to maintain," Rannie agreed.

"I need values. Some basic manners, not attitude."

"Deportment."

"I don't need to be getting in somebody's face to make a point."

"Low-key management," said Rannie.

"It's like a philosophical thing," Bubba complained. "You get no discipline from kids out of today's high school and broken family setting."

Rannie stifled a yawn. "Tough to keep your core values intact."

"The boy's built, I tell you that. Looks like he'd test positive for that steroid – what's it called? Stanzolol?"

"I think so. Yeah." Rannie thought, you ought to know. You sell truckloads of steroids to the high schools.

"Put him in a suit, maybe he could work for an escort service."

"It was just an idea," said Rannie. She thought, what is your problem? You don't need a patsy? A fall guy? Did she have to spell it out?

"Some of the stuff he was saying, well it ain't what you call a confidence booster."

"Like what?"

"He was talking about stealing Civil War stuff. Selling it to collectors. I'm figuring it's like, this cain't be real."

Rannie thought, Civil War. Then she thought of her brother Collier's extensive collection of books, diaries, and maps.

5

"YOU HAVE A SACRED DUTY TO STAND BY YOUR HUSBAND IN THIS TIME OF crisis," pronounced Mary Canty Ralston, not dramatically, but in a very matter-of-fact tone and very loud. She wore a five-carat diamond on her hand, four or five heavy gold bracelets on each arm.

She had the Charleston accent. Duty was doody.

"I'm not changing my plans," Dale replied firmly. She couldn't believe she had run into her mother-in-law grocery shopping. Collier had been indicted by the federal grand jury the day before. It was all over the morning paper.

They were pushing carts in the East Bay Harris Teeter in the five o'clock crush, Dale a good six inches taller than the old woman with the turkey gobbler neck and creases on her lips from smoking. The East Bay Teeter was a restoration project built into an old brick warehouse. All the downtown society people shopped there. They looked stylish and pampered.

Mary had so far selected a case of Miller and eight bottles of red wine. Her signature drink at the Yacht Club was a concoction of Irish Mist, *crème de menthe* and blended scotch. But she would drink anything. Collier's vapid sister Moira had been left in the bakery section indecisive between pumpernickel and rye. Moira lived with her mother. She had spent a year in college and then just come home. Probably couldn't find the classroom.

Mary either didn't hear what Dale said or didn't care. She just steamrollered on as she always did. Demanding this, ordering that, and condemning the other. She had been drinking since noon at the Yacht Club and was loud as usual.

"Divorce between you two is simply out of the question now. It would look like you were turning on him just because of this wretched sting thing or whatever they call it. People would strongly disapprove. I couldn't live with that kind of situation."

Dale was cool. "Do you know what Collier was doing when the FBI walked in on him?"

"Some kind of ghastly man stuff, I suppose. His father was just as bad. All men do it."

"Collier always knew a bandwagon when he saw one."

"I never took an interest in my late husband's romantic affairs, and I don't see why you should be so obsessed with Collier's. Far better to suffer in silence."

"Don't squabble or yelp? Help keep his bawdiness low key? Sure. It's the least I can do. A small way of apologizing for being a woman."

Mary Canty either didn't hear or else believed Dale was serious. She said almost grandly, "I simply won't be responsible for Collier's fol-de-rol. He was a millstone around my neck for years, and now he's yours. For keeps. I have passed on the torch to the new generation."

Dale wasn't really listening. She said to the wall of canned vegetables, "I'm going to have to get a job, I guess."

"That's certainly advisable. Someone's got to earn the money to pay Collier's defense fees. I certainly can't afford it."

Dale looked around. "Rannie's defending him. Why is it costing money?"

"Rannie has a living of her own to earn. Office and overhead and all that nonsense she insists on getting so wrapped up in. She can't just take time out from that to babysit Collier. She's got to bill for the hours. Otherwise things would simply become impossible."

What Mary Canty really meant was that her husband, old Collier Sr., had left her a humongous downtown house with thirteen-foot ceilings, a dining room that would seat fifty, and no other assets. Naturally, Mary couldn't imagine selling. It was one of those houses in Charleston that entitled the owner to social prominence. So now she lived off Rannie. And Mary wasn't about to disrupt that cash flow. Mary also couldn't imagine reducing her lifestyle. Rannie paid for the cook Yulonda, the maid Tamzie and two gardeners, not to mention the hefty bar tabs at the club.

Mary Canty's voice transmitted like a loudspeaker. "Poor Rannie. I truly feel sorry for the pathetic girl. Always wanting to be like her Daddy as though that might cause him to approve of her or something. Just had to become a lawyer when she could have married almost any boy in town. Married a lawyer if that was her obsession. Her career is an endless series of headaches for me. Just when I think she's got it basically under control, something ghastly happens. That wretched Calvin what's-his-name being murdered. Now she has no one to run her cases." Mary was nearly bellowing. Even in the Harris Teeter where people were used to her, a lot stopped and stared.

Dale knew little about the law, but she did know that you could get disbarred for paying people to bring you clients. Mary was beyond being a drunk. She was a drunken fool.

Mary Canty said, "He was shot dead in a hole in the ground. Found with buzzards flapping all over him. Just grisly. Honestly, the kind of people they allow on Kiawah you wouldn't believe. It's all that

31

public right of access to the beach nonsense I suppose."

They went down the next aisle, Dale getting dill pickles and Mary getting cocktail olives. Dale said she was going back to New York. Mary said she couldn't possibly return to fashion modeling. She was too old. Dale said she wasn't a model.

"Well whatever it was. Collier thought you were a model. That's why he went so crazy over you. Poor fool. He never could resist a pretty face. Just like his father."

"I was a stylist. I set up the backgrounds for the shoots. Got the props together. Found an exotic location. I guess I've only told you that twice a week for four years."

"You'll have to go to work for Skip Rightenberry. Get your real estate license and sell houses. All the distressed wives of ruined husbands do that. It's the only suitable thing for you. I'll call him myself."

Dale cringed at the image of Skip with his toupee and fat cigar. He staffed his office with ex-debutantes whose ex-husbands were in prison or barred from various lines of professional work or who had flushed their inheritances down a commode.

"Of course you'll be living in reduced circumstances, but what else can you expect? I've certainly had to make adjustments since the death of my late husband." Mary Canty never used her husband's name. He was always "my late husband" or "Mister Ralston." He had been one of the prominent old-time solo practitioner lawyers. Mary was, what sixty-two? Sixty-three? She had her debut in 1952 as she never tired of telling. Collier, Sr. had been much older. His youth was back during the Depression.

"The romance of poverty is greatly exaggerated," Dale said, but Mary didn't hear. Dale was inhumanly patient as she always was with her mother-in-law.

Mary Canty went to war with the meat counter, digging to the bottom of every stack as though there were some perfect chop hidden there. Pushing people aside. Raucously protesting the rise in prices. Flinging things around. The butcher retreated into the freezer locker to avoid responsibility for any riot she might create.

When Dale had moved to Charleston and married Collier in the big St. Michael's Episcopal church, she had thought the town deeply romantic. She was from midstate. Charleston held a mythic, otherworldly quality. The harbor and ocean. The antebellum chunk of town at the toe of the peninsula. And her time in New York built on that image. Charleston was the only southern town outside of Palm Beach that New Yorkers considered free of pellegra, hookworm, illiteracy, and murderous redneck lynch mobs.

She had quickly learned that the town was a mess of sprawling modern suburbs, military bases, and dirty industry that had created the worst air pollution on the east coast. That she could live with. She had survived the Big Apple after all. The real problem was the pocket of gentry who clung to their little South-of-Broad Street enclave socializing with one another purely because they had been born in a tiny geographic region of half a square mile. Dale was expected to fit in.

That meant tolerating the social snobbery and the obsession with genealogy tracing back to the seventeenth century, who was cousin to whom. Listening to tedious accounts of what family had lived here and there. Admiring the heirlooms that had no validity as objects outside of a chain of custody through the family for ten generations. This she could handle.

What grated on her was the lack of alliance with her husband. Not just the momma's boy aspect. Collier, the sensitive lad who had sought his mother's protection from a tyrant father, paid the price of utter obedience to his mother's whims. But the snooty chill that would descend on a room if Dale dared question any aspect of the historic past. Collier the history major who quoted whole chapters of Shelby Foote and had spent a year doing research on blockade-runners—Collier who collected Civil War artifacts – Collier, heart and soul, was *one of them*. And Dale was "from off" as they said.

Moira came drifting up like she was wading through the Milky Way collecting stardust in a string bag. Stark-raving-Moira as Dale called her in private. Dale thought of Moira—other than as deranged— as belonging somewhere prior to 1955. Or at least 1965. She was only twenty, but she seemed to live in some time warp up in the ozone. Bubble-flip hair-do. Big floppy hats on Sundays.

Dale had always been pretty certain that Mary had fucked around in her youth and the children were fathered by different men. While Rannie had flame red hair and all the aggression that is said to go with it, sister Moira was pale blond, vague and vapid. She would make little sighing noises when she entered a room or sat down or got up. She read historical romances and took her Charleston ancestry very seriously. She was a cream-filled pink candy in a Whitman's Sampler.

"I do hope they get it right," she said. She clasped her hands and gazed off somewhere above the fish counter like she was seeing the Assumption of the Virgin.

Dale knew what she was talking about. Moira had talked of nothing else for the past month. Another movie company was coming to town to do yet another Civil War drama. Ante-bellum romance was a popular theme for TV mini-series, and Hollywood had latched onto Charleston as a living set populated by rubes thrilled to perform as extras at non-union wages. And owners of historic homes who snatched at the dollars offered to rent them as film sets.

The mayor shamelessly pandered to the deals in a pipedream of making Charleston a kind of Hollywood-Southeast. Rumors said this one was another Civil War soap opera. Dale knew the company—Jazz-Bo Productions. The Traub brothers. American filmmakers with a fresh and distinctive voice, as they described themselves. In truth they were rip-off artists extraordinaire. They churned out schlock knock-offs of current hits for video release. Both of them afflicted with potty-mouth to the point of La Tourette's syndrome.

Dale had once clashed with them over the use of a mansion on the Long Island Gold Coast. The elder Traub had told her to get fucked, and followed with, "If you can't grasp that, the teaching aids are my cock up your ass." A real charmer that man. No chance of her renting her house to him for a movie set no matter what her destitution.

"No one is renting out her house this time," pronounced Mary Canty. "We know where this is leading, and we're determined to stop it."

Moira blinked at her.

Mary railed, "That filthy little mayor turning us into a tourist attraction! Now we're to be held prisoners by movie companies. It's got to stop."

Moira's hand flew to her mouth. She looked stricken.

Mary Canty fixated on an amethyst ring on Moira's hand. She said, "Dear, if you die before I do, I want that ring."

6

MOIRA THOUGHT IT WAS JUST TOO TACKY THE WAY HER SISTER-IN-LAW
Dale had eyeliner tattooed on her eyelids. The little things—they might
seem petty to some people—were clear indicators that she'd never fit
into the family. And now poor Collier forced into some legal imbroglio
because Dale just wasn't adequate for him. She had tried to warn him
at the time of the marriage. Dropping little hints. But to no avail. The
creature had bewitched him.

The salt smell of the harbor filled the air. High up in her sunlit
third story bedroom with walls of creamware white, Moira felt she was
floating above her peerless view of the sea. When she stood on the long
piazza, she could reach up to the robin's egg blue sky and spread her
arms and just drift weightlessly up into the white wispy clouds.

Early morning was her favorite time to write, and she was working
on her forgeries. Not that she called them that. They were an exercise
in the author's craft. She wasn't plagiarizing. Or stealing. Not exactly.
She just needed a little boost with the public to become known. All
those tiresome rejection letters from editors who clearly didn't read
beyond the first page or two. They were probably too busy going to
their analysts or whatever New Yorkers did.

She had two manuscripts very nearly completed. In one—*Southern
Gale*—a hero very much like Rhett Butler is a blockade-runner during

the Civil War. It dovetailed exactly with *Gone With the Wind* just as if Margaret Mitchell had intended it as a prequel. Or had written it before and then abandoned it. In the second—*South Blows the Wind*—two people very much like Rhett and Scarlett run guns to Maximilian's Mexico and then take all their money and buy a plantation in Cuba.

Both were written on paper from the 1930s. Moira had discovered it in a storeroom of her father's law office along with ink of that period as well. It would stand up to any laboratory test. She was going to plant one in her brother Collier's Civil War collection. The other she wasn't sure where. But when they were discovered, it would be such a big find. Experts proclaiming them authentic Margaret Mitchells. Press trumpeting the news. Then she would come forward and claim authorship. The world would learn that a new Margaret Mitchell had been born. All those girls at Sweet Briar who had been so mean to her would know they had made a big mistake.

The nice man in that rare book shop in New York had been very interested in Collier's collection when Moira called him. Said if she would send him an inventory, he would fly right down and have a look at it. She would have to put her mind to the task and complete her novel very quickly.

Using a fountain pen, she wrote, *"With the greatest of rejoicing, we passed under the protective guns of Fort Sumter and drew near to the church spires of the Holy City. Having once more eluded the blockading Union fleet, we were safe among friends and countrymen. The crew gave up a great 'huzzah,' and I indulged them in their enthusiasms. My thoughts were occupied with Bland McMurtry, the treacherous Irishman. I knew I would be forced to call him out and meet him at dawn when the tendrils of mist wove their way among the trees—meet him on an open field with 'pistols for two and breakfast afterwards for one'."*

Moira ran her fingers over the blue steel of the 1861 Colt navy revolver that lay on her desk. It was lighter than the Colt army, and for a woman, a viable step up in firepower from a derringer. A reproduction admittedly, it was nonetheless an exact replica. And a working model. Walnut grip. Seven and a half-inch octagonal barrel. Fixed brass bead front sight, rear V-notch hammer sight.

Her pistol was made before the invention of the fixed cartridge. You loaded it using the hinged loading lever under the barrel. Turn a chamber of the revolving cylinder into line. Pour in gunpowder from a brass flask. Ram it with the lever. Insert a lead ball. Ram that in. Then cap the nipple with a copper percussion cap. The revolver's hammer struck the cap, creating a spark to ignite the powder and fire the gun. It was a lengthy process and yet somehow strangely satisfying.

Scarlett O'Hara had used just such a weapon to kill the Yankee scavenger who was intent on looting Tara. Scarlett had done so many brave things, but that was the bravest. The scene, however, was strangely unsatisfactory—one of the few lapses in *Gone with the Wind,* a book otherwise perfect for its verisimilitude. When Scarlett kills the Yankee, she simply thrusts the pistol at his bearded face and pulls the trigger. That was it. No further description. Margaret Mitchell—however accurate her writing was on Southern life of that period—had simply no firsthand experience of killing a man. Nor did Moira. And this bothered her. She was conscious of her own future place in the literary pantheon and wanted her research to be precise in every detail.

She sealed the envelope with the list of Collier's collection and his address. She hadn't made a complete inventory, Collier had so much. But what she had listed she knew to be extremely valuable. Of course she didn't sign her name. She couldn't have anyone connecting her with this.

She'd get Tamzie to put it in the mail. If the manuscript dealer got it in a few days, took a few more to make his plane reservations, then she'd have ample time to finish writing her book. Except for the research on killing a man. And she had that pesky dueling scene to do for her climax.

Moira went out of her room and called down the stairs. "Tamzie!"

Honestly, where was that girl?

Working for the Ralstons, Tamzie would nod and say "uh-huh" to all the "dear Tamzie" shit. At least with Miss Moira you got errands to run, and that meant she could get out of the house. Walk the streets, stop in the shade and talk to the other black gals pushing the little white babies in strollers.

Tamzie Jerome was twenty-seven. In summer, she wore a gray uniform with white collar, in winter a black one. Her momma Mozelle had worked fifty-four years for various Ralstons and finally died. She always carried an umbrella in the sun. One day she forgot it and fell over with heat stroke right at the corner of Broad and Meeting. When Tamzie had come back from New York for her momma's funeral, Miz Ralston had come rushing up to her in the AME church. The woman said, "Thank God you've come. There's so much to be done. You may start tomorrow."

Nothing about sorry your momma died after working her hands to the bone all the years for me. Just get going with the upstairs carpets because the servant problem has gone all to hell. Tamzie was so floored she just said "uh-huh."

Tamzie had moved to New York on the occasion of her husband Debone Wigfall getting ten years for some kind of killing less than first degree murder. While she was there she got divorced and took her maiden name back. She'd been in housekeeping at the Beverley Hotel on the East Side, so the work wasn't much different. Plus she had practically grown up in the Ralston house on Legendre Street and knew the routine: work like a dog and get next to nothing in return. Sometimes along with pay, they'd give her stuff that was cast-off, wore-out, or half-eaten. Like that parrot with no feathers name of Rosco that was the only pet Tamzie ever had growing up.

Tamzie took Moira's letter up to the Broad Street post office and got in a long line. In front of her an ancient white man fumed and fidgeted, kept turning around to look at the people behind him.

"I wonder how many other clerks they got in the back doing nothing," he snorted.

Tamzie didn't make eye contact. Even down south, folks were getting New York crazy.

"Playing pinochle!" he said even louder.

By the time she got to the window, Tamzie was so tense that she didn't pay much attention when the clerk had her sign for a special delivery letter. Normally she was alert to zip codes that signaled jury duty or over-due bills looking for her.

She was halfway back to Legendre Street before she realized the letter was from the IRS and addressed to her. She read it real slowly several times. The Atlanta branch of the U.S. Treasury was telling her she hadn't filed income tax six years before. This caused her to detour west up to her little frame house on Cannon Street and search through all her papers. Finally she found a copy of the 1040 form that H&R Block had filled out for her. She knew why she had erased the memory of the ugly thing. That was the year she had had to mail the government a check for $800.

Tamzie spent the day scrubbing bathrooms and thinking about

the problem. At lunchtime she sat eating a chicken salad sandwich and looking through the newspaper. Bail at $50,000 was set for some dude for strong-arm robbery on Nassau Street. This made Tamzie think of her ex-husband Debone up at Central Correctional Institute.

She phoned Debone up and had to wait forever before they got him out of a cell. It didn't particularly matter because the red bitch Rannie used the phone a lot for calling various prisons on behalf of clients, so old Miz Ralston never looked at the bills. Rannie paid them anyhow.

When Tamzie explained the problem to Debone, he said, "Woman, the sum total of your talents is a fine ass and tits. That's all. You don't remember whether you sent that money in or not."

"You took the money, didn't you, Debone," she said.

"I might have. I had a lot of expenses at the time. Jew lawyers don't come cheap. Even the ones what get you ten years in the slam."

Debone not being much help, Tamzie called a toll-free number in Atlanta, which was on the IRS letter as a place to refer questions. She had to punch in numbers depending on what she wanted to talk about, then listen to music while a voice kept butting in saying they was all busy serving the taxpayers and would get to her soon.

Finally this man come on to say he was Chet Rinser and how could he help her. She said she knew she had mailed the money in. She had paid every year before and since. Why would she short the government that year? He said she should put her social security number and the taxable year on the check.

She explained, "That was the year my sorry-shit husband went to prison which made it a casualty loss kind of year. And anyhow, I know every seven years the government forgets whatever went before. Since this was nearly seven years ago can't you just drop it?"

He said, "Once we have the check, we'll send you a notice as to interest and penalties or else you can calculate them yourself. The penalties are five percent a month up to twenty-five percent of the whole."

She said, "I can't do the math on that right off hand, but I know I don't have that kind of cash and I ain't in the instant-money crime business like my former husband."

Chet asked, "Is there any other way I can be of assistance?"

She said, "All these Republicans in government now, I figure it's time to downsize the IRS. Maybe start with robots like you."

He said, "Once again, my name is Chet Rinser and I was happy to be of service to you."

Tamzie sneaked a Sam Adams beer out of the refrigerator and sat drinking it, the man staring at her from the label like he was thinking heavy stuff. No matter what angle she looked at the thing from, she saw only one solution. She'd have to go to the red bitch for money.

7

WHILE DALE WAS WAITING TO SEE JACK CAMDEN, SHE HEARD A WOMAN IN his office say, "You say what's my contention? It's my contention that all's he does is what he damn well pleases or thinks is a good idea. I hate all this sneakiness, and if I had the money I'd go all the way to the Supreme Court."

"All that's true," said Jack Camden. "But money talks and bullshit walks. If you'll excuse my French."

"There's nothing legal about these actions, and you can bet if I'm ever asked I'll say what's on my mind."

"Um, did you hear my last statement?"

The woman was a washed-out blonde with a cigarette dangling from her lip. She slammed two doors on the way out.

Dale was having her last minute doubts about divorce. Other women in town put up with infidelity. One of her friends got a twenty-four inch Mikimoto pearl necklace from her husband just before he confessed an affair. She took it to Croghans', exchanged it for a pair of earrings, and went on with her life. Croghans was the society jewelry store. If your husband didn't know what to buy, you gave the store instructions on what to show him.

Jack Camden ushered Dale into an office of antique furniture and framed maps of the Lowcountry. He said he had been expecting her and it would be a privilege to serve her as he did so many of the better class of citizens of the lower peninsula. Jack Norcross Camden, IV—he liked to use his entire name—was the carriage trade lawyer in the divorce arena. He was a bowtie, willowy body, smooth as silk kind of guy. He charged by the hour and he charged a lot. He called it "a high level of service at a reasonable cost in the ongoing effort to separate fact from fiction."

He sat back in his chair and steepled his fingers. Said it would be the usual man-caught-in-adultery deal. She'd get the house, the furniture, whatever bank accounts weren't cleaned out, pretty much everything. They'd do a motion for temporary support until the alimony figure was arrived at. Sure, Rannie was a pit bull, but there was nothing she could do to save her brother on this one.

Dale said, "The night before the wedding, I signed a nasty prenuptial agreement."

Jack told her, "Not to worry. Fraud, duress, mistake. Any or all three of those will get it set aside."

"Collier's flat busted," said Dale. "His family wants me to pay his legal fees to Rannie."

Jack actually paused and blinked at that one.

Dale told him, "Among other problems is the matter of numerous items Collier has stolen that are in the house—rare vintage Civil War books and documents. They fill several walls in his study. I don't know what they're worth, but they have to have some value."

Jack breezed right past that. "Don't confess to any crimes or I can't represent you. We must seek a higher level of ethical behavior as we approach the twenty-first century."

Dale said she didn't feel good about the legal process.

Jack did a little turn-up smile at the corners of his mouth. "Divorces can be described as divisive at best." Looked at her like he expected her to laugh.

Dale trudged home in the blistering sun. A new heat index combined temperature with humidity for a general misery quotient. At that moment, the total was 104.

Tamzie Jerome used to come on Saturdays and clean, but Dale had had to lay her off. Collier had emptied their joint bank account. Just closed it down. What he didn't know was she had her own with some meager savings from the New York years and bits she had put aside from household accounts. Maybe $8,000. Wouldn't last long with mortgage and car payments. She didn't feel bad about her secret stash. She wasn't exactly stealing. Just keeping a private insurance fund.

A couple of power walkers strode by swinging their shoulders and the hand weights they carried. They waved to Dale and she forced a smile in return. Two women from down on the Battery. Their lives were exercise, car pools, and Junior League.

Collier had never pressed Dale to join the Junior League. She could at least say that in his defense. Or maybe it was just that her mother-in-law had resigned in a huff.

Mary Canty was fond of telling how Liz Petrie had come all the way across Broad Street to demand, "and I mean *demand*" her recipe for caviar avocado bisque saying she had a party. And the next thing Mary knew it turned up in the *Charleston Receipts*. All members were required to submit "receipts" as they were called in Charleston—not recipes—and Liz had stolen hers. When Mary Canty had jumped her about this, Liz had said no one can own a receipt, so she couldn't call it stealing. Well that cured Mary Canty Ralston of the League.

Dale knew the League—or the JLC as they called it for Junior League of Charleston—did charitable things and sometimes felt a twinge of guilt about not pitching in. She couldn't handle the members though. Women with the bit between their teeth. At that precise moment, she got a fresh reminder of this. Midgie Carolton, the banker's wife, came right up the walk behind her on Legendre Street and asked her to join JLC.

"Well not really join," said Midgie. "But perhaps you're in need of a paid position. As a manager of a store. With League volunteers to help you out."

"Well . . ." Dale hemmed.

"You know our motto," said Midgie, just vivacious as all get-out. "'It's not just *one's family*. It's *family*.' And what with your . . . well, problems, we thought you could use some help."

Dale invited her in, asked what she had in mind exactly.

Midgie said, "The JLC is considering a clothing store – well, really, a very upmarket boutique—called The Bee's Knees. It'll be a spin-off of our annual 'Bee There' charity sale. It seems more profitable than a tea room or some messy children's festival and profit is the bottom line in charity work, you just have to admit."

"Yes," Dale admitted.

"I've just been to a National training session in Richmond, Virginia on thrift shops. Everybody there was just darlin' and made us feel so welcome. Upmarket/downmarket was roundly debated and the National was pretty clear on steering us into upmarket as the wave of the future." Midgie held up her hands like a picture frame. "Can you picture it? A big sign that says 'twice-loved clothing.' Isn't that just a darlin' slogan?"

Dale said yes, she believed she could picture it.

"Since you're not a member, you can be much tougher on people than we'd be able to. Make sure all quota is properly pressed or dry-cleaned. Be sure the volunteers all wear red shirts, and be adamant about enforcing that one. You know how they'll come in from exercise class wearing god-knows-what. And along with it, around holiday times, we'll sell our Charleston basket. It's been redesigned to have our Lowcountry tea, oatmeal lace cookie, a Charleston scene jigsaw puzzle, and the JLC's own *Charleston Receipts* cookbook. You know we had to sue somebody for stealing our receipts. They are all copyrighted. And with all the lawyers we're married to, it was a pretty easy thing to do. We put a stop to their piracy nonsense in a hurry, I can tell you."

Dale asked Midgie if she'd like some iced tea.

Midgie said, "Of course I would. It's been such a morning. I had men scheduled to come and lay new carpet and wouldn't you know they went to the wrong house. I swan I don't know how I take the stress."

While she was getting out the ice, Dale decided she'd go into real estate.

Other than the occasional seersucker, Rannie's suits were always linen, dark colors, with shoes in colors to match, pumps or canvas espadrilles—a shell top—none of those silly women's ties. She sat filing her long nails and looking out her office window at the late afternoon traffic on Broad Street while her brother Collier, out on bail, flipped through old issues of *Field & Stream* and fidgeted.

She was on the fifth floor of a six-story bank building that had been modernist architecture in 1905, but now just looked ugly. What was good about the location was some of the windows had views of the flat blue sheet of the harbor and Fort Sumter on its island. The area would soon provide the backdrop for the latest film project in South Carolina—a made-for-television movie that would begin shooting later in the month.

Rannie's office looked to the rooftops of Broad Street and south, the old homes of the city. Her daddy had had his office here, and the happiest memories of childhood were meeting him as he came out and walking home with him as the town began to thin out and grow quiet. He'd hold her hand and he'd be hers and hers alone.

The Fed Dubiel had been by to deliver her a personal copy of the FBI sting video, which she had requested under a Brady Motion to produce. She told her brother Collier she was looking forward to hours of viewing enjoyment. Collier said he didn't need any more punishment. He was not feeling well. He had just driven back from the state capital in Columbia where the House of Representatives had suspended him pending his trial.

Rannie said, "Next the Supreme Court'll pull your law license. Not that you ever used it gainfully."

Collier told her he had done that debt collection last year that netted them seven thousand dollars. He sounded peevish.

Rannie rolled her eyes. "Well, that restores my faith. After you've done your time, you can apply to get your license back. What does it take? Five additional years." She laughed. "Your little fantasies of partying up in Columbia while a big firm does all the work and pays you a rain-maker's share. What did we end up with? You and me. And when you were in the office, it was like a potential accident zone."

Collier sulked. A sibling rivalry begun in childhood had tilted totally to her advantage. Rannie took the opportunity to stress that Collier owed her $40,000. As a professional courtesy she had cut her usual fee by ten thousand. She had to play the daddy role while Collier took a bullet train to prison. The only passengers it was stopping to pick up were more of his asshole buddies who couldn't wait to squeal on him about other bribes he had taken. His one and only hope was she could maybe take out a bridge somewhere down the tracks, dig up some tricky criminal procedure to derail the sucker.

"And to do that," she stressed, "I need the forty thousand. So you need to get a job. Work in K-mart or a lumber yard or something."

The notion of actual work truly terrified Collier. "That doesn't pay forty thousand," he squeaked.

"Well your spoiled wife can go back to fashion modeling."

"She was a set designer," he said truculently.

"Whatever. And let's get your house up for sale before unpaid mortgage payments eat up the equity. Skip Rightenberry will take care of it for you."

Collier said Dale had joint ownership of it. He couldn't sell without her approval. Rannie said the self-serving bitch better get her head straight. The house would have to be sold during the divorce settlement anyhow.

Collier's mouth opened. "What?" he protested. "I'm not leaving Dale. We've had our differences. But the marriage is solid. We're just doing a short separation."

She reminded him of all the stuff Dale didn't know. The statutory rape charge from the sixteen-year old legislative page. Slew of ethics charges by female divorce clients who said he took his fee through sexual favors. Half-dozen malpractice suits that had to be settled by his insurance carrier. The drunk driving charge with the naked woman in the car that the highway patrol commander had quashed. A private detective would turn up at least some of those. And she had every reason to believe that was about to happen. The word was on the street that Dale was shopping for a divorce lawyer.

"And," she added significantly. "Once she tells him about your . . .

archive collection . . . the fat will be in the fire. So you better sell it off now. Call up that bandit Blake Huston. He'll buy the whole lot. Get rid of all traces."

Collier's eyes bugged out.

"Yes, brother dearest, I know how you got most of your collection." She flexed the fingers on her right hand. "The old five finger discount. You and that brainless hunk fourth cousin of ours, Hunter 'Hootch' Gibson. Aptly nicknamed. You know I just got him out of the bug-house. Blitzed out of his mind from a weeklong drunk. Shooting out streetlights. What a buffoon."

Collier stood in the doorway looking round-shouldered and beaten. "Hootch seemed like a promising young man at the time I hired him as an aide. Had solid recommendations. A member of Kappa Alpha. And he was a relative . . . however distant."

"Sell the collection," said Rannie firmly. "Do it now."

"No," said Collier stubbornly. A mean look clamped on his face. The same look he'd get when they were little and she'd take his toys away from him, dare him to fight back. He said, "Did you ever think maybe Daddy wasn't really your father? Like all the rumors would say?"

He ducked out before she could throw something at him. Rannie knew he had said that just to set her off. And it did. He had always wanted to take her Daddy away from her. Be the eldest son. The heir apparent. The important one. While she was just a girl. Supposed to get married and take on somebody else's name. But Collier was a nincompoop and a failure. So he'd echo all the ugly rumors. Rannie was a bastard. Some red-haired man was her daddy. She wasn't a real Ralston.

She started pacing the room. Everyone always told her to calm down. Like having a lot of energy was some affliction. Sure she had a lot of energy. She worked hard. Sometimes way into the night. Jogged.

Played a vicious game of racquetball. Worked on the restoration of her house. She just didn't need a lot of sleep, that was all.

She had a mother who went out and mortgaged her house when she wanted money and then expected Rannie to pay it off. Clients that 'effing mugged people while waiting in her outer office. Haughty. Arrogant. They'd say I don't need to give you a fee because all the world will flock to your door after you defend me against these unjust allegations by corrupt officers of the law.

Well fuck them all! Fuck every godamned one of them!

8.

"YEAH, ALL THE DISGRACED WIVES WORK FOR ME," SAID SKIP RIGHTEN-
BERRY, THE REAL ESTATE BROKER. "NOT A LOTTA FANFARE ABOUT IT, BUT
THEY'RE ALL HERE WITH THEIR LIFESTYLES SCALED BACK DRASTICALLY."

Dale sat in his office on Broad Street with the tropical garden
behind showing through a big window. She was being interviewed as
a property manager. The idea was she'd do that while she studied for
a real estate license, then start selling houses. Skip saw her looking at
the garden and asked her if she liked it. She said it was lovely. He said
there was an apartment upstairs. Paused to let that sink in. Added that
he often spent the night there, told his wife he was out of town on business.

Dale had never been much good at handling vulgar men. She still
cringed remembering the run-in with a Yankee version of Skip, that
movie producer named Mendel Traub. Now Mendel—of Jazz-bo Productions—had booked a lot of downtown Charleston to do one of his
schlock films.

Skip wore a toupee with a green sport jacket, red tie, and tassel
loafers. He put one foot up on a chair and stood holding his crotch the
whole time he talked to her. He called her "little lady." He told two
jokes, one about a man standing in a line to donate sperm and the other
about an Indian naming his kid 'Two Dogs Fucking.'

The women in the office dressed pretty well, linen layered in neutral colors or all black. One of them Dale knew. Her husband was in jail for bank fraud. They used to have a big house on Tradd Street, would entertain lavishly. Before the husband got sent off, Collier was always trying to tap him for campaign contributions.

Skip touched on Collier's "current snafu" and casually mentioned the price of Rannie Ralston. He had checked out the mortgage on Dale's house and the financing statements filed on a variety of personal property. He said his agency would be able to sell the house pretty easy, get the equity out of it for her. And he laughed and said he figured the repo men would be hauling off her Mercedes SL pretty quick.

Dale thought, yes, it's a perfect symbol of my fall from grace.

"But clouds got silver linings," said Skip. "You'll need a bigger car for clients, anyhow, little lady. Maybe a Mercury or an Olds. I'll he'p you finance it. It's part of our family atmosphere here."

Skip talked to her about the profession, telling her tourist totals were up, but the big angle now was Yankees who figured if they bought a big house they'd crash Charleston society. Kind of like buying a stately home with a title attached in England, he said. Culture and old world charm was the Charleston motif for current demographics.

Skip said, "Some folks say a real estate license is a license to steal. I can't agree with that. We're value-added with a twist." He did a little twist of his hips. Then he went over the seven percent commission that she'd split with him as broker, said incomes varied widely according to hustle and moxie. It didn't take her long to see it wasn't the best deal in the world.

"Let me get this straight," she said. "I give you half of every commission. With what's left I run my own car. Set aside a niggling retirement. Pay insurance. Pay my medical benefits. And buy bread and salt."

Skip shrugged and smiled broadly. "You got some alternative? Like, you wanna go to med school, feel free."

At lunch, Skip said all his salesgals had trouble with the dimensions of houses they sold. He held up his thumb and forefinger an inch apart. Laughed. "That's because all their lives they've been told this was six inches!"

Dale ate the Chicken Wadmalaw. Normally she wouldn't have had anything so big for lunch, but she was worried about bills and this was free. Halfway through she quit eating, telling herself she was being foolish. Skip asked her if she wanted a doggy bag and then made some crack about 'doggy-style' that she didn't listen to.

That afternoon they drove out to Sullivan's Island to see a house Skip said was for sale with a potential buyer coming to look at it at 2:30. He wanted her to start watching sales, be ready to transition in the minute she had her license.

Going over the causeway across the marsh, Dale was quiet, watching the distant flashes of water. Skip said she should loosen up, practice making conversation with him so she'd be able to

handle clients. "No more hoighty-toighty afternoon teas for you, little lady," he said. "It's launching time into the work-a-day world. Waist-deep in toil and worry like the rest of us."

Sullivan's is a barrier island that shapes Charleston harbor. From the south end, you can see Fort Sumter where the Civil War started. The houses are old two and three-story frame houses buried in a century of foliage. Mary Canty Ralston always rented a house on Sullivan's in the summers. It was Charleston tradition since before the Civil War to go there or up to Flat Rock in the mountains. Originally they did it to escape mosquitoes and yellow fever.

Collier had expected Dale to stay out on the island all week with him coming on the weekends. Dale had always balked at that because it meant spending days with her mother-in-law and Moira. Plus even from the beginning of the marriage, she had suspected Collier liked to get her out of the house so he could meet women.

The house Skip stopped at looked like it had been built maybe in 1920 when there was still no bridge, everybody coming out by ferry. The yard was thick Bermuda grass with palmetto trees and yuccas. Skip used his car phone to tell the office he was looking at warehouse property in North Charleston and to not bother him for a few undisturbed hours. Dale didn't make any comment on that, but he knew she had caught it.

"They can't make a decision on their own," he said, fishing in the mailbox for the house key. "If I don't lie to them, they drive me nuts. They think majority rules or something. Like because they outnumber me they're in charge." He looked at her. "So don't overreact or nothing."

"I've got my passions under control," said Dale drily.

"Yeh, but you were thinking plenty of dissident stuff."

Inside, the house had the salt smell of the beach, but seemed bathed in the green of the plants around it. A big fireplace with andirons and a ship model on the mantle dominated the living room. The furniture was ratty and worn.

"There's furniture in here," said Dale.

"It's a furnished rental."

"You said it was a sale."

"So I lied."

"And there's no client coming for an appointment."

"Correct."

"And the idea is that you get me in a bedroom, and I surrender to the inevitable and put out for you."

"You're a sharp cookie. Just think of it as an interface initiation. All my girls go through it. Maybe we'll get on famous in the random moments of each day. Folks could call us Skip and Dale. You know. Like the chipmunks in the cartoons."

"That's Chip and Dale," said Dale.

"Whatever turns you on."

He had his hands on her waist, big hands with freckles and tufts of red hair on the knuckles. She was taller than he was, but she was taller than a lot of men. Dale pushed him off, but he kept coming, grabbed hold of her shoulders. She wriggled away from that. He started to unzip his pants like he wanted to wow her with his equipment.

A big glass lamp packed with seashells sat on an end table. Dale was surprised at how heavy it was when she picked it up.

"Hey, put that down," barked Skip, his hand inside his fly.

She heaved it at him. He dodged easily, but it did shatter, sending shells all over the floor.

He clenched his fists and rolled his shoulders threateningly. "You stewpid twat!" he yelled. "That's coming outta your pay!"

That was when she cracked him across the shin with the fire poker and sent him sprawling and rolling on the floor wailing with the incredible pain. "You bitch, you cunt!" he wailed.

She stood over him ready to hit him again, said, "I'm going to take advantage of your good mood by borrowing the car. So give me the keys." He handed them over, watching the poker all the time.

As she was starting the car, he hobbled out onto the porch. "We're talking grand theft auto here!" he yelled after her. "You'll never work real estate in this town!"

"Thank God for small favors," said Dale.

She drove the car back to Charleston and left it in the lot behind the agency. The girls in the office were buzzing and talking behind their hands. Skip had called and said something to them about her.

Well, real estate was out. So there was really no alternative. She'd have to rent her house to the movie people. Which meant she'd have to deal with Mendel Traub. Either that or become an ordained minister by mail.

9.

GENERAL SESSIONS COURT HAD HELD A LONG, SLOW DAY OF GUILTY PLEAS, AND RANNIE'S CASE WASN'T LIKELY TO BE CALLED UNTIL LATE AFTERNOON. WHEN THE JUDGE ANNOUNCED A RECESS, RANNIE CLIMBED DOWN OUT OF THE JURY BOX WHERE THE LAWYERS ALL SAT AND WENT OVER TO HER CLIENT IN THE MOB OF THE GENERAL SEATING AREA. IN A LOW VOICE SHE SAID IT WAS TIME TO GIVE HER THE ENVELOPE.

A week before, she had told the scumbag to get $5,000 in a big manila envelope and have it the day of the plea. "And don't ask me what it's for," she added. When he had started to talk, she reiterated, "I said not to ask me what it's for." He had nodded all knowingly.

Now he handed it over. Dirt bag with his t-shirt rolled up over his shoulders, tattoos all up and down his arms thinking he was some heavy metal rocker or something. "Roll down your sleeves," she said. "Try to look halfway civilized."

Rannie took her briefcase and the envelope and walked back behind the judge's bench to the little door that led to his chambers. His office was open and filled with lawyers arguing motions in civil suits. The hall was crowded with waiting lawyers, the endless snarl of an overburdened justice system.

Rannie locked the envelope inside her brief case, stood around chewing the fat until the recess was over and then came back out with the lawyers to take a seat in the jury box again. She gave her client a thumb's up signal. He looked real pleased. Fool, thinking she had bribed the judge. He had swallowed it without dispute.

If he had argued with her, she would have said, "You want something out of a judge, you got to do something for a judge. And let me tell you, a guilty plea's not a contract. You ignore this prudent advice, once you've pled, he can sentence you to whatever he wants. He's real liable to ignore the deal I've got set up, and you won't be getting a heavy suntan for ten or so."

Her client got five years. "You'll be out in three," she said. "A man who jails as well as you can do that standing on his head."

"What I am is cool," he said, acting all cocky. Damn fool sucking up the flattery for what a hard-ass he was. Easing the transition as the bailiff snapped cuffs on him and moved him into the courthouse lock-up for transportation to the county jail and then to another facility of the state of South Carolina.

At close to six, Rannie had a drink out of the bottle of desk bourbon like her daddy had always done—Jim Beam—and walked home the same route he had always taken. She took an odd comfort in following his routines, thinking maybe he was watching her from on high and was proud of her. Tell other angels, that's my baby girl down there all grown up. My son Collier never amounted to much. But Rannie's special. She will try a dam' case. Lemme tell you.

She went over to her mother's house where she ate supper only because Mary Canty was always passed out drunk by then or soon afterwards. Sometimes she had to put up with her dingbat sister Moira, but not usually. A few well-directed ugly remarks and Moira would retreat to her room and barricade the door.

Rannie piled a plate with cold lamb and potato salad, poured a stiff

Jim Beam in a short glass and sat down before the TV news.

Bertha Lee Hewitt of the United Church League Against Gambling was standing before a large group in an auditorium. Her voice echoed as she said, "We are here in numbers and with attitude. I know I speak for all of you when I say I am against dog tracks and against putting dog tracks before God. We don't need that kind of thing."

That segued into the story about state representatives pocketing money to vote for dog track gambling. Dubiel smirking with the U.S. District Attorney. Then Collier Ralston's face loomed up jabbering frightened nonsense. "The FBI is trying to send a message that the mature voters of this state by and through their lawfully elected representatives are not going to be permitted to make up their own minds about dog track gambling. We are moving in a wrong and dangerous direction. Society is on trial here. Not me."

"You're cute," said Rannie to the screen. "Cute'rn that kid in *Home Alone.*"

Rannie watched herself next, identified as Randolph Ralston, attorney for Collier Ralston. She said to the camera, "I don't bother to conceal the totality of my disgust here at this FBI saturnalia. We are witnessing incompetence so gross on the part of federal agencies that it overshadows any alleged—and I stress 'alleged'—crime they say's been committed. We intend to go to trial and are looking forward to our day in court."

Rannie knew it was great advertising. A phenomenal number of people watched local news. Fuck the prevailing ethical sentiments. Rannie Ralston takes no prisoners.

Rannie snapped off the TV and was ready for a night of work on her house when she saw the maid standing there. It surprised her that Tamzie was still around, the girl usually beat it out the door as soon as Mother dozed off. Tamzie stood there with her head ducked and mumbled the IRS said she had to get in compliance.

Rannie asked how much. Tamzie told her. Rannie got out her checkbook.

"They's interest and penalties," Tamzie added.

"There always is," said Rannie. She wrote out a check for the full debt. "I believe that will fully compensate the IRS," she said all sugary. "However . . . I want you to give me a mortgage on your home. I've got the form right here in my briefcase. Just a little security on the debt. And you know what else?"

"What?" said Tamzie suspiciously.

"You really don't have to pay me back this money."

"Yeah? And then you take my house."

Rannie gave her a saccharine smile. "No. That's not the idea at all. In fact . . . I'll tear up this mortgage . . . once you've done me just the smallest, teensy, little favor."

Tamzie looked kind of sullen, which ordinarily would have pissed Rannie off. Like her mother, Rannie was loud on the subject of the ingratitude and trifling worthlessness of the servant class. She could hear Tamzie laughing with her friends, saying yeah, girlfriend, you just ack dumb, the white folks pay all the bills. But this time, it was all playing into her hands.

"I want you to bring me some of the things you stole for my brother Collier," Rannie said oh-so-sweetly. "The Confederate archives."

Tamzie was stunned. "How'd you know we thief them?"

"Caught your act on TV," said Hootch Gibson, loud enough for everyone in the bar to hear. "Looked like you didn't know whether to shit or go blind." He laughed, hovering over Collier Ralston's table. Hootch had been looking for someone to pick up his drink tab and Collier seemed a likely prospect.

Juleps was popular with the young professionals and at eight o'clock was packed with lawyers and bankers in suits. Cigar smoke hung heavy in the air.

Hootch pulled out a chair, turned it backwards then sat down, arms resting on the chair back, admired himself in the mirror over the bar. Set his rum and coke down. Collier looked peeved, being with a young and very pretty girl not his wife.

Hootch looked her right in the eye. "I like these gangster bars. All the lawyers hanging out. This one belongs to Bubba Spainhour. William T. Spainhour. You don't call him Willie-T. He says it sounds like that jig in the old beach song 'Sixty-minute Man.' You know that one?" Hootch sang a few lines off-key.

The girl looked at Collier quizzically.

"Say, are you a hairdresser?" asked Hooch. "I could use a little trim."

"Are you deliberately trying to be an a-hole?" the girl asked. She screwed up her face in disbelief. "Is this some kind of act you do?"

Hootch blinked. Someone else had called him an asshole recently. Was there, like, a conspiracy going on? "Hey, I know Bubba. We're tight." He frowned as if reluctant to let her know the full story. "You see, I'm going to be doing some . . . uh, business with him."

The girl forced a little sickly smile at Collier. Said she thought she'd take the opportunity to go "winky-tink." Come back when his friend was gone.

"You want, I could put a contented smile on your face," said Hootch as she left. She looked back and rolled her eyes disgusted.

"I'd appreciate you not emphasizing my current predicament,"

Collier said tersely.

Hootch said, "You got serious cash-flow problems, huh? How about me? Rannie don't cut any slack even for cousins. Maybe we ought to sell off some of our collection. Raise a bit of ready cash."

Collier said, *"Our?"*

"Sure, good buddy. We kind of put the whole kaboodle together as a team didn't we? I figure we're partners."

Collier chose his words carefully. "I can vaguely recall you making . . . a few minor contributions during the time you worked for me up at the Legislature." He gave Hootch a hard white grin. "And let's remember that relationship. That you're an erstwhile college boy who once had an aide's job with me."

Hootch looked around doing a confused act. "Did I mis-hear the news? I thought you just got disemployed and indicted and whatnot? Kind of took the wind out of your sails."

Hootch smirked, watching Collier do a slow burn. Collier finished his scotch, sucked his teeth and held up the glass signaling the waitress for another. Hootch waved his glass, even though it was full. When Collier wasn't looking, he slid his bar tab over near the girl's drink.

"There's a ready market out there," said Hootch. "I make a few calls, we can move the merchandise, no problem."

Collier gripped Hootch's forearm fiercely. "You want to talk your way into jail? You name any of the pieces of the collection and a dealer is liable to smell a rat. Go straight to the cops. Or if he's shady, use the leverage to beat the price down to nothing."

Hootch didn't lower his voice. "So what's the point if you don't liquidate it when you need to?"

Collier sounded like he was explaining to a child. "That collection is being put together for posterity. I'm leaving it in my will to the

Historical Society. Keep it here in Charleston where it belongs and out of the hands of northern libraries or the Getty Museum or some place. Can you imagine it in California? Absurd."

"Your will? You planning on dying?"

Collier let out his breath, disgusted. "No. Not any time soon."

"Oh. I thought maybe it could be arranged if that's what you wanted." Hootch made his thumb and forefinger into a pistol. Laughed like he thought he was the funniest guy on earth.

The waitress came with the fresh drinks, started setting them on the table with little white napkins and a bowl of mixed nuts.

"I figure I need to work up a business plan on this one," said Hootch, standing up with both his drinks. "Maybe even a mission statement. What do you think? Huh?"

"Do you want to take that bar bill with you when you go back to wherever you were sitting?" Collier said archly.

Hootch did an exaggerated double take, looking at the bill like he had never seen it before. "That's not mine."

10.

DALE GOT UP OUT OF BED WHEN SHE HEARD THE FRONT DOOR OF NUMBER 18 LEGENDRE OPEN AND CLOSE. IT WAS BARELY SIX IN THE MORNING AND BIRDS WERE SINGING IN THE BACK GARDEN. UP ON THE ROOF, GULLS WOULD PERCH. TAKING THE BREEZE. SCOPING OUT SOME EDIBLE GARBAGE IN THE STREET. NOT GIVING A HOOT ABOUT THE SOCIAL DRAMAS GOING ON IN THE HOUSE.

She went downstairs in her nightgown, light spilling through the Palladian window above the front door. At night the moonlight came through it as white as snow.

When Dale had first seen where she was going to live as a married woman, she had stared in awe. A classical English Georgian of perfect symmetry that opened in back through French doors to a green garden of spray roses, nandina, and holly. It seemed like some priceless museum where generations had lived in utter joy and would infuse her own marriage with their essence. Collier had said he didn't often think about his Charleston heritage, but he guessed he was comfortable with it. Which was a lie. He thought about it all the time, and he was bothered he wasn't as important as his ancestors. He had planned on running for the U.S. Congress, then maybe Governor of South Carolina. Now those plans were on hold.

Down in the kitchen, Collier was making coffee in a French filter machine. He wore a summer weight gray suit but no tie. The tie stuck out of his side pocket. The clothes were wrinkled like he had slept in his car. Once she had thought him the best looking man she had ever seen. And this from the perspective of working around the top male models.

She remembered his maiden speech in the legislature: the importance of keeping the Confederate flag flying at the capitol. Tradition. State history. Heritage not hate. The Civil War was something of an obsession with him, which she always thought a bit odd because he had never served a day in the armed forces. But he had had a lot of ancestors in it. Mostly the navy. And blockade-runners like the mythical Rhett Butler.

"I thought we agreed on a separation," said Dale. "Meaning you don't live here anymore."

Collier grunted at her by way of greeting. He was in an accusatory mood. "I understand you belted the crap out of Skip Rightenberry. It's all over town. He's threatening a civil suit. Do you have a brain in your head?"

Dale crossed her arms defensively, leaned back against a countertop. "I could use that as a provocation. I'd then mention your recent encounter with the law. But I'll bite my tongue. I did love you once."

It was true. Their first meeting in New York occurred in a restaurant when he had bumped into her table and knocked her wine over. Apologized in a smooth artful manner that recalled the South and everything she missed about it. That velvet Lowcountry drawl that was really a brogue straight out of England. House came out hoose; about aboot; Moultrie Mootrie and the Cooper River was the Cuppa.

And he was so unbelievably good looking. They had started talking. Both were from South Carolina. He was just out of law school, in the city with some buddies to see the Yankees play. She was doing her thing with the fashion models.

They dated at a rib place and reminisced about barbecue and baked shad and undergrad days at the University of South Carolina where they had both gone, him a few years ahead of her and doing it much more stylishly in the fraternity set. He went home. Wrote to her. Phoned her a lot. Came back to see her. She went to visit him in the awesome Ralston mansion at Number 1 Legendre, a block down from where she lived now, with its panoramic view of White Point Gardens and the spanking blue harbor. The famous Fish and Stars gate that led to a lush garden.

They did a vacation together on Edisto Island. Made love poorly. Laughed about it lying there shy and looking at the ceiling. Made love a lot better, feeling each other that time. The next day when he asked her to marry him she felt a sense of relief. Like life was laid out now with no more big question marks.

The night before the marriage he had sprung the pre-nuptial agreement on her. Told her in a hard voice she would sign or the marriage was off. Eyes like flint. The contract was a Rannie Ralston special. Dale effectively got nothing in the event of a divorce. She signed because she couldn't think of anything else to do. And Collier had managed to be faithful to her for a full month after they were married.

Dale dismissed her memories. Collier was talking about something she hadn't been listening to. Draining their assets to make bail. The broker saying it was a lousy time to sell stocks but having to do it anyway because they had to live. *They* had to live. He was figuring her in the equation just like his mother had. "I've got to raise the money for my defense. I can beat this thing. I know I can. Then we'll go back to normal."

She let that pass too. Normal was gone for them forever. She asked why Rannie was charging him. He said she had overhead. Expenses.

She couldn't just drop everything and attend only to him.

Dale said, "And now Calvin Whitesides is dead."

Collier scowled. "Don't start your little ethical digs on that. So he was her runner. Father had one. Every successful lawyer has one, and nothing is ever done about it. Everybody knows Calvin ran clients to her. Knocked on the doors of car accident victims. Picked up some of their more pressing bills. Got the hook sunk deep before she really stuck it to them for her fee. I honestly don't know what she's going to do now. Her whole practice could fall apart."

"You always can find the time to worry about the less fortunate," Dale said drily.

"She supports Mother."

Dale gestured at the house. "You'll have to sell your antique guns. And all those books and signatures and maps and things."

Collier looked horrified. She waited for the lecture on family heirlooms and traditions. All the sweat he had put into the Civil War collection making it of national significance as he called it. Leaving out the stealing part.

Instead he said something odd. "If that swine Blake Huston comes around trying to make an offer for the entire collection, you shut the door in his face. The man is a vampire, a blood drinker. A damned black-mailing, bottom-feeding, scum-sucker!" The veins were standing out on his neck.

"Who's Blake Huston?" said Dale, amazed at his vehemence.

"What I said. A total crook."

"As opposed to you pilfering those books from old coots who didn't know what they owned? Blake sounds like the very person to sell the stuff to."

The coffee was steaming now, but Collier ignored it. He lifted his chin slightly like he was taking a superior posture. Talking down to her in a chilly voice. "That would be very poor judgment."

Dale looked out the kitchen window where birds were splashing in the little cement goldfish pool. "Poor judgment," she said. "Like being videotaped naked?"

Collier slapped a cup down, poured coffee aggressively, spilling a lot on the counter. "I can't expect you to understand that. God knows I've tried to talk with you about my problems. The stress of running a law practice while sitting in the legislature. Driving back and forth to Columbia. I feel like I spend my whole life in a car."

She still didn't look at him. "Or a hotel."

"I'm never home. I get lonely and frustrated. Always worrying myself sick about money and financing the next campaign. I just go crazy."

Dale studied her fingernails. "I don't know. Maybe it's like a phase you go through."

"Going crazy?"

Finally she turned and met his eyes. "No. Going to prison."

His nostrils flared. A glacial chill descended utterly. "That's an unconscionable remark."

Collier sometimes used big words like that. She wondered how it went down in a legislature of bubba-boys.

Both of them heard the tow truck at the same time. One of those long flat beds that cranks a car up onto the bed rather than pulling it behind. Two ugly men in t-shirts were hooking up to the Mercedes SL.

Collier ran out screaming at them. They bellied right up to him like they wanted him to take a swing at them, and he got quiet. Stood there limp and watching. They were taking both cars. The SL and

Collier's 450 with the cellular phone and the Confederate flag bumper sticker.

Dale went to the phone and looked up the number of the South Carolina film department, a special little agency designed to help bring movie deals to the state. Nobody was in at that early hour, but she left a message on the answering service.

Collier came back inside beaded with sweat. The heat was already bad. "Who are you talking to?" he demanded.

She told him she intended to rent the house out for the Civil War movie. They were paying $50,000 for two week's occupancy.

"You can't do that," he said.

"Why?"

"Mother will be furious."

II.

TAMZIE KNEW IT WAS A MISTAKE DRIVING UP TO CENTRAL CORRECTIONAL IN COLUMBIA TO TALK TO DEBONE THROUGH THE PLASTIC. BUT WHAT WAS BUGGING HER WAS THE RED BITCH RANNIE TELLING HER TO WALK OUT WITH THE BOOKS AND STUFF JUST LIKE SHE'D DONE BEFORE. WHY WAS IT SO SPECIAL? DEBONE HAD BEEN IN ON IT. HE WAS THE ONLY ONE SHE COULD TRUST. WHAT SHE LEARNED INSTEAD WAS HER EX-HUSBAND WAS ABOUT TO BE RELEASED AND EXPECTED TO MOVE IN WITH HER.

"You can divorce my ass much as you please," said Debone, his face looking all blurry through the screen. "Makes no difference. You the one wanted all the stand-up-in-church bullshit. But when I get out of here, I'll be needing a bed and roof. Get me on the road to rehabilitation with some reasonable style. Buy me a set of wheels. You still driving that junked up Chevette? A man's got to have some pride."

Tamzie couldn't believe what a fuck-up mess the prison system was, a man like Debone could kill three people and be let out in four years. How he could behave himself all that time was beyond her. She told herself the bad news of his pending release had been headed her way anyhow, so she had to quit being superstitious, thinking that visiting him had maybe brought it on. Her momma Mozelle, rest her soul, would have told her even thinking about that sorry sack of shit might bring him down like a curse from a root doctor.

Tamzie's momma had kept her indoors, a sheltered youth in the Jackson Street project, so when Debone come along about eleventh grade, he seemed like a good idea. She figured she had done a Beauty and Beast routine on him, reforming him, making him stand up in church and get a job bartending at private parties and do the furniture lifting for her and Mozelle cleaning house. Problem was Debone liked to do another kind of lifting. Watches, silver, cars. Sell it at flea markets, the cars to a chop shop up in Lake City.

Debone would make wax imprints of car keys so he could come back later and boost the BMW or the Cadillac. Not many. No more than two a year because in such a small area folks got suspicious real easy. Rule-of-thumb, half book value of a mileage-depreciated vehicle. Gave him a tax-free income of $20,000 a year without breaking a sweat.

The rest of the time he'd deal light dope for that Bubba Spainhour man, which was why he had to end up killing the three dudes, not in one big gunfight, but spread out. One of them not even business, just some badass outside a club waving a gun around. That was the only one he got convicted for, and everybody—judge, solicitor, cops—all agreed the victim pretty much needed killing. Parole board thought so too, so they were letting Debone out in short time.

Tamzie had to admit she'd made use of the stolen car money. Even done some minor thiefing herself. What it was, Collier Ralston would give them a name of a Confederate book he wanted. While cleaning, they'd search through rows of books in folks' libraries down South-of-Broad, walk out with it. As far as she knew, no one ever missed anything she took. Collier would scout it out while socializing, get the exact location down. Then he would pay them twenty, maybe thirty dollars tops for it. Just a book. Or some old bunch of papers bound up with ribbon. It wasn't exactly stealing, because the truck was so worthless. Tamzie'd buy herself a half pint of Tanqueray for Saturday night.

This was why she had driven up to Columbia. It bugged her that Rannie wanted her to risk jail to steal those books for her. She asked Debone how that Confederate bullshit could have any value. Was Collier crazy?

"Say *what?*" said Debone. "I mean we are talking 'bout a man what dress up in Rebel *costumes* and play Civil *War.* That old bat Miz Ralston reading stories out loud *in Gullah.* Singing negro spirituals with a bunch of yacht club drunks all trying to sound black."

Changing the subject, Debone said, "I hear they's a car call a Range Rover line up three deep down South-of-Broad now. Man got to *have* one cause it say he's like British royalty and own a plantation. The thing retail for round $55,000. Drive one a' them muthafuckers up to Lake City and get my finances back mod'rately *on the level.*"

"I'm through with all that," said Tamzie.

Debone snorted. "You best get over disrespecting me or I be likely to take a dim view of your continued good health. Whup up on them kidneys until you need you a adult diaper."

When the time was up, Tamzie left the dirty plastic and brick of the visiting room. Place stank like a sewer. Worn out old white men with guns on their hips eyeing her ass as she started to strut just to show them. The state was building a new prison, going to tear down CCI. Tamzie wondered if any of the lifers would miss the place. Had come to think of it as home. Worthless bunch of trash. The kind your momma warn you about.

The only pet Tamzie had as a child was a Amazon parrot name of Rosco that had first been a Christmas gift from Miz Ralston to her daughter Rannie. It was a mean parrot and would bite anybody who got close. Then it started to eat its own feathers and became a bald parrot. So they give it to Tamzie because it was wore out and half-eat up.

Funny thing was, Tamzie had loved that bird. She was real tore up when one day she came home to find a heavy drinker current boyfriend of her momma had cooked and eaten it. That being kind of the last straw, Mozelle had thrown him out and warned a weeping Tamzie about keeping a part of you separate from men. That way you never totally belong to them and could cut loose if need be.

She hoped the muffler wouldn't fall off the Chevette on the way back to Charleston. Last thing she needed was more bills. All the way back she kept wondering why the red bitch Rannie wanted those books so bad. Paintings you could almost figure, some Japan dude paying millions for a bowl of flowers. But books made no sense. Maybe a Bible John the Baptist once owned. But these were Civil War books. Only some fool like Moira Ralston would want them.

"I know you're in there," said Mary Canty fiercely. "Now open this door!"

Moira flinched at the shock of her mother's voice. She could flee a mechanized world in the sanctum of her bedroom. She could fill her personal space with family portraits and artifacts—her spoon collection, her mounted Confederate medals—but nothing was magic enough to ward off the evil witch.

Her grandfather's gold Elgin pocket watch lay open on the desk. Twelve noon. Time for her mother to go to the Yacht Club and begin the day's drinking. Sighing, she got up from her roll top desk and unlocked the door to allow the demon into her third floor home up in the clouds.

Her mother swept in bringing anger and distrust and dissatisfaction.

"There are no locked doors in my house. You know that."

Moira said, "As wildly preposterous as it may sound to you, I need privacy to write." How could she possibly explain to this person who called herself her mother that writing was the bread of life to her? How could it be otherwise? She had been raised in a house an ancestor had built in 1832. Lived each day of her life with portraits and age-spotted mirrors, the mellow glow of old wood and timeless elegance. Chippendale scuffed by the boots of southern cavaliers and chewed by generations of retrievers.

"You always have your nose stuck in a book. How do you expect to catch a man like that?"

The jeers of derision. Moira's clever lines always failed her at these moments, leaving her with the stubborn voice of a stunted adolescent. "I'm only twenty years old."

"You're twenty years old, and you are living out in a world someplace where I have never been." Mary Canty turned with a flourish. "And simply do not want to go to." She did another half-turn, lifted her hands to invoke the heavens. "I have paid. I have paid the price as a mother. I have written out checks for the finest education one can buy. I send you to Ashley Hall. I send you to Sweet Briar—and this is the part I simply cannot understand—you come home after only a year when there are all those nice boys at the University of Virginia. Washington & Lee. Hampden-Sydney. All from fine families. Many of them gentlemen farmers. You would have adored the life there."

Moira talked through a small pout. "I don't need to be married yet."

"When you were at Ashley Hall, they would call at the house. Young men would come around, and you would act hopelessly backward, say something inane to them, talk about your writing or whatever you call it, and they would slink off. Typically, I would never see them again. When you went off to Sweet Briar, some of them—the more backward ones—used to at least ask about you. Now they've given up asking."

Moira felt the vibrating pulse on her wrist. It jumped as though it were trying to leap out of her flesh. "I have heard all this and heard it and heard it."

"Whatever became of that nice young Bradford boy?"

"He had jug ears."

"He most certainly did not."

Moira flared. "Did you measure them? Is there some dimension you require before they're jug handles? His ears turned out on either side of his head. He looked like a Toby mug."

Mary paced the room. "I must start drinking decaffeinated coffee." She wheeled. "I always had this lurking fear that you would take up with someone inappropriate. Some sort of dreadful brown person. Someone on that scale from Jewish down to negro. Now I think I would welcome it. I could be like Barbara Bush with Mexican grandchildren."

Moira flinched. "You mustn't talk about such things, mother."

Mary showed her teeth in a feral way. "Why not?"

"I'm going out now."

"I hope you're not going in that outfit."

"What's wrong with this?" She was wearing a floral print chintz sundress, pretty standard attire.

"I expect you to change. I require it."

Sometimes when Moira cried, she thought she was making pools of tears on the floor. Little mice would come out at night and drink from her misery. She cried because she was afraid of palmetto bugs and death and the loneliness of being creative in a world of hateful mothers.

The fear turned her inside out and made her think she would lash out and do something violent. She eyed the Colt navy revolver on her desk and imagined pointing it at her mother's head.

12.

"LET ME GIVE YOU SOME ON-THE-SPOT GUIDANCE," DRAWLED RANNIE RALSTON FROM BEHIND THE HUGE DESK. "THE RESPONSIBLE DECISION IS TO BACK DOWN. GO LICK YOUR WOUNDS AND SHUT UP. WOMEN HAVE BEEN WANTING TO RACK YOUR BALLS FOR A LONG TIME. DALE GIVING YOU A FEW LICKS . . . WELL, IT ALMOST CAUSES ME TO RESPECT HER A LITTLE."

"You can't stonewall me," Skip Rightenberry huffed. His right leg was in a cast up to the knee. His eyes kept cutting to the nude painting of Rannie that hung behind her head. They were in the inner office where she admitted clients when she wanted to psyche them out in a special way. The picture was a devastating element in what was otherwise 1960 attorney decor. Framed Declaration of Independence. Her father's law license like he was still there as the senior partner. The old out-of-date case reporters that no one used now. Everything exactly as he had left it.

Rannie had been up working on her house until the first streaks of orange were in the sky. She felt fresh as a daisy. She didn't need sleep like other people. She swiveled about in her chair to gaze out the window. "Ever since I went into practice with my daddy, I've been something of a role model for aspiring professional women in this town. My very life is a method of erasing misconceptions about the weaker sex. What would become of that purpose if I allowed you to bully my sister-in-law over your superficial wound?"

Skip raised his voice belligerently. "I got agony that won't quit. Bones don't knit right for a man my age. It's a goddam permanent disability."

"The cast is a fake," she said, still staring at the view out the window. "The day you file a lawsuit I'll subpoena the doctor into a deposition and prove it."

He slapped the arm of his chair. "You don't know that. I've got a compound fracture. I can barely walk. I stay up for an hour, I gotta lie down for two."

Rannie turned back to Skip and smiled faintly. She wanted to tell him he looked like he had a head-on collision with a truckload of dog shit. What she said instead was, "Don't imagine I don't share your concerns. But I'm very busy right now with the realities of the marketplace and don't have time to deal with you."

Skip was tense, pressing his lips tightly together. "If this is gonna be hostile . . . if you can't see reason . . . you'll deal with my lawyer."

Rannie sounded thoughtful. "You know when you think about it, if there's a profession that's more disliked than lawyers, it's probably realtors."

Skip snorted.

"It's what you read," she said. "In the press and other vehicles of opinion. I know. You make enough money to live with the grief. But you get complacent and satisfied. Forget how vulnerable you are in a world of yeasty change. How many folks out there got a hard-on for you. I guess what I'm trying to say is that if you continue to aggravate me, I'm going to make you my life's work. You won't make a sale in this town that the buyer doesn't sue you for fraud. You win some, you lose some. But with deposition time and a poisonous reputation in town,

Skip Rightenberry should be in bankruptcy within, oh, two-maybe-three years."

Skip was thinking and staring at the painting. Rannie wasn't showing her snatch in it, but her boobs were on full display. "You can't give me one positive justification for . . ."

Rannie put a finger to her lips to silence him. "We're not going by conventional wisdom on this one. None of that go-along and get-along small town stuff. I'm asking you whether you want to continue working as a realtor."

As Skip limped out the door on his crutches, Rannie said, "I'm sure your decision's the right one. It'll ensure the public's confidence in the real estate profession. We can greet each other courteously on the street. Smile. Pass on."

He didn't wave goodbye.

One down, one to go, Rannie thought as Dale came in.

It was really hard to picture Dale wielding a fire poker. She was incredibly good looking. Lightly sun-tanned. Mouth wide and sensual. Wide apart deep blue eyes setting off the dark hair. And a sense of repose about her running right down to the fingers. But then she sat around all day doing nothing. A little gardening. Some interior decoration. No stress. Very cool, too. Crossing those long legs just so. Trying to not look at the nude portrait.

No pleasantries. Rannie launched right in, telling Dale she liked to think that she conducted her practice in a way that was both ethical and sensitive to the needs of the modern woman. She was convinced she could serve both Collier's and Dale's interests. She recognized that they were now two distinct camps, but both sent a single message. Any pragmatist could see what that was. They had a profound need to reach a just result at the lowest possible cost in resources and additional human suffering.

Dale kind of cocked her head to one side, giving her a wary look. They all did that. You just kept going and led them through to the end.

Rannie said Collier was out on bond, which took the last bit of his liquidity. It meant he was placed on hiatus until trial time. Without some serious defense work on her part—and that required substantial funds—he was headed for one of the holding pens for the antisocial. In with all those urban predators who make things so uncomfortable for the white middle class. Which would be a tragedy, she was sure Dale would admit.

Perhaps Dale really didn't care about four years of marriage down the drain. Collier was beginning to believe that. Consistent with these profound suspicions, he had reported Dale's reluctance to sell the house to contribute to the defense fund.

Dale started to speak, but Rannie raised a hand to silence her. "I know. You say you can't afford it. But really you can't afford not to. Sell the house. Find a small place to live. No need for a dingy hotel room or some trailer park in North Charleston between a bowling alley and a go-cart track. You don't have to sink that low. Get something decent in a nice suburb. Marsh view. Real estate didn't work out, go to work at something else. Think of it as a job-creating incentive."

"Hew out my destiny," said Dale.

Rannie cocked her head and eyed her opponent. The bitch must have collagen injections in those lush lips. "Yeah. Something like that."

"How about if you cut the shit, Rannie?" Dale flashed a good girl smile.

Rannie pondered her for a moment. "You need to sell all of Collier's Civil War collection. It's worth a lot of money. Blake Huston will buy the whole lot. I'll broker it for you so you don't get skinned."

"Who on earth is Blake Huston?"

Rannie leaned forward like a conspirator. "Society blackmailer. My parents' generation. Early in my practice of law I used to take him payoffs. Disguise it as personal loans being repaid. My clients were all from the best families. Had to marry off a wayward daughter and didn't want it to come out she had had an unfortunate first marriage. Or a series of abortions. Or an affair with a . . . you know, a negro. He's a Civil War collector as well. Fanatic about historic documents. So much of his best dirt has come from them after all."

"It's all stolen, Rannie. You know that. Collier probably snagged something from every home South-of-Broad. Hootch Gibson, that cousin or whatever he is of y'all's helped him with some. Tamzie did some. It was a regular little thieves' den. And I'm not selling the house. That's the advice of my lawyer, the semi-legendary Jack Camden."

Rannie kept a poker face at the name of the preeminent society divorce lawyer. He was a big one for the protracted battle and the endless hourly billings. Which would make a real fight of it, but Rannie always enjoyed a fight. She changed the subject, shifted her position without missing a beat. "I understand you're renting the house for the movie. Good. That should cover the mortgage for six months. Mother will be furious, but business is business."

Dale was looking at the nude painting.

"Yes, that's me," said Rannie. "Do you look that good with your clothes off?"

"Why? Are you lezzie?"

"No, and I'm not into incest either. But I know for a fact my brother is a lousy lay."

"You've seen the video," said Dale.

13.

TAMZIE'D ALWAYS SNEAK *MARTHA STEWART LIVING* OUT OF THE
RALSTON MAIL AND READ IT FIRST SO'S SHE'D KNOW WHAT MOIRA WAS
ABOUT TO HIT HER WITH. THE JULY/AUGUST ISSUE SAID BEFORE STEAMING
CLAMS OR MUSSELS YOU SPRINKLE THEM WITH CORNMEAL AND SOAK IN
LUKEWARM WATER. THAT WOULD CAUSE THEM TO SPIT OUT THE SAND.

That was fine. Moira didn't eat clams and mussels, but she'd send
Tamzie out for some up to Crosby's fish store and tell her all about how
to get sand out of them. Which was fine. Tamzie could go "yes, ma'am"
and act all amazed at how smart Miss Moira was to know all these
practical things. Soaking mussels don't break your back.

Then there was the knife-sharpening article. Moira would want
Tamzie to sharpen all the knives, would stand over her telling her what
she was doing wrong and how a sharp knife was less dangerous than a
dull one cause you didn't bear down so much. Which was fine. Tamzie
didn't mind sharpening knives, and she could control that impulse to
stick one in Moira.

But the "seeds of plenty" article looked dangerous. It was all about
what they called a "potager" garden, which seemed pretty much a plain
old vegetable garden. It said there was joy in growing too much stuff
because your friends come over and cook vegetables with you using
their own special recipes. That sounded like a lot of hot work, but

Tamzie had herself a ace in the hole. Miz Ralston's garden was flowers and the two gardeners that the red bitch Rannie never tired of saying she pay for had right precise instructions on what went where in the ground. The momma-daughter fight over that one would stall things until Moira'd lose interest.

The fool Debone was getting out. He had phoned collect from the prison to tell her to pick him up and to score him a gun. Have it waiting for him. He said the TEC-9 had surpassed the Uzi in popularity and he'd like to field test one. Also he was ready for some hydraulic jackhammer getting it on with her.

Bad enough that men and their aggression shit was unleashed all over the world. All in love with their selves instead of just one woman. But Tamzie had to live under the thumb of the red bitch Rannie who was in love with her daddy's ghost instead of a man like she was supposed to be. Tamzie had called the IRS to check if Rannie really paid the taxes and was told that they wouldn't process it and put it in the computer for eight weeks. So she had no way to know if Rannie was lying or not. And Rannie wanted that Confederate stuff stole back from Collier's house pretty damn quick.

What really got to Tamzie was how the IRS man ended the conversation saying, "Once again, I'm Chet Renser with the Internal Revenue Service. I hope I have been of assistance to you."

Enough to turn you into a Republican.

At five, Tamzie wheeled the drinks caddy out onto the piazza for Miz Ralston and some of her friends, all of them yacking away at the same time.

One of the old biddies said, "My mother always said the morals of young people move in the opposite direction of hemlines. And she should know. She lived through the 1920s."

They all laughed and the ice tinkled in the glasses.

Tamzie sneaked a hit out of a bottle of vodka in the kitchen, changed out of one uniform and into another and walked uptown to the College of Charleston. The old buildings and big trees were pretty, but the sight didn't do much to lift up her spirits. Taking the job night cleaning so as to pay off the red bitch made her wonder if it was about time to go out and suck on the exhaust pipe of her car.

Her first night, some administration fool read to her out of a federal manual on dangerous chemicals, introducing her to her equipment and then actually demonstrating how to put a plastic trash liner in the cans. Tamzie was thinking about movies where all the Miami drug cowboys get shot to bits at the end. She wondered if that gun that Debone wanted would cause that kind of damage.

The fool assigned Tamzie to the library, a big new building but all closed in with trees and bushes so it seemed old. Her supervisor got her vacuuming the upstairs in a kind of special area with its own glass doors and real old-looking books like Collier had her and Debone steal.

Thinking about the red bitch Rannie made Tamzie attack the carpet like she wanted to rub it raw. Making her sign a mortgage. The bitch had just took the house right out from under her. Tamzie would live in it and pay the bank, but her debt to Rannie would keep building until one day she'd have precisely nothing. Old man Ralston, the red bitch's daddy got famous for that kind of stunt. Always carried a deed and mortgage form in his pocket. End up with his name on more pages in the courthouse deed books than anyone in the history of Charleston. Tamzie shut off the vacuum and started emptying the trashcans.

"I bet you look real fine in civilian clothes," said a black man's voice. A deep and suggestive voice.

Tamzie looked up to find a kind of medium-skinned brother. He was fat, no getting around it. Height wise he was only so-so. But the face had possibilities of being handsome with that tight-trimmed full beard. He was holding a big panama straw hat and a walking cane with a silver knob head on it. The man was a dude.

"You look like a man who like to cook," said Tamzie.

He stroked his beard, thinking about it. "I make a right wicked Hoppin' John. Spoon bread is kind of a specialty. I'll float cornbread in white bean soup." He looked her over in a way that said you being cruised, girl. He said call me Thaddeus Wyndham and what's your name?

She said Tamzie Jerome. He said he was the archivist and to be sure and lock up when she finished because Special Collections had valuable stuff. The Audubon Birds were priceless.

Tamzie didn't know about archivists so she asked what he did exactly and he said he bought rare books and manuscripts for the library. He liked to collect rare stuff. A treasure hunt with somebody else paying the bill.

"I mean you got a regular job here?" said Tamzie. "You're a for real librarian?"

"For true."

"Got state benefits and health insurance?"

"You bet."

"Retirement?"

"Shore."

Tamzie checked him over. The man don't look half so fat as before. "What church did you say you go to?" she said.

14.

MOIRA WAS NOT HAPPY WITH DALE. HER BEST EFFORTS REBUFFED AGAIN, SHE QUICKSTEPPED HOME IN A SERIOUS SNIT. DALE WAS NOT PLAYING THE ROLE AS INTENDED TO DISCOVER THE MANUSCRIPT. EVEN AFTER A TEDIOUS HOUR OF MOIRA HINTING AROUND ABOUT THE CONDITION OF COLLIER'S ARCHIVE COLLECTION, OFFERING TO SORT IT OUT, CHECK FOR MOLD OR SILVERFISH, BUT OH NO, NOT MISS DALE. IT WAS LIKE SOME FOOLISH SISTER-IN-LAW RIVALRY. DALE JUST BEING WILLFULLY STUBBORN. JUST WOULD NOT LOOK THROUGH THOSE BOOKS AND GO 'OH MY GOODNESS WHAT IS THIS? MARGARET MITCHELL? *SOUTH BLOWS THE WIND?* DO YOU THINK IT COULD BE GENUINE?' AND HERE THE NEW YORK BOOK DEALER MIGHT BE ARRIVING ANY DAY NOW.

Moira's mother had always said Dale was nobody's idea of a model matron. Mother was always a great one for cataloging deficiencies in someone. Still, she often had an unerring eye. Dale's tendency to go barefoot in the house. The over-familiarity with the servants. It was so easy for them to get the wrong ideas.

Not that Moira hadn't done her best to be good friends with Dale over the years. Giving her little hints that would help her fit in better. Praising her taste in literature, saying that mother only read ghostwritten tell-alls by faded movie starlets. But Dale never would ask about Moira's writing even though it so clearly might have been a common ground between them. And now when she returned the copy of Mac-Donald Oxley, *Baffling the Blockade,* to Collier's collection, Dale had looked at her like she had stolen it.

Among other matters of business, Moira had gone over there to praise Dale's courage in renting out her house to the movie company. Moira announced she had invited the producer to dinner in a show of the famous Charleston hospitality. She wasn't utterly sure of the distinction between a director and a producer, but knew the producer was higher up the social scale.

The morning mail lay on the silver tray in the hall. Moira took it to the drawing room and sat down to go through the new *Martha Stewart Living.* Cleaning mussels and clams. Sharpening knives. Potager garden. And then there was an absolutely fascinating article on peaches with the origins of all the hybrids explained. Moira loved rolling the names on her tongue. Red Top. Suwannee. Canadian Harmony. Cresthaven. Belle of Georgia. Indian Blood. They sounded like the names of romantic novels. Dealing with the twentieth century was so difficult for one of a passionate and romantic nature. Very few people shared her love of cricket serenades and the wild flights of the swifts in the evening peace of the gardens.

Rannie always made vicious japes and jibes at her. Rude, crude, and socially unacceptable, their father used to say about her. Distasteful as Moira considered the subject of bastardy, she couldn't help but speculate that Rannie was not a true Ralston. The idea that Daddy liked Rannie best was a pathetic fantasy of her sister's creation. Moira and Collier were his preferred children. Rannie had been treated almost like a foundling. Or a poor cousin being raised in the family out of charity.

She turned back to the article. It said tree-ripened peaches had much more sugar than the supermarket ones that were harvested before they were ripe. Of course everyone knew that. But what was truly fascinating was it warned that a peach picked before it was ripe should stand at room temperature until it was soft. Moira practiced saying that with a little sigh in her voice. "Whenever I have an unripe peach, I let it stand at room temperature until it is soft." That sounded almost sexual. And goodness. Such receipts. Grilled peaches with balsamic vinegar. Delicious although not very southern.

She would have to plan the dinner menu for the producer very carefully. And Martha Stewart's calendar had her ordering roses for the fall planting. There was so much to do. It was a world of mounting difficulties.

"Tamzie!" she cried out. "Tamzie!" Moira was fuming again. Where was that foolish girl? Moira never used the dreaded n-word, but "nigger in the woodpile" had been one of her father's expressions and honestly at times it seemed very apropos.

The interstate stretched away the long miles as Tamzie drove Debone back from Central Correctional.

"You still looking good, *woman*," Debone purred, blowing cigar smoke out the open window. "You giving up on our marriage was bad wrong. Change your name back however you want, you always a Wigfall to me."

Tamzie wanted nothing to do with Debone, but the man was dangerous and you didn't just high-hat him. And you didn't get all worked up, go running to a woman's shelter where those washed out white women answer the phones, tell you you need self-esteem counseling. Or go crying to Miz Ralston wanting to sleep in the bedroom behind the kitchen. No, you got to be cool about it, do sly things that make him want to move out. Think he's putting something over on you when he does. Sliding like a lizard over to some other woman.

Debone figured they should drive direct to "their" house for a little love, sex, and fulfillment. He said what pass for poon-tang in prison he don't want to think about ever again. She said she wanted him checked out by a doctor, make sure he's not carrying nothing from that prison. She wasn't even going to ask what his tool had been up.

"And anyhow, we won't have *my* house for long if we don't thief back that Confed'rit shit from Collier Ralston."

Debone said don't bother him with her worries. Prison had allowed him to develop a life-skills program, in keeping with which he'd be needing the use of the car until he reestablished his credit. She said no way. Debone said she must have the case of bad memory. He had rights in her. He said, "Overall, my soul don't feel comfortable with that divorce business. Violating family values like that make me want to lash out and do you harm. The kind of spontaneous violence my parole officer gone say I have to watch."

Tamzie said not to get in a forceful way or anything.

Debone asked, "You ever listen to the words to 2 Live Crew's 'Bad Ass Bitch'? The one the Congress is so work up over 'cause of the words about beating the shit out of women? Well, lemme tell you something. The song don't lie."

15.

TO DALE, THERE WAS NOTHING YOU COULD REALLY PUT YOUR FINGER ON ABOUT "HOOTCH" GIBSON THAT MADE HIM DIFFERENT FROM ANY OF THE OTHER N'ER-DO-WELLS IN THEIR MID-TWENTIES WHO LIVED ON THE FRINGES OF CHARLESTON SOCIETY. THE KHAKI CARGO SHORTS AND TEVA SANDALS. T-SHIRT WITH A MARLIN ON IT. FADED SWORDBILL CAP. A UNIFORM THAT SAID HE WAS A SPORTSMAN KIND OF GUY WHO KNEW HIS WAY AROUND BOATS AND MAYBE DUCK BLINDS IN THE WINTER.

Somehow he had attached himself to Collier and been a legislative aide a couple of summers. It had bothered Dale, one of those little signals that maybe her husband needed hero worship. Collier said he had to give a job to a cousin. Not that Hootch was closely related at all. But in Charleston, even the most distant relative was claimed as a cousin. And Hooch was in KA. The brotherhood of the Order was all-important. And like Collier, he was a Civil War reenactor.

What was startling about Hootch was to find him in her study going through the stuff in the middle of the day, pulling down books and thumbing through them. The shelves ran floor-to-ceiling with rifles and swords mounted between each set, which gave him plenty to look through.

"Oh hi," he said, his cap on indoors, the bill pulled down level with his eyes. He pushed it up a bit with a thumb. Leaned up against the roll top desk.

Dale thought he's better looking than most. Lifeguard type body. Who did he resemble? Could it be Brad Pitt? No, he had an edge of dissipation on him. She had seen him really sloppy drunk a lot of times. And there was something almost sinister about his eyes.

"Uh, this is still my house," she said, crossing her arms in a defensive posture. As tall as she was, her eyes almost met his at the same level.

Hootch did a shuffle. Pushed his cap up a bit more. "Yeah right. Oh you're wondering why I'm here. See, Collier asked me to stop by and check on the collection. See if there's any silverfish or mold. That stuff's murder if you don't catch it early. Can't be too careful. And he wanted me to pick up a couple of things for him as well."

That little touch made it almost believable. That Collier would send him over to pilfer the collection, get it out of Dale's clutches. But still, something was off just a tick. Dale said, "You really ought to call before dropping by. And ring the bell rather than just walk in. It's a new age and all but still customary. Otherwise I might get the wrong impression. Call the cops and have you arrested, not knowing it was a social or business visit."

"Hey, no problem," said Hootch. "I got an attorney. You know my cousin Rannie. Your sister-in-law. Rannie's handling my false imprisonment case. Which kind of like puts her on a retainer for whatever other difficulties I might get into."

"Rannie would kill you for first-naming her," Dale said.

They were talking like that. Light banter as though nothing were out of line. Dale suggested, "You might like to put the book you're holding back on the shelf where you found it and go on back out the door, closing it behind you."

That was when the tension clamped down on the scene that made Dale feel like she was back in New York confronting a street whacko. Just an odd animal cunning look he gave her. Hesitating. Sizing her up. Wondering how she'd react if he just picked up an armful and walked out. Whether she'd really do anything. Then the moment passed and he was putting the books back, saying sure no problem. He could see where she was coming from. But say, what was this?

And he pulled out a big stack of pages tied up in blue ribbon, flipped through them. It seemed to be a handwritten narrative of some sort. "I thought I knew the whole collection by heart," said Hootch puzzled.

Dale could smell liquor on him. She turned up her nose, took the pages from his hand and stuck them back in their place. She edged him towards the door, but he dawdled, looking out the windows to the garden, running his hand over the latches.

"You don't have an alarm system in the house do you? The reason I ask is most houses down here do. Crime's pretty much running rampant. You go off for a couple hours and burglars back a truck or van up like they're working on something. Folks in the neighborhood are accustomed to seeing that because the houses are all kept up so well. Immaculate almost. Not like years ago when things were still pretty shabby and you even had pockets of spades living down here.

"But the way things have gotten, they'll take pretty much anything. Settle for new-laid sod or swimming pool equipment, garden ornaments. No gnomes or flamingoes because we're too upscale. But you get plenty of decorative fountains with herons or egrets on them. You can figure half the retail price for stolen goods. That's what they pay at the flea markets and places."

Now he was looking at the swords and Civil War rifles that

mounted on the dividers between the bookshelves, asking if Collier ever oiled them, did anything to keep the rust off. Then he moved to the front door, gave her a wink and said, "I'll catch you later. Maybe you and Collier got your signals crossed. I know you aren't doing well together. Couple gets married, and they come off the same starting blocks. Then run at different paces."

Dale decided Hootch was a bigger asshole than she had figured. The type who'd get roped into a crime and have the whole thing hung around his neck. Be the one standing there when the cops arrived. Dust settled and everyone else cut and run. He'd be blinking wondering where they had all gone. Just the sort of patsy Collier would use for his dirty work.

She had repressed something really nasty about him. When she and Collier were first married, Hootch had put a bloody deer head in their bed. Antlers. Tongue sticking out. Glassy eyes. Bloody gore soaking into the bed. He thought it was a real howl. A little prank he had picked up from that mafia movie *The Godfather*.

That had put Collier off him and gotten him barred from the house. She didn't know what their relationship might still be, Collier leading his secret life in Columbia and all.

Hootch was still hanging there. Dale said, "Well, I see you're not too adept at concealing your intentions. But what I'm wondering is if you're silly enough to think you're playing a board game. Like Monopoly. And think maybe you've got a 'Get Out of Jail Free' card."

He looked at her intently. Big crease between his eyebrows. Struggling for a retort that wouldn't come.

16.

DEBONE PUFFED HIS CIGAR, SAID IT WAS CRIMINAL HOW KIDS RODE THEIR BIKES BAM UP ON THE SIDEWALKS, WHAM BACK DOWN IN THE STREET, DARTING IN AND OUT OF TRAFFIC. THEY'D COME TO A RED LIGHT, KIND OF WOBBLE BACK AND FORTH AND THEN DASH ACROSS IN FRONT OF SPEEDING CARS. HE HAD HAD TO SPEAK TO A WHITE COLLEGE BOY RIGHT SHARPLY ABOUT SUCH NEGLIGENT BEHAVIOR. THAT LED TO SOME WORDS BETWEEN THEM AND DEBONE SMACKED HIM ON HIS ASS AND TOOK THE BIKE.

The fancy mountain bike had made it easy for him to score some heavy jewelry, chains and bracelets, things a man needed, out of a car at the Meeting Street Piggly Wiggly parking lot where somebody was always selling shit out of his trunk. Just dart in and out of the parked cars, the dude yelling after him. Debone said he didn't like stooping to petty theft, strong-arm robbery shit, but a man had his appearance to worry about.

Debone was a one-man crime wave. Tamzie told him, "You look like a total fool in them hip-hop clothes. Man your age ought to have a job in an office. Wear a suit. Maybe be a librarian or something."

Debone gave her that cocky smile and said he was stylin'. "And it's an open question whether you know shit from shinola about male fashion." And then he said *"Library?* What is this library shit? Emptying the trash over at the College got you interested in finally reading a book? Man work in a library got to have his balls tied off with a rubber band."

"I read plenty," Tamzie argued. "I'm getting up to page fifty-five in a book called *All God's Dangers* which is about our black heritage. And men who work in libraries seem just fine to me."

"I catch you messin' round," he warned, "it's 'Goodnight Irene' for you."

The day before he had smacked her ten feet across the room, so Tamzie knew that was no lie. If her money problems weren't bad enough, she now had to feed the man, him just putting down ribs and fried chicken and baked potato all at the same time like he never had a meal seven years in prison. Ordinary liquor wasn't good enough for him. He had to have that "Sweden vodka" which cost more than any mortal man ought to ever have to pay for a drink. If she didn't get him out the house, she'd be over at Beneficial Finance just to pay for groceries.

Tamzie worked on that problem, thinking about it most of the hours at work. She figured maybe let drop to the red bitch that Debone, this recent felon, had force his way into the house that she, the red bitch, virtually owned. The man talking plans to turn it into a crack house. That would get Rannie going to the cops, moving him out, and he couldn't blame Tamzie. She'd say to Debone let her know when he found some other home. Not let on she had romance plans for when after it had happened.

She thought maybe invite Thaddeus Wyndham over for barbecue chicken. Wear her metallic tunic and palazzo pants. The big hoop earrings with the gold-tone acrylic and rhinestones. Tell him she believed the old saying that we should all occasionally pamper ourselves.

Thaddeus was like a walking bookstore, but not a showboat about it. He'd talk normal, tell her about the collection, who had donated it, what he was trying to get somebody to donate. He liked talking to her. The fact Tamzie didn't have a master's degree from the University of South Carolina didn't take away her ability to attract men.

Tamzie said folks seemed to donate stuff, didn't Thaddeus ever buy nothing? He said they had limited budgets, but on occasion he'd made a purchase. That let her ask about who would buy stuff like he had in the collection. Assuming somebody had some for sale. He got right stiff at that, maybe thinking she might lay plans to walk off with something. Try to fence it on the street. He asked what particular piece of the collection was she thinking of.

She said, "No, it's something I got at home. Or rather something somebody's going to give me any day now."

He kept looking at her, knowing for sure she was going to boost something. "What you mean," he said "is something you're going to purloin. And that raises concerns."

"It ain't really *stealing*," she argued, screwing up and telling the truth without intending to. "Nobody ever look at the thing. Not like in here where you run a library."

He was stroking that beard like a grandfather wondering how this younger generation got born. "Did your momma ever ask you 'What if everybody did it?'"

That made Tanzie feel about five years old and lower than dirt. "It's nothing but ancestor stuff," she said.

Thaddeus smiled at that one. "Ancestor stuff is the record of the human condition. All our warts and blemishes. Our angel wings too. Did you know your ancestors, I mean direct forebears of Tamzie Jerome, were freed long back before the Civil War?"

"You serious? How'd they pull that off?"

"It's a long but interesting story. You know something else interesting?"

"What?"

"Once they got free, they bought slaves of their own."

17.

"WHAT YOU MEAN," SAID DEBONE "IS SOME WHITE SLAVE OWNER NAME OF JEROME DONE PORK YOUR GREAT-GRAND-GRANMAMMA, HAVE A SON BY HER. NOW THAT'S WHAT I CALL A REAL SOURCE OF PRIDE."

Tamzie and Debone walked down Legendre Street to where Dale's house sat across and just up from Miz Ralston's.

"That's part of it," Tamzie sulked. "But my ancestors were for true Africans. From the Gold Coast. The man was a iron worker and saved a penny here and a penny there. Bought his wife's freedom. Went on to own businesses and farms."

"So where did your family go wrong?" said Debone.

"You mean holding other folks in bondage?" said Tamzie.

"No. I mean how come they lost all they money and you ain't rich?"

Tamzie did not like what they were about to do. She imagined Thaddeus looking at her like the dirtiest of sinners. Knowing she was up to something. The red bitch Rannie doing that thin-lip smile that said she had a mortgage on the house. Her momma Mozelle watching from on high saying how come you can't pay a tax and keep hold of what I work so hard to give you, get you out of the Jackson Street project.

She said, "Why don't you just go steal a car, get caught, and go on back inside the jailhouse?"

"I'm using a combination of resources to fund my program. I figure to get out of hock before I die."

Tamzie was disgusted. Debone had spent the day before in the Strom Thurmond Federal Office saying he wanted to manage a midnight basketball program. They give him so many forms to fill out he give up and leave.

Now Tamzie and Debone were thinking to walk in Dale's house and take stuff. Dale was always nice. She didn't like giving orders and standing over you while you worked, saying you missed this or that. Usually she'd arrange to be out of the house until you were done. Which would make the stealing job easy. Few hours of cleaning and they could take whatever they wanted. Rearrange the shelves so there were no holes where you'd notice stuff was missing.

Tamzie was so tense that when Dale answered the door she started talking way too fast saying she knew Miz Dale was needing help and they thought they'd pitch in and clean the place from top to bottom. Have it looking like a spring morning.

Dale looked at them a little puzzled. She said, "It's nice to see you back, Debone."

Just like that. Not nice to see you back out of prison where you been for cold-blooded killing a man. Not I'm sorry to see they let your worthless black coon ass out 'cause you could use a good seat in the electric chair. What he deserved to have said to him.

Debone give Tamzie a look.

Trouble was, Dale was firm she couldn't afford them. "I'm doing my own cleaning now," she said. "It's better that way. You know what's going on in my life. They keep no secrets over there." She kind of gestured with her chin down Legendre to Miz Ralston's house.

"We just do it once more for old time's sake," Tamzie insisted. "No charge."

"You know I can't accept that." She gave them a decent smile, looking right at them. Dale was always like that.

Debone said well if she change her mind just give a hollar. They drop whatever they doing and be right over. Then they back off and the door close.

Disgusted, Tamzie said, "Miss Dale's scared of you in them hip-hop garments. Maybe next time we try to win the woman's confidence you might do even better. Come wearing dreadlocks and a wool cap pulled down to your ears. Get mauled by drugs ahead of time so you drool and stagger more."

"You got to learn to control your moody, evil ways," Debone shot back. "The problem encourages more close scrutiny, but it can be overcome. And thinking on it done caused me to remember the one thing we sold the man Collier that was legitimate. That diary that belonged to your momma Mozelle and come from way back in the family. I mean it's ours, ain't it? We can legally siphon it out. If you worrying about the morality of the thing, we leave the woman a twenty dollar bill. Just like we got. Maybe throw in some compound interest."

"What's this 'ours' shit? We been divorce."

"Not in the eyes of God where you put us with that AME church wedding. Besides, I ain't give up on y'all yet. Family values. Safe sex. Anti-drug message. That's the new Debone."

That was when the white dude in the short ponytail and seersucker suit came up the walk. Body like a fireplug. Something snapped in Tamzie's brain. Miz Dale had already phoned the cops on them, and here he was.

"How y'all?" he said nicely. Walked right past them.

"Fine, just fine," said Tamzie. She relaxed a bit. They went on down the walk, glanced back. He was up ringing the doorbell.

"You think he's a cop?" she asked nervously.

Debone looked over the man's car like he was wondering if it was worth stealing. "Nah. I knows a cop when I see one."

Tamzie said, "Most of the cops you met been kneeling on you cuffing your hands behind your back. Maybe you didn't get such a good look at the time. Get to study the way they move particularly."

Dale's doorbell rang for a second time. Her visitor was a white man in a suit, moderately short with a small ponytail and clean-shaven face. Not real short, but a couple inches below Dale's height. Dale had always had trouble with short men. They felt like they had to come on strong to prove their manhood. This one was very polite, although he was perspiring in the heat. Temperature in the mid-nineties outside. He said don't be fooled by his southern accent, he was Josh Mahoney from New York and had come to survey the manuscript collection as had been arranged.

A warning bell went off. Dale said she was real busy and had nothing for sale. If Collier had called him, then he needed to get Collier to work through their lawyers. They were getting divorced. He would understand those things.

She closed him out and stood there with her back to the door trying to figure, thinking, Collier? He would never sell his collection. Rannie? She might have done it. Try to force the issue with a cash offer out on the table. Then she thought—*Moira*. Little sugar lips Moira must have something to do with this. Moira had been coming around almost every day borrowing this and returning that. Mooning around handling every book on the shelves. She was up to some daffy scheme.

Dale went into the study and pulled out the ribbon-bound stack of paper that had puzzled Hootch. She found a hand-written manuscript of a novel. *South Blows the Wind.* The name Margaret Mitchell as the author was a dead give-away. That lunatic Moira had planted the thing.

Dale flipped through it reading a page here and there, all about Scarlett and Rhett in Maximilian's Mexico. Dale had read a book about that once. Some Confederates had left the South during Reconstruction and started a colony there. Got involved in a mess with the French, who had Maximilian on the throne. Moira had used it as the basis of a fake Mitchell novel. A sequel to *Gone With the Wind.* Even written it on what appeared to be old paper in case someone wanted to authenticate it. Like there weren't handwriting analysts in the world.

Vintage Moira. Moira with the cashmere twin sets and pearls and doing her nails every day. Moira with her helpful advice. A round dining table is a godsend for a politician's wife. No one guest has a seat of greater honor than the others. Moira had been over to the house yesterday, pretty much like everyday, saying how brave of Dale to rent her home to the movies. This courage inspired Moira so much she had decided to invite the producer to dinner. She had used her calligraphy on the invitation so he would realize she had something of value to contribute to the project. She thought it would be uplifting for him and help authenticate the film. Hollywood seldom got movies historically accurate.

And Dale now remembered that she had come in with something in her arms and gone out empty-handed. The something had been a manuscript. Moira had settled upon Dale as suitable to play a role in whatever little drama she had cooked up. But as a first step she had planted the manuscript and called a book dealer down from New York to discover it just as the movie crew hit town. Was Hootch part of the plot? Was his walking into the house the same as breaking in?

She looked around the room at all the things Collier had collected. A framed map of the Mason-Dixon line. A recruiting poster that read:

TO ARMS! TO ARMS!
YOUR COUNTRY CALLS!
Mounted Volunteers
Wanted!

Underneath a silhouette of a man galloped his horse while blowing a bugle.

And all the tedious books. She ran her fingers over some of the titles.

Charles Coatsworth Pinckney. *An Address Delivered in Charleston Before the August Society of South Carolina.* Printed by A.E. Miller in 1829. 24 pp. One of eight volumes.

Confederate War Journal Illustrated. Vol. 1, No. 1

William W. Chamberlain, *Memoirs of the Civil War.*

Benjamin Lundy, *The Civil War in Texas*

Hootch Gibson wanted the collection or at least part of it. Dale didn't know what was valuable and what wasn't. But Collier would be a walking catalogue on that. Were they in league?

How bad would it be for her to sell a few books? The owners had never missed them. They were all affluent. No destitute widows and orphans in the lot.

Dale sat and stewed for a while and then phoned Mary Canty. The clock said noon, but true Charlestonians didn't eat dinner until two or even three. They preserved a custom that dated to plantation days before electric lighting. Mary would be having the first Plymouth gin and tonic. Gin for summer. Scotch for winter.

"I don't know why I'm talking to you," rasped Mary Canty. "You've broken my family into warring camps. But I'm always the one to bend over backwards to keep open channels of communication."

Dale let that pass and asked about Hootch Gibson, who his parents were and all.

"I think he's a bit young for you," said Mary acidly.

Dale counted to ten, took a deep breath, and said she had recently found him in her house and she wondered if he was dangerous. Was there anything in his past? Mary Canty, if anyone, would know.

"He's a cousin of some sort. His parents lived on Tradd Street. Drank heavily."

Mary Canty always thought of others as drinking heavily.

"Are they still drinking on Tradd Street?"

"Certainly not. They died some years ago, the father before the mother. Drinking will do that. High blood pressure. Strokes. Hunter, or Hootch as he seems to be called, has a trust fund."

Dale asked where he lived, and Mary named a carriage house on Dubose Street, a little place behind a big mansion. "But of course you want to know if he's dangerous. Everyone wonders about that dreadful incident of him shooting out the streetlights and being committed. I believe the reason given was collegiate debauchery."

18.

THE AEROBICS CLASS THAT DALE COULD NO LONGER AFFORD WAS FILLED WITH WOMEN WHO SHARED FANTASIES OF LAUNCHING MINI-INDUSTRIES. ONE TALKED OF CREATING A WINDOW BOX BUSINESS. WITH FLOWERS. GO AROUND AND WATER AND WEED THEM FOR THE HOMEOWNER WHO LACKED A GREEN THUMB. OTHERS HAD THE COOKIE-SHOP-IN-THE-MALL DAYDREAM. AND THE HIGH-TONE RESTAURANT. THE CONSIGNMENT JEWELRY SHOP. DOG-WALKING. RAISING HORSES. OF COURSE NONE OF THE DREAMS EVER MATERIALIZED UNLESS THERE WAS AN M.D. HUSBAND WILLING TO FLUSH MONEY DOWN THE DRAIN.

Dale had always been hard on the women for their lack of realism. They had everything, lacked for nothing. She had been like that once. Now reality had intruded sharply. The movie people would be coming in a week, but as big as their rental fee seemed, it wouldn't go far. She had a whopper of a mortgage on the house. Either she found a way to make money or goodbye house and treasured possessions. Goodbye to lemonade and tea in her garden, to the quiet of Legendre St. and sleeping in the big bed with the rice designs on the posts. She thought about this as she embarked on an enterprise of semi-crime. She didn't know how to dress exactly, but decided on tight jeans and a t-shirt, neat vest, and silk jacket. Tennis shoes. She guessed that would be okay.

The College of Charleston had an archives collection. They could

tell her some values on a Civil War collection. Fanatic collectors—
Blake Huston or whoever—were sharks. Collier was walking proof of
that. They'd spot her ignorance in a second.

The College library had palmettos outside and a narrow quadran-
gle that ran up to the really elegant Randolph Hall, the oldest structure
of the campus. The wind rose as a summer storm approached, whipping the trees and bushes. Thunderheads like gray whipped cream
leered high in the sky.

Special Collections was upstairs behind a glass wall with its own
door. Rows of old books and heavy tables. A marine architect's side and
top views of a Civil War era ironclad in a glass case.

A man's voice behind her said, "That's the USS Keokuk. It was
sunk by Confederate batteries during the siege of Charleston. Went
down as they said 'riddled like a colander.'"

She turned to find an enormous black man in a beard and bowtie,
a faint contented smile on his face. He said powerful as it was, the
union fleet could neither force an entrance into the harbor nor totally
seal it off. Blockade-runners entered and left pretty much at will until
the last year of the war. Dale said she had heard that but forgotten it.
He said he was the curator. Thaddeus Wyndham. Of the Orangeburg
Wyndhams.

Dale froze with white liberal guilt. She had to ask this descendant
of slaves about Confederate archives. She took a deep breath and asked
him what a Bedford Forrest diary would be worth. Kind of short. Less
than a hundred pages. Covering late 1862 into mid 1863.

Thaddeus kind of squinted with one eye. "Bedford Forrest was
virtually illiterate."

"It might be an illiterate kind of diary."

"Might be?"

"I've never really seen it. Don't even know if it exists."

"It doesn't."

He had caught her cold. She had made the diary up. "I have, like, a project." She swallowed hard. "For the Junior League. To make a list of ancestral papers of the members. Try to decide what's valuable and what's not. I was trying to get some ideas. Guess I'm not going about it the right way."

He said Confederate materials always brought two and three times Union ones. The romance of the cavalier South. At least one historian had analyzed it as the Celt battling the Saxon. The battle of Culloden brought to American shores. He thought there might be something in that.

She asked how about one of the original drawings for the Mason-Dixon line?

She watched his eyes bulge. He said, "That belongs to Frannie MacAlpin. Lady down on East Battery. I've been trying to persuade her to donate it to our library." He stroked his beard. "She says she's misplaced it."

"Uh, yes. Right. It's hers."

He showed her a book guide called *Book Prices Current—Civil War.* Said they varied according to the fanaticism of collectors. For some reason Jefferson Davis seemed to bring more than Stonewall Jackson. She should take her time, make notes, whatever. Dale sat at a table and read:

"Bartlett, Napier. *Military Record of Louisiana*—$3,500.

DeBray, Xavier Blanchard. *A Sketch of the History of Debray's 26th Rgt. of Texas Cavalry,* 26 pp. original printed, blue wraps, first ed. rare—$3,200.

DuBose, Henry Kershaw. *History of Co. B, 21st Rgt. (Infantry), SC*

Volunteers—$2,500."

Dale sucked in her breath. Collier easily had two hundred books. Thousands of dollars each. She flipped through pages of book titles. Then she saw what really rocked her.

"Original Drawings, A Plan of the West Line or Parallel of Latitude which is the boundary between the Provinces of Maryland and

Pennsylvania [sic]. One of two orig. drawings for the Mason-Dixon line.   [26 Dec. 1767-29 Feb. 1768]—$360,000."

Outside, the storm broke with a crash of lightning and torrent of water. Ceiling lights began to flicker. Thaddeus burst out of the back very concerned about the computers and the humidity system. He rushed out and downstairs, leaving Dale alone.

She sat looking at *Book Prices Current*. It was a reference book. Couldn't be checked out. But there was no tattle-tape in the book. It wouldn't set off an alarm. She wouldn't really be stealing if she borrowed it and brought it back. She slipped it in her purse.

That was when Hootch sauntered in wearing a swordbill cap, poplin vest with a lot of pockets on it, and khaki shorts. Used his cap to brush off the few raindrops that had caught him, put it back on his head. He was the last person Dale wanted to see, so she stepped back in the shelves of books and watched him through a gap. He was going around the room picking up books, looking at them casually. He strolled over to the big glass case with the Keokuk in it, fiddled with the lock and suddenly the lid lifted. He slid out the map and rolled it up, put a rubber band around it. Closed the case. No alarm had gone off.

Dale stepped out, her mouth open. She might have been watching muggers operate in broad daylight on crowded streets in New York. You just couldn't believe the gall.

He was walking towards her now, looked a little startled, then recognized her. "Hey, what're you doing in here? Family genealogy?"

"I let Collier handle that. And Moira."

"Yeah, they're nuts about family history. Well, see ya. I'm in a hurry." He stepped around her.

"You'll never get past security with that," she said.

He looked at the rolled up drawing, eyes open, surprised. "With what? This? Just paper. Won't set off any alarms."

"Because I'll walk down with you and tell them what you're carrying."

He gave her a smug look like there was something between them. "You're crazy about me, aren't you? I always noticed that about you. Maybe now that Collier is going off to do jail time, you and me can get together."

"That doesn't hold much appeal. But right now you've created a problem that I can't just ignore."

"You remember Sunday School? Bible stuff? Among the Hebrews when a man died, his widow had to marry the next brother. Collier always said I was like a brother to him."

Dale was cool. "That's nice you know the Bible. Maybe you can get religion in jail. Many of them seem to."

Hootch gnawed on that for a moment, then reached out and took her by the throat with a big hand. He was too quick to dodge. His fingers and thumb hooked under her jaw pinching in. There was something glittery-crazy looking in his eyes. He'd been drinking. You could smell the booze on him.

Hootch was so big he blocked Dale's view of Josh Mahoney, who just reached up and kind of pinched a place at the base of his neck. A wave of pain rushed through Hootch and his knees buckled. Josh guided him all the way facedown on the floor. Held him there. His little ponytail was sticking up like a geyser. He said he guessed she should call the downstairs desk. Have them get security. Dale did that using the phone right there on the desk. All the while watching Josh. He was built really powerfully. And his face had nice lines.

"Nice shirt," Josh said to Hootch. "Guess it's pretty cool in all this Charleston humidity."

"It's an open-mesh weave," grunted Hootch, head twisted to talk back over his shoulder. "This is your teal color. I've got one island blue as well." Hootch looked hopeful. Color came back into his face. He tried to get up. Josh pinched him in that spot again, harder, and Hootch screamed. By then the brown-uniformed security guards were coming in.

Hootch started yelling, "It's just a ol' piece of paper! I found it on the floor. You can't do this. I got rights."

"Don't be a self-dramatizer," said Josh.

19.

"HOOTCH GIBSON," MARY CANTY DECLARED IN THE MIDDLE OF SUPPER. "ALTHOUGH I CAN BARELY BRING MYSELF TO PRONOUNCE SUCH AN ABSURD NICKNAME. I THINK HE COULD BE THE ONE FOR YOU. EVERYONE AT THE CLUB AGREES. HE'S QUITE HANDSOME."

Moira dabbed her lips with the napkin and folded her hands in her lap. Her mother seemed to be leering at her from across the crystal and china, drinking iced vodka from a fluted champagne glass, leaving the roast beef on her plate untouched. Moira could never imagine herself growing older and assuming that character, impersonating her mother.

Her sister Rannie was bolting her food down, trying to get away from them as quickly as possible. She would go out in that smothering heat, mosquitoes so thick you couldn't move, and bang and slam away at her house. No one could stand to work for her, so she had to do most of it on her own.

Mary Canty was wearing a gold pin in the shape of a tree with pearls on each branch. She said Hootch wasn't a close cousin so there'd be no problem with co-sanguinity or whatever it was called. His parents had been heavy drinkers, but sensible with their money. Left Hootch a trust fund of some sort. He was doing business studies at the College. He was quite handsome. Kappa Alpha fraternity.

Moira became attentive. KA was after all, the fraternity of the old

South. Founded at Washington & Lee when Robert E. Lee was president just after the Civil War. "Didn't he serve as an aide to Collier at one point?" she queried.

"I'm sure he did," said Mary Canty. Not that she knew. "Full of promise that young man. Very trainable for a girl with the will to do it."

"He's in Collier's Confederate reenactment unit as well," added Moira thoughtfully. She could see his face. He was handsome. But he drank to excess. Rather like her mother. She could picture the pair sitting together on the piazza with a pitcher of gin rickeys.

"You're actually interested?" said Mary Canty, astonished.

"Do you ever get laid?" Rannie asked her sister. "I mean when you went off to college, did some guy even put a finger in you?"

"Randolph, I won't have this vulgarity," declared Mary Canty. "You're worse than common trash."

Moira felt as though she could reach out and touch the discomfort in the air. It was palpable. Her sister obsessed on the animal side of human sexuality. Rannie was not a Ralston, but something else. Some spawn of a red-haired monster and certainly not of their perfect gentleman father.

"I'm just trying to be helpful," Rannie blandly told their mother. "You want to marry off the Virgin Moira here. Maybe we should get her hymen cut by a surgeon. Reduce the potential for hysteria on that crucial wedding night."

Moira tittered. She didn't like tittering, but Rannie always made her do it. Made her feel balanced on a high wire and might just give up and pitch herself into a vast chasm below.

Rannie pointed her fork at Moira, "Once that's over with, you don't have to worry about your other problem."

"Excuse me?" Moira squeaked.

"Perhaps you'll both excuse me for being so explicit. But the vagina is very flexible. Within the first thirty seconds of intercourse it expands or contracts to fit the penis. Whichever is needed."

In her house, Dale sat bathed in the light of the TV. watching the news. Her mother had always said she'd ruin her eyes if she watched it in the dark, but Dale preferred it that way.

State Representative T. C. Polsom pled guilty to bribery charges resulting from the FBI sting "Operation Chump Change" and was sentenced to forty-six months in prison. He said he hoped to soon be released to a halfway house where he could perform community service fighting illiteracy. His attorney begged the court to not send Polsom to the new Broad River Correctional Institution but rather to a federal minimum-security facility for white-collar offenders. Polsom's wife Donna said, "I'm not trying to glorify my husband, but he thought he was serving the state and his home district in what he did. Now he's only looking to find his peace."

And there was that yokel Dubiel telling the press microphones that the prosecutions were moving forward as planned "from the git-go." He was wearing his gun. You could see the bulge under his armpit. He added, "Heads we win, tails they lose." Guffawed showing his molars.

Dale cut off the TV and sat in the dark listening to the crickets in the hot night. To save money, she didn't run her air conditioners, trying to get by the way people did before. The thick, soupy air seeped into the house and hung in a stagnant mass.

Collier had called up furious once again. The movie people scared him. They'd be coming into the house and maybe messing with all his stuff. He demanded she move every personal item of his into the library and padlock the door. Guns, uniforms, everything.

He said he'd come over and do it himself, but she said no, she wouldn't let him in. He said he'd hold her personally responsible if anything got pilfered. She said fine, whatever.

Collier gave more loud warnings about Blake Huston. How the thieving swine shouldn't be let in the room with the books. Shouldn't be allowed to even look at them through the windows. Dale said she'd like to get to know Blake. Anybody who could rile Collier so thoroughly had a style worth studying.

Life had its oddities. In the first year of her marriage, she had wondered about Collier's occasionally dressing up like a Confederate and reenacting battles. She decided it was no sillier than social events with tuxedos. No bigger a waste of time than men watching NFL football. And in a world of women writing Ann Landers about cross-dressing husbands, certainly less worrisome. So she just put it out of her mind. It was a hobby. Like golf.

At age twelve Dale thought she'd grow up to marry Lanny Parsons because she liked the way he wore shirts and socks the same color. In college she had liked Randy Allison because of the white navy uniform he wore to ROTC events and the whites he wore playing tennis. Collier was Confederate gray. She wondered if there was some color associated with book dealers. Velum red? Orange calfskin? She had never thought of a book dealer before. Or if she thought of one, she pictured a stoop-shouldered old man in a dusty shop. Never saw him as ever having been young and vibrant.

The book dealer Josh Mahoney was really broad shouldered, reminding her of wrestlers in college. She wondered if he had done that. One of those man things that some of them do. Nothing glamorous about it. No cheering spectators. Pursuing a goal all your own in a series of lonely gyms. Testing yourself for your own satisfaction.

Josh had a real quiet side to him. And a way of talking without letting out much about himself. Did that come from bargaining with people for books. Or just long hours in quiet places? He had pulled Hootch off her in the library. Used some martial arts nerve grip. Dale had never had a guy fight for her before. She had to admit it gave her a little fluttery feeling.

Dale went into the study and turned on the light. The map of the Mason-Dixon line seemed to be mocking her. $360,000. How could she possibly sell that? She wouldn't know where to begin. Dale knew why Collier didn't feel he was really stealing to have taken it. Frannie McAlpin had about eighty squillion dollars and no heirs. She was very loud about how she was leaving everything to a cat hospital.

Collier had a long list of rationalizations, which Dale had swallowed over the years. Southern heritage was the chief excuse. Greedy heirs would sell the artifacts to the highest bidder. The Getty museum would end up with it all. The records of the Old South would be moved to California. But Collier also wanted a monument to himself. A special room in the Historical Society named for him and his collection. He frequently mentioned the Morgan Library in New York as a model for his far-sighted vision.

Dale began pulling books off the shelf at random and looking for an entry in *Book Prices Current*.

> "*Fleming, Francis P[hillip]. Memoirs of Capt. C. Seton Fleming of the 2nd Florida Infantry, C.S.A.—$1,200.*
>
> *Casler, John O. Four Years in the Stonewall Brigade—$850.*
>
> *MacLeod, George H.B. Notes on the Treatment of the War in the Crimea with Remarks on the Treatment of Gunshot Wounds. Rare Confederate Surgery Manual.—$4,200.*"

Even the most excruciatingly boring stuff was valuable.

Pickens, F[rancis] W[ilkinson] Message No. 1 of His Excellency F. W. Pickens to the Legislature, at the Annual Session of Nov. 1861. Columbia, S.C. Charles P. Pelham, State Printer, 1861.—$2,000.

And the personal letters were worth even more. Collier had three Stonewall Jackson letters and a Jefferson Davis all neatly kept in clear plastic binders. *Book Prices Current* listed:

"Jackson, Thomas J. ("Stonewall") 24 Sept. 1862. 2 pp., to Samuel Cooper Recommending Col. W.E. Jones for promotion.—$21,000. Davis, Jefferson. 1 Apr. 1865, 4 pp. to Gen. Braxton Bragg. Reflecting on the weakened military position of the Confederacy.—$60,000.

Dale thought she would choke. She couldn't believe the gold mine she was sitting on.

What got her out of the house after dark was to go over to Rannie's construction site to purloin some strips of lath to stake her tomatoes in the garden. Dale had seen all kinds of wood scattered in Rannie's yard and in the big dumpster on the street from the major gutting and renovation of the old house. It wouldn't be stealing exactly. Rannie was her sister-in-law. She could spare a few sticks of wood.

Even in the dark, the heat was nearly suffocating. A thirty-eight-year-old record high had been broken. The thermometer had registered 100 degrees and the heat index made it 112. Legendre Street was silent, lights in the windows of the houses. A truly elegant street with trees so old no one remembered when they were planted, and residents who thought they were pretty much at the center of the universe.

Well-to-do people always seemed kind of trapped by their family ties. Life was too comfortable to make you want to strike out for a strange city and try something different. When Dale was twenty-one, the choice was obvious. Her boyfriend was Naval ROTC and had cruised off on a ship without bothering to ask her to marry him. She had a degree in English literature that would get her a teaching post in a junior high school where kids cussed you to your face. Nothing but a long dreary calendar of facing each day trying to make it through to a holiday.

And here she was after four years of marriage all enmeshed in the same toils. She couldn't quite bring herself to go back to New York. The South was too comfortable. And the fact was, she liked the town. She liked the old houses with shutters and long porches they called piazzas. She liked the giant oaks and the palmettos and the vines that twisted all around things.

Dale turned into the narrow little Rantowles Lane that was mostly filled by Rannie's house, a big Queen Anne with fishtail shingles. Rannie had the plumbing and electricity all done and was living upstairs in a pair of finished rooms. No lights showed. Rannie had gone out. The front door was off its hinges leaving a hole of silent emptiness. Dale stepped through the opening into the yawning dark. She stood there enveloped in black velvet until her eyes could make out shapes. A police car cruised down the street, playing a spotlight over the house. Dale ducked back out of sight feeling like a prowler. The car drove away.

Sawhorses and stacks of lumber littered the downstairs. The dining room seemed finished. Light fixtures in place. Wall sconces and a big chandelier. Nice wainscoting with mural wallpaper above it. Enormous wine rack at one end of the room with bottles in it. Dale's mind flitted back to Josh Mahoney. She wondered what you'd talk to a book dealer about over the dinner table. Would he take her hand and draw it to his lips? Maybe suck her fingers?

The wine rack along the wall of the dining room seemed out of place. You didn't put your wine on display. Restaurants did that, not Charleston homes. Certainly not South-of-Broad homes. Dale wasn't trying to snoop. The wine rack moved almost by accident. It was mounted on a wheeled track. And behind it in a hiding space sat a big green plastic garbage bag loaded with wads of . . . of cash! "Kow-a-bonga," she said. Then she said it again. "Kow-a-bonga!"

She dug in it up to her elbows. Big fat stacks of currency, fifties and hundreds, but without bank straps. This was used money held by thick rubber bands. It was dirty money. Dirty meaning illegal. Rannie had gotten it from somewhere not very nice and was not about to report to the IRS this humongous transaction way over the $10,000 that triggered the requirement. Dale knew about the ten grand rule from Collier, not that Collier ever earned money in that sum. He just liked to fantasize.

This is not stealing, she said to herself. Rannie is my nasty, tiresome, witch sister-in-law. This is a family matter. This is definitely not stealing. She kept counting out the money. Hundreds and hundreds of dollars. There was so much it didn't even make a dent.

Then she froze. She had reached thirty thousand and fear had set in. She had never stolen anything in her life. Well certainly not of this magnitude. But she had a semi-wicked thought. She'd take enough to pay Rannie the stinking fee she was demanding to defend Collier. What a burner on her that would be. And it might keep Collier out of prison. Much as she would enjoy seeing him behind bars, he couldn't pay her alimony while locked up and the mortage was daunting.

Well, maybe she'd take just a bit more. She needed to buy a car.

20.

"I TOLD YOU I FOUND THE SUM-BITCH ON THE FLOOR," HOOTCH GIBSON INSISTED. "I WAS ON MY WAY DOWNSTAIRS TO TURN IT IN JUST LIKE A GOOD CITIZEN OR A DAMN BOY SCOUT. I GOT RIGHTS. HE CAN'T JUST WHIP UP ON ME BASED ON SUSPICION. HE'S NOT EVEN A COP. I DON'T KNOW WHAT HE IS."

At the end of the day at Ralston & Ralston, No. 6 Broad Street, Rannie always liked to sit at her desk and have a Jim Beam on the rocks the way her father had done. As a little girl when she'd meet him to walk home, he'd have a slight whiff of bourbon on his breath. She'd hold his hand and feel like he was hers and hers alone.

Hootch was there with his absurd alibi for how he wasn't really stealing a drawing out of the College of Charleston library. Offered a drink, he sucked down three in a hurry. Rannie knew she shouldn't drink with a client, but he was a cousin. That counted for a lot in Charleston. Ferocious set of pecs on the boy. He looked distantly like somebody from the movies. Matthew McConaughey? Brad Pitt? She'd like to have a man who looked that good. But what a lout. She had to tell him to take off his damn cap indoors. They all did that now. Little in-your-face college brats. Thinking they're above good manners.

Down below, Broad Street was getting quiet. By six, all the lawyers were going home, the banks letting out. It hadn't been an easy day. One of Rannie's clients had just drawn twenty years for shooting a highway patrolman point blank in the chest. The trooper had been wearing a bulletproof vest, so he wasn't hurt except for the impact, which left him with sore muscles and bruised ribs for a month or so. Still it was not a very civic-minded thing to have done. In the middle of the plea, the fool turned to the trooper and said, "For what it's worth, and I know that's not much after all the rigmarole I put you through . . . I just want to say I'm sorry."

They all tried to pull that. Act contrite. Get going with the rehabilitation act. Rannie had only been able to clip him for $5,000. But for a couple hours work it wasn't bad.

Rannie told Hootch he was an imbecile to try to steal from a library, patrons everywhere, half of them moralistic liberals. And she said they needed renewed attention to his legal bill. The five hundred he had given her for handling the streetlight shooting incident was a pittance.

Hootch scratched his face, said it was easy to understand her conflicting emotions—sincere desire to protect the innocent Hootch Gibson versus need to earn a living. "But bottom line is my allowance is tapped for the next six months." He helped himself to another drink and asked about his lawsuit for false imprisonment.

Rannie looked at him over the rim of her Old-Fashion glass. "The state of your mental health would not stand close scrutiny. That lawsuit's going nowhere."

That riled him. "What am I? Bat shit? There's nothing wrong with my head."

"You shoot out street lights. They take you in for observation. You tell them you're having a heart attack. Then try to check out by ripping the EKG leads off your chest and running out the door. That was real stable behavior."

"What's that got to do with anything? I don't like being shut in. I'm an outdoors kind of guy. Believe in all the traditions of American liberty. That's what we'll tell the jury on this trumped-up larceny case. I saw that drawing lying on the floor and instantly knew it was part of our valuable heritage. I felt a moral obligation to turn it in to the proper authorities. Cause I respect heritage and shit."

Rannie scoffed. "Tell the jury? You watch a lot of TV? You think I'm going to put on a full-blown trial for your sorry hide? You'll take the plea they offer us and pay a fine. Do some community service."

Hootch hunched over, swatting at his boat shoes with his cap. "Around this town, we trust fund boys are like an endangered species."

What a clown. She could hear him telling that to little honeys in bars. Just kind of dropping into the conversation that he had inherited wealth. Then trying to stiff them on the bar tab.

"This fee business," Hootch said, sucking an ice cube. "Don't you have any alternatives?"

Rannie stared at him, thinking about the angles. He was dumb, but it might work. "You ever thought of working as a runner?"

He said she had already sent him over to Bubba's. They hadn't shared his vision. Rannie said she meant run cases for her. He'd need to get a CB radio in his car, listen to the police channel for accidents. Meet the victims in the hospital ER or later in their homes. Strike up a conversation. Act sympathetic. Stress the permanent nature of their injuries and the difficulty of dealing with insurance companies on their own. Steer them to her office.

The fantasy took flight with no problem. Hootch started talking countywide marketing. Said he reckoned he could up her volume, wipe out his debt in the first month.

She opened the bottom drawer on her desk and fished out Calvin

Whitesides' Smith & Wesson .38 revolver using a pencil through the trigger guard. Held it dangling in front of him. "Sometimes you're out late at night, things can get rough."

His eyes lit up. He hadn't held a gun for far too long. Not since the cops had taken his during the psychiatric evaluation. "I wouldn't want to stall innovation."

She reached it over to him, using the pencil.

He hefted it, getting the feel of its weight, pointed it at the portrait of her father on the wall. Then he dropped the gate, let out the bullets, counted them. When he came up one short, he sniffed the barrel.

"It's been fired recently."

"It's off the street. Who knows where it's been."

Hootch reloaded the gun, got up and shoved it into the waist of his trousers, pulled his Absolut vodka t-shirt over it. Gave her a 'man, don't fuck with me' look.

Hootch was such an waste-wad. She couldn't believe her mother proposing this muscle-bound clod as a marriage prospect for delicate little Moira.

Then her own predicament struck her. She couldn't remember the last time she got laid. Well, she could, but she didn't like to. The experience was too ghastly.

Big deal guys that managed mutual funds, big-league tort lawyers, medical doctors—they all wanted bimbos. A successful career women like herself had to settle for sex without love. Sex without even respecting the bedmate. It was a wry twist on the old "put a bag over her head" quip. With Hootch you'd have to put a bag over his brain.

"You don't have a girlfriend do you," she ventured cautiously.

He looked at his shoes. "Naw. I been turned inside out by bitches in my time. I'm taking a breather."

Rannie said, "It's funny when you think about it. Strapping young guy like you. Peak physical form. High sperm count. But maybe getting a bit old for the coeds. They always want guys their age. Clowns with skateboards or the yahoos holding up the porch posts on the frat houses."

"Ain't that the manifest God's truth."

"Then one day they're married and suddenly know how small a paycheck is."

Hootch thought he was following her there for a moment, but now he wasn't sure. "Say what?"

She used the pencil to give her hair a little flip so it fell over one eye. "I'm wondering what you do for nookie."

Hootch looked like Christmas and his birthday had landed on the same date.

*

In late evening, Tamzie vacuumed the Special Collections area real slow, and sure enough, Thaddeus Wyndham came out on his way home. He carried that walking stick and a straw hat with a little green visor strip across the front of the brim. She didn't have to think up jive to lay on him to hold him there. He had this way of looking at her like hunger and thirst all merged in a slow burning heat. All that business of treating her like a thief seemed behind them.

Without any lead-in, he said, "Despite the handicap of a minor weight problem I been working on, I like the out-of-doors."

Tamzie said, "I ain't done much of that since I was a kid and used to stay summers with my grands on Daniel Island. I miss it, but it's part of my life that's behind me."

Thaddeus smiled. "It could bear further consideration on your part."

She liked the way he talked. The man had got some word chemistry in him.

"I'm right fond of fishing," he said, "maybe because I enjoy eating fish. It's rewarding work. I get right smart catches of flounder in this area if I drift the ocean inlets when the tide's incoming. Mud minnows make good bait."

"Sounds interesting," said Tamzie, wondering if this was an invitation or what.

"But your flounder is famously slow on swallowing the bait. They like to take it by the tail, then turn it so as to swallow head first. That takes some time."

Tamzie said, "Un-huh."

He was standing real close to her now. His eyes were half-closed. "So what you do is count slow to ten. Then set the hook."

Tamzie gave him a bedroom look. "What number you figure you're up to now?"

21.

It was first thing in the morning at No. 6 Broad St, secretaries down on the pavement carrying coffee and bags of pastries from the Iron Kettle Café. Pigeons cooing on the windowsills, drinking from dripping air conditioners. In the office of Ralston & Ralston, Dale listened while Rannie told her about her new client, a woman whose baby swallowed crack cocaine and died. Charged with homicide by child neglect.

"She says she's a good mother because she and her other children

125

benefit from her drug dealing. They have a higher standard of living than they otherwise would." Rannie looked thoughtful. "Homicide by neglect requires extreme indifference to human life. I doubt the state can show it. But as they say, who gives a flying whatever? She's barely able to come up with a few thousand dollars. Lying about it. Got money stashed somewhere."

When Dale had married Collier, old Collier Ralston, Sr. had been dead a few years. Rannie kept alive his sacred memory and fought to provide for the family. Dale might have admired Rannie except greed always hung around her like a miasma. And she couldn't really judge the continuing rite of grief for the father. Nor her sexless nature.

No, it wasn't that. Rannie had sexuality. But it was libido like some barbarian queen of legend. Red haired like the Irish. Maeve of Connaught who led men in battle in a mythic age. Or some ruthless Olympian goddess who descends to earth to copulate with a handsome shepherd and then destroy him. Not at all like the other Ralstons Dale knew.

During her marriage, Dale had seldom come to the law office because Collier was so seldom there. He preferred the old Wade Hampton Hotel in Columbia with the legislature in session, drunk politicos and lobbyists stalking the halls after dark in bed sheets like Roman togas. All night poker parties. Naked coeds from the university prancing from room to room. He once told her that he was a novice legislator when for the first time he witnessed a man take the cap off a quart of liquor and throw it out the window. The cap. A declaration that they intended to drink it all.

While Rannie was talking about the crack client, Dale opened the airline bag and counted out forty thousand dollars onto the desk. Enjoying her little moment of malicious triumph. Rannie stopped in mid-sentence, looked stricken. The reality of the cash couldn't quite penetrate her understanding. She accepted its presence almost grudgingly.

All that was left in the bag was *Book Prices Current.* Dale's next task was to sneak that back into the library. "That's it, isn't it?" she said. "The fee you demanded?"

Rannie had an expression on her face like poison was slowly seeping through her system, realizing she should have set the price higher. She had no idea that Dale was a closet altruist. Or ridding herself of any possible sense of guilt in the marriage break-up. Or whatever she was doing. She clicked her teeth together, said, "Mother is determined to get Moira into the Junior League."

"That's nice," said Dale evenly. "Get her out of the house more."

"She can't possibly handle it," said Rannie. "Spend a whole year as a provisional member. It's like a sorority pledge year. Doing scut chores. She'd fall apart."

With Rannie's grip on her broken, Dale almost felt a female kinship. Wanted to ask her about lost illusions and romance and abandonment. She checked that impulse. You don't stick your hand in the water with a piranha.

Rannie picked up one of the wads of money, riffled it, threw it back down on the table, really chewing over it. "It's funny," she said. "Being a criminal lawyer I see a lot of men get sent off to prison. Wives left behind. Somehow the women seem to live without visible means of support. I always figure the man buried some cash somewhere. Lied to me about not having funds for my fee. That's why I require the money up front. They always have it. They always lie to you and say they're broke. And once you've agreed to represent a client, the judge won't let you off the case. You have to stick it out. And then the client is in control. Instead of accepting the plea, he can demand a jury trial that might take up to a week of your time. Make you work for next to nothing."

"Is there something you want to ask me?" said Dale.

"You want to tell me about your secret stash?"

Dale thought a moment. "No, I'm not into sharing and sisterhood at the moment."

*

Tamzie told Debone they had to find a way to pay the red bitch Rannie back for the IRS debt. Get her house free again. They were in need to come into some money. Maybe Debone had a secret stash he had kept from her and now could bring out at a good moment. Or maybe he could get a job.

Debone wasn't big at taking hints. He lay around the house in the late morning watching "Reading Rainbow" on TV. He said, "Hey, this is a pretty good story. This king got a whole river of gold that flows."

Tamzie said her momma Mozelle used to tell old Miz Ralston Negro stories like that. How the good Lord made all folks black but some of them rushed into a big puddle and washed off and got white. And the colored folks were too late and all they do was get the palms of their hands and the soles of their feet pink. Miz Ralston would eat up that shit and say she going to write a book of Gullah stories one day. Debone looked at her hard. "You think it really happen like that?"

"What?"

"How we got black?"

Tamzie knew for sure the time had come to go upscale. Make a move on a more educated man. Debone was so dumb, just listening to him put wind underneath her flying wings.

Tamzie said, "Let's stick to the subject of money and how to get it."

Debone lay back on the plastic covered couch, hands laced behind his head. "Some good things going on and some better things in the pipeline. I'll soon be realizing my potential. Any day now I expect a contract for a new car the chop shop gone need."

Tamzie allowed she was ready for him to go his separate way. He said to don't upset him, woman, he envision having several options. Debone said he was interested to note that paint colors had changed on cars in his absence. Purple was a lot hotter. More red in it. And your classic maroon had more blue in it, more like a purple grape.

"You planning on stealing a purple car? If so, I don't want to know about it. Or ride in it."

Debone flipped TV channels with the remote. All kid shows. "You got to take a close look at the incentives. The luxury sport utility vehicle is your route to take. Your Chevy Blazer. Your Jeep Grand Cherokee. When it come down to it, your Land Cruiser is about the best deal with a retail of around thirty-eight thou. Your Lexus LX450 is just the same thing costing twelve thou more. A discriminating buyer can figure that out no sweat. Ask why he need to pay the extra juice."

Tamzie vowed the stealing in her life was behind her. And she hadn't really believed it was stealing at the time. Taking those old books and papers. More like cleaning up. Throwing out old stuff.

"Car theft ain't exactly stealing," said Debone. "It's more like a business. Especial here in the booming Sunbelt markets."

Tamzie said she hoped he enjoyed whatever new mental state he was in.

"To the casual observer," said Debone. "I'm existing in a state of limbo here in this semi-urban bungalow. But I expect a final resolution of that problem soon. When I acquire the necessary funds I intend to buy me one of them Pontiac Trans Ams. Now that's a power plant. Got the same engine as a Camaro or a Corvette. Best push-rod engine in the world. Like a motor on steroids. Figure red

with a black interior. It will look and feel special. Always draw a crowd. Especially of the well-endowed she-males of the skimpy attire persuasion."

"Among that crowd which draws," said Tamzie, "be your parole officer wondering how you come by this deluxe lifestyle."

"All this fretting, girlfriend," said Debone. "You doing a disservice to progress. The spirit of exploration and risk-taking what make this country."

The midday news brief came on TV. State Representative Preston Landis said he pleaded guilty to bribery charges because he wanted to "tell the truth as I understand it to be." He said he "did not have a timetable on his planned rehabilitation, but he hoped it could be done quickly."

His estranged wife Beryl in prepared remarks told the press it was "not right to turn us into a nation hunkered down and fearful of every government snooper. This land of ours is in some trouble. Government incurs more power at the expense of the people." She added that subsequent to the sale of the family home at a tax auction, she would shop for a mobile home.

Assistant federal prosecutor Dave Dubiel said that was a "dad-blame 'nother one down" and cracked his knuckles near the microphone so it sounded like gunshots.

The weather map registered a scorching ninety-six degrees.

"The problem with them legislate dudes," said Debone, "is they violate Debone's first law of operation. They try to steal too much. My motto is be hungry, stay humble."

22.

Debone had been talking for some days about boosting a car and driving it to Lake City, get himself liquid again. He said the entire nature of the car theft business had changed during his absence. What was big now was "strip and run." You steal a car, strip the parts, and then ditch the frame. Cops find the frame, close the theft case. Then you track the frame down using the I.D. number. Buy it at an insurance auction. Put it back together and sell it same as new. Big money follows.

Tamzie said, "You gonna do all that work?" He said, "Only the first part." He said he believed in growth industries. He had read a car got stolen in the U.S. every twenty seconds.

Sure enough Debone had come by Tamzie's house in a this-year Jaguar XJ6 he had stole and was going to drive to Lake City to sell. Key right in the ignition. Debone didn't believe in hotwiring cars. He said you're driving along obeying the speed limits and some cop figures you aren't good enough for a car of that quality. So he pulls you over and when he looks inside there be those ripped loose wires and he's made his case. You're climbing out of the car at gunpoint moving your hands real slow to a flat position on the roof of the vehicle. If you stole the key and wore a suit, you claim the owner told you to take it out on the interstate and blow the carbon out of the pipes. You just a chauffeur. A house nigger.

Tamzie thought she would shit. He had taken Miz Mary Canty Ralston's car. Walked right in the house big as life, said 'how ya'll doing?' to the other help. 'Seed Tamzie around? No? Well just tell her

I drop by.' And walk off with the car keys. One stop shopping. He said when he had the cash in hand, he'd be dropping back by for a little pleasuring.

Tamzie said he must have rented his brain out to someone else.

*

At the College library, when Tamzie finished cleaning, she found Thaddeus still working late, having his dinner at his desk. She told herself that despite her troubles she was considerably blessed.

She asked him what he was eating, and he said a seafood salad he had concocted. Little squid. Shrimp. Snow peas. Twist pasta. Vinaigrette and a fresh lemon squeezed over it. She told him he had real style, and they shared the meal sitting there at the desk, eating with the same fork. He allowed he liked to take a drink in the evening although he was not a cocktailer in after-five lounges. She said she didn't sit parked on a barstool neither, although a hit of Seagrams in the evening went down fine.

They talked music a bit. He appreciated the historical importance of jazz, it being a true creation of the African-American, but it bothered him all the same, music notes spilling all over each other like they falling up and down the stairs. A profound challenge to appreciate. What he truly liked for basic relaxation was the blues. Chicago style.

She could tell he was seriously checking her out. A man of untold powers. She said she was not afraid to look down some new roads. He said, "You know you got razor cheek bones?" His hand brushed the edge of her face, then slid down her back to hold her rump.

She didn't push his hand away. "You holding onto a different set of cheeks. And anyhow don't you maybe got some business to attend to?"

He raised and lowered his eyebrows. "I got business right at hand."

"I'm having trouble breathing. I think lust is sucking up all the air."

"Anybody ever told you you could be Miss Black America?"

"My momma used to say my face was brown like a paper bag."

"I'd like to see you in a red dress that would unzip all the way down to the bottom." His mouth went on hers and took away still more of her breath.

What happened on the desktop Tamzie would remember and dream about for many days. The man had some equipment. He put it to her for what must have been forever until she was in a total meltdown. The whole time she was hearing "Fever" by Chaka Khan. Or maybe it was the original version by Martha and the Vandellas. She weren't sure which and it don't matter. She walked out of there dripping. The night was hot, breathless, and deep blue.

All the way home to her house on Cannon Street she told herself she had long ago progressed to womanhood. Knew how to cross the street by herself. Was nobody's fool. But if this wasn't love, she didn't know it.

When she got home, the phone was ringing off the hook. Debone said the chop shop was still operating although on different premises. The deal had gone down, and they had sent a man to drive him back to Charleston in a late model Honda Civic. Socially responsible kind of vehicle. Just off the old Cooper River Bridge where it dips down through the east side project, they got smacked by a drunk with no headlights. Debone was down at county hospital telling them he hurt too bad to walk and needed a disability report for his lawyer.

Tamzie said she was asleep and he'd have to be disabled without her assistance.

Debone said, "Woman, you get your big coon ass down here with

the car or I be liable to meet your objections with some harsh consequences."

*

During the day Collier called up hysterical saying he had learned
from Rannie that Dale had paid his retainer. What had him gripped
with frenzy was the fear that she had sold part of his collection. If she
had dared sell his map of the Mason-Dixon Line, well, she'd be sorry
if she had. He was going to come out of being pilloried and be back on
top again.

Dale tapped her nails on the butcher block in the kitchen. "You
know at first I thought maybe you had called to thank me. The way I
helped with your urgent need of cash."

He didn't catch the sarcasm. He screamed she was blank ignorant
of the value of the items and would get ripped off by sharks. She had
no business trying to deal in the rare book market. And she was never,
never to go near Blake Huston. The man was like a shrew. He ate five
times his weight a day.

She hung up. Why was Blake Huston such a terror? She tried to
remember Collier's soul mates. A face didn't come to mind.

Dale spent the evening wondering whether Collier or Hootch or
both would try to break in and loot the collection. Close to midnight
she got tired of jumping at noises and locked her bedroom door and
went to bed. An hour later the shouting downstairs woke her up. She
had the worst of all scenarios. Collier and Hootch were both there and
in some kind of a fight.

As she came down the stairs, Dale could tell one thing. The two
weren't in league. Or else they had had a right savage falling out.

"This is my house!" Collier screamed at Hootch.

She flicked on the lights just as Hootch grabbed Collier by the lapels and slung him around. Collier's head struck the wall with a crack.

That was when Josh Mahoney stepped into the room and put Hootch in some kind of a hammerlock and cuffed his hands behind his back. Hootch said what the fuck. Josh was wearing a suit with a necktie. He reminded Dale that he was Josh Mahoney the rare book dealer. Said he was staying at the King Charles up Meeting Street.

He had been out for a walk, saw the two of them break in, but independently, one following behind the other. He said maybe with the cuffs on this one they could now proceed in a somewhat less frenzied atmosphere. He bent down to take a close look at Collier. Remarked he wasn't your standard rough trade that one found breaking into houses. These two weren't even tolerable imitations of burglars.

"I'm going to withhold comment on this," said Collier from the floor. Dale wondered if that glazed look in his eyes meant he had a concussion.

"I know," said Hootch. "You're wondering what motivated me to come in here at this hour. It's quite a story, I can tell you." He stood there shoulders hunched forward, hands locked behind his back. He reeked of booze even from where Dale was standing.

Collier sat up holding his head with both hands. "Ordeals like this leave me weak. We've got to put these budget battles at the Statehouse behind us and get the public schools the money they need." They all stared at him and then each other. He was delirious.

Hootch shook his arms, said to Josh Mahoney, "I understand what you've done is a natural reaction, but what've you got on my thumbs?"

"Professional thumb cuffs. They're designed for police work. No risk of nerve damage to the wrists the way handcuffs will often do."

"Cool. Say, are you some kind of cop?"

"You can buy them in your army surplus stores. Pawn shops."

"Cool."

Josh said, "Now some people might think this was taking the law into my own hands, but . . . " He punched Hootch hard in the gut doubling him up. A really vicious blow. Then led him by his hair outside to vomit in the yard. Josh left him retching and came back in. By then, Collier was swimming up out of his trance. He had turned angry, yelling at Josh.

"What I want to know is are you sleeping with my wife? I have a right to know!"

Dale was totally disgusted. "You've done it, Collier. You've managed to sink to septic-tank level."

Josh looked around the study thoughtfully. "I wonder," he mused, "as long as I'm here, I might as well take a look at the collection."

23.

Jason Traub the movie director said, "So I tell the guy, *I'm* pushy? That raises more questions than it answers."

A little knot of sycophants laughed dutifully. Dale was brushed aside as the movie people came into her house at five o'clock in the morning to set up for two weeks of shooting. The director wore a t-shirt that said "Free T-shirt" on it and a cap with a cloth neck cover. Bulgari wristwatch. Nike running shoes. He was having an ego-fest with a cluster of assistants, mostly shapely babes, just kind of wallowing in their adoration. Dale could smell the tension and the backstabbing.

Back when Dale did the sets for fashion shoots she had clashed with the Traub brothers. They were shooting *Bitches of Wetwick* out in the Hamptons at the far end of Long Island. The name, as it implied, was an incredibly shameless, tacky rip-off of *Witches of Eastwick*. Worse, it was a sex-spoof.

A week before they were entitled to, the entire movie company bulled into the mansion Dale and her group were using. When Dale argued with them, Traub said, "Hey, go be bulimic or something. Stick your finger down your throat and puke." When she said she'd call the realtor who had rented the house to them, Traub offered her a job on the spot. Said he'd double her salary. Then laughed raucously. "But you have to blow me."

Dale called the realtor, but he was already in Traub's pocket and wouldn't back her up. Traub shoved a hundred people into the house, just knocking Dale's crew aside. She gave up and left. The incident had stuck with her. She had always wanted to exact some sort of revenge. But she had to keep it in perspective. How do you hurt somebody with the sensitivity of a toilet seat? *Bitches of Wetwick* went straight to video anyhow.

Traub was chiding the coffee drinkers. "Let's get this work shift moving, good people! Are we having a power breakfast here? Wake up radiant, people!" Men with buckets and ladders and big rolls of wallpaper were coming in the house. They were all ready to redo the dining room in red flock wallpaper. They were just going to slap it up. Some kind of ghastly cathouse looking stuff.

Dale said stop, what are you doing? The flunkies clustered around her in an aggressive little knot saying she needed to adopt a more community-based outlook.

"This is my house," she reiterated.

They say is this some tactic to intimidate and harass? It's in the contract. Fine print, but in there. We get to redecorate at our pleasure. It's in writing, it sticks. This is a nice house and all that, but we'll sue your ass.

Dale said, well, antebellum style meant Greek revival. You could do Irish linen curtains that let the light filter in, reflect on the heart of pine floors. Give it an amber glow. A woman standing barefoot on it in a transparent peignoir. Almost like . . . well, soft porn movies.

Traub rose to that image. "Hey, is this high concept, or what? We been searching for just that kind'a *je ne sais quoi.* We're mediocre schlocky up to this point. I figure I'm surrounding myself with successful people here. Is the guy with brains and class a no-show? I'm gonna pursue this arena. You're hired, sweetheart. We're putting you on the staff for aesthetic advisement. Say, fifteen a week."

"Fifteen thousand dollars?" said Dale.

"Is that what you want? You got it." He looked around the room. "Nobody questioning my decision?" Back to Dale. "Of course not. I got mythic status."

"It's a deal," said Dale.

"You could'a held out for twenty." He guffawed. "But for that much you'd a had to blow me."

Dale realized he had no memory of her. The Long Island fracas had joined the blur of all the people he walked on. Traub went kissy-kissy with a girl in tight jeans. "Oooo you *bambola* you. Had our tits cosmetically accentuated have we?" Then back to Dale.

"Okay, move aside. Go off and tell your neighbors about your blinding stellar success. Say if they want your pinnacle, they gotta have your level of dedication." He put on a southern drawl. "It'll make 'em reeeaaal pissed off."

Dale moved aside. A golden shower had fallen on her sensibilities.

*

Nighttime brought no relief from the heat of the day. Sticky, humid air held a smell of garbage in the streets. Hootch had the top off his jeep cruising the streets of Charleston drinking a few brewskis out of his cooler. He was pissed about being smacked around for the second time by the ponytail dude—what's-his-name Josh Mahoney—so he wasn't in the best frame of mind when he made his first bid to run a case to Rannie Ralston. Plus, he had endured a real fucked-up kaleidoscope of a week, flagging a marketing test, professor asking him why he was in college. Saying he ought to go ahead get into sales. Maybe aluminum siding. Half-ass bastard. Working on a piss-ant prof's salary, trying to play philosopher king.

Rannie had been on the rag all week. Somebody had stolen her mother's car and the cops had their thumbs up their asses. The old bitch Mary Canty wanted Rannie to drive her to the Yacht Club daily to get soused. Rannie threw a brass duck paperweight through her office window. Nearly skulled a tourist down below. Screaming about her lush of a mother and how Hootch better get out there and bring her some auto accident paraplegics. She wanted three million dollar structured settlements that would bring in income for years.

Rannie was crazy when you thought about it. Couldn't get it out of her head that Dale was selling Collier's Confederate archives and they had to be gotten away from her in a hurry. Hootch hadn't told her about how his break-in had been aborted due to interference by outside parties. Didn't want her to know he had his own plans for the collection.

And then that tight asshole Moira sent a kind of a pre-invitation to dinner at the majestic Ralston mansion. Little note saying he would soon receive a more formal one. This was so he could get his Confederate army dress uniform dry-cleaned because he would be meeting a Hollywood producer.

The Civil War reenactment part of his life had gotten confusing. When he had started out he was a freshman in college. Some of the brothers in KA were into it. Go to battlefields and shoot off antique guns and do some underage drinking. The older men would buy you liquor. They had seemed cool to him then. Guys who never quite grew up. One in particular Hootch had admired. Wore a caped greatcoat and drank rum out of a wooden canteen. He used to say, "I like being an alcoholic. I groove on the mood swings." Now Hootch was starting to see them as losers. Dead-end job types—machinists, postal workers—who were living in a rebel dream world.

Hootch drove his jeep Wrangler south on Rutledge past the baseball park ready for his first job. He had been drinking at the Ark where the Citadel cadets hung out, put about six drafts in him. Rannie had warned him to stay away from funerals. The bereaved were seldom in the best frame of mind to consider the solace of a wrongful death action. The benefit of that would only become apparent a few days later when the funeral bill came in.

He had gone out and bought a $3,000 800-megahertz portable radio that would tie him in with the countywide radio system. Also a $300 VHF marine band portable and two walkie-talkie batteries. That had drained his trust fund check for the month, but this top-level gear had given him his first serious lead.

Cannon Street was one-way between Rutledge and King, right in the heart of the spade neighborhood. Hootch briefly wondered about the rebel flag license plate on the front of his jeep, then figured fuck 'em if they can't take a joke. Plus he had his Smith & Wesson if things got rough.

Little frame houses with plants on the porches. Some kind of lodge. The Loyal Order of Tents. Man, spooks got some funny names for things. Made him think of *Amos 'n Andy*.

Pickaninnies still playing on the sidewalks in the dark. He spotted the house. Ratty little wood frame shotgun job with big banana plants in the yard. No wracked-up Honda. Some kind of junky blue Chevette. Maybe the Honda got towed to a junkyard. Probably totaled. Replaced it with the nigger rig.

Hootch went up and bammed on the frame of the screen door with his fist. Fucker putting on his neck brace as he came to the door. Big black dude with a cigar between his teeth opened the door a crack and looked out suspiciously like he thought Hootch was a bill collector or an insurance investigator checking to see if he was really hurt. Fucker had a build like an offensive lineman.

Hootch said he was Hootch Gibson an *accident* investigator. He stressed the word 'accident,' said he didn't work for an insurance company so relax. He had been looking into an ancillary matter and noticed the terrible incident of last Tuesday just off the Cooper River bridge and was he Mister Debone Wigfall the party in the Honda Civic?

The man said "Uh-huh," flicked his cigar ash down on the step and smeared it with his shoe. To do that, he had to open the screen door wider.

Hootch said he had seen the police accident report and figured the prospects were very good for a sizeable settlement without going to trial. He handed him Rannie's business card. Debone studied it.

"It's like the high-end law service in the county. Your courthouse insiders all swear by her results. Her clients are bonded to her. You'd think they were joined at the hip. A solid money-maker creates that kind of loyalty."

Debone looked at the card some more. Hootch wondered if he could read.

"Phone in and a secretary will assign you a time slot for the initial free consultation. You park in the parking garage, bring her the ticket, she picks up that tab."

"Uh-huh."

"Of course you want your Civic back better than new. That goes without saying. But we're talking the larger largesse. You got kind of a casual atmosphere here at your homestead, which is fine. But you could repaint in brighter hues. Rejuvenate the look of the place."

"You done been beat to the punch."

"Say what?"

"I got me a lawyer. Good one."

"Well, I'd say that 'good one' shit was mostly in the realm of the-ory," Hootch ventured cautiously.

"I got me the man what advertises on billboards and TV. Man got a regular factory of young counselors churning his cases, beating the shit out of insurance companies. He say they get to eat what they kill."

"It's a volatile market out there," Hootch argued. "There are plenty of questions to be answered before you ally with a particular firm."

Debone gummed the cigar, slobber on his chin. "I'd say the on'y pressing question is how much?"

"How much what?"

"How much you spot me now as advance on the settlement?"

Hootch got a little testy at this. Jeezus what an argumentative pain in the ass. "I mean what's the agenda we're talking about? How much you gotten? Or been offered?"

"I ain't saying."

"Now look here," said Hootch. "There are dishonest folks out there. Some of them flagrantly so. Many of them will come across with the up-front money but lag in the later revenue. I hate to sound stern, but we can't have a valuable discussion without clearing the decks of the sludge. Why don't you give them a call and say you've changed attorneys. Then I'll be in touch with my party and we can come up with a figure."

"Hunh," Debone said. Kind of like a grunt that was also a laugh.

Hootch asked him what that was supposed to mean.

"It mean getchore ass outta here, buckra boy, or I'll put the Rott-weiler on you."

The more Hootch drove around, the more steamed he got. Son-of-a-bitching blue-gum talking down to him. He opened the small cooler in the well of the passenger seat and popped the top on a tall Bud, chugged down half of it.

Hootch drove and finished the beer. By the time he was back down Rutledge and left onto Cannon again, he had formulated a plan. He shut his lights and left the jeep idling. Went up to the house and rapped on the window, then walked back to the car. Black bastard sitting in there watching TV.

Now he was getting up. Bag of shit standing there in the window smoking that cigar. Hootch decided to shoot it out of his mouth. With the light behind him, he was a perfect target. And he couldn't see who was outside.

Hootch took a double-hand grip on the Smith, rested the butt on the roll bar of the jeep. It was an easy shot. He squeezed the trigger. Bam. Window glass shattered and Debone jumped back just seconds apart.

Real quick the gunshot brought people out on their porches. Dogs were barking. A woman started screaming.

Hootch hauled ass in the jeep, turned left on King Street then right in front of the big Post & Courier building and right on Meeting where he blended in with the traffic. He had the bad feeling he had missed the cigar. By the time he had driven all down into the maze of little streets south-of-Broad, it had turned into a good feeling. He figured he'd stop by the KA house and tell them how he had winged a spook and had a woman lawyer with crowd-pleasing knockers who wanted to do some parallel parking with him. That's right. His own lady lawyer wanted to take her fee in good solid dicking.

Something struck him as familiar about Debone, but then they all looked alike, didn't they?

24.

The Jaguar being stolen had thrown the whole Ralston house into turmoil. Bad enough that Moira was subjected to her mother's long harangues on the decline of American morality, but she had to accompany her to some dreadful car lot to pick out a new Mercedes. Even Mercedes dealers seemed sly and uncouth. Of course Rannie had been utterly unreasonable about the price, as she was about most things, and the stress had taken its toll on Moira's work.

The movie company had arrived in town, and Moira was just beside herself with the excitement of it. They were laying dirt down in a big stretch of Legendre Street. An antique horse drawn brougham drove across it with a woman in a crinoline dress. She didn't recognize the actress. Moira hoped this wasn't a low-budget production. But surely the mayor of Charleston wouldn't allow that to happen.

Outside, the sky was a blue dome. Moira nibbled a perfectly quartered apple. She liked to write with a staff pen and India ink. It gave her a link to the past, and different pen nibs permitted such graceful calligraphy.

As she sat at her writing desk preparing dinner invitations, she looked again at the movie producer's acceptance. It was a bit casual, a scrawled reply on her own invitation: "Be there with bells on!—Mendel." He hadn't preserved her card to place with others on a mantle, but she supposed he didn't have a mantle at the moment. And it was doubtful he was invited out in Charleston society.

She pictured herself presiding at the head of the table, but deferring to Collier as the reigning man of the household. "All these hard-jawed women who want to change the world," she would say. "I have no desire to join their ranks decrying the rule of men. I devote my days to preserving what is left of beauty and gentility."

Now with the producer's acceptance firm, she could proceed with her other guests, promising him as the prize of attendance. She wrote an invitation to Hunter Gibson and addressed it to the KA house. She couldn't bring herself to call him Hootch. Hunter was such an elegant name. And "Hootch" evoked the grape-stained mouth of Dionysus. Or even worse, the intoxicated fraternity lout. Moira had always been very firm with men about her requirements in this area. They were to set limits on the number of drinks they had and stick to them.

She wrote with careful penmanship, *"As it will be an opportunity for us to become acquainted with the creative life of Hollywood—and perhaps exert a beneficial influence upon its gross commercialism—I am making it a theme dinner. We will dress in antebellum costume."*

She put down her fountain pen and ran a finger along the 1861 model Colt navy revolver. By removing the percussion caps on each chamber, she could leave it loaded yet harmless. It gave her a little frisson to handle it. Like a defanged snake. No, that was not a good image. Like a rogue male brought to heel. Masculine and powerful, yet tamed by a skillful disarmament. A Rhett Butler so desperately in love with Scarlett that he lived only to serve her.

When Moira was still at Ashley Hall, Hunter had once come to the house. She remembered him looking at her in a disdainful way. He and Collier had come from deer hunting and had great bloody slabs of venison. They wore camouflage clothes dotted with beggar lice. Their guns smelled of cordite. That hint of masculine menace. The rogue male. They had both been drinking. She had given Hootch a haughty toss of her head.

How did one go about reforming a drunk? Literature seldom treated the subject except for depressing slice-of-real-life books. All those dreadful naturalists starting with Emile Zola or Theodore Dreiser or whoever it was.

Outside, the midday sun was blazing hot. Three stories down below in the garden, the men toiled at weeding. Moira wondered how they stood it. All that African skin, she supposed. They were designed for hot climates.

*

Dale figured she was supposed to earn her fifteen thousand dollars from the Traubs, but none of her suggestions had much impact. She'd say something, nobody seemed to hear. Finally one of the honey assistants came over and asked, "Are you trying to win plaudits for originality?" She said Dale would get paid no matter what, so why didn't she just take a powder. Dale shrugged and gave in.

For Dale, the best thing about Charleston was living in a city, but virtually at the beach. In the fall and spring she could go over to Sullivan's Island in mid-week and there'd be nobody else on miles of white sand. Now at the height of summer vacationers were plentiful but not overwhelming. She lay on her towel wearing a white bikini and let the sound of the surf take her thoughts drifting. The feeling soothed like an adolescent dream of love. A sense of being cared for and nurtured.

When the shadow came over her, she looked up to see Josh Mahoney and knew he had followed her. He tried to be casual, say hi, surprise meeting you, but the signs were there. Dale had had guys running into her casually like that since she was thirteen.

He sat down in the sand beside her looking pretty good in his red bathing trunks with his shirt off. She closed her eyes, but she could feel his gaze going down her body, lingering on her navel. Then her crotch.

She said the haze was deceptive. She had factor-fifteen suntan oil if he wanted it. He said he didn't burn. She said she'd heard that one before.

He was reading the *Post & Courier*. He said not much was going on. Somebody got his nose shot off in a drive-by shooting. But none of the real depressing stuff you read every day. He turned a page, paper flapping in the breeze before he got it folded tight.

Dale said she was getting a divorce, but her depression had bottomed out. She was on the upswing. Opportunities she believed in ten years before still remained.

Josh asked if romantic passion had torn her away from a vital career. She said no, it wasn't much of a job. You traveled. You met some famous models. You found exotic locales or unusual props. Once she had to locate a boa constrictor. But it hadn't been hard to give it up to marry Collier.

"Our love affair wasn't flashy," said Dale. "It was about coming home mostly. Getting out of New York and back to a place you understood. Or thought you did."

Josh said if he wanted to exploit the situation he could tell her at that point that she was a beautiful woman.

She kept her eyes closed, being cool. "If you did, I'd reply I've got small tits."

"I don't like women whose tits are the whole focus. Yours are harmony, understatement."

She draped a hand on her chest. "My heart's racing."

He didn't have a clever comeback.

Dale opened her eyes and propped herself on one elbow to look him over. His chest was incredibly broad with big shoulders like he still exercised a lot. Nice mat of hair on it. She wondered what it would be like to sleep with him in a wash of starlight. She thought about the kiss scene in *From Here to Eternity* with the surf splashing over them.

A thoughtful look settled on her face. "You know what's funny is I had a roommate in New York. She worked as a stock analyst for Paine Webber. A real career type, but with the ordinary desires of a woman. She wanted to be in love, maybe consider marriage eventually. Single men being such a scarce commodity in that city, she scaled down to what you'd classify blue-collar I guess."

"Electricians? Plumbers?" asked Josh with a flicker of curiosity. "Many of them make more than your average Wall Streeter."

"Real blue-collar. A cop. When he did narcotics duty, he had this, well, casual look."

"Like a derelict?"

"Yeah. Like that. But the oddity was he didn't mouth off all the time. His social behavior seemed, well, he had this way of watching and listening. Like he was in the habit of picking up information and stuff. Men aren't normally like that."

Josh laughed. "Usually trying to impress you. Tell you their fund of stories that illustrate why they're heroic. Strong but sensitive."

"Right."

"So what's your point?"

She lowered her sunglasses to give him a long look. "Are you some kind of cop?"

He thought about that and said no, being a cop had never been an ambition. Not even as a kid. The Dalmatian dog had briefly attracted him to the fire department. He asked how she and Collier had seen their marriage when they started out.

Dale closed her eyes again, lay back. "It was all very traditional. I served as domestic infrastructure. He played at statesman. Not that he had any strong stances. When opinion polls indicated widespread opposition, he was opposed."

"But that didn't work out?"

"By most objective standards, I guess you'd call it abysmal. He had affairs. We didn't have any kind of disclosure standards. So it all came out in one big rush."

Josh said he had heard the same thing happening in Albany, New York. Men away from home for long periods of time get up to shenanigans.

Dale kept her features calm, being cool and vaguely cynical.

"There's an indigenous culture up at the state capital. It includes little college girls all infatuated with the corridors of power. Most of the legislators see life up there as their personal bacchanalia. Collier always went with the crowd."

"Again," said Josh, rubbing his chin, "if I were trying to make a move on you at this point, I'd say I can't believe a man would need anything more than you."

"I didn't provide the artistic stimulation or whatever it was he needed. The most recent disclosure has him caught in an FBI sting with a . . . well, with a woman whose profession doesn't sit comfortably with family values."

A couple of kids ran by chasing each other on the edge of the surf. Josh said it was hard to miss the news on Operation Chump Change. Every day some poor stiff was pleading guilty.

"Maybe it was a welcome slap in the face," said Dale. "Lot of bills are coming in. Contingent liabilities that he hid from me. It'll force me back into the job market."

Josh folded the newspaper a couple of times. "You could get into the rare book business," he suggested.

She laughed, still keeping her eyes closed against the sun's glare. "With you as my illustrious mentor? A crack at the big-time?"

"A crack at potentially doing time, really. Considering."

"Considering what?"

"Considering that all your inventory is stolen."

Dale opened one eye and looked at him. He did look awfully good with his shirt off. "Are you sure you're not some kind of a cop?"

25.

"That sorry shit mully-fucker," said Debone, letting Tamzie know how pissed he was at his parole officer. "Telling me how lenient he being on me. Telling me he could pull my ticket anytime he wants. Yassuh, Mister Man. Yowsuh."

Tamzie said, "Un-huh."

"I say, hey. Looka here. A clear message been sent. Man, I is so straight I can't hardly sit in a chair no more."

Tamzie had been waiting outside the parole office building in the heat. He made her climb over the gearshift and let him drive. She was thinking she had had about all of this she could stand. The man was back less than a week and gets shot at. Bullet actually clipped off his nose.

She had taken him to the county hospital where they did the folks without medical insurance. Even with all the gunshot wounds and cuttings, nobody had seen a nose clipped off like that. They brought three more white coats over to look at it. Debone was bleeding like a stuck pig, and it took an hour to stop it. He would need plastic surgery, rebuild his nose somehow. They also were obliged to report a gunshot wound to the police. Which meant the parole officer was informed.

"You listening to me, woman?"

She nodded. Yeah, she was listening. She was paying attention like she knew a woman had best pay it around a man who'd smack the daylights out of you just for fun. Put your tits in a wringer or pour lye on you.

"So I say to the man, why we wasting taxpayer money spending your time with me when they unreformed folks out there roaming the night?"

Tamzie asked what he had done with his unreformed money from

Miz Ralston's Jaguar. She needed to pay back the red bitch Rannie or the house might be taken out from under them. He said that was her problem to keep a roof over them. Maybe she should get a third job like at a car wash or somewhere.

Debone pulled over at the corner of Beaufain and Coming Streets near the little grocery that advertised Jamaican jerk beef. Some dudes hanging out there drinking Schlitz Malt Liquor, cans in brown paper bags. "You're on free time now," he said, putting Tamzie out of the car. "Later this evening you'll get some hands-on experience with my loving."

"I don't want my car associated with no 7-eleven stick-up," she said. "Stealing copper wire from some construction site. Whatever you got in mind."

"Woman, this car so slow it drive like it's in reverse."

*

Tamzie still had two hours before her night job at the College, so she walked over to Bull Street. Thaddeus carried on a lot about the Avery Institute, an archive depository for Black history. He said big museums like the Getty out in California bought up everything and local folks never got a look at it. Which made small places like the Avery so vital.

Live oak trees shaded the rows of old houses on Bull Street. An old technical college had been repainted and turned over to the Avery. Inside, Tamzie ran smack up against Thaddeus himself and went weak in the knees. She felt drab in her pale green maid's costume, wondered if he'd be ashamed of her.

He said, "Girl, you look good as quail on toast."

She said this place sure was something. He said, "We've come a long way, but a long way ain't all the way." Then showed her around for a first exposure to African-American archives.

An old photograph captured black women in long dresses outside a rundown church under big oak trees with Spanish moss. She could almost hear them singing "Come by Here, Lord." She told Thaddeus how during summers she used to go to a church like that. They'd leave broken crockery on the graves. He said that was an African custom they brought over.

In another photo, he pointed out how the slave cabins made a little avenue that went up to the big plantation house. It was big but not real fancy like Tara in *Gone With the Wind,* which was phony, just something Margaret Mitchell made up. This house was just three stories of clapboard, a little trim around the windows.

She said the cabins didn't have room enough to cuss a cat. He said that was true, but it was funny, the dimensions were what the slaves built just as in Africa. Nine-by-nine for those from Benin, eight-by-eight in Angola, ten-by-ten in Senegal and Gambia. African families lived in intimacy. He had his hand on her arm. She looked at him, and he didn't move his hand. His touch made her pants wet.

Debone was just trash saying come here woman lemme put frequent flyer miles on your pussy. This man had class. He said for vacations, he liked to go down to the French islands in the Caribbean, Martinique, and Guadeloupe. Talk French with them. What he called 'Creole patois.' He asked would she like to go one time? See where her Huguenot ancestor—Alphonse LeDell Fournichelle-Jerôme—come from. Big slave rebellion down in Santo Domingo had sent Huguenots as refugees to Charleston. They had to start all over again up here, but they didn't give up the slavery habit.

Thaddeus showed her the manumission papers on her ancestor, the court documents that set him free in 1816. He said, "His name was Cato, but his real name was Kouami which means Saturday, the day he was born. The masters named the slave children because they knew that giving names gave them power. So the slaves kept secret names.

"When he had a son Deacon, however, we have no record of a secret name. That's because he named the boy himself, and Deacon was a free man. He had another son Quash and another one Hardtimes. Another one Esau. Daughters Cupid and Pemba and Mimba.

"Cato-Kouami was what was called mulatto. His father—Alphonse Jerome—was white and apprenticed him to be trained in iron working, later set him free. We have no record of his mother. He took the name Jerome, bought the freedom of his wife Tremba. After the Denmark Vesey slave rebellion in 1820, manumissions were outlawed. If Cato wanted labor, he had no choice but to buy slaves and keep them in bondage."

Tamzie picked up a coil basket of dried palmetto fronds wrapped around bundles of sweetgrass and pine needles in an African design. It had been used for rice. Now tourists bought them on Meeting Street near the courthouse. She said her momma used to say, "Promising talk don't cook rice."

Thaddeus said that in fact was a Hausa proverb. He said slavery was a carefully planned operation. Before cotton, they grew rice. North of Charleston along the Waccamaw had been wealthy plantations from Winyah Bay to up above Murrells Inlet. The seed rice came from Madagascar and the technology for growing it from Senegal. Gambia and Senegal provided many of the slaves because they already knew rice culture. They were brought over due to their skills. They felled the giant trees, hauled out the logs. They cut the big dikes, sowed, harvested and milled the rice.

Thaddeus said slavery was not humane, but it was human. Real people were involved. Anyone takes pride in accomplishment. In an odd way, the slaves felt they owned the land they had tamed, felt they owned the product of their toil.

He showed her the work of the WPA Federal Writers Project way back during the Depression. They went around talking to folks who had been slaves, gathering their oral history. One of the former slaves, showing off the big rice dikes, had said, "Missus, slavery time people *done* something."

Tamzie kept thinking about the stuff she and Debone stole for Collier, speculating on its worth, but still getting intrigued by the history. She had had a cousin named Founchelle Jerome. That name must have come from Fournichelle. Another cousin was named Viola LeDell.

A framed poster read:

Land, Negroes, and Stock
AT AUCTION
15 to 20 Likely Negroes
1000 or 1200 Acres of Land

Thaddeus called the poster a broadside. Said it dated to 1852. The Avery had bought it last year. Paid two thousand dollars for it.

Tamzie said a man she used to clean for had broadsides. Mostly recruiting posters for the Confederate Army. They'd say 'To Arms! To Arms! Volunteers Needed!'

Thaddeus said the Civil War was a particular hobby of his. The colored regiments held his fascination. The 22nd Colored Infantry that fought at Petersburg. The 54th Massachusetts that was in the movie *Glory*. William Carney, a black sergeant who won the Congressional Medal of Honor for saving the regimental colors during the disastrous attack on Morris Island. Thaddeus was helping the Avery build up their collection in this area, trying to get donors to contribute.

He opened up the Avery's copy of *Book Prices Current—the Civil War*, showed her items he was going to buy when he had the budget for it.

Regulations for the Medical Dept of the US Army, 1860.—$2,500.

Cary, R[ichard] Milton, *Skirmishers' Drill & Bayonet Exercise*, First Ed, wallpaper wrappers, rare—$2,200.

Rutherford B. Hayes's copy of *Anthology of Passages from Lincoln's Greatest Speeches and Letters* with Hayes's signed inscription on the title page—$5,200.

(Lincoln, Abraham) Broadside, Ford's Theatre . . . Friday evening, April 14, 1865 . . . Our American Cousin . . . Very good condition—$3,800.

Gardner photograph of the execution of the Lincoln Assassination Conspirators—$4,200.

Tamzie said, "What I'm wondering is, are we speaking in terms of getting a real hard read on prices here?"

26.

Rannie sat in the courtroom next to Lenny Womble waiting for his bond hearing. Ahead of him came a woman who had stabbed her husband in the chest as he climbed through the bedroom window. Her lawyer was saying, "Your Honor, she's really no danger to anyone in the community save and excepting your abusive male crawling through the window."

Rannie was not in the best of moods. Legendre Street was lit up by big floodlights way into the night as they did filming for the movie. You had to park your car somewhere else and couldn't enter or leave your house except at special times. Tempers on the street were short. Mary Canty was bellyaching about the horror of it every night. When Rannie would see that slimy jerk of a director, she'd feel like putting her fingernails into his eyeballs.

For a lot of years Rannie had had her nails cut physician-short. She figured she had to act like a man to compete in a man's world. That foolishness was behind her, and now they were long and bright red to match her hair.

Lenny turned to her and said in a conversational tone, "I had plenty of time to read while incarcerated."

"I'm sure," said Rannie, sotto voice. She tried to ignore him. Silly smile on his face. Lenny had descended from frat boy to drug meltdown in record time. She figured it was a distinct possibility that Bubba Spainhour would have him killed soon as he got out on bail.

Lenny studied the ceiling as though fascinated with it. "When you wouldn't take my calls, I was thinking of sending you audiotaped messages. But then I didn't have any audiotape equipment. You'd think they'd provide that. Some kind of First Amendment right or something."

Rannie closed her eyes and took a deep breath to control her exasperation. "Go whine to a liberal about it. Maybe go on Oprah. Or Sally Jessie."

"I see where the post office has launched a campaign against dogs biting mail carriers. Makes sense really when you consider the thousands of dollars in lost work time when a carrier is bitten."

She turned on him. *"Will you please shut up?"*

He didn't seem to notice her swelling anger. "I mean it's not like they're anti-dog or anything. They just want owners to take responsibility for their pets."

The judge looked up kind of disgusted and told Rannie to instruct her client to be quiet.

Rannie hissed at Lenny to shut his yap.

When Rannie was a little girl she used to sometimes watch her father try cases before juries. She was so proud to be his daughter. She wanted to grow up to be just like him. All the men on the street tipping their hats to him. Men wore hats back then. Not the dumb caps that mouth-breathers like Lenny wore. And a Lenny would have gotten clear off the sidewalk for her father. Now she had to sit there telling him to be quiet. She got no respect. Girls never did.

For a brief moment she got a vividly detailed image of Calvin Whitesides lying dead in a hole. That was one dirt bag who had pushed her too far.

When her turn came, Rannie got up and did a spiel she figured to be moving but not teary-eyed. She said her client had a quart a day liquor habit. He drank because of the pain from the hole in his nose that cocaine had produced. She more than understood the public policy of slamming shut the revolving door of our prisons, but Lenny needed rehabilitation. She mentioned that it cost $18,000 a year to keep a criminal in a high-security prison. A valid sentence couldn't be arrived at without preliminary alcoholism treatment which she had arranged.

The judge set bail at $150,000, and Rannie went out to the pay phones in the hall. Behind her, Lenny was saying he always saw leadership as being an opportunity to serve. Nobody was listening to him.

In the hall, Rannie dropped a quarter in the phone and dialed

Bubba Spainhour's private line in the back of *Juleps*. Bubba picked up at the first ring. He had been waiting for the call.

She said, "The judge responded in a positive way. Lenny gets out soon as you put up one-fifty large. And then there's my service charge."

Bubba always had a flat voice, no emotion. "You seem to be bringing things right along."

"I like to think I operate in an understated, efficient way. I also want you to know that I'm willing to work with you on payment of my fee."

Bubba sucked his teeth. "By and large folks in my walk of life distrust their attorneys. It's an indication of successful transition that we're able to get along like we do."

"I'm sure that's true. And as value-added, I'll point out that Lenny has a difficult time keeping his mouth shut."

Bubba sounded thoughtful. "Lenny has long been a problem employee. But we're just gonna have to snap a losing streak here."

"We can waive the right to a speedy trial," Rannie said helpfully. "Let the prosecution diddle around as long as they want. You make the call. Figure how much time you'll need."

"That depends I guess. Like watching ACC basketball and a player does one of those game-ending alley-oop attempts. For that one little moment you just hang suspended with your heart up in your throat."

When she hung up, Rannie was thinking Bubba would have to put up ten percent as the fee for the bondsman to get Lenny on the street. But the rest of the money wouldn't be forfeit. Lenny's appearance would be a moot issue. She was certain they were going to snuff him.

Rannie knew her life was one of unstinting, brutal sleaze. She had her flaws, she'd get PMS-y sometimes, but she could take it. She was linked by temperament to her father. She was the unassailable Ralston.

Mary Canty and the attendant liquor bottle, Moira chattering like a gerbil in a cage—well, who could say what they were exactly.

*

"It's a whimsical gathering," Moira gushed.

Dale was trapped by her sister-in-law on Legendre Street. The mistake Dale made was stopping to look through the iron gate at Mary Canty Ralston's garden. She couldn't resist because it was always a showplace of blossoms with two gardeners working full time. Roses spilled down from the trellises. The Traubs were dying to use it in the movie, but Mary Canty refused to talk to them.

The gateway was forged of cast iron, the famous fish and star gate that Mary had borrowed back from the Smithsonian and now refused to return. Originally part of the house in antebellum days, the gate had been sold during the Great Depression. The Smithsonian was ill-advised enough to let her mount it during a spring show of homes. Dale remembered the big to-do of it being shipped down on a train. Also the spate of letters from the Smithsonian, first incredulous, then irate when she wouldn't return it. Mary Canty had once replied to them: *"I cannot understand your intent. You write to me as though I were involved in some memorabilia craze."*

Moira was running on without taking a breath. "It will pay tribute to the past, elevate the tone of an otherwise commercial enterprise, and provide a haunting reminder that history is made by real flesh-and-blood people."

Dale thought, oh my God, not one of Moira's parties. And somehow she had corralled one of the Traubs for dinner. And wanted Dale to attend. Along with Collier and Hootch Gibson. Yuck.

Moira's antebellum theme parties—typically on the birthday of Gen. P. G. T. Beauregard—were famous South-of-Broad. Weeks before the date, people became tense expecting the invitation and began frantic efforts to find other social events so they could decline. And this in a city which had a large element of Civil War worshippers and white people who gathered in chorales to sing Negro Spirituals.

The problem, as everyone saw it, was Moira. And what persona she would slide into as the evening progressed. One minute she was trilling the Southern belle vocabulary of blissful and darling and cute. The next—her voice utterly changed to a version of Sarah Bernhardt—she'd wax dramatic and say she seized her life and held it to her trembling breasts with both hands. When she got mad, she yelled in Mary Canty's voice. It was like a demon possession.

Dale found she had to state the obvious. "Collier and I are getting divorced."

Moira stared with blank incomprehension.

"Divorced," said Dale. "As in no longer married."

"But Mother insisted you wouldn't."

"Your mother's wrong."

"How utterly rueful."

Dale thought, rueful?

"You feel no pangs of regret?"

"Well sure, but . . . "

Moira virtually drowned her in froth. "I'm not confounded by this. You know I'm a notorious perfectionist in these matters. I think artistically. I mix and match fine things. The party's all very tightly scheduled and I simply will not take 'no' for an answer. You know I'm Collier's biggest cheerleader despite all his problems and such. And I know your life has been a long climb from Irmo to Charleston, but I'm also a fan of yours. Let the barrage of criticism come from the small-minded. Divorce is certainly human folly, but Moira does not subscribe to poisonous gender politics."

Dale looked up and down the street as though searching for an escape route. "Really, Moira, I ... "

"It's so important that Mister Traub realize the Southern Confederacy is not grave dust to be swept away by the broom of history. And you know, there's this funny, little rumor going round that Mister Traub is interested in historic writings, and since you have Collier's collection in your home I envisioned that you two, you three, might want to converse on the topic, and ... "

Dale had the odd feeling that Moira was so wrought up she was going to levitate off the ground. "Moira, no one can be allowed to see that collection. Collier stole it all."

Moira shifted from a sizzle to a splutter. "What a mean, hateful, spiteful thing to say about my brother!"

27.

Tamzie saw it was time for her to go down and open the big fancy iron gate Miz Ralston had stole from a museum, drive the car out, go back, and close the gate. Then drive the woman over to the yacht club to sit there drinking until she'd call Tamzie to come get her round four. Then came early cocktail hour that would run 'til seven or eight, when she'd pass out. The woman could sure do some drinking and never throw up in the morning like a man would.

When Tamzie was a little girl, she'd often complain to her momma about how mean Miz Ralston was. Ask how she could stand working for the woman. Her momma Mozelle would say, "Honey, I sucks my teeth from the time I goes in that house in the morning to when I gets home at night."

Her momma used to tell Miz Ralston darkie proverbs. It seemed to calm her down somewhat. "Trouble made for man. Ain't goin' fall on the ground. Goin' fall on somebody." Old Miz Ralston always said she wanted to put them in a book.

Whenever Tamzie saw one of those Ralph Lauren Polo ads, she thought of the Ralston children. And white people say black folks are sullen. Those Ralstons hanging around with hair drooping in their faces, giving the world scowls like they so superior.

The way things were in the South, Tamzie had been raised around them, helping her momma with the work. Collier was kind of sneaky, never playing with boys, always walking around with one hand in his pocket talking to himself like he was in front of a jury like his daddy. About sixth grade the girls started to tell him he was cute, and he found a whole world where he could operate.

Rannie was mean. She'd kick and bite until she drew blood. Her daddy always said she should have been the boy. Rannie was scared of nothing except him. She lived for attention from him and he never gave her any at all. Word among the servants had Miz Ralston fucking some other man way back when—some red-haired man—and Rannie came from him instead of old Mr. Ralston.

About the time when Rannie hit sixteen, Tamzie walked in on her going down on a high school boy in the study. Rannie was so scared Tamzie would tattle to her daddy that she made herself scarce for a whole month.

When the phone rang in the kitchen, Tamzie said "Ralston residence" and heard Thaddeus on the other end say "How you, baby?"

She said, "My body just know when it's the weekend."

"How about some more magic touch?" he asked in a real low voice.

She said, "My mind is weak for you but I gotta stop it."

"And here I got such interesting news. I been doing some excavating over at Avery. It seems Cato's wife—Tremba—she was literate. The woman could read and write. We got what's called a slave pass here that she wrote out. It gave a slave permission to travel off the plantation. It's just three lines with her signature at the bottom. Dated October 15, 1822."

"Yeah?" said Tamzie.

"Don't you get it? Laws forbade teaching slaves to read and write. If she could do it, she'd be right rare in South Carolina at that time. If she left any kind of writing at all, it'd be worth a fortune."

Tamzie thought about that book her momma gave her when she graduated from high school. Two books really. One was a St. James Bible with a cover of olive wood from the Holy Land. The other was the old thing with the cracked cover she'd sold to Collier Ralston for twenty bucks. She had never looked inside either one.

She got ready to say how about you define 'fortune' when she looked up and Miz Ralston's standing there staring, giving her that fish-eye look. For just a second Tamzie wanted to tell her white ass off. Say she was dating a college professor type man and she had an ancestor who was just as important as any ol' Ralston. Instead she said "I best be going now," and hung up the phone. Put on her servant face and drawled, "We 'bout ready to go now, Miz Ralston?" The woman talked to her crazy. "I can see my way clear. I will stop this infamy. I'm going to have to play the role of Lady Godiva and ride my high horse."

Tamzie wondered what that meant. Lady Godiva was some kind of chocolate candy.

28.

In the middle of a lonely supper, Dale suddenly put a face on Blake Huston. Over the years, Collier had often had other collectors to dinner. Typically they hated each other, but were drawn together by their shared passion. Dale would sit and smile as they talked of Civil War campaigns. Be the good domestic woman. Ask them if they'd like some brandy with their coffee. Very dull. But Blake had been one of them. She knew he had been to their house. A big man. Bigger than Collier, but kind of stooped with age. And hooded eyes like a lizard. He had watched her every move with those eyes, leering, undressing her.

She searched Collier's address book and sure enough found Blake's name and number. She called him up, identified herself, and said she wanted to sell some of the collection. He took so long to speak she wondered if he was deaf. But he seemed nice enough. Not the fang and claw feral beast that Collier described. He said he was old and couldn't get around. Asked her to drive out to see him on his plantation down Highway 17. His voice was slurred, but he didn't sound drunk. He gave her detailed directions.

As Dale hung up, she told herself, you're not really committed to anything. Just exploring. Listing your options. If it seems dangerous, a nasty risk of prison, you just back off. You haven't done anything criminal. Well, not totally.

Dale had in fact used a portion of Rannie's stash to put a down payment on a new gunmetal blue Mustang. She drove in it south over the Edisto River, through Jacksonboro, over the Combahee and onto secondary roads after Pocataligo. The directions led her without a hitch onto a dirt road and finally a sandy drive.

Live oaks shaped a canopy of dull green leaves, hanging with the gray beard of Spanish moss. The white house sat at the end like a metaphor for seeking a path back into the past. Dale came to the end and parked in front of boxwoods. Getting out, she walked up a brick walk that bisected a sunny lawn of thick Bermuda grass. Magnolias and japonicas. An arbor heavy with fat green grapes.

A black housekeeper led her down a cool, shady hall into a room of portraits and chintz couches and a vernacular fireplace mantle. Blake Huston was sitting in a wheelchair paralyzed down one side from a stroke, which explained the slurred voice. He said, "I don't want to sound like I'm at death's door, but you see I've got more than a minor problem. Being left here in the lurch. Waiting around, that's no fun. I just sit here and don't think much."

Dale helped herself to the sherry he offered and sat in a Windsor chair across from him. The room was really pleasant. Timbered ceiling. Windows with leaded glass.

She showed him a letter from Jefferson Davis to Queen Victoria dated 23 Sept. 1861 informing her of the appointment of James M. Mason as ambassador to Great Britain. She also had a Robert E. Lee to Gen. Jos. Hooker, 2 Apr. 1863, arranging the return of a wounded prisoner.

Blake asked if she could guarantee their authenticity. The eyes had turned sly, perhaps lustful. Caressing a path down her body. Dale said she wouldn't know authenticity if it hit her in the face. She just took Collier's word on things.

Huston was in his seventies, maybe eighties. He had been big once, and the hair that was mostly iron gray still contained traces of its original red. He did a cackling laugh. "Let's just own up to the truth and call a dog a dog. This one can bark, but he can't hunt."

Dale waited.

"Collier's going to jail."

"Perhaps," she allowed.

"And he needs money real bad. But he can't sell his collection publicly because like so many private collections it's mostly stolen. All that stuff Collier has . . . " He waved his good arm around the room. "I've got a ton of it. Everyone asks me why. They've asked that for the last fifty years. I give them the same answer. You do it for the hunt. The discovery. The special gem that no one else can find."

"Yes."

"The meat in the walnut."

"I think I get the point."

"And to scare the living piss out of people."

"You lost me there."

"If they're scared enough, they'll pay your price. No haggling."

Dale was about to say she was still lost, but then she saw the nest of silver framed photos on the little table next to her chair. Sun faded black and white of people she didn't know. Men wearing fedora hats and vests with their summer weight suits. Women with upswept hairdos.

There was one color photo in the group, but faded either with age or the process from the early days of color photography. Mary Canty Ralston stood between two men being young and sassy beautiful in a way Dale had never known. One of the men was Collier Ralston, Sr. Dale had seen plenty of pictures of him. And the other was Blake Houston, much younger, but him without question. Blake saw her staring at the photo.

"Ebullience," he said. "That was me." In a rambling monologue he took her back on a timeline to his youth. He told her about the University before the Second World War, about fraternity hazing and riding in jalopies and drinking moonshine liquor.

Dale thought we all continue to live in rooms of our mind where life is frozen at age twenty-one. That perfect moment just before reality slaps you in the face like a wet fish.

Then he came forward to graduation and the difficulty of earning a living in the Depression-era South. He talked about various jobs he held and lost, cotton broker, ship chandler, railroad executive. Mostly he told her about blackmail. Finding family skeletons and implying they might be brought leering out of the closet. But for those interested in buying archives, they could remain safely hidden. With their sense of tradition, order, and social correctness, the Southern gentry were easy marks. The reverential tones properly described ancestors. Not mockery.

"A touch of the tar brush," he cackled. "That was the trump card. Oh sure, cowardice in battle, bastardy, criminal behavior, those were all very well. But coon blood always got them reaching for their checkbooks."

She looked again at the picture of Mary Canty, wondering about her link with this crippled old man.

He said, "There's colored folks roaming the landscape that can claim kin to the Ralstons. You find me evidence of it and I'll pay your price."

"Why is that?"

"I'll turn around and drain Mary Canty Ralston dry!"

He was still cackling when the colored woman came in to say it was time for his medicine. He said, "All this government upset over smoking. When you're driving back, you ask yourself would you rather come up against a man who's drinking or one who's smoking?"

Dale said he might have a point. She left and got into her car, driving back over the great salt marshes of the Combahee River, home of the blue crabs and mussels and shrimp. She remembered the traces of red hair. In the photo, Blake's hair had been thick and a bright Celtic red. She made a guess, yet it seemed like a true one. Rannie Ralston had been worshipping the wrong man.

29.

In the back office of *Juleps*, Hootch Gibson leaned forward in his chair and made another sales pitch for why he should take Lenny's place as the society dope dealer. Hootch had just come from his entrepreneurship class and had on running shorts and leather walking sandals with tire tread soles. Leather bottom book pack lying at his feet. He had downed a few quick belts of Finlandia vodka before the meeting, and he was feeling relaxed, confident, a whole lot smarter than Bubba Spainhour and Randy Travis. Bubba cleaned his nails with a match end, listening patiently.

"Sure, I hear Lenny's out on bond. But my in-put is sorely required. The region's economy continues to grow, but your supplier deliveries are flat. I'm ready to establish my own identity. Meet the unique needs of your customers. Let the position reach its full potential."

Bubba interrupted. "Rannie Ralston tells me you're in trouble with the law again."

Hootch gave Bubba a wary look. What was this? Rannie didn't know he'd shot the big spook.

"In the collich liberry. Was that part of your project to steal all this big money Confed'rit stuff?"

Hootch waved it off. "Oh that. Little altercation. No big deal."

Bubba had mesh tops to his white loafers. He said Hootch was an easy winner in the bullshit competition, but what he heard was Hootch tried to steal something. Got his ears pinned back by some ponytail dude. Man look like one of them far-out college professors.

"My assailant sucker-punched me," said Hootch defensively. He hunched his shoulders and went into a pout. "Plus he has martial arts training."

"Yeah," Travis smirked. "I hear Chuck Norris don't make much of a personal appearance neither. But he tends to bring a commitment to excellence."

Hootch knew he was being poked fun at. "You don't need to get tense," he said, speaking directly to Travis. "I'm not trying to flatten the hierarchical structure." He figured the man, being such trailer trash, was easily threatened, worried Hootch was bucking for his job. As if Hootch longed to spend all day hanging around Bubba Spainhour. The man had the brain of a damn farm animal.

Bubba lit a menthol cigarette and held it cupped in his hand. Hootch rattled on about cocaine dealing. "Once my presence is in place in the village-like atmosphere of downtown, the first phase of redevelopment will follow. Fast approval of customer credit. A stable manager will make the business of buying and selling more orderly and less open to abuse."

Travis interrupted. "Say, what color do you call those shorts you're wearing?"

"Uh, I think it's periwinkle."

Travis repeated it deadpan. "Periwinkle."

Bubba said, "They take a little getting used to."

Hootch plunged on. "What Lenny does is give customers a five-day window for payment. This being recreational drug product that routinely includes a weekend. This stretches it out to seven days. You're losing major interest on the float. The savings realized would be substantial. I'd have to do the numbers on it to tell you exactly. But you want ballpark, multiply your gross by the prime rate."

Bubba said he couldn't use banks with the volume of cash he generated. And nobody had such an efficient laundry that they worried unduly about lost interest short term.

Hootch said he got the point. But did Bubba have, like, a communications advisor or anything of that nature?

"No," said Bubba, "but I think you just got lucky."

"How's that?"

"We're phasing Lenny out permanent-like. You get the inventory and existing accounts. Whatever additional market share you pick up. There's only one hurdle."

"What's that?"

"Lenny won't be exactly agreeable."

"You mean this is kind of like a hostile takeover?" said Hootch.

"I hope and figure we can end it here for a very long time. When Lenny is permanently absent we'll schedule to close the transaction— get you his old franchise—within thirty days."

Hootch grinned and stood up. Thinking, well aww-right. He had his career on track and his own criminal lawyer callin' for a ballin'. She had flat-out propositioned him. Meaty-looking gal that one. Big set of gazongas on her.

"Travis will get you a clean piece."

"That's okay," said Hootch. "I got one of my own." He liked saying that.

Bubba said, "And lemme give you a little hint. When you sack a quarterback, you don't dive at him. You don't leave off your feet. What you do is you run right through him."

*

Dale remembered Collier liking to hang out in PJ Clarke's in New York on Fifty-fifth and Third, telling stories, posing as Charleston landed gentry to anybody who'd listen. But he wasn't really. The Ralstons hadn't had any big property since the Depression, when the bottom fell out of the cotton market. They had just walked away from thousands of acres, lost it to the county for taxes. Collier would have no recollection of those days at all. He had heard all the stories and really sucked it up. Made it part of his being.

Dale devoted an afternoon to the Register of Mesne Conveyances looking up the history of the family's holdings back to the first boat. The Ralstons had indeed come early, up from Barbados in 1703. Most of the deeds were on microfiche now, but the ones Dale wanted were so historical you had to go back to the old books.

The old woman who helped her wore a button that said "Ask me about my grandchildren." She said she didn't care for the way things were done now. She thought the boss exhibited a distressing failure of institutional control. Dale didn't ask her what that meant.

In enormous old books with cracked covers Dale searched plat maps from the early 19th century. They held an air of mystery, a flavor of a vanished past, a sense of the raw, untamed land with vast forest and marshes seething with wild life. Then she hit upon a huge tract on Daniel Island around 1812—Longboat Plantation. A female Ralston had brought it as a dowry into a marriage with a French Huguenot named Jérôme.

The deeds referenced by the map showed that the plantation had been conveyed in 1816 to Cato Jerome, freedman by his father A. LeD. F-Jérôme. The dower rights—the interest of a wife in her husband's property—had been signed to Cato by an Annabelle Moira Ralston Jérôme.

The old woman was talking national politics and federal subsidies for the mohair industry. "I defend everything the Constitution stands up for and the flag, and that takes in the right for folks to disagree with me. Sounds like socialism to me. Communism. Marxism. One of them 'isms'."

Dale agreed that government ought to get out of financing private industry. Then she found the will and the manumission document freeing Cato in 1810 and the mystery became clear.

A Jerome and a Ralston were married. But Jerome had an illegitimate son by an unnamed black slave woman. That would be Cato Jerome. The white Jerome set his son free, and upon his death in 1816 willed a tract of land to him on Daniel Island.

So there was no black blood in the Ralstons of Legendre Street. Not what you'd call prime blackmail material for Blake Huston. In a way, Dale felt relieved.

Then it struck her. Jerome. That was the maid's name before she married Debone Wigfall. Tamzie Jerome. Tamzie must be related by blood to Mary Canty and all the rest. Pretty distantly related, but still they'd shit a brick if they knew that.

"I hope what you're looking for pans out," the woman said.

"Thanks," said Dale. Smiling. Really kind of amused.

"I often take time to pause and reflect and thank God I'm born in this great nation of ours. Which it is despite aggravating circumstances."

"That's a good point," said Dale. "Too many people take it for granted."

30.

Sure, it's a glamorous life," said Mendel Traub, holding his glass of Wild Turkey that he had insisted on pouring Coca-cola over. "Being consumed by unending foreign travel and first class hotels, creative accounting."

Rannie thought, what is this bullshit? It's not Beauregard's birthday. She had come in from work to find the fat Hollywood toad wearing a Hawaiian shirt; Moira, Collier, and Hootch Gibson in Civil War period costumes. Rannie poured herself a Jim Beam, not Turkey which was far too sweet. Over ice. No cola muck in it.

Traub talked real loud, which made Moira wince and sometimes take a step backwards from him. She had on her *Gone With the Wind* dress, a big-hooped crinoline with a plunging neckline. Rannie knew the evening was headed for disaster. Moira's dream world and the Hollywood ego had to clash at some point.

Rannie thought her sister was such a dip. Their Daddy had taken Moira duck hunting once, and she refused to get out of the car. Then the dog rolled in something disgusting, jumped on her, and she threw up. Rannie had gotten two ducks that day. A left and a right. Bam bam. Daddy had been proud of her.

Moira was saying, "I know. You're silently laughing at my poor beleaguered nostalgia. But I live for the long perspective. Poor men. They simply don't know how to handle me."

Mendel said yeah, whatever, and changed the subject. He said the Lowcountry has been featured in a number of Hollywood films in recent years, but only as a backdrop for location shots. The state had lost millions of bucks that could have been spent locally if producers had access to a local studio. The city had to get its shit in a pile and provide one. Moira winced at the word 'shit'.

"But, hey, no charge for these wisdom nuggets," said Mendel. "You good people need to think of me as the point man for the local economy. You're all caught up in worshipping the risen Elvis. The second coming of Elvis. Whatever. Can't think about commerce like you need to."

Outside the night was silky black and wet with humidity. Night birds and little bats darted and swooped in the garden. Moira said soon the moon would rise and flood the land with its light. In the darkness the crickets will call and you will swear you hear the tiny creatures rustling in the grass. Mendel Traub said, no shit, you can hear them?

A vast array of candles lit the dining room, ricocheting from one mirror to the next in a zillion points of light. White flowers floated in crystal bowls on the table, filling the room with their heavy odor. Rannie never knew the names of plants. Their mother was the gardener, so Rannie rejected it instinctively.

Collier and Hootch were decked out in their rebel reenactment uniforms, Collier's with frogging across the front of the blouse and a wine red sash. Collier said to Hootch that what he really hated about women was how when you'd go into a restaurant together and the headwaiter would offer them a table, women stand there and look over the room. Like they thought there might be a better table hidden somewhere. But then they couldn't just eyeball the room and ask for something better. They'd stand there and take forever to make up their minds. And if you asked—having normal sensibilities and being aware of the irritation being caused—if the table was okay, they'd just keep looking. Not say anything.

"I hear you," said Hootch. "Man, I been there and back." He had been drinking before he came, and now the bourbon on top of that slurred his speech.

"And if you ask them why they do that, they say they were wanting the man to take charge. Meaning you. Like you weren't being forceful enough in telling the headwaiter 'Yes, this will do just fine.' Or 'No, this stinks. Get us something better or I'll kick your ass.'"

"Man, I been there and back," Hootch reiterated. He swayed slightly on his feet.

Rannie stared at Hootch, but he wouldn't return her gaze. What a fool. She couldn't believe she had offered herself to him and he had made no move to take her up on it. God, that uniform. The last thing in the world she was interested in was role-playing. She poured herself another hit of Jim Beam. If they were going to get bombed, she may as well too.

Moira told Mendel Traub that Charleston had long had a very distinguished Jewish community. It had produced writers and musicians and jurists.

"Izthat a fact?" said Traub. He stood uncomfortably close to her, trying to look down her décolletage. She offered him another drink. As she poured, she told him that the word "cocktail" dated to the American Revolution. A New York hostess—a Tory gentlewoman—used to give innovative parties. She mixed punch—which was all different flavors of alcohol in one potent drink—and put a rooster feather in the glass. Hence the name cocktail.

"Kinda like a B-52," Hootch interjected. "Cointreau and a bunch'a other shit in it. Power one of those suckers down and you got a jolt for the evening."

Mendel said he was happy with the beverage component of the meal so far. So a lag time between that and the food was okay by him.

Rannie thought, why doesn't Hootch look at me? Or even this Hollywood scumbag? I've got a provocative style. Should I listen to them more adoringly? Where is the turbocharged sex drive that's supposed to be so controlling in men?

Moira said she was reminded of a Civil War story dear to the hearts of all Charleston women. Rannie rolled her eyes knowing what was coming—the old Sherman spares Charleston canard.

Moira said General Sherman had been stationed in the Holy City before the war as a young lieutenant just out of West Point. He had fallen in love with a Charleston girl who had spurned him. Later after he had taken Savannah, he turned northwest to Columbia, which he burned to the ground and left Charleston intact. His former love—now married to a Confederate officer—received a letter by post. It read: *"My dear, I give you the city of Charleston, South Carolina. Signed, William Tecumseh Sherman."*

Traub said, "Hey, that's rich. Wedge a sex scene in there and you'd have a right fair storyline."

Tamzie served the dinner of baked chicken, black-eyed peas, collards, and cornbread. She was sullen as usual, but you had to expect that.

Moira explained that the silver was Repoussé, which is a very old pattern. It had been in the Ralston family since the 1700s. Faithful slaves had buried it in the yard when Sherman swept past the city. Charleston girls either inherit their silver or they pick the pattern quite young, perhaps when ten or eleven years old.

"None of this health food craze for you guys," said Traub. He seemed to enjoy his meal. And he was looking down Moira's dress again.

Moira said Atlanta's beloved Margaret Mitchell spent considerable time in Charleston. Local legend held that she wrote a sequel to *Gone With The Wind,* and the manuscript was lost. Buried in some collection in a library of one of the great houses of the city. And wasn't that an amazing thought, Mister Traub? A priceless manuscript lying within reach.

Rannie thought, What is this shit? I've never heard that.

Traub said call me 'Mendel' and nah you'd have to deal with Mitchell's heirs on the copyright business. And they were a bunch of bandit low-lifes. He hired his own writers. Screenwriters were generic trolls. Give them a dish of food and a bottle of cheap whisky and chain them to a typewriter. Or word processor. Whatever it was they used. Fucking quill and scroll. Anybody could write. He'd do the job himself, but he was busy with important stuff. Moving money around.

Moira strove desperately to tolerate this gauche being. Choosing her words carefully, she said a number of ladies in the city knew the Civil War era intimately . . . and were also writers of some ability. Perhaps some of them had manuscripts he might find of interest in his project.

"Can they write zebra sex?" asked Traub with his mouth full of peas.

"I beg your pardon?" said Moira.

He chewed, pointed at her with a fork. "Zebra sex. Black on white. Big sweating black buck overseer and the panting white vixen in the big house. *Mandingo* meets *Pretty Woman.* Southern Debs Do Biloxi. That line'a shit."

Moira put down her fork. Her blue eyes were very round. She started to giggle, but it trailed off into a kind of strangled whine.

"The concept presents its challenges," said Traub. "You know what I mean? To do it tastefully. Make a statement about the American condition. And yet still get in some sweating and heaving. A lotta good audibles as he puts it to her."

Moira closed her eyes, opened them, and seemed to be looking through the wall at something in the distance. Without a word, she stood up and left the room, her dress rustling.

"Hey, did I do something?" said Traub. He looked from Rannie to Collier to Hootch. "Did she cringe at that analogy or something? You'd think I farted maybe."

Rannie said she had two hulking redneck clients from up in Berkeley County who buried a man alive. They thought they had killed him and were going to dispose of the body. When they threw him in the pit he moaned. So they just covered him over.

Traub said is there some point to the story? A moral or something? Rannie said she couldn't help but think what it must have been like when Robert E. Lee marched north with 85,000 galoots like that. Kind of men who could come at you with bayonets over an open field. No wonder Yankees often broke and ran.

"No shit?" said Traub. "Buried him alive, huh?"

Moira swept back into the room, her chin high and haughty.

Traub looked up. "Did I prompt some worries or something? Hey, I'm meeting my obligations. I'm here chowing down. Doing my best to be amiable."

Rannie said not to worry about it. Her sister was an ambulatory dingbat. Then she saw the Colt navy revolver Moira held by her side. Her sister's eyes were bulging, teeth grinding. She directed a total, insane fury at him.

"Hey, whatcha got there?" Mendel said.

Rannie half stood up.

Moira swung the big pistol upwards, but it went off prematurely with a huge boom. Traub flung backwards in his chair, crashing to the floor.

Collier leaping up yelling, "What have you done *now*, Moira? What have you *done?*"

"Fucking-A!" said Rannie, slamming her palms down on the table. "You are a pathetic heap of excrement!"

Traub rolled on the floor clutching his thigh, blood spurting out between his fingers, screaming, "I'm going into shock, goddammit! I'm going into shock!"

Moira placed a finger on her chin. She spoke very quietly. "For the life of me, I cannot understand what has produced this moral lapse."

31.

The movie company didn't show up the next day, and no one called Dale to explain. She cleaned out her kitchen cabinets, scrubbed down the wood with Ajax and straightened everything. As the afternoon heat died down, she mixed herself a vodka tonic and turned on the six o'clock news to see State Representative Sheldon Ritter plead guilty to bribery. He told the judge he didn't know what shelf he had placed his conscience on when he took the bribe. He had been preoccupied and confused by personal problems as well as by those of his constituents such as beach renourishment and the restoration of the Fawcett Creek spoil disposal area.

"I have long been criticized for being too outspoken, but that is my way. I was trying to keep my commitment to my home people and the thousands of jobs that depend upon proper development of state resources."

His wife Jacki said she was living one day at a time while preparing a personal letter to the State Supreme Court. "I ask the Lord to guide us on the right path. I trust and believe. Trust and believe."

Federal prosecutor Dave Dubiel gave two thumbs up and a mule eating briars grin. He said, "It's a slam-a-lam clean sweep, and you best believe it."

Somehow they managed to work all that into a 30-second spot. An ad came on for a "Moonlight Madness" sale. Dale cut off the TV.

The doorbell rang and she opened it to find Collier standing there. She didn't let him in. He said Moira hosted quite a theme party, laughed nervously. Dale didn't understand what he was talking about and wasn't really interested.

Collier shuffled his feet, looked at the drink in her hand like he wanted one. He said, "It's like I'm sitting in the penalty box while the game of life goes on without me. I feel twisted up like a pretzel. Damn litany of legal gymnastics."

Dale listened to his gabble. He was hurting. No doubt about it. But she didn't feel any guilt. Sure, she had read all the articles by anthropologists on how men were programmed to want sex with dozens of women. But the same articles said woman's role was to control the man. She objected to his extra-marital sport-fucking because that was nature's plan.

He said the legislature, his law practice, these were all vital sources of income. Now they were gone. He was angry. He was worried. The perpetual discord got him down.

He said, "It wasn't like a marriage in name only. Not a monument to idealism, sure, but we were happy. Then we fell into a gap of misunderstanding. I did some questionable things. But I've drawn the lesson correctly. I know what I won't be repeating. But you seem to want to punish me. I don't need this retribution. This ostracism. The facts don't quite justify it."

Dale guessed his design. He wanted to coax her into making peace. Then he just came out and said it.

"Look, I'm trying to articulate an apology here. Get us back together even in a temporary and limited way." He smiled at her.

Dale didn't smile back. "I don't know what women fantasize about in these situations. What scenario they want. The man surrenders. He gets down on his knees and pleads. He cries. Or does he shamble like a little boy and mumble an apology? Or maybe comes sweeping up in a limo with flowers and diamonds. But none of it quite works for me. His image of strength is gone even in the one with the diamonds. However it's played, the man is still a heel. The romance is gone."

"Look, goddammit, you don't have to be such a heavy about all this. You're doing okay. I know you've got sources of income. Something you've hidden from me all these years."

Dale cocked her head, suddenly very attentive. "You're bothered I paid Rannie for your criminal defense."

He stared at her. "Of course I'm bothered. You handed her forty thousand dollars. Now where did the money come from?"

"Let's not talk about it."

Collier grabbed her arm. "Not talk about it? What is this? Would somebody please tell me what's going on around here? Tell me you didn't sell that map of the Mason-Dixon line. You have no earthly idea what it's worth."

Across the street a house up, a young blond girl sat in an antique red M.G. Looking straight at Dale. Even with the sunglasses on, Dale could feel the eye contact. It zapped her brain. Collier had been driven over by some little honey. Some ditz brain who was still impressed with big Mister Legislator. Or maybe some ditz brain who liked to fuck outlaws and was such a ditz brain she thought Collier was a real outlaw.

It wasn't hard for Collier to read her thoughts. "She gave me a ride," he said testily. "Okay? I don't have a car as you know. And I needed a ride."

"She's one of your honeys," said Dale, her voice rising.

"There's little reason for you to think that."

Dale made a sarcastic grimace. "Should I invite her in? Let her make an independent evaluation of our marriage?"

"You're sounding very strident, Dale. You're very angry underneath, and it keeps showing."

"Should I be warm and fuzzy? What would you have done if we had reconciled? I swallow your crap and throw myself into your arms. I want passionate sex. How would you have gotten rid of her? You go, 'Take your clothes off, sweetheart, while I scoot out and tell my driver she can have the evening off?'"

"She's a friend. Okay? I have to have someplace to live. I can't live with my mother and crazy sister. I mean, Jesus. Moira shooting movie producers."

Dale pushed him backwards out the door. "How about you just leave? Okay?"

He stood and stared at her sullenly.

Dale said, "Are you pretending to have a hearing problem?" She caught the Yankee sarcasm and didn't care. She was really steamed.

The girl out in the car called Collier's name. She was impatient sitting out there in the heat. It seemed to galvanize him into action. "Hey," he said angrily to Dale, "you want out of our marriage. Fine. Go back to Irmo and marry a car salesman."

Dale gave him a look straight in the eyes she intended to drill through his skull. "You could be a method actor. You've certainly redefined the role of shithead."

*

Tamzie had driven Miz Ralston back staggering drunk from a long afternoon at the Yacht Club and now stood out in the garden sneaking a cigarette. She was down to five a day and planned on cutting out smoking altogether because Thaddeus didn't approve. For a man who ate so much, he was real big on health habits.

As she smoked, she thought about what an awful time she'd had scrubbing the blood stains out of the carpet in the dining room. They never really come out no matter what you use on them.

It had certainly been an exciting night. The big boom of the gun brought Tamzie bolting out of the kitchen into absolute pandemonium. Folks yelling and hollering and rushing around. Collier on the phone shouting for an ambulance. Cops charging in.

Miz Ralston got woke up by the noise and came downstairs so drunk she could barely walk. Made Tamzie mix her a stiff Plymouth gin and tonic and bulled right into the mess.

"Of course it was an accident," she said loudly. "She had brought the pistol down to show him and it went off. I suspect the fool man grabbed at it and caused it to fire. Men have no sense around firearms at all. My late husband always said . . . "

EMS came and Traub was carried out on the wheeled dolly. He ripped the oxygen mask off his face and screamed at Moira. "You bitch! You cunt! I'll sue your asses off!"

Tamzie laughed just thinking about it. But then all of a sudden her investment in a little moment of free time started to yield a bad return. Moira came out and cut her off from the house. Tamzie snuffed the cigarette and put the butt in the pocket of her apron.

In her patient, talking-to-servants voice, Moira told the gardeners that it was time to deadhead the roses and order bulbs for fall planting. They said, "Yes, ma'am, Miz Moira" and went on weeding. She had a basket on her arm and scissors. She intended to dry flowers for arrangements. Tamzie knew this because the *Martha Stewart Living* calendar advised it was a good day to do it. Then sure enough, she spotted Tamzie and came over.

"Well, what did you think of our little altercation last evening?" she asked. Her pink tongue ran along her lips as she waited for an answer. "Do you think I had adequate justification for my contentious behavior?"

"I can't give hindsight to the scales of justice," said Tamzie.

"Justice is indeed the *mot juste*. He was tried and convicted of common vulgarity right there at my dinner table. It did not rouse me to a state of exultation. Yet I feel I did right to emphasize my disapproval of everything he stood for."

Tamzie said uh-huh.

"The black slaves contributed a great deal to our Southern culture. Okra soup, greens, red rice, and cornbread are our common cuisine. Their woven rice baskets are still a popular tourist item sold on the street corners. When we share food we communicate a common heritage."

Tamzie said yes'm, she supposed they did.

"You're so lovely, Tamzie," Moira said. "Your skin's as smooth and brown as apple butter."

Tamzie got real wary in a hurry. She didn't even say "uh-huh."

"You could be milk chocolate. The blood of some brutal white slaver must flow in your veins. I'm not proud of the ugly reality of history. I merely choose to focus on the good and the pure."

Moira snipped a flower viciously. Her eyes looked like two holes in her face. "Have you ever shot a man before?" she asked.

Tamzie said no, no she hadn't had the occasion to do that.

"There's a moment there—just a split second as you pull the trigger—where you feel you have total control of the situation. For the first time in your life."

32.

Mary Canty Ralston was so loud that she was always given a corner table in the dining room of the Yacht Club. Even so, the entire lunch crowd could hear her conversation.

"So I told the pathetic little man that she was perfectly sane. And that simply closed the matter."

For some reason the shooting didn't make the news, but everyone South-of-Broad was buzzing about it. Dale had been subpoenaed to the court-ordered psychiatric evaluation hearing for Moira in the Probate Court. She had testified that yes, Moira did spend a lot of time alone, but she had the ambition to be a writer. No, she didn't seem particularly isolated. She got out of the house. Did things.

The psychiatrist had testified that schizophrenic episodes are typically triggered by a traumatic incident. It detonates latent tension existing between delusions of grandeur versus feelings of inferiority. Schizophrenics often exist under the authority of a parent figure who has taken a decision-making position for the child.

"Horseapples!" Mary Canty barked out in the courtroom by way of rebuttal.

Moira lied with a perfectly prim little mouth, saying the whole thing was an accident. She bore no ill will towards anyone. She didn't hear voices or feel any compulsion to violence.

Somehow though, everything had gone okay, and the judge had freed Moira from the threat of the loony bin assuming that the civil suit would settle the issue of who fired the shot. Afterwards, Mary Canty had commanded Dale to join them for a celebratory lunch at the Yacht Club and without thinking she agreed and then immediately regretted it. The trio sat at a corner table while Mary Canty downed her fourth gin and tonic and unleashed the full daunting range of her contempt for the mental health profession. Dale's comfort level was not high.

"Such a ludicrous encounter," Mary Canty said. "The silly man had the gall to ask me if we lived—how did he put it?—'somewhat in the past'? 'Of course we live in the past,' I said. 'It's Charleston.'"

Dale could understand how things had once stood. American history moved fast when you thought about it. Some folks in their sixties now had grandfathers who fought in the Civil War. Go back to when they were growing up, the "Gallant Lost Cause" was on everyone's lips. That would have been in the 1930s-40s. Life remained pretty traditional. Rural. Stable. Small population.

Then you move right on up to the big segregation fights of the 1960s. Baby-boomers became teenagers. Economy rocketing. Suddenly nothing was the same. Rock-and-roll. Mary Canty had never even adjusted to that. Called it "ain't nothing but a hound dog music" from the old Elvis song. But that was the least of the changes. Farm populations shrank to nothing. Suburbs sprawled across both rivers. Malls. Super highways. Poof. The traditional South had vanished.

"Men used to write such nice historical novels," said Moira sadly.

"Oh sure, there'd be a sex scene. But it would be a few lines and fade out. None of this graphic bodice-ripper stuff."

As usual, Mary Canty wasn't quite listening. She said, "The Ralston family has nothing to be ashamed of. We did our best to stabilize the price of cotton and keep a decent living for all our tenants. Turning to the legal profession was a matter of necessity for my late husband. And as for all of this modern dirt we're so fond of digging up . . . the Ralstons freed their slaves. We had a record of that."

Dale thought, yes, when Sherman swept through.

Moira talked mostly to herself. "I tried to explain to the doctor that my writing depicted heroic male archetypes. I do not subscribe to the modern feminist view of man as some belittled figure of fun."

Something the shrink had said came back to Dale. He said schizophrenic episodes were an attempt to reorganize the personality in a more holistic way. A small sub-group of victims were often emotionally restored. Had he meant Moira was better now? Hard to believe that.

Mary Canty's loud rant was only interrupted by her frequent trips to the restroom. Age and heavy drinking had wreaked havoc with her kidneys.

"Your mother is never ambiguous," said Dale in her absence.

"I have to accept that," said Moira. "Or else live in a dream world where someone else is my mother. Pretend I'm a foundling left on the doorstep by elves."

Dale looked at Moira sitting all etiquette school straight. Knees together like evidence of what a serious, good person she was. She could be pretty if she tried. Her skin was really perfect. Wanting to make over another girl is a standard female vanity-fantasy. You know you're attractive to men. You see some girl with potential, but she can't get her act together. But it's a fantasy because you can't truly explain it to her.

She's that way for a reason after all.

Still, the temptation to play the mentor lurked for Dale. Take Moira shopping and give her a quick guide to what's sexy, chic, and wearable. Dale could tell her the bubble flip hairdo went out in the early sixties. And your clothes are like Jackie Bouvier would have worn before she became a Kennedy. Little top-handled handbags that match your shoes. Not like she expected Moira to appear in a skintight tube dress that barely came below her ass. And Moira wouldn't start showing décolletage on the street. Or wear leather miniskirts. No fashion vanguard stuff. But maybe she could get her into shorter skirts. Padded shoulders in her jackets.

What was the difference between Moira and all the other hyperchirpy wealthy women, their lives all smartly on track? Only marginal, really. Moira wrote. They restored furniture and made crafts and flower arrangements. Moira didn't power walk with a weight belt. She belonged to the old no-exercise school. No tennis. Despite her historical interests, no horseback riding even. Certainly no in-line skating or beach volleyball. Too déclassé. So she always looked kind of washed out. Devoid of color. But she shared their other major preoccupations. Pedicures. Facials and massages. Home redecorating. Piling up closets full of shoes.

Dale put aside her ludicrous impulse. Dale who didn't fit in herself trying to mentor her spinster sister-in-law. Train her for break-neck days of social organizing and charity work.

"We live," Moira said, "in a period of continuing and deepening cynicism about our national past. It is the duty of the writer and historian to bring the nation together."

"Well, that's true," Dale agreed. "But you also want to be a commercial success. Right?"

Moira looked very prim. "I am not personally seeking fame or adulation. But commercial success is after all an index of the impact one is having."

"Then it seems to me, the thing is to go with the market. Quit trying to fight the trends."

"What are you getting at?" said Moira cautiously.

"Perhaps you should try your hand at nonfiction. Write the true histories that interest you so much. I'm told they're easier to sell."

"Moira must join the Junior League," boomed Mary Canty from halfway across the room. "It's the only solution."

*

"You're a wild, crazy bitch, you know that?" said the Fed Dubiel. It was late in the day and everyone outside the courthouse had that relieved-to-be-headed-home look.

"I'm underwhelmed at your homespun flattery," Rannie said. She knew she looked good. She was just coming down off the high of a three-day jury trial. The action always got her juices going non-stop. She didn't bother to sleep more than an hour or so each night. Rather than wearing her out, tension made her glow with divine fire.

The client was typical for her. North Charleston dirtbag beat his girlfriend to death, stuck her in a shed out back, and went on living in the house. The cops found the corpse naked except for white vinyl boots with stacked heels. Her client had sold the girl's clothes. He was staying there while he also translated her car, furniture, and kitchen appliances into cash. This ended up providing the necessary fee for his defense. When the dead girlfriend's trash relatives came around wanting to know what happened to all the stuff, Rannie said she had no idea. But she gave value for money. Rannie had actually convinced the jury to bring back a verdict of voluntary manslaughter instead of murder.

Her client looked at her and said, "I have to be frank and say I'm disappointed in the verdict."

"After that there display of jury hoodwinking," said Dubiel, "I know when to quit asking for a plea on Collier."

"Do you even have the authority to bargain a plea?" Rannie asked drily. Dubiel was such an upstate hick. Even as horny as she was, almost crazed in its intensity, she wasn't tempted by him.

He rubbed the back of his head and gave her a good ol' boy shit-kicker grin. "I know, I know. Technically speaking, I ain't fully in charge of this here Chump Change operation. God I love that name. Chump Change. Yeah, we got lines of authority running to Columbia and Richmond and even Justice up in D.C. They groove on lines of authority. Yes they do. Religious about it. What I think is some of these legislators were in deeper than others. I think your boy better plead and do his time. Maybe he needs a heart-to-heart with us. Afterwards we'd evaluate his information, see if he's eligible for the witness protection program."

"Okay, you've gone through the confusing set-up that's designed to tease me along. Now I'm supposed to ask what you're talking about."

Dubiel wiped off his brow. "Whew! Thought you'd never ask. But that's okay. We got there anyhow. What I'm trying to say is in my line of work you get accustomed to watching the topography. Seeing who's who and what's what. You get to where you can spot somebody who's out of place.

"Like that book collector dude staying up at the King Charles. Registered under the name Josh Mahoney. He has an odd resemblance to some out-of-town talent that's been known to be hired in situations like this. You know? The ones where someone knows too much but maybe won't keep his mouth shut. Never actually carry his piece so there's no point in frisking him, shaking down his motel room. He'll pick it up in a bus locker. Somebody leave it for him there. Then ditch it after the job."

"You're telling me there's a shooter in town."

"I'm checking on it. But you can never be sure one way or the other with the professionals. Never any priors on them. If they get a conviction, they're pretty much out of business in that line of work."

"You're full of shit," said Rannie.

"For Collier's sake, I shore hope so. Not that that counts for much." He paused a beat. "What do you do after hours?"

"What's it to you? You gonna ask me out for a drink because you're too cheap to spring for dinner? Maybe a couple of drinks depending on my tolerance. See where it leads. Somebody in your office think you're consorting with the enemy, you say you're trying to work a deal. That way maybe the drinks go on an expense account."

He stared at her, kind of rolling his jaw. "I like that. My assessment stands. You're a wild, crazy bitch. I like it. Body so tough it's savage. Big set of welcoming hooters."

Rannie thought, well at least he notices. "You pretty impressed with the equipment between your legs?"

"There're no negatives to it. Typically it delivers satisfaction. Lot of groans and moans. Sometimes outright lavish praise."

As she turned to walk off, she said, "I bet your dick looks like it needs baby powder on it."

33.

WPAL on the radio was playing the old Delfonics "Didn't I Blow Your Mind This Time." Driving her junky old Chevette up the interstate, Tamzie was thinking on summers when she was growing

up, she had spent with her grandparents on Daniel Island along with a dozen boy and girl cousins. The long months were a lazy time of soft rains and mosquitoes and bullfrogs at night and walking barefoot up the road to a little store to buy Kool-Aid and eat it dry out of the package.

Back then, big old Dan Island had stuck out in the upper part of Charleston harbor like another world. Just little farms and woods where men used to hunt possums and coons. She'd help her grandmomma scrub clothes in a big iron pot over a fire, hang them on the line in the backyard. Nights they'd catch mating fireflies in a jar and set them way off in the woods and say they were ghost lanterns or the plat eye trying to lure you to doom.

Now that the new Mark Clark Expressway passed over the top end of the island, the white realtors were all excited about carving it up for housing subdivisions with boat docks. A big billboard with Skip Rightenberry's face on it said a "controlled growth community" was on its way.

Tamzie turned her car onto the little dirt track. Over on one side across a fallow field you could look across to the Navy base where the big submarines came out. She used to sit scrunched down on the edge of the water with her boy cousins and listen to them say they were going to join the navy and see the world or grow up to be bad-ass boxers like Muhammad Ali.

The old house sat rotten among a grove of pecan trees, roof caved in and all the windows broken out. Grape vine and blackberry thorns tangled it up. Behind it was the blacksmith shop where her granddaddy had made ornamental ironwork and talked about goings on in Charleston and all the big city growth as "unusualness" he wanted no truck with. Tamzie stayed amazed by what Thaddeus had said to her. That she had an ancestor who was an iron worker and bought his freedom and had his own slaves working for him in a foundry. Even owned a plantation here on this very island.

She thought of her grandmomma snapping beans or making flapjacks on a big iron skillet. Without electricity, they never had a TV up there. But her grandmomma would say, "You gets you TV and folks just talk to it 'stead of each other." When Tamzie'd ask her grandmomma for a quarter for candy, she'd say, "Chile, I got more good sense than I got money to waste." And they'd go catch crabs with a chicken bone on a string or pick blackberries and not worry about store things.

Tamzie thought about being a little girl again with her hair in plaits lying in a field of daisies. Watching the ants crawl in and out of their mound. Big creamy clouds drifting by. Thought about syrupy blackberry pies and sardines and sharp cheddar cheese on soda crackers. The world had dumped all that out with the trash. Skip Rightenberry's controlled growth community was going to take its place.

She saw the car first, over near the blacksmith shop, big new deep green Mercedes, then Dale and Moira motioning for her to come over. What on earth were they doing up here? Moira was almost dancing with excitement.

"You won't believe what we've found," said Dale looking real pleased.

Inside the shop was all dust and broken things. Sweetpea vines had crept in through cracks. But propped up against the wall was a Fish and Star gate. Just like the one that hung at Miz Ralston's.

34

Tami Wyrick said, "So I'm like, '*Really?* Well then *puh-leaze* just shut up.'"

Everyone laughed.

Waiting for the Junior League meeting to begin, Moira decided Dale was certainly full of surprises. The girl seemed so simple and uncomplicated. Lower middle class certainly. But she did have some very exciting ideas. Going up and finding that gate on Daniel Island was just wondrous. Those years in New York must have infused her with the creativity of the big city. She should be encouraged to join the JLC.

All the rude things Collier was saying about her, well, he was just wrong. There was no way she would do injury to his archive collection. She valued their Southern heritage far too much. And all that business of who got what in the divorce was just too confusing. Collier shouldn't get divorced if it was going to disturb him so much.

The JLC made you be a provisional member for a year, so Moira had to really put herself into it because you were voted on at the end. Of course all the things on the list of charitable activities sounded positively ghastly. Cleaning out cages at the animal shelter. Running a workshop on protecting families from salmonella poisoning. Doing a puppet show on sexual abuse for the public schools. She shuddered to even think about that.

The history project had sounded like a natural for her until she discovered it was nothing more than going to the historical society and photocopying documents from regular paper onto non-acidic. Moira decided she would just have to design her own history project. And why not? She had her special talents.

Here she'd been just totally committed to fiction writing for so many years. Had her plans for launching *Southern Gale* so well laid. But then no one came to discover the manuscript and then that filthy movie producer was so ugly and she had to shoot him just a teensy bit to make him see reason. And out of the blue Dale had said why not use your expertise on Southern history and culture to write nonfiction. Everything just clicked into place. Crystallized, really.

The presenters were all sitting on the stage waiting to be introduced and to tell what their projects were going to be. Talk was about how gift registries were no longer just for brides. Toys "R" Us had a baby registry. Other stores were opening a full range from births to graduations, retirements, you name it. Tami Wyrick, whose husband owned a new car dealership, said there was just an appearance of tackiness about it. Moira certainly felt constrained to agree with that although she thought the way Tami spelled her name was truly tacky and selling cars was simply beyond the pale. Tami was known to have returned underwear to Victoria's Secret after Christmas.

When Tami was introduced, she outlined a ten-step plan to get beyond idle talk and into action launching the "Bee's Knees" clothing store with all proceeds going to charity. It would sell used clothing but of a very high quality. This was stressed. The items for sale would be *very* selective. League members would not be hesitant to shop there.

Tami's plan received such enthusiastic support that a motion to require each member to provide $50 of "quota" was made and passed by unanimous voice vote. Many murmured that Tami was just a ball of fire. Tami said that good promotion and high standards could double sales for any business. She knew this from her husband.

Moira was next up. For the occasion she wore a Laura Ashley

bib-chintz dress that some people would have said was way-too-long and way-too-full, but Moira thought was just right. Of course everyone knew her and her mother, although Mary Canty had dropped out of the JLC years before. Moira said her mother's absence at the meeting did not signal any change in the Ralston family thinking on charitable works. Developing a broad appreciation for community history was a key element for getting everyone—the well-off and the not-so-well-off—pitching in with community projects.

Family was the key to community. The history of family—genealogy—had come to absorb Americans of all walks of life in recent years. Charleston—with some rather glaring gaps—had led the way in recording genealogies and demonstrating the past they all shared. Here at the edge of the twenty-first century it was time to fill in those gaps and make the historical record complete.

She paused and scanned the room with a pleasant smile. "I think it's high time we mentioned the unmentionable."

They all looked a little curious at that, exchanging glances, shuffling their feet.

"Mis-ceg-e-na-tion," she pronounced firmly, giving each syllable equal weight. "Or at least that's what it used to be called. I don't know if there is a name for it anymore. Interracial child production?"

The whole room fell silent.

"Every one of you has mulattos in your family tree and you know it."

*

A ceiling fan barely stirred the nighttime heat in the finished upstairs bedroom of Rannie's house on Rantowles Lane. The central air conditioning wouldn't be in for another month. Rannie had her blouse off, a drink in one hand, watching the eleven o'clock news, trying to unwind a little.

State Senator Collier Ralston still refused to plead and was expected to go to trial. His attorney who was also his sister—Randolph "Rannie" Ralston—said her position was "no retreat."

Rannie switched off the TV. Hootch lay fully dressed and sprawled on the big four-poster bed, ankles crossed, a Jim Beam with the ice mostly melted in it resting on his chest. He yawned. "I was going to tell Bubba and Travis we needed team leaders and workers to dress the same, but with dirtbags like them, what can you do? I mean, I don't see myself going out and getting tattoos or wearing nylon shirts."

Rannie nursed her bourbon and water. Hootch had slugged down about five of them. If he had any more she figured he'd get into that wild stage where he'd drink continuously until he passed out. She remembered fraternity boys doing that in college. Going face down in a big washtub of Purple Jesus. Had to be dragged out before they drowned. Those were the days when guys still put the moves on her. She didn't want to believe it was because they were blind drunk.

Her father had always taken his bourbon with sugar and water in the old way. Sit and sip it waiting for dinner. He read the evening paper rather than the morning one. Kind of like a summary of the day's events. Keep his deaf ear turned to mother yapping away at him about the servant problem. He'd use that deaf ear as a trick in court. Pretend he couldn't hear when an opponent said something damaging. Make him repeat it louder and louder yet.

Hootch said, "Bubba's not looking for me to act as a human resource person, but shit, I can't figure how he expects to grow at even an average rate if somebody doesn't get a handle on the personnel."

Rannie ignored him. The day had not been kind to her. She had called Bubba to goose him into paying Lenny's bill, said in the aftermath of all the work she had done she felt it ought to be cleared up. Bubba said she sounded full of frustration and discontent. She replied she was not Miss Manners. He said all the same she could use a personality implant. Pissed her off.

Rannie knew she was going to have to pretend Hootch was someone else the whole time they made love. Maybe a big corporate raider, and they were in a Caribbean resort together. Just focus on his body. Virtually keep her eyes shut. Hope he kept his mouth shut.

Hootch was saying, "Speed is going to start having a big local impact soon. Methamphetamine. Crank. I mean, the advantages are obvious. Coke gives a rush and then you go down. With meth, you stay awake for days. You can set up a lab here in town. Home brew it with ephedrine and such chemicals you derive out of gasoline, rubbing alcohol, pool-cleaners, drain cleaners. Not have to deal with those killer Colombians. And no smuggling. No borders."

Rannie unsnapped the front of her bra and showed him her big breasts. He locked onto them with his eyes, but otherwise didn't do anything. Just took a hit off his drink.

She put her hands on her hips. "Hootch. Will you just shut up, take your clothes off, and fuck the hell out of me? Okay?"

He sat up, got slowly off the bed. "No problem-o. I'm no stranger to the stud-in-the-bedroom routine." But he put more ice in his drink.

Rannie was thinking they ought to legalize castration for men below a certain I.Q. The phone rang and she barked 'hello' into it.

Mary Canty just started right in saying Moira had made a complete hash of the Junior League. She had missed two meetings, which got her a $100 fine. And then she created some uproar about mulattos.

Mary Canty had never gotten a straight story on that one although god-knows why not because the whole town was talking about it.

"I'm the last to know anything. It's my cross to bear in life. Three children who never get along and haven't the slightest gratitude for all my sacrifices."

Rannie stood beside the telephone table tapping it with long red nails.

And then if that wasn't enough, Moira had taken Mary Canty's ultra-suede suit—a skirt and jacket—and a purple silk blouse and given it to the JLC clothing store. The suit had cost $800 and all Moira was supposed to provide was $50 worth of quota. Mary Canty had adored that suit and couldn't believe it was gone just like that.

Rannie checked her watch. Her mother hadn't passed out yet. But she was sure enough drunk and said she didn't understand why Collier kept coming around asking for an allowance like a teenager. Why couldn't Dale give him money?

"They're getting divorced," said Rannie, trying to hold onto her patience. Crazy menopausal old lush.

Big pause while Mary Canty tried to have a coherent thought. "Well we can't have that. It would be scandalous. They must get back together."

Rannie took a deep breath. "That's not going to happen, Mother. They hate each other. It's gone just like your suede suit. So get over it."

"I can't afford this," Mary wailed. "You know the straits of my finances. I had a hysterectomy last year. I need a facelift."

Rannie started to lose her cool. "Do you think I don't know the consequences of your spendthrift lifestyle? You trying to run a Hanging Gardens of Babylon like we were in the last century and the darkies showed up and worked for fatback and cornpone. It might have slipped your mind I finance your whole operation."

"You shouldn't be rude about your brother," Mary said sharply. "You've always been jealous of him. Ever since you were a little girl."

That really pissed Rannie off. "Why don't you take a feminine hygiene product and shove it up your posterior!"

Rannie slammed down the phone. Her mind was racing. Angry about the way Daddy played her off against Collier. Almost wouldn't let her go to law school. Angry that her mother had wanted it that way. Rannie would come out at St. Cecilia's and marry a lawyer who would join the firm. Ralston, Ralston & Somebody. Collier would go into politics and play. Never have to take a hard look at the numbers like Rannie did every day. And in that most compelling example of his inanity, racking out with a federal informer. But that obscured the larger point. He was born and would remain a flake.

Outside, the moon had climbed up into the dead center of the sky. She swung her tits around to Hootch again in significant offering. This was what passed for torrid romance in Randolph Ralston's life, she thought. A clandestine coupling with this utter lout. He better be damn good between the sheets.

He folded his arms defensively, stood there with a dopey smile on his face.

Then it struck her. "You're a twenty-six year old virgin, aren't you."

35.

Tamzie soon found that old Miz Ralston had no interest in the Fish and Stars gate Tamzie and the others had discovered. Mostly she occupied herself being mad about the movie company out in the street and up at Dale's house. Soon after the big hymie got shot she had phoned up the movie folks and said since they were endangering her household with their discharge of firearms she was canceling their right to use her son's house at No. 14 Legendre St.

They go, "Come again?"

So she repeated it a lot louder the way she normally talked to black folks like they be retarded or deaf. Finally one of them came on the line and say a contract is a contract and that's that.

Some days pass by with Miz Ralston going on about rude, ungrateful children and how nobody understood her position. She'd do her daily drinking, maybe go shopping at Elza's and come back with a St. John knit dress that cost about a half-year of Tamzie's wages. Then she'd get on the Lady Godiva thing and her duty to the community. Then she'd call the red bitch and get hung up on.

The day they were making the movie on the street, Miz Ralston told Tamzie to start up the lawn mower and keep it going 'til she come down. The gardeners weren't there that day, but Tamzie could start a mower easy enough. She give the cord a couple of good yanks and stand there with it roaring.

Tamzie thought, The woman is sure enough drunk. But then she lives drunk. Got so much alcohol in her she be drunk when she ain't drinking. And mean. Let me tell you.

Meanest thing she ever did to Tamzie's momma was have her write out place cards for a big dinner crowd that was coming. Mozelle could barely read and write and didn't know how to spell all those names. So she lettered them out best she could, and of course they were all wrong. But Miz Ralston used them anyhow and all the guests laughed over how their names were spelled and said wasn't Mozelle just precious and wasn't she darling. Laughing at the poor old darkie and feeling all superior.

Mozelle had said, "I felt lower than a snake, and let me tell you, honey, they crawl on the ground." Other times she'd say "Honey, hell ain't no pit. Otherwise it'd fill up, so many white folks going down in it."

Well sure enough life had its surprises. Miz Ralston came out of the house buck naked, big gray bush between her legs, big old titties hanging down like they about to bang up against her knees. She was wearing tennis shoes with little short socks had bitty pom-poms on the back. She takes the lawnmower from Tamzie and starts to mow back and forth. By then the movie folks had been drawn over by the roar and were looking through the gate. They like to shit.

"Shut that filthy thing off!" Jason Traub yelled. He shook on the gate like the bars of a cage, found it was open and came in, six, eight people right behind him. He was the brother who hadn't been shot so he could walk fine. Miz Ralston kept on mowing. Woman had never mowed a lawn in her life, but there wasn't much to it really. Just go back and forth.

"Do you need it fucking sign language interpreted?" Traub reached out to grab her as she went by, then held back. The woman was naked. He yelled, "Won't somebody pick up the ball on this? Do I have to handle every detail?"

Somebody said the cops were called.

Traub stood there with his hands spread, talking up to heaven. "Do I sit here on permanent stand-by? Is this just the beginning of the pernicious shit I must eat? My budget gets eroded while even bigger costs lurk below the surface?"

The cops showed up with flashing blue lights the way cops do and couldn't believe their eyes. They threw a blanket around her and she threw it off. They took hold of her and she had to let go of the mower so the engine shut off. She's screaming about rights of private property. Finally they had to cuff her and take her away in the patrol car. She yelled out the back window she'll pay a fine every day until the movie is run out of town. Tamzie thought California is supposed to be full of crazies. They'd never been down South before.

The fat producer—the other Traub brother Mendel who got shot—had a hip cast and was carried around by two big goons in his chair like some Egyptian king. He remarked they couldn't ask for better publicity. "But I see upbeat headlines," was what he said exactly.

When Tamzie told Thaddeus about the woman naked, he laughed and said I guess that's what you call doing more with less.

*

"And just who are your witnesses to the alleged battery?" asked Rannie Ralston. She paged through her file as though looking for names. She was fed up and didn't half have the energy to enjoy teeing off on these turkeys.

Two nights running, Hootch Gibson had passed out drunk on top of her without even getting it in. She'd leave him in the morning snoring. This morning he had phoned her at the office and said he woke up with a hard-on so big it pulled his eyelids back inside his head. He really thought he was some kind of stud horse. She told him he had the dick of a chipping sparrow.

Everyone sat around the long polished table in Rannie's office library with the walls lined with yellow volumes of Southeastern Reports and the tall windows looking at the harbor. Rannie used West-Law for her legal research—on-line and CD-ROMs—but she kept the books because they had belonged to her father. The three big-firm Broad Street lawyers turned to Mendel Traub sitting there in his hip cast.

"You know damn well who was there," he said, looking from them to Rannie. His hands scooped the air like a stand-up comedian, saying gimme some help, I'm dying up here.

Rannie smiled, gave him the smooth, level stare. "And which of those witnesses are supporting your story of the events that evening?"

He started up. "What? I shot myself? Is that your spin on it?" He twisted around in his seat, hands spread apart, looking from one lawyer to the next like he was totally confused. "One of you help me out. I think I'm partying with the right people here in town, they shoot the shit out of me. I'm ruined. I'll probably never walk again. My tennis game—and I'm speaking with bitterness here—my game is finished. This, like, special occasion with high Southern society ends in a freakin' disaster for me. My story, which no one but a stone liar would dispute, is the bitch aimed the thing at me, pulled the trigger and fired it. If I hadn't'a tried to jump out of the way, I'd be dead. And what happens when I come in here to resolve things amicably? I get rhetoric spouted at me."

Rannie was thinking of Hootch and Moira on a wedding night. Hootch snoring. Moira not knowing if she was deflowered or not.

"Are we failing the honesty test here?" Mendel said. "I mean I'll approach a vagary with some relative detachment, but I mean jezus-tit."

"Excuse me," said Rannie mildly. "Can we get to what you're prepared to offer to settle this?" She watched the man, his face frozen in mid tirade, his mouth hanging open.

He said, "You're real funny."

She acted surprised. "Yes? I wasn't trying to be."

"I pay *you*? Is this it? I get shot, nearly die, and this is the smart mouth I get?"

Rannie said a ballistics report had the pistol being very undercharged with gunpowder which was why his wound was so superficial. He said you'd rather my leg was torn clean off? Rannie ignored this, said as she saw it, he had been drinking heavily that evening, five straight bourbons according to the servant. Her sister, a girl of very delicate disposition, was nearly scared out of her wits by him waving a gun around like a crazy man. When he shot himself—however unfortunate that turn of events—he absolutely terrified Moira. She was under a doctor's care now and seemed likely to remain so for the indefinite future.

Rannie turned a page in the file. Said next issue was the matter of the savage attack upon Mary Canty Ralston by agents, servants, and employees of Jazz-Bo Productions. Poor woman getting on in years. In and out of senility. They chose to humiliate her and have her dragged off in handcuffs. American society had become rather coarse lately, but an entire movie crew jeering and hooting at the mentally ill made her sick to her stomach. Even aside from the fact that the victim was her own mother.

"Is this fucking la-la land?" railed Traub. "I thought Hollywood was berserk. This is over the edge. I'm in a, like, mental implosion."

Rannie said she wanted a straight hundred thousand for the injuries to her mother. She was being conservative because the dear woman really was not fully conscious of what had been done to her. As to her poor sister, that claim would remain open pending a full psychiatric report.

Traub went beyond indignant. "You're nuts," he said furiously. He looked at his lawyers who seemed almost awed by her brass and said,

"She's fucking nuts!"

Rannie laced her fingers together and rested her chin on them. "Oh, and I want Dale Ralston fired from whatever job she's doing for you. The consulting thing."

Traub yelled at his lawyers. "Am I supposed to take this abuse? I pay you to make me sit here and take it? Am I a stakeholder here? When did I become the fucking big bad wolf?"

One of the lawyers cleared his throat.

"I don't need your legal jargon," said Mendel. "What I need is for you to kick her ass, and if that feat is beyond your modest capabilities, then you can start selecting an outplacement firm."

Rannie said impassively, "What I'm sure your learned counsel will advise you—once you're all out of the room—is that I will stand in front of a Charleston County jury and say, 'I'm Miss Rannie Ralston. You all know me. You knew my daddy.' And sure enough, they'll all know me. And then I'll proceed to kick *your* ass."

She gave him her sweet girl smile. Kind of a simper. "We'll take two hundred thousand dollars to settle both cases without going to trial."

36.

First thing in the morning while the movie crew did the scramble to get the day's shooting going, Dale was fired right off. Not by Jason Traub. He was busy having his hair done.

Some under associate assistant canned her, a willowy guy in a silk scarf. Etiolated was the word that came to Dale's mind. You're decertified was how he put it. She said, "Excuse me?" He said, "You're out. Kaput-ski. The dogs bark, the caravan moves on."

She said, "But this is my house."

He said, "Did someone say it's not? We've got it under contract. As to the other thing? Got something in writing? Of course not. *Capiche?*"

Dale asked if just by chance her dear sis-in-law Rannie had something to do with this. He said, "Is a bean green? Does James Brown get down?" He turned to scream at a lighting man. "What are you doing with that? Open a dialogue with me!"

She stood there, now a non-person, as the movie people used her house. Dale Ralston the no longer well-compensated. Fade in; fade out. She felt a surge of anger. The world and her in-laws were sure enough whipping her around. Her marriage continued a daily test of putting up with the vulgar, the rude, and the crude.

He turned back. "Hey, the key to outplacement is keep it upbeat. Stress your enthusiasm. You got a lot to showcase. Don't burn your bridges." He turned away again shouting, "Yes, yes, do we have an encore problem here? Hey, that really and truly sucks!"

Dale went out and sat on her piazza while the movie crew came and went. She had to find a way out of this morbidity. Otherwise she'd end up dead of dismay and self-loathing. She got to thinking about Josh Mahoney, wanting to go see him, not to bellyache, but just curious about him. Was she just trying to reinvent herself through a man?

By nine o'clock the heat wave had locked the peninsula in its suffocating embrace. A chemical spill had stalled traffic, turning the interstate into a blistering hot parking lot from five miles out of town all the way down onto Meeting Street. Car engines boiled over. People passed out from heat stroke.

Dale walked up Legendre onto Broad and then Meeting Street. The Queen Anne was the last of the 1950s motels in town. They had all been replaced by inns, rustic or regal, all varieties. Audubon bird print decor. But this was straight out of the architectural style book of the tacky decade. Big neon sign. Flat roof. U-shaped of glass windows with the beige curtains always drawn because the rooms faced each other across a parking lot.

She didn't particularly expect Josh Mahoney to be in his room, but he was. He said come in out of the heat. It's brutal. He had his shoes off, barefoot on the carpet. He used a scrap of paper to mark his place in an old-looking book. She went in, looked over the generic motel room. The cool of the air conditioner brought instant relief.

Josh looked good to her, and she had an impulse to kiss him. She bet it would be like drinking from a clear stream. Instead, she asked him if he was doing any business. He handed her the book. C. M. Calhoun, *Liberty Dethroned*. It seemed to be about the Civil War. She set it down on the dresser.

"I'm hanging in there," he said. "Getting a few things accomplished. You'll see some stuff, not be able to make up your mind quite. Never realize how much you want it until the offer gets revoked."

"Is it fun?"

He patted a laptop computer like it held state secrets. "One big serendipity treasure hunt. Life's an open-ended feast."

She leaned up against the dresser with the TV on top. Opened one of the dresser drawers at random. No particular reason. Just an idle movement. And there was the gun lying right on top of some underwear and socks. She knew nothing of guns. Never even used one as a prop in a fashion shoot. This one was a revolver. She knew that much.

He watched her looking at it. "What? What did I do?"

She was cool, didn't raise her voice. "Playing at John-boy Walton and you carry a gun. Are you a crook or a cop or what? Some kind of a killer? Stick-up artist? One of the Feds putting my husband in jail? "

He said he often carried valuable stuff. Sometimes certified checks. There were crazy people out there.

She studied him, said she'd really like it if he wasn't a crook. So she was going to put him to the temptation test. Collier's collection was all stolen. A library full of fool's gold. Would Collier get in bed with him to sell it off? Collier was good at getting in bed, but no, he'd never sell. But if Josh wanted it, he could have it. No charge, no commission for her. Just rent a truck and drive off with the whole accursed lot. Or if he wanted a sidekick, he could use Hootch Gibson the same way Collier had. As a patsy if something went wrong.

"Who's Hootch Gibson?"

"A jerk. He's in the phone book. Hunter Gibson. Hootch is a nickname. If you're a crook, you'll get along fine with him. He's the jerk you beat up twice already. You've established your authority."

Josh said, "My business doesn't lack for crooks. You can meet them by random phone calls to dealers in New York. But I try to keep basically legit. Rare books always have chain of title problems. Sometimes I hit a minor scandal, but I've been virtually germ-free. Knock wood." He rapped on the veneer of the dresser. He didn't try to get close, make a grab for the gun or anything. Nothing threatening about his posture.

Dale took the gun out of the drawer and held it. He didn't go all nervous. Just stood there cool. But she wasn't waving it around. She asked if he'd get fired for losing his gun. Did the boss know he carried it? He said he tried to look at things logically. If he kept the job, he kept it. If he lost it, then he did that.

She unzipped her pocketbook and stuffed the gun inside. She wasn't sure why she did it. He looked puzzled. She opened the room door and went out into the blinding heat.

He followed her out in his bare feet. The pavement was ferociously hot, and he stepped back to the doorframe. "You really ought to give me that back."

She crinkled her nose at him like a teenage girl flirting. "Why don't you come over for dinner? We can discuss it then."

37.

Hootch sipped a banana daiquiri at the bar of the Mills Hotel as evening came on, crunching the fine ice and sugar. The bar was a good one, big and solid, set at one end of a dining room that belonged to the last century. French windows opened out onto the tropical growth and the fountain in the courtyard. The scene resembled the French Quarter in New Orleans, and yet it was genuine Charleston too. True antebellum. Hotel had been built before the Civil War. You could find it in the pictures of that time. Old engravings in *Harper's Weekly*. Photographs of the city after the Yankee bombardment.

Hootch often thought he might make this his business headquarters. Sit in here much of the day. Have lunch, a few drinks. Take calls on a cellular. Very upscale place with extremely high-priced drinks. That kept out the riff-raff. When the weather cooled off, he'd sit out in the spacious quiet of the garden. Maybe wear a Panama straw hat. That blond honey bartender would be a problem. Be all over him wanting a date. Rannie was enough trouble for one man. Talk about demanding. Girl had a pussy on her like a damn Pandora's box.

He was meeting the pony-tail dude, one Josh Mahoney as he identified himself. Strange, the man calling him up out of the blue and saying the contretemps of the past were a mistake. Set a bad precedent for future conduct. Because what they needed to do was pool their resources and score some serious Civil War documents.

Hootch had said if Mahoney was a buyer then Hootch-man could deliver. He had an entire organization behind him. Some very heavy people had picked him as a person of vision and given him real autonomy. Mahoney said he had spotted Hootch as quality from the first. Knew he wasn't just some talking head.

Thinking about the impending deal, Hootch liked to remember when he first stole something for Collier. Working for him as an aide at the State Legislature in Columbia. The object in question was a Confederate blouse, double-breasted job with velvet collar sent out from the state museum for dry-cleaning. Hootch pilfered the claim ticket and walked off with it cool as you please, thinking he had just played a prank. He learned quick enough that the value lay in its having been worn by Wade Hampton, the major Confederate hero from South Carolina. Collier's eyes had lit up like a kid in front of a birthday cake. At that moment Hootch knew he held all the cards. Just like a crack-head, Collier had a drooling junkie's needs. And ol' quick-fingers Hootch could always come up with a bag of candy.

From there on it had been smooth sailing. Hootch had gotten whatever he wanted. Free booze for him and his under-age buddies. Loan of cars to go out on dates. Being ignorant, he had set the price far too low. He wised up later during a Southern history course. Despite flagging his final grade badly, he did learn the magnitude of what he had been stealing.

The recruiting broadside would bring $4,500. The Fort Sumter documents a couple thousand. The account of the Shenandoah Campaign with marginal notes in Stonewall Jackson's handwriting was worth ten grand. A Jefferson Davis letter held an incredible market value of thirty thousand. The numbers added up in the most amazing way.

When Mahoney came in wearing a suit, he walked past the piano very smooth, a man at ease with himself, stood next to Hootch. Hootch studied him as he ordered a Maker's Mark straight up. The man knew how to drink in the old time way of Hooch's father. None of these fruit-flavored drinks. Maybe some value there. Kind of a signature style that should be imitated. Hootch felt a little underdressed in his "Right to Keep and Bear Arms" t-shirt, Desert Storm camo cut-offs.

They moved to a table. Mahoney said it was a good bar, and Hootch agreed with him. Mahoney said, "You know sometimes I think it's more interesting to think about visiting a bar than it is to actually visit it. I go to Sloppy Joe's in Key West once. It's basically like I pictured it, but they're having a Hemingway look-alike contest. Fifty white-bearded old men. Kind of freaky in a way. Pilgrims at a shrine somewhat like myself. But no mystical experience. You know what I mean? The spiritual vibes long dead. I mean they sell t-shirts for shit sake."

"Yeah," said Hootch, awed by the dude's insight. "What a tear-jerker."

Mahoney took a pull on the drink. "So. Does a life of crime agree with you?"

Hootch gave him a look, finished his daiquiri wondering if he should change drinks. "I ride to work each day on a sunbeam. How 'bout you? You don't seem like any New Yorker I've ever known." Hootch held up his glass to signal the waiter he was sticking with daiquiris.

Mahoney's eyes were smiling. "I'm southern. That means I'm polite and sincere even when I'm ripping you off."

"None of what you'd call moral qualms?" said Hootch. "No nervous tension where you get to feeling you'll get hurt bad because you're doing something bad?"

"There are moments," said Mahoney, "when I'm hanging out there carrying a couple hundred thousand in a satchel that prompt strange feelings. But basically, I'm comfortable in this role."

"As a crook?"

"The rewards are often problematic. A lot of ill-advised entries into the field are trimming profit margins here and there. Sometimes a sure deal gets truncated. But it's a complete life in its own way. Stultifying desk jobs are not my game."

Hootch liked the way the man talked. Very cool. "Give me a time and place to meet, and I'll have a thing or three to show you. Kind of a start-up vehicle."

Josh raised an eyebrow. "What are we talking? Items in the one to two thousand dollar range? We can go a lot higher. My buyers are not cheapskates."

The waiter brought Hootch another daiquiri, slid it onto the table with a napkin under it. Hootch waited for him to leave, said, "If we agree on price, I imagine you can boost your production far more than that."

"Do these rare materials in question belong to Dale Ralston? Or is that not a particularly appropriate question? Well, no mind. Don't want to bring up a touchy subject. What we'll do is we'll meet at a neutral spot out in the open. You may want to carry a gun. You'll be happy and I'll be happy. We're not in the medium of children's entertainment."

Hootch liked the gun part. The dude was cool alright. "How about you give me a wish-list?"

"What we're really looking for"—Mahoney raised and lowered his eyebrows several times—"is your African-American stuff."

Hootch stared at him open-mouthed. "You're shittin' me. Who would want that? I mean . . . what would it even be?"

Mahoney leaned forward, resting on his elbows. "This is business, right? Not sentiment. So we have to examine what drives the market-place at the moment. Sure rebel artifacts bring more than four-to-one to Yankee of like-kind-and-quality for your basic collector. But there's a new player out there."

"Nigger lovers?"

"So to speak. The federal government. Non-profit foundations. Big universities."

"Federal faggots," said Hootch disgusted, the whole thing taking a while to really sink in.

"And everything to them is the black man. They are pouring out money like you wouldn't believe to build black archive collections. Then the Getty's always involved. That museum out in California. They got so much money they have to spend with both hands to keep their non-profit status. Prices are going through the roof. With no questions asked."

"Lemme think on this," said Hootch. "But I'm pretty sure we're in the same ballpark."

He didn't have to think long. Hootch knew the collection. And right smack in the middle of it was one of the few legit items. Some coon diary Collier had bought off of that maid Tamzie Jerome for twenty bucks.

*

Dale had been to the post office which was in the same building as the federal court. She had gotten used to being fired, but she had to stay out of the house a lot because of the filming. The Fed Dubiel came around the corner from the courthouse and stood there looking at her.

"You know it's funny," he said. "I was always real active as a kid. Played three sports in high school. But I never broke any bones, never any injuries at all. No surgery. Except once. We were warming up pre-game. Did I say it was baseball? Well it was. I was throwing long balls to one of my buddies and the other team's doing batting practice. One of them pops a fly ball. Somebody yells 'Heads up.' I look around to see this gray blur rocketing at me. Catches me smack on the nose."

He used two fingers to wobble his nose back and forth. "Broke my nose. Fractured my cheekbone. Had to get out-patient surgery."

"Is there some point to this story?" said Dale.

"Yeah. Things come at you from all angles. The unexpected ones are what's dangerous."

"You want to quit playing guess-what-I'm-thinking? Maybe spell out your message?"

"You need to persuade your husband to plead guilty. Rannie's just going to strip you of whatever assets you have and then sell him out. That's the way she operates. A forthright cunt, that girl."

Dale thought on that, got slightly steamed. Trash mouth hick thinking he was telling her big revelations about the Ralstons. "This getting caught blindsided," she deadpanned, "that works for everybody. Right?"

She walked home and found the movie crew packed up and moved on somewhere else for the day. She sat looking at the telephone wondering just how much she truly hated her sister-in-law Rannie. Finally made up her mind and called Blake Huston. She said, "Don't pop the champagne corks, but I think I might have what you want."

"Black blood?"

"Somewhat. Cousins. The two families have been split apart for a century and a half."

"Every family that owned slaves has got that relationship."

"Still, it's a fact."

Blake made a snorting noise. "So maybe they should have a chance to get back together. Get to know one another."

"True."

He said, "It's odd. I was reading in the newspaper y'all got a parking garage up there in Charleston with a big crack in the cement. Had to close the top floors. But they figure they can repair it with epoxy."

"Isn't that glue?" said Dale.

"That's what I thought. The world's changing in ways I can't figure out. Is that the point I'm trying to make?"

"Are you asking me?"

He said, "I told you I'd pay. Name your price."

Dale said, "I don't want money. I just want you to drop in on somebody. Maybe . . . like you said, put a family back together."

38.

Debone said, "Prison has been kind of a distraction, and now I er, uh, feel I can concentrate on my career again."

Hootch sat in the back office of *Juleps,* his wooden chair tipped back against the wall. Watched while Debone made his pitch to Bubba Spainhour and Travis, trying to get back on the payroll. He had been an enforcer for Bubba before he got sent off. Big gauze patch over his nose. Sure enough, the very one Hootch had shot. Hootch kept a hand over his mouth, thinking it was funny as hell.

Now that Hootch was hired to whack Lenny Womble, he figured he was in the inner ring and strutted around the bar most days, hung out in the office. Naturally, he didn't notice what a nuisance he was making of himself.

Bubba said, "I don't wanna stop any kinda overture to open a dialogue. But you just being recently out on the street makes you a little too conspicuous for current employment. At this point in time you're just not what I'd call a good game matchup."

"I'm trying to take the whole thing in perspective," said Debone. "I do my time. I come out thinking I'm on top of the situation. Gonna pick up where yesterday left off. Then I get this backhand slap. It's like loyalty is a word nobody salutes no more. Looka here. Did I say something wrong? I mean, what's the roadblock here?"

"There's nothing in particular that you've said that's kind of sealed my opinion. We're in a rebuilding stage, I grant you. Physically, you look like you could play the position. But I think I'm gonna have to keep you red-shirted for a while. Leastways until your parole officer starts to treat you as routine."

Debone was whining now. "C'mon, man. Gimme a chance."

"I think I done decided on that already once."

Now sucking up. Telling the man he was a loyal darkie. "Say.

Looka here. I'm gonna remain on my toes. Keep my calendar clear. Be at the telephone waiting for that call."

Bubba breathed out kind of tired, then turned to Hootch. "Ain't you got some house cleaning chores to take care of? How many days on this assignment has it been? Two? Three? So when're the results gonna match the hype?"

Travis had to jump in. "You sucking hind tit on that one, Hootch boy."

Hootch saluted Bubba. "Yeh-boy, chief. I'm good to go." The fuckers always wanted everything done yesterday. Travis giving him that look that was supposed to make him afraid. He'd get to Lenny in good time. He had to keep his eye on the big picture.

Hootch slid out the office door and went out to the bar, ordered two Miller drafts and looked at the boat ads in a newspaper he folded down the middle of the page.

23' 1991 Mako Centre Console, 225 Johnson, float-on trailer

25' Chriscraft inboard, 1978 model, $1500 OBO

Seeing Moira shoot the shit out of the producer had certainly been a laugh and had made him the center of attention at the KA house for several nights running. He had followed Rannie's script, lied to the cops and the loony-bin court about what happened.

The Ralstons were one high-gear dysfunctional family. Collier like a one-legged man in an ass-kicking contest. Mary Canty bombed on some weird drink she made—the woman could drink some damn liquor—telling him Moira was "available for romantic interests." He guessed he knew what she meant.

Damn Rannie had sure turned into a Class-A cunt. Endless nagging about his performance in bed. Accusing him of being a virgin.

Which he sure as hell wasn't. Not that he could remember the details on a lot of sex he had had. But he had sure enough waked up naked beside girls in bed before. Well, fuck her and the horse she rode in on.

The big question on Hooch's mind was whether to get an earring. Five, six years back he would have said no, folks would think it was some kind of international queer signal. Out trolling for dress designers. But now everybody seemed to have them. Not just the little wanna-be Seattle grunge kids who hung out around Marion Square. But all the college boys.

The door to the back room opened and Debone came out. As he drifted past, Hootch slid the extra Miller in his direction and said he should come quench his thirst. Maybe it was a good opportunity for them to get acquainted both on and off the job. Debone said he believed he would.

"So how did you get on in prison?" Hootch asked.

Debone gave him the cool dead-eye look of a convict, but then decided to play along, see where it went. "Well, you have some years to gather your thoughts. You get to know a lot of guys and then you get out. Don't see them no more. It's kind of a shame in a way."

"How's it feel? Preparing for the rest of your life?"

Debone looked thoughtful. Took a long drink and wiped his mouth with the back of his hand. "I know I got my weak points. I let everybody see my heart. You always know where Debone stand on an issue. Your basic white boss got trouble dealing with that sometime."

Hootch looked thoughtful. Asked him how many men he had killed. Debone watched all the yuppies in the restaurant, the young lawyer chicks in their suits and skirts that were short but not too short. He said he had a career high of three.

Hootch said Travis was the primary muscle now. Maybe Debone

could take him out. That would leave a vacancy. Debone stared at him real suspicious. "Or," said Hootch, "you could develop a whole new attitude. Do a little B&E on my account. Go in clean. Take something nobody will even miss."

Debone straightened up and looked down on him. "You after that Confed-rit shit too, huh?"

39.

"We, uh, have a minor problem with the Traub settlement," the big firm lawyer said in a hesitant voice.

For Rannie it was always a moment of quiet triumph when defense lawyers called up whining and wheedling about settlements. She knew she had them by the 'nads. Sit back in her chair and enjoy listening to them squirm. This time it was particularly good.

It seemed the Traubs had a long history of liability problems. Jazz-Bo Productions had suffered a spate of arson, drug arrests, car wrecks, and rape charges by minor starlets. Their insurance carrier was threatening to cancel their policy. They wanted to settle it on their own. No insurance company involved.

"Don't propose I accept less than the agreed upon $200,000."

He sounded fatalistic. "I won't."

Rannie thought for a minute.

"Are you there?" he queried.

She snapped her fingers. "Okay, here's how we'll work it. My sister Moira fancies herself a writer. Romantic treacle. Sighing in the afterglow. Stays cooped up in her room waltzing with the sea breeze and churning out bilge. You do up a contract, buy some of her trash."

He mumbled around on the other end. Dithering. He couldn't

imagine the Traubs producing a film based on anything Moira had done.

"Do you know anything about Hollywood? Any company, no matter how small, options or outright buys dozens of scripts and rights to novels a year. Most of them never get produced. They're thrown on the slag heap. It'll be perfect. You keep your insurance, and you get a tax write-off for the purchase.

"And I tell you what else. My brother is a member of a Confederate reenactment regiment. They're authentic down to the last trouser button. The Traubs can employ them in the battle scenes. No battle scenes? Write some in. It's not a full regiment as you might imagine. Not that many people like to play dress-up. There's only a hundred of them. You may make out one check to me as their attorney."

Rannie was really amused. She could imagine those clowns messing up the Traubs' movie. Making them run over budget. With any luck that fool Hootch would probably manage to shoot someone.

    *

Hootch asked the bartender of *Juleps* if he knew how to make a Mojito. The bartender said no.

Hootch said, "It's light rum, mint leaves, splash of 7-up. Sugar cane stick."

The bartender said, "Yeah?"

Hootch said how about laying in some sugar cane for his next visit. The bartender said how about drinking up and getting out.

Hootch watched the early lunch crowd, having himself a second rum and coke and thinking he had a lot on his plate. He had to wipe Lenny—man, Bubba and Travis were getting shirty about that. He had told them he was a little behind schedule of the point where he'd like to be, but they were being hard-asses about it. He couldn't figure on much respect around that Travis in his fucking new pair of snakeskin cowboy boots. Indonesian rock python he said. Talk about tacky.

Then he had to get the coon diary for Mahoney. But that was under control. Debone told him he was developing a plan. Put his fiancée Tamzie into Dale's house as a maid. Get her to start sliding out stuff a little bit at a time, replacing it with other old books. Nobody would notice. Useful tool, Debone. You want something stolen, get yourself a nigger.

He didn't want to go out in that heat, but a man's gotta do what he's gotta do. Yes, Hootch could keep two balls in the air at once. And today was Lenny removal day. Then he'd get back to Josh Mahoney.

The way Hootch saw it, the problem with Lenny went way beyond his coke and Quaalude habit. The boy had no style. Wearing a striped Casey Jones railroad cap and singing that Grateful Dead song about cocaine all the time off-key. Hard to believe he had been a KA.

Hootch knocked back his third rum and coke in the bar and went out into the glare. The seats in his jeep were scorching. He had a new bumper sticker that said "This vehicle insured by Smith & Wesson." It matched his gun.

Hootch squinted a bit in the sun despite his photo gray UV protection shooters sunglasses. The heat was already pushing ninety-four in the shade and the jeep had no roof on it. He turned his swordbill cap backwards because it was action time. The booze was kicking into his system, giving that hundred-yard-dash feel.

He had chosen his gear just right. Air Force survival vest with ammo clips in the deep pockets. Smith was in the big pocket in the back. Israeli combat boots with cotton canvas uppers and his athletic socks coming up to his knees. He had it all figured out how he'd work the hit on Lenny. Drive around 'til he saw him. Take him for a ride out into the country. Drop him with one shot to the back of the head. He might bury him if it wasn't too hot out. No sense in breaking too much of a sweat though.

"Let's catch some rays at the beach, dude," he said aloud, practicing his deadpan delivery. "Maybe score some shit and smoke out." His voice was moving too fast. It was going to be hard to act cool.

Hootch found Lenny standing outside the little grocery on Queen Street propped against the wall. Really stoned. Black t-shirt sleeves rolled over his biceps to show a Spiderman tattoo. A long time ago back when they were in college a lot of girls had thought him good looking. That was ancient history. Ol' Len was, like, totally wasted now. "You really got to get rid of that tattoo, man," Hootch said. "You're scaring off the clientele." He revved the engine a couple of times. It had a bad tendency to knock off.

Lenny answered in a voice so thick and stoned he could have been holding his tongue with two fingers. "I hear they got lasers now that will take them off with no scars. Seven to nine treatments about, oh, a month apart."

Hootch delivered his lines. "What're you doing hanging out here? Climb in. We'll catch some rays out at the beach. Cool off in the sea breeze."

Lenny shook his head in the negative. "I've got like a major deal to do, then got to get home to see *Baywatch,* man. That's my idea of beach. I mean we talking bikinifest babes."

"Where you're going, I imagine they only have the Disney Channel," said Hootch. "What'dayou mean deal? You got a customer?"

"Breakfast, man. I'm gonna score some L'il Debbie snack cakes. They're like the best sugar high around."

Hootch jumped out of the jeep leaving it idling. Looked up and down the street. Other than the little grocery on the ground floor of a big frame building, Queen was residential. Big shady trees and old houses. He walked around the jeep to the passenger side, holding the Smith against his leg. He told Lenny they would be saying farewell to the Twinkies. Say bye-bye, now. He put the gun in Lenny's gut. Its deadly significance didn't seem to register.

Lenny said, "Hey, you remember when we were kids the *Six Million Dollar Man* on TV? Where the dude is half computerized? Like it's gonna be reality soon. I was reading where scientists are going to link the human brain to, like, silicon chips. Grow nerve cells right onto the chip."

Hootch drew the pistol back to smack Lenny across the mouth with it, but Lenny suddenly sprang into the passenger side of the jeep and climbed over the gear shift to get under the wheel.

"Hey, lemme drive, man," he said all invigorated.

That was when Hootch shot him right in the rib cage. The report was surprisingly loud, even making a little echo down the street.

Lenny lurched back into the passenger seat. Hootch told him to buckle up for safety as he walked around the jeep and got behind the wheel. The engine knocked off. It seemed to take forever to get it cranked. Hootch popped it into gear and drove off. Somebody had come to the door of the grocery, but he didn't see the face.

Hootch showed his irritation, cursing when he'd have to grab Lenny by the shirt to hold him in place. He had told the dumbass to put on his seatbelt. Lenny said he was fucked up bad. Something wasn't working right at all.

"How's your pain threshold?" said Hootch in a chatty voice.

They caught the red light at Beaufain too far back to run it. Some spades in baggy shorts were idling against the fence around the old project being cool. Looking him over with half-lidded sleepy eyes. Giving him the 'fuck you, man' look. Hootch took the opportunity to belt Lenny into the seat. The shoulder harness would hold him up. Lenny was gasping like he had a plastic bag on his head. Great long gut-wrenchers.

Hootch looked over at the spades with a frank expression. "My colleague here has bad allergies. Pollen count is up today." He turned his cap around forward and pulled the bill low on his eyes. "*Adios* mutherfuckers g'bye."

He was laughing like a maniac when the light changed, and he roared up Coming Street to catch Calhoun and head on over the Ashley River Bridge. It took a half hour to get out of the traffic and over the Wappoo Cut and then across the little bridge on the Stono River into the country. Nobody took a second look at Lenny. Just a kid passed out. Probably drinking in the middle of the day. Hootch had the momentum going for sure now. He let out a rebel yell. Yee-hah!

Past the marsh along the Stono, the trees made a shady canopy over the road. Traffic was moderate, fancy cars going down to the resorts at Kiawah and Seabrook. Hootch only shook that when he turned onto the dirt road, the jeep bouncing in the ruts. On impulse, he had decided to show off his kill to Bubba Spainhour. Let the boss know he was worthy of trust.

Bubba lived in a suburban ranch-style house in the middle of deep woods. Hootch had been there once before. The man had no style at all. Shag carpet like a motel. Kept the plastic K-mart covers on his lampshades. Satellite disk in the yard. His idea of decoration was ceramic elves.

When Hootch pulled up in the yard, Travis came out almost

immediately. Lenny's head was rolling around like the neck was broken. Kind of a bubbling noise came out of his throat.

Hootch peeled off his shades, and dangling them, pointed a finger at Travis. Ducked his head and raised one eyebrow. "Just call me the bounty hunter," he said in a theatrical TV voice.

"You stoopid, mully-fucker," said Travis. He didn't sound pleased.

40.

Tamzie watched chuckling to herself as Moira Ralston lectured the Smithsonian Museum people who had come all the way down from Washington. As a photographer clicked away, Moira said, "The gate is the symbol of entry into a garden of earthly delights." She stretched out her arms to the Fish and Stars gate, posing for the photos. "It opens the enclosure to a magical space for outdoor living."

Tamzie and Thaddeus were all dressed up for the Smithsonian people photographing the new gate and writing an article on slave craftsmen in antebellum Charleston. For the big event, Moira had gotten her hair cut in a layered shag and wore a slim dress and cropped jacket. This had been a fashion suggestion from Dale Ralston who had a lot of personal style, no question of it.

As the Ralston maid, Tamzie had been an eyewitness to Miss Moira's new liberalism and how it resulted in a final break with the Junior League. Each member was supposed to bring $50 worth of "quota" as they called it to the JLC clothing store, the Bee's Knees. So Moira had taken Miz Ralston's ultra-suede suit and purple silk blouse out of the closet and given it to them figuring it was way over the limit and she'd get extra credit or something.

Then Tami Wyrick called up and said Moira owed them $50 and

of course Moira was floored by this news and wanted to know what was wrong with the suit and blouse. So Tami—whose husband owned a new car dealership—said they were trying to be very selective and just couldn't have it in the sale. Moira asked what was wrong with it, and Tami Wyrick said it was wrinkled and needed pressing.

So naturally Moira said she'd come pick it up and have it pressed. But Tami Wyrick said it's too late, she'd already given it to Goodwill. Well Moira was almost speechless at that. And Tami Wyrick kept stressing that they had to be "very selective" in their clothing line. Then she finally came out and said, "We sure don't want the kind of clothes that bring black people into the store."

To which Moira said, "Well you sure let them on your husband's car lot!"—and slammed down the phone.

"In winter," Moira gushed, "a gate is as bare and stark as the leafless trees. Yet its stolidity and strength holds the promise of permanence, and in that constant guardian role, the certainty of the coming spring."

The Smithsonian Museum people actually wrote down what she said. They had come lickity split to see the new gate and to crate up the old one and take it back to Washington. They weren't about to look that gift horse in the mouth. They called Charleston an historical treasure trove of black craftsmen. Tamzie was amazed at the interest in her ancestor Cato Jerome and the heritage of iron-working passed down through the generations to her grandfather. The museum folks called Cato gifted and influential.

Thaddeus was carrying charm in buckets talking about black heritage and black historic preservation, pointing out carpenter's lace and handcrafted wood trim on the porches of houses on Legendre Street. He had his beard trimmed, wore a white suit and big straw hat. Just impressed them up and down.

Moira didn't take any backseat in the matter. She called herself a stabilizing influence in preserving a vanishing way of life. She said she used cedar chips, newspapers, or lavender flowers instead of moth balls for storing winter clothes. Her customs were more traditional and less harmful to the environment. And those nasty commercial drain cleaners were banned from her house. She preferred boiling water, baking soda, and vinegar.

As they were having iced tea and cookies among the flowers, Moira gave out little pots of basil as gifts. She said it was an old Charleston tradition.

There it was, thought Tamzie. Old Martha Stewart makes her entrance. That was in the May issue.

Then she thought, oh shit here comes trouble. Debone showed up looking like the veteran of the calaboose that he was. Baggy pants sagging down his ass, t-shirt with Tupac Shakur on it, some gold chains he had thrown on. Big gauze patch on his nose like a man would who got shot in the nose.

She told him she could see he didn't bother to polish up his image none. He shot back she could control her mouth or he'd put her in the obituary funeral part of the local news.

He said, "Anyhow something funny's going down. That red bitch Rannie Ralston been around the house on Cannon Street with a realtor. Told me she'd be foreclosing on a mortgage since you ain't come across with Collier's collection. Then on top of that I got that dumbass white boy Hootch saying he'll pay for a particular article in the collection."

"Which is what?"

"That thing yo' momma give you. Which I might add you sold for twenty bucks. And bought liquor with it."

"It took a ocean of liquor to put up with you."

"Yeah? Recollecting our marriage, I feel a tug on my heart too." Debone rubbed his chin. "Yeah, that diary. They's sure enough things to think on here. And maybe a real sweet deal to double-cross with Hootch."

"What deal?" Tamzie demanded.

"I lie to the muh-fucker. Tell him we been slipping out a book here and there from Dale Ralston's house. Making a little stockpile."

"What's the point of that?"

He didn't answer because at that moment Thaddeus strolled up looking fortified from a big glass of iced tea. He had put on little half-moon reading glasses she had never seen him wear before.

Tamzie like to died introducing them, saying this is Thaddeus in charge of ancient books of great value at the College library, and this here is Debone who, well, is, uh, self-employed in the automotive resale business. All the time silently praying please dear God don't let Debone open his fat, dirt-talking mouth and say we living together. But Debone had his mind focused elsewhere.

"Books, huh? Like that history shit?" Debone got animated. "Man, lemme tell you. I been getting this, like you call, collector mania. And what I wonder's this. Listen here. What would you say is your most valuable line in, er uh, them Civil War books?"

"Confederate documents primarily," Thaddeus said drily. He looked past Debone, nodding at where the Smithsonian folks were drifting away through the Fish and Stars gate. They smiled back at him with that white liberal look. Kind of like sick cats.

"Confed'rit?" went Debone. "You serious? What about black folks? I mean I know the brothers got their pedestal place in history. We did the math on them pyramids in old Egypt and all that."

Thaddeus gave him a over-the-top of the glasses look. "I don't believe the historical record truly supports that."

"What? What kinda shit you layin' on me? Eva'body know that."

Thaddeus folded both hands over the head of his walking stick. "I have some powers of discernment." He looked at Tamzie like he could see right into her soul.

"Yeah but supposin' . . . nothing immediate to offer . . . but lemme raise this matter anyhow. Supposin' somebody had a long-lost diary. Kind of written by this slave person. Gimme a bottom line on that. Kind of a price profile."

Tamzie cringed, thinking, shut your dumb mouth, niggah.

Thaddeus gave Tamzie a slow look like St. Peter on Judgment Day. "You're really incorrigible," he said.

Tamzie didn't like the tone of that. "I'm what?"

Debone says, "He's saying you can't make no silk purse out of a sow's ear. The man talking down to you, girlfrin'. All his white suit and that walking stick and all talking at you high and mighty. Saying you not a success story like him."

*

Rannie asked, "What did you do to your hair? You almost look human."

Moira carried the tray with the tea pitcher and the glasses into the kitchen. Everyone had gone home. She answered crisply. "Today has been a tender look at the richness of life. I am indelibly marked by it."

Following her in, Rannie opened the cabinet, got out the Jim Beam and poured herself a pop. "Just wondered. I mean it's not like I expected any intimate physical stuff out of you. I can't believe any man is itching to get into your pants."

Moira sniffed and went on cleaning up.

Rannie knocked back her drink. She felt soiled from hauling that fool Skip Rightenberry up to Cannon Street. Tamzie was being stubborn and slow about looting Collier's archives. Rannie figured the sight of the realtor would give her a good prod. Talked to that sleaze Debone who was out of the joint now. Told him to goose her into some action. Just fling her ass out of the house if she didn't get it in gear. Moralists could quibble about her methods, but the results spoke for themselves.

Rannie paused and examined her sister. There was a distinct sense of style there. Moira must have resisted her inner voice and listened to a hair stylist. Then she thought, Dale. Shit. "It's Dale isn't it? She did this."

Moira floated past. "She has spurred my entrance into a realm of infinite possibilities. For that I shall always be grateful." The kitchen door swung closed.

Rannie watched the blank door. Thought about having another drink. Why not? It was almost five o'clock.

Ms. Long-legs collagen lips Dale was behind all this museum gate business. Little priss-pot Moira had latched onto her like a remora fish. Like some berserk version of *folie à deux*.

The door swung open again. Moira hefted a second tray. "You could help," she said sourly. Clapped down the tray on the counter top.

"Yes I could," said Rannie, but she didn't budge.

Moira stood in the middle of the floor, hands on her hips. The scene took on the edge of a teenage squabble. "Sometime in the third millennium, I suppose."

"I'm sure you tire of me telling you, but I work for a living. You might try it sometime. The energy flows. Gives you a lift. But then I guess there aren't a lot of job opportunities for psychotics."

Moira violently twisted on the water tap, began banging things into the sink. "No argument there," she said angrily. "I'm crazy. You all tell me so. But be sure to take out all your lingering resentments and regrets on me. It always makes the bully feel better."

"Well excuse me for being the salt of the earth," Rannie told Moira in a world-weary voice. "You might be interested to know I've sold your book"—she waved a hand vaguely—"any book you want really. Pick one out of the pile of rejects. It doesn't matter—to Jazz-Bo Productions."

Moira whipped around, her face a mask of horror. "You mean the Traubs?"

"Yes, the Traubs. Did I underestimate your ignorance? I know it's vast."

"You will not commandeer my life's work!" Moira shrieked. "You will get out of it, tear up any contract, whatever you've done, immediately. I refuse to participate."

Rannie was really out of patience. "Stupidity has always been your specialty. But this is over the top. You need a sanitarium and shock treatment."

Moira hit a real seething emotional high. Her eyes bulged and her face turned livid. *"I'm* insane? What about you? All of your vulgar . . . *coloratura!* Your rapture of open sexuality! Is that some defense mechanism? I don't notice a lot of men asking you to marry them!" She stormed out leaving the door swinging in her wake.

"I don't need defense mechanisms!" Rannie shouted after her. "I've got curves! I've got tits! I don't need reconstructive surgery!"

41.

Sometime past midnight Rannie got her second wind and went on hammering and running the skill saw despite the neighbors yelling at her to knock it off. She was not ready to sleep yet. Not until she got really tired.

That afternoon she had pleaded a woman guilty for shooting her husband in the gut with a 12-gauge shotgun. They had been arguing over who would drive to the store to get more liquor. When the judge asked if she had anything to say, the client said, "I just hope your honor'll take into account I called an ambulance as soon as I done it. I didn't really want him to die. We just had an argument. I think if I got alcohol counseling I'd be okay and become a valuable member of society again."

The judge gave her twelve years and Rannie took her house and car. The car was garbage, and the house wouldn't net but maybe $20,000 because of all the debts on it.

After that, she had played three hours of really cut-throat racquetball until her opponent, a middle-aged lawyer with a big firm, decided he was having a heart attack and had to lie down. Then about six straight hours of work on her house.

The mercury had peaked at ninety-seven at midday, and night brought no relief. Rannie's body ran with sweat even in the dark. Screw the neighbors. You hear me? I mean it. She went on with what had to be done to get the job done. Nobody could ever quite seem to understand that about her. Her freeloading family sure didn't. Freaking mother spending the day buying out Talbot's. Try to do something nice for Moira and she has a shit-fit.

Her t-shirt sweat-plastered to her body in the humid night, Rannie nailed up sheetrock. Stick the nail on the board, wham with the hammer. Stick-wham. Stick-wham. Stupid-ass sister. Stick-wham. Like to nail fucking Moira's ass to the wall. Stick-wham.

She couldn't believe it when the jeep drove up without lights, the engine shut off, and three men got out carrying a big bundle. Just walked right in the front door of her house.

Rannie went straight down the stairs, hammer in one hand, big flashlight in the other. What were they up to? If they thought they could crash in her house for the night, smoke crack, whatever it was they had in mind, she'd straighten them out on that. Have the cops on them like ducks on a Junebug.

She snapped on her big flashlight, caught them all squinting at her, free hands trying to block the flood of light. Bubba Spainhour and his red-neck hoodlum Travis and that stupid Hootch. They were carrying a damn body wrapped up in a plastic sheet. You could see the feet sticking out.

"Whoa-there, hoss," said Hootch. "This looks like a prelude to a conflict." He drifted back into the dark. Gutless. Like a kid caught cutting up in school. She couldn't believe she had taken her clothes off for him. Actually lain down and spread her legs. The humiliation of it all.

"Stay the fuck out of the dining room!" Rannie bellowed at him.

Hootch stopped. Held up his hands in a placating way. "Okay it's cool. Enough of this vocal display shit."

"The floor's torn up," Rannie snarled. "I'm not having you fall through a hole and then turn around and sue me."

Bubba was wearing a white leisure suit in the heat, the cuffs on the jacket sleeves turned back. He said if Rannie was through sharing her thoughts with downtown Charleston, maybe Travis and Hootch oughta heft the body out of there. They did as ordered, grunting a bit with the dead weight.

Then Bubba turned back and talked to Rannie in his Big Daddy tones. Said he liked the smell of wood shavings, and she seemed to be doing a first rate job. Told her he didn't realize it was her house. They were just driving around and saw a dumpster was all. Noticed the house was open.

Rannie was incredulous. "You're telling me you'd put a body in a dumpster? This is what you do? You are a fool. You are a class-A, high-test buffoon."

Bubba rubbed his jaw, refusing to get riled. "It's a interestin' business I'm in. You get to meet all kinds of folks from all different parts of the country. High risk. High yield. But you got to own up to your errors and then focus on the successes. You know what I mean? So I'm sorry about the mix-up. I'm man enough to say it. I can name others who wouldn't be."

This really hacked Rannie off. Him trying to dump a stiff on her and then talking down to her. "I accept I got to deal with low-life," she said. "Most of your Episcopal Bishops have no need of a criminal lawyer. But I draw the line at you bozos."

Bubba toed the sawdust on the floor. "When you've cooled down, you'll reckanize there's no harm done. We ain't no flu epidemic."

Rannie said, "I think I can get past my anger. But what I'm going to tell you right now, you no-account bag of excrement, is you're fired!"

Bubba kind of squinted at her. "Say what?"

"You heard me."

He pointed a finger to his chest. "You're firing *me?* I'm the client."

"You don't pay your bills—you compromise me—make me an accessory to your dumbass criminal behavior—I mean that's it. Finished. Over with. I will never represent you again."

"I've never liked a gal with a smart mouth. I know, I say things I later regret. But there's got to be a level of control."

"Are you telling me I'm losing control?" Rannie demanded. She knew her voice was cracking and fought it.

Bubba rubbed the back of his neck. "Lemme tell you a little something. I guess you're what's called a strong personality, but I guess I am too. I'm pretty secure in what I stand for and what I represent and what I believe. And what I believe is this. Lemme tell you."

She pushed a sweaty hank of hair out of her face. "Yeah? What is it?"

"There's a limit to just how scary you are, little lady."

For a split second, Rannie was paralyzed. Nobody threatened her. Her mind started racing. If she lunged at him with one furious whack, she could drive a nail into his skull. Right between the eyes. She had to hold her arms rigid by her side, fists trembling to stop herself from doing it.

As they went out, Hootch stopped, took a big swig out of his silver flask. "Hey, babe. How's your cooze?" Made a pumping motion with the heel of his hand.

Bubba and Travis saw it, exchanged a look.

At that moment, Rannie decided she was going to kill him. By God almighty she was going to kill Hootch. And it would give her a great deal of pleasure to do it.

*

Dale got out of bed at one a.m., the doorbell ringing, to find Moira standing there twisting her hands, lips trembling, face streaked with tears.

"She's sold my treasured work to that . . . that horrible movie producer!" she wept.

"Traub?"

Moira wailed, "Yes! How could she do such a thing?"

"Sell your book?"

Moira plunged past Dale into the house, flung her body around, forging a new standard for histrionics. She jabbered through a tale of Rannie doing her ruthless routine of shaking money out of people. And there was some tax thing Moira didn't understand and it all got twisted around and . . . and . . . she was polluted. She was defiled. She was dragged through a sewer. Rannie was vindictive, cruel, ruthless. Rannie was a master vulgarian. Her . . . her *whorishness* was deep and abiding.

Moira reserved some of her harshest criticism for Mary Canty who had brought that squawling bundle of toxic waste called Rannie into the world. Mary was a calamity. She was a society wrecking ball. She was a perverse joke of motherhood. Under her critical gaze houseplants died and pets got colic.

Dale couldn't disagree with this, but she had a weakness for the practical. "How much did you get?" she asked.

Moira didn't seem to know. But the question brought her down from the heights of hysteria.

And Dale saw her opening. This was a golden chance to rescue Moira from her worst instincts and stick her thumb in Rannie's eye as well. Very slowly, because she could never be certain just how dense Moira really was, she explained that this was Moira's chance to actually sell a book. Dale knew a literary agent in New York who would be thrilled that a book was already sold to Hollywood.

Moira flatly refused. She insisted it was a crucial point of principal. She would not stoop to moral dishonesty. She would not even be devious.

"As opposed," ventured Dale, "to forging a Margaret Mitchell novel to be discovered in my house?"

Moira's brain seemed to be channel-surfing. She couldn't grasp that Dale had figured out her stunt. "I can't live with the thought of that wretched man as the wellspring of my success."

Dale wanted to say, you idiot you're not a success. Or maybe, you don't know the meaning of paying your dues. She wondered about telling Moira the anecdote of Marilyn Monroe becoming a movie star and saying now she'd never suck another . . . well, Moira wouldn't like the analogy. "You develop amnesia," she said instead. She thumbed through her address book for the number.

 "But it's past midnight," Moira protested.

Dale spoke with total certainty. "She'll take the call."

Dale dialed the agent at her home in Larchmont. At the whiff of a deal, the agent woke up in a hurry, said she was spiritually enhanced, jumped on the opportunity like a hungry barracuda. Hollywood— even the Hollywood of the Traub brothers—was a lure as powerful as pheromones.

Moira seemed mesmerized by how easily it had been done. "But she hasn't even read it."

"They don't have to read it," said Dale.

42.

Debone had been to the plastic surgeon, come back saying he was gone get himself a Michael Jackson nose. Make all the white girls want him. Have himself a foxy chick at least as good as Elvis's daughter what's-her-name. Priscilla. Yeah, that was it.

Tamzie was studying the want-ads. She read:

Gorgeous white Cathedral Lake, Demetrios Wedding Gown,

size 3 w' lots of beeding/secquence, never worn, clean/pressed, ready to
wear, Pd $1200 asking $400 OBO. Matching beeded

shoe sz 61/2 incl.

She was thinking when she married Thaddeus she'd like a nice church wedding wearing white. Just pretend the first one to Debone never happen. The paper would say Mrs. Thaddeus Wyndham was wearing white Cathedral Lake. Young as she was and the age of Thaddeus, she'd be like a trophy wife. Everybody saying man you robbing the cradle.

True, they had had that ugly little scene when the Smithsonian folks were here. But that was all Debone's fault. Get him out of the picture and the sun would come out from behind the clouds.

Debone rooted in the freezer saying what happen to all the Haagen Daz frozen yogurt fruit bars? The phone rang and he snatched it up. Listened a while and said, "Hootch man, lemme check the inventory." Then stood there holding his hand over the receiver and nodding his head, patting his foot as time passed.

After awhile he spoke into the phone again. "You just got lucky. I am looking at it right now. Oh yes indeed I am. Very fine piece of workmanship this one. Whole buncha pages in it, all of them with stuff written on 'em. Offhand I would say this is the freedwoman's diary experts can't do without."

He listened to somebody on the other end, then said, "Let's nudge the price up to about double. You get the idea."

Pause.

"Well why don't you seek some financing?"

Pause.

"You're starting to earn your way now. Yes, I'm getting cooperative on this one."

Pause.

"I'll introduce a full plan on that later on."

They talked some more, Debone saying yeah he knew the dirt path off Cane Slash Road out John Island. Round near the big tomato fields. Yeah, they could meet there back in the woods around two tomorrow afternoon. Make the swap.

Debone hung up. He said that honkey asshole Hootch had a buyer for their family diary. And after that he wanted to begin steady sales of all of Collier's collection.

Tamzie said, "How much?"

"How much what?"

"How much is he paying you for what you don't got?"

"Enough so's I can quit scratching for money. Get away from the social stigma of food stamps."

"Your welfare program seem to begin and end at my refrigerator," said Tamzie.

Debone didn't answer. It meant he was thinking. Trying to figure if Tamzie knew something key to the deal. Had learned what the diary was worth working around the library nights cleaning. Maybe he should call the white boy up and renegotiate.

Debone went back into the bedroom closet and came out with a snub-nose blue-steel pistol, showing his intentions to get into the rough stuff with Hootch. Tamzie said to get that gun out of her house.

"Control your stress level, woman. This experience is a learning one for me. Getting into the stolen archives business is tricky."

"You a real stand-up comedian," said Tamzie. "Maybe they take you on at the Comedy Club. Talk about your career path and job prospects."

Debone opened the gate on the revolver and put in bullets. "I always have this reputation for absorbing some hard shots, but I may need to hand out a death penalty on this one. Put a sign on his eyes what say closed for the duration. For two reasons that come to mind straight off. A: I don't have the diary in question so it highly unlikely the white boy will want to part with his money except when staring at the business end of my piece. Two: that white bread shit-ass the one what shot off the end of my nose necessitating all this surgery."

"How'd you figure that out?"

"I just know it."

"You better not kill him," Tamzie warned.

Debone grinned. "Don't come apart on me, woman. I don't need to kill him. He's got a real familiar problem of he can't run to the cops."

Tamzie's voice rose. "I swear you best not kill him. I ain't harboring no fugitive in my house."

"Do I hear some concerns voiced? You know it's funny. All the time I'm up at CCI, I'm thinking get an education. See them ads on TV. Become a graduate of NEI Truck Driving School. Get on with Conway Southern Express. But it's clear after this phone call that self-employment is still the best way to go. Yes, I want to build on this opportunity. Use it as a stepping stone and not a stumbling block."

"I imagine your parole officer would love to share all your career ambitions. Put you back in state issue dungarees. Blue work shirt with a number on the back."

"You get out of line, woman, and I won't need to request any outside assistance. I'll handle your discipline internally. And afterwards you'll be needing reconstructive surgery on your whole body."

Tamzie was unfazed. Debone had really started to wear on her. She said, "I see here in the paper they got one- and two-bedroom furnished apartments in Donaree Village starting at $465."

Debone stuck the pistol in the waist of his baggy shorts. Practiced drawing it out real quick. "You planning on moving out of your own house? Think that'll improve your quality of life?"

"No, you're leaving. Cause I've decided to let a man ask to marry me."

43.

When Josh Mahoney showed up for dinner at Dale's, he brought it with him, a take-out called a "Steve's Special" from the Greek café on King Street. Meat, shrimp, and flat bread and salad with olives and feta cheese. Bottle of *Retsina* wine.

The outside of the house was banked around with pipe towers and equipment covered over with canvas tarpaulins and sheets of plastic. A threatening thunderstorm had driven the movie crew off for the day, and the heavy clouds brought darkness early. A pair of security cops sat in a little air-conditioned trailer on the street.

With the bulk of the house inside dominated by movie equipment, Dale and Josh sat propped up against the headboard of her bed eating and watching TV. The six o'clock news had another state representative pleading guilty.

"If I could long ago have been provided with professional assistance for my drinking problems, none of this would have come to pass. I accept and am prepared to live through the judgment that has been passed upon my head even as I continue to grieve for my tragic mistakes."

"Here it comes," said Dale. "He's gotten religion like the rest of

243

them."

"I have long espoused that this country should get back to the basics among which is human and divine forgiveness. The Holy Bible should be our guidance in these matters. Joseph of the coat of many colors forgave his brothers, and Esau forgave Jacob. Long term psychotherapy from caring health professionals is a form of state forgiveness."

The camera switched to Dave Dubiel and he vowed it was a "sure 'nuff barnburner."

Right after that, the electricity went out. Josh said he liked the murky landscape. It would make his seduction routine less obvious. Dale said he should at least tell her the story of his life.

Josh turned over on his side, his head propped on his hand. He said he had gone to Sewanee. Real isolated Episcopal college for rich snots. He wasn't personally a rich snot. His father was a minister and pastor to rich snots so the environment was familiar. Seniors wore gowns like at an English university. Everybody lived with their heads so far up their elitist asses that he figured majoring in classics made sense. The choice didn't thrill his parents, but at that age you don't pay a whole lot of attention to them. So he went forward with a self-inflicted wound.

Dale said, "I understand that one." Cocked a thumb at herself. "I'm English lit."

He nodded sympathetically. The only job he could get was an insurance underwriter. They hire warm bodies and pay couple thousand below the white-collar market rate. He handled personal lines—homeowner and car—which is the butt-end of even that industry.

One day he got this big scheduled listing because the homeowner collected valuable books and art. They had to be listed and appraised separately because of their value. He looked at the books and realized he had done research on many of them for term papers. It intrigued him. He got out of insurance and into working for a bookshop.

He asked Dale, "You bored yet?"

She said no.

"By now, girls in bars have recognized someone across the room they have to talk to."

"I'm hanging on your every word."

He asked how she was taking the dissolution of her marriage. She said when she was a stylist her job was to create illusion. They'd do a shoot in the Museum of Natural History with a painted scene of the African veldt behind the models. It would look like they were there. Set up exquisite people in a sidewalk cafe being very cool and hip. Ten feet away, winos were panhandling. But you couldn't see the derelicts in the final product. A perfect illusion.

He said, "This is a metaphor, right?"

She said, "Yeah. Something about the difficulty in telling truth from fiction. This house, a life of leisure, was all real. The love was an illusion. Admitting that means I have to dramatically change the way I do things."

"So how do you pay for this?" He gestured around the room.

"I have a secret trust fund."

He got a faraway look. Dale realized she wanted something to happen between them. She wanted to move in slowly. Signal her availability. What came out she thought afterwards was silly. At the time it didn't matter.

She asked, "Who did you first have sex with?"

"You mean other than the lies high school boys tell?"

"Right."

His eyes held on hers. "A girl at Sewanee. My freshman year. She asked me if I wanted to learn about sex with her."

Dale grinned wryly. "Learn about sex. That's a nice approach."

"Given the terms of the offer I had no trouble admitting I knew nothing about it."

"She was shy probably."

"Shy?"

"Wanted to be in love with you. But had to seem hip and modern. Empowered. Whatever it's called now."

"She wanted to learn how to do oral sex. But I guess she was just shy. Really wanted to learn missionary position but couldn't admit it."

Dale studied him and knew he was laughing. "You're skating the edge of being a smart-ass," she said. "But I like the thin line. So far."

The air was tense and heavy, the thunderstorm at the towering cumulus stage. Pretty soon it would rip loose with all its violence. A flicker of distant lightning seemed to add to the sexual charge in the room. He moved closer to her on the bed and kissed her gently. "You know you're really kind of over the top, looks-wise."

Dale felt dizzy with desire. She kept her face close to his, her lips slightly parted. "It's good you should have to meet higher standards occasionally. Why don't you take your clothes off and leave me breathless?"

The storm broke as they were tangled together in her bed. She soared so high into rapture she felt she wasn't touching the earth. Afterwards, Dale lay there gasping, her heart pounding. "You could live on your laurels from that one for a long time."

"Thanks," he said. "You're a reminder of why the sexes remain attracted to each other. A magisterial reminder."

He spread his big hand across her narrow pelvis, thumb touching one pelvic bone, blunt fingertips on the other. "I'd like to think this is more than one of those so-called get acquainted sessions. I don't know about you, but I'm sinking in the quicksand of love."

Dale's pulse was getting back to normal. She rested her hand on his. Her life seemed more vaguely defined than ever. Or maybe it was purely defined in terms of her adversaries. Her lush of a mother-in-law. Collier the wounded lizard. Rannie the flaming curvaceous cutthroat wearing her power suit dominatrix costumes. Unattached to a man for reasons yet to be disclosed other than her incurable nastiness.

Outside, the rain had slacked and a chorus of little tree frogs racketed away.

Dale said, "Assuming all that stuff is stolen, what's the penalty if I get caught selling it?"

"Considerable."

"That much, huh?"

*

When Hootch explained the importance of planting the body on Rannie's property—why they had to go back and do it when she was gone—Travis said he wanted nothing to do with it. Hootch couldn't believe it. Here Rannie had insulted Bubba right in front of the staff. They couldn't let that pass. Had to send her a message. But oh no. Travis says Hootch should stick the thing in a crack house up on Bogard Street. And he better do it that way or Bubba was gone be plenty pissed.

Hootch figured when Travis applied for work with Bubba he checked the 'yes' box under the "Are you dumb?" question. That qualified him for the job.

The body had sat all day under black plastic in the back of Hooch's jeep while he drank in a variety of bars where the air conditioning was adequate to his needs. He felt good. His first confirmed kill under his belt. Lenny's book of business soon to be his. And Debone just sitting there on a diary that was about to be translated into big bucks. Yessir, that was one audacious jiggaboo. Maybe had an extra chromosome in there.

After dark, Hootch went back to his apartment and got on his gear. Rain pelted down, so he wore his Ranger Boonie hat, USMC camouflage nylon poncho, military issue speed-lace boots with the silicone sealed seams. Plastic surgical gloves for the messy but necessary task.

Lenny was a bitch to lift, but Hootch heaved him out of the jeep and dragged him into Rannie's ground floor. Unrolled the plastic. Snapped the leg irons on Lenny's ankles. Then the thumb cuffs with his hands behind his back. Mahoney had been right. You could buy them in plenty of pawnshops up on Rivers Avenue.

There. All the little touches to give the cops something to scratch their heads over. Go up a hundred blind alleys. Bonehead Travis had no eye for this kind of detail. Go with his direction, he'd turn the organization into some kind of Three Stooges theatrics.

Hootch patted Lenny's ghastly face. "Sorry ol' buddy-row. Playing second fiddle to you was a strategy I couldn't emotionally keep going with. No hard feelings though. Me? I'm—what's the word?—ambivalent about it all."

Now just a few minutes to snoop around using his 18-inch Maglite, every cop's favorite. Starkrypton lamp adjusts from flood to spot. See what else he could do to unsettle the bitch if she needed any further unsettling. Let her know their association was history.

Once he had his business rolling he'd hire big firm lawyers to provide for his legal needs. You couldn't work with a whore who wanted sexual pay-offs. Always yanking your pants down.

When she realized he was serious, she'd probably cut up nasty. Treat it like a broken romance. He'd be cool, low-key. Say something like, "Just accept it as a learning, growing experience." Or, "There's no call for self-immolation." Something like that.

She had told him to stay out of the dining room. There were holes in the floors. But he didn't see any holes. Everything seemed intact. Maybe he'd drag the body in here. She'd make the connection all right. Slap up-side the head. Let her know that the Hootch-boy don't forgive and forget soon.

Well jayzuz-tit. Here was Rannie's wine rack filled with its aged bottles of vintage stuff. He'd walk off with six or ten. Later bring her a house gift of one of them. See if she recognized it.

It surprised him when the rack moved in his hand and he realized it was on little rollers. What have we here? A secret hidey-hole? His light played over a big green plastic garbage bag. He looked inside it. "Sham-a-lam-a-ding-dong," he said under his breath.

Hootch had to take his hat off, hunker down, and think about this. Damn it was a bunch'a cash. The question was did he take it all now or just take some and come back for the rest later? Rain was sure pissing down outside.

Under the poncho he was wearing his fourteen-pocket safari vest. The Hootch-boy had the right kind of gear for these split-second opportunity situations. Fill those with wads of cash. Damn, it was a shame to leave so much of it. Why not take it all? The plastic would keep it dry until he got back to his place.

Shit, was that a cop car going through the lane? Playing a spotlight on the houses. And Hootch keeping company with a corpse. He dropped his Smith & Wesson into the bag. He'd gotten good mileage out of it, but time to ditch. If the cops found it on him, they could tie him to Lenny.

The cop car went on up the lane. Hootch slid the wine rack back into place. He counted to two hundred and sprinted back into his jeep and fired the engine. Rain coming down so hard he could barely see. What he had back at the house—in the piles of army gear he'd buy at random from catalogues—was a twenty-one-inch high-density plastic mortar tube with flexible rubber handle. What soldiers carried a mortar barrel around in. The lid screwed with a watertight gasket. He'd put the cash in that and it would stay free from mildew, rot, whatever. Get maybe ten, twelve more of those tubes for when he came back for the rest of the money.

In the meantime, the cash would come in handy for various things he needed. What he wanted to do with it first off was order one of those OMON Scope/rangefinders he had seen in a catalogue. Thing cost $169. Manufactured for the Soviet Special Forces so it could operate in Siberian cold and desert heat. A man needed a lot of super-cool gear in this world.

And he'd require a weapon to use on Debone. Maybe a target pistol. A nice Ruger MK-10 in the Silhouette model. Ten-inch barrel. A Ruger would do for his immediate needs. He didn't have the time to shop around for an Olympics-level competition weapon.

44.

Rannie was furious. "How about bagging this goddam stiff and getting it out of here? It's drawing flies."

Cops were prowling all over making measurements, taking photos.

Yellow police tape around her house. Despite the torrent during the night, the stinking heat was back in force. Mother Nature seemed to be engaged in some general retaliation.

She knew who had done it, that knuckle-dragging, simian Hootch Gibson. His idea of humor. At one point in college, he would sneak into people's swimming pools at night and take a crap. He had put a bloody deer head in Collier and Dale's bed on their wedding night.

The cops didn't exactly jump to obey her orders. They spent time asking her pointless questions about what Lenny did for a living. She said they knew full well that Lenny worked for Bubba Spainhour. They had already gone round to see Bubba, who claimed he hadn't had contact with Lenny in months. He worried about Lenny, though, because the young man had this habit of staying out late at night. It was bound to lead to trouble. Mixing with the wrong crowd and such. The cops said that to her deadpan just like Bubba had said it to them. Which was to say far and above the usual deadpan.

"This killer, well we got ourselves a brazen boy here," said a bald detective, inspecting the work she was doing on the kitchen wing. "If the houses didn't cost so much you'd think the neighborhood was spiraling downwards."

Rannie said the body had been dumped there. Anyone could see that. Gunshot wound in Lenny's side and no blood trail. A wadded-up sheet of plastic he was wrapped in.

She knew they were laughing at her. Thinking since Lenny had been her client the killing was a warning to her. Break her grip on serenity. Bullshit. That bug-brain Bubba had left Hootch unsupervised for five minutes and this was the result. She'd fix Hunter "Hootch" Gibson's red wagon. She'd think about nothing else night and day until she had fixed him.

Rannie said from a personal point of view she didn't marvel that polls showed seventy-six percent of Americans seldom or never trusted government to do the right thing.

The cop scratched at his bald head, pushed his sunglasses into place with a forefinger. "You know, putting up with people like you the way I do—excusing my way through life and all—I ought to get a medal rather than a crucifixion."

Rannie didn't listen. She knew she'd have to move Lenny's drug money. Nosy cops poking into everything. Soon as it got dark she'd haul the garbage bag over to her mother's house. She'd practically have to sit with her back to the wine rack all day to keep them from finding the secret chamber.

Then little rosy Moira showed up, really putting the cap on the morning. She smelled like she had bathed in Arpège. Said oh my goodness gracious what is all this about?

Rannie expected her to faint at the sight of the corpse, all bloated with gas leaking out of it. But Moira glanced at it and looked away. Didn't even seem to register the morbid horror. She needed Rannie's assistance in a professional capacity. Had a contract she wanted her to look at.

"Are you buying something?" Rannie snarled. "You don't have any money. And I won't co-sign a note. Unless you're buying a shock collar I can fit around your neck. Give you a near lethal dose of electricity every time you do something stupid."

Moira got a fey little smile. She seemed composed, serene. "Well that's all changed. Thanks to Dale."

Rannie snatched the wad of papers from her sister. "What's changed?"

"I have prevailed in a modern world," Moira said radiantly.

Rannie's whole body seemed to be vibrating. She was going to freak out. She was going to have a psychotic reaction. Moira—little twinkle-toes Moira—had sold a book for a $500,000 advance from a major publisher!

*

The way Debone figured it, they'd shake hands. He'd say, Mister Hootch, I presume? Hootch'd say yeah right. Then Debone'd say sorry I can't offer you no drink, but we're way out here in the woods where you wanted to meet. All pleasant and smooth. Big smile. Nobody stone-faced.

Debone'd be carrying the red canvas athletic bag with his gun in it. Nice Taurus .357 Magnum with a 4-inch barrel. The white boy'd have the money in something, have his gun in the back of his pants under his shirt. He'd be nervous the way white boys be when they go out on the street to score dope. Debone just give 'em the slow, cool-nigger grin and let them perform.

Debone would say he presumed Mister Hootch would like to inspect the merchandise. Unzip the bag without waiting for any tension to rise. Pull out his piece and cap the mother-fucker before he could get his cleared. Before he even realized what was going down. The money would be somewhere in the car. Yowsuh. Debone knew how to protect his high rankings.

Debone drove Tamzie's Chevette up the dirt road past the tomato fields and into the pines. And wouldn't you know the air conditioner would quit working. Just a breath of hot air blowing.

The white boy and his jeep were setting there waiting for him. Debone stopped twenty yards away and shut off the engine. The thing shook and rattled and coughed before it finally quit. Flat embarrassed him. He knew the white boy'd be smirking at him, thinking he held the edge because he drove a superior motor vehicle.

Hootch waited in a folding lawn chair beside his jeep. Fucker trying to be cool sitting down relaxed. Wearing shades and some kind of Walk-Man looking plastic earmuffs. Had a cooler next to him, sipping a brew. Listening to tunes. Oh yes he was super-cool. Gone on vacation and not going to pretend otherwise.

Debone slung the athletic bag strap on his shoulder. Things moving right along. Go at him with the smile all ready on his face. Get the job done.

Hootch raised up a long-barreled pistol in his right hand. Fucking Wyatt Earp pistol.

Whoa, things were suddenly tense. But the boy was way too far off to take a shot. Just letting him see his iron. Case Debone had any bad thoughts in his head. This would make it a bit trickier. Maybe time to pitch a temper tantrum. Yell that if the boy don't trust him they'd meet somewhere else another time. Get in the car and sit there until he pitched his gun out into the leaves. Maybe crank up the engine to show he meant to drive off if they didn't get things resolved.

Debone yelled, "Hey, man, what this badass shit? My network don't inform me we was gonna play rough."

Hootch rested the pistol on his forearm. Shit, that barrel was long.

Debone heard a little pop. But the sound had come after the sting in his chest that made him take a step back, kind of stagger. Knees going weak. A huge burn starting to spread through his whole body. Debone wanted to get the zipper open on the athletic bag, but the strap had slid down his arm. The bag lay on the ground. He tried to reach down and get it. It seemed a long ways off.

He took two more stings straight through his chest and went over backwards. The sky showed real blue up over the treetops. Crows were flying up there cawing. Settling on a branch. Debone lay gurgling. A shadow covered him over.

Hootch said, "Is it hot out, or is it just me?" lifting the canvas bag. Unzipping it and finding the gun inside but nothing else.

"Shit a brick!" yelled Hootch, flinging the bag onto the ground. He was not pleased.

But Debone was beyond hearing.

45.

"I will not have you further involved with that . . . that negress," ordered Mary Canty Ralston. She was wearing a raw silk Carlisle suit and her big diamond. "Tamzie is hired help. You know how they get above themselves in a second."

Normally her mother made her feel like a rabbit trembling in tall grass. But Moira was stronger now. Her new status as a recognized author was like a long, strength-granting drink of nectar. She said she didn't enjoy confrontations, but she had to reject her mother's suggestion. Mary Canty said if Moira didn't stop shooting the guests, she'd end up rejected by Hootch Gibson. And if that happened she swore she didn't know where a replacement could be found. Moira said good riddance. Mary Canty said good riddance? That mind medicine the doctor gave you must have utterly eliminated your brain.

"The boy drinks far too much to be good for him," said Moira dismissively.

"Nonsense," argued her mother. "He scarcely touches a drop."

Moira said, "By comparison."

Her mother said, "By comparison to what?"

"To someone in this room."

Mary Canty gave her a mean look and said, "You know, Moira, I really do want that ring if I outlive you."

Moira truly no longer cared what her mother thought. Her family caused all the stress in her life. Rannie so mean and spiteful just because Daddy never loved her. Collier having a panic attack because Dale might sell his books or his map of the Mason-Dixon Line, as if she'd do such a tacky thing.

Moira determined to not let these people impose their problems on her anymore. And she wasn't about to take that silly lithium the doctor prescribed for her. She felt just fine without it. So many things had to get done in her busy series of days, and the medicine just made her tired.

And she had so many things on her mind. She would be needing a photo for the dust jacket on the book. It had to strike just

the right note. Should she wear period costume? Stand in an open window looking towards the sea. A gold-hued light bathing the look of poetic melancholy on her face.

And then how to describe herself. Some authors said they were based somewhere. They tried to communicate that they travelled the globe in search of glamour. Moira Ralston is based in Charleston. Absurd. She was from Charleston. Her roots were in the Holy City. She wasn't based anywhere. Divides her time. That sounded better. Moira divides her time between her ancestral home in Charleston and . . . where exactly? She didn't own a plantation. Or a flat in Paris or London.

When the phone rang, she answered it in a rush: "This is Moira Ralston the author, currently based in Charleston." Which she realized was wrong. Which got her a little in a dizzy whirl and it took her a moment to realize she was talking to her agent. The woman had such a pronounced New York accent. Rather coarse really.

"They've put your book to the marketing department," she said. "And they have just one question about the storyline. Which I frankly couldn't answer."

Moira thought, haven't you read it yet?

"Is there any zebra sex?"

Moira dropped the phone. The floor seemed to suddenly rise up to meet her.

*

Hootch answered the knock at his apartment door, thought, holy shit! Almost jumped out of his skin.

A uniformed cop and a plainclothes detective stood there. They spooked him at first until he realized they couldn't have gotten onto him about Debone so fast. They had come around to ask Hootch about the death of Lenny Womble, whether he knew of any fellow drug dealers or addicts who might have had it in for him.

Hootch didn't invite them in. Gripped the doorframe because his hand was shaking from the scare they gave him. He said he didn't care for his good friend being characterized as an addict and dealer. It made his life less worthy somehow. The detective said they characterized Lenny as a drug addict and dealer because it was a fact.

Hootch said, "When you've got a pal and something horrible like this happens to him, and you always liked him, this is a real painful thing. I don't know about his background although we were in college together, but I've never seen anything to cause me to believe he took part in criminal activity. If I had, I would have severed my friendship with him on the spot and reported my suspicions to the police department."

He added he guessed all good citizens wondered and would want to know how such a brutal murder could happen right in the heart of downtown residential Charleston. The cops said, well, shit happens.

Hootch said he would be happy to be interviewed by the FBI or appear before the Grand Jury. If anything good could come of it, putting the city in a more positive light, whatever, he was willing to volunteer. The cops said they'd keep it in mind.

"Oh, and one other thing," Hootch added.

They turned back to listen.

"You might be interested I'm changing attorneys. Rannie Ralston—well, having to sexually service her—let's just say it's less than gratifying."

"Excuse me?"

Hootch was really pleased with himself. "Can't keep her clothes on around me. Always jumpin' for a humpin'."

The detective gave a little bark of a laugh. "Miz Ralston hear you say that . . . well, she'll cure your smirking problem for you."

46 .

"Okay, Joe Hollywood," Collier snapped at Hootch. "Will you take off the goddamn sunglasses?" Collier looked real authentic in Confederate Colonel's uniform wearing a fake imperial—drooping mustache and goat beard that ran in a straight line from his lip down his chin.

Hootch scrubbed at his beard stubble. He had let it grow a bit for the movies, give him that rugged look. "Sho' thing, pod'na," he answered. "Soon's that fag director says 'action', the shades will be lost."

The men all laughed. One hundred rebels were lined up in ranks in a broomsage field rimmed with pine trees. Gray and butternut uniforms with blue trim. Blanket rolls. Slouch hats and képis. Springfield rifles and socket bayonets. A lot of them wore beards or were unshaven. Clumped in the field twenty yards off was all the movie equipment. Vans, trailers, cameras mounted on 4-WD vehicles. A little crane for aerial shots.

Collier felt tense of course. Like most folks under a disability, he lived in isolation and dependence, this movie his only source of income at present. For Hootch, it was a vanity issue. Tell everyone you had a role in the flick. Look, there I am. The one acting dead there. And who could tell? Might get discovered. Go Hollywood big time.

Although barely nine in the morning, the temperature had already climbed up in the eighties. The margaritas Hootch had poured into his canteen had turned warm, and he seemed to be sweating more than the rest. He tied a red bandana around his head, put his képi back on top of it.

The movie people had some kind of snafu and told them to get under shade until they were ready to go. The men broke ranks and went back among the pines where their cars were parked.

Hootch felt pretty rough around the edges. Up partying all night before at the KA house, presenting his new image as a serious businessman hell-bent on a growth strategy. No tip-toe into the water approach for him. It was head down and straight up the middle.

Hootch had told the brothers that college kids today didn't understand hard work. They felt content to just coast. And he was shocked at some of the antics they were allowed to get away with. That was when the house president had reminded him again about not paying his affiliate dues.

"So," said Hootch, "did you take your acne medicine this week?" That rocked them. They couldn't deal with his quick and cutting wit. And they had no idea he had notched up two confirmed kills. The big jungle-bunny had tried a double-cross; Hootch had popped him. True, he didn't have the diary that Josh Mahoney wanted, but that could be arranged.

Hootch figured when the big bucks started to roll in he'd begin a small program of gift giving to the College of Charleston. This would build over time until he gave a really big gift. Have them name a media center or a wing of the business school after him. They'd press an honorary degree on him. Be draping him with the Doctor of Laws hood when he'd flash a sterling silver flask, take a hit, and say "Par-tay down." That would bring down the house. The brothers would love it. Establish him as the untamed Hootch Gibson of Kappa Alpha story and legend. In his speech, he'd tell the audience he liked to drink. It repackaged reality in a way to give him deeper insights into life and shit. Yeah, he'd lay the total Hootch philosophy on them. The wild man drops pearls of wisdom before swine.

Identifying his current profile no longer posed a problem. He didn't want to think of himself as a professional hitman. No, that sounded psycho and dirtbag. What he'd call himself was a hard-charging entre-preneur in the archive game. Set to be a tycoon while still on this side of thirty. Folks might describe him as tough and demanding to work with, but he didn't apologize for those characteristics. Once he got a few of the projects off his desk and had the cash to show for it, he figured he'd go on a hunting trip. Maybe kill a black bear up in the Smoky Mountains with a pistol. If he got that under his belt he might move up to knife hunting. Nail a wild boar with a Bowie knife.

Collier sat on a tree stump fiddling with his sword knot looking real despondent. Hootch figured to give him one last chance to join the new strategic focus.

"Collecting's funny when you think about it," said Hootch strolling up. "It's all kind of personal and confidential. You don't exactly get hordes of tourists in to look at your collection. In an inverse kind of way, that's what drives the market. A Wade Hampton blouse in a museum display case, buncha rubber-necks just wander past, give it a glance, uh-huh, move on. 'Bout all they'll say is look how much smaller folks were back then. Doubt that blouse would fit anybody they knew. Way too small. But dangle the thing in front of a private collector, and he sees hours of viewing pleasure."

Collier looked up irritably. "Is there something you want to tell me?"

Hootch said he had a serious buyer for the archives. He needed to take over the entire collection, do an evaluation of inventory and start moving the stock. Due diligence time.

Collier snorted. "That's an exercise in futility. Dale isn't about to hand it over."

Hootch squatted down and took Collier by the bicep, squeezing tight. "What you do, buddy-row, is you walk in there, say shut up and sit in a corner, bitch. Walk out with the stuff. Load the trunk of your car as many trips as it takes. Then you've got the chore out of the way."

Collier jerked his arm away. "What do you think I am? Some misfit? My little aide who can't manage to graduate from college can just order me around now?"

Hootch gave him a slow grin. "Hey, don't go dyspeptic on me. You figure I'm not the wave of the future? Well, I'm not real flashy. I prefer what I call controlled expansion. I've had like two career victories. Moving on up ready for a third one. The first one, no doubt about it, I had some trouble. Unfamiliar weapon. I lacked confidence. But now dominance has crept in. The second one I took decisively. Real bad-ass Zulu boy. Situational shooting at its finest. Twenty yards. First shot square in the heart. An unbiased observer would have to feel good about me being in charge."

Collier twisted his mouth in distress. "Why can't I understand what you're talking about? You've killed somebody? Is that what you want me to believe?"

"Yeah," said Hootch, standing up real cool. "Yesterday."

Hootch liked saying that, watching Collier look like a dam' dog shittin' peach pits. And another funny thought struck him. If Collier wasn't going to be helpful—if he in fact was of no use at all—then he was just an impediment. He and that spade Tamzie were the only live witnesses who knew how the collection got stolen. Oh yeah, and Dale too.

*

"Sure, come on in," Dale said to her husband. But she didn't let him any further than standing in the hallway. Collier's rebel uniform was stained with sweat from a long, hot day of movie-making. Dale had made herself a martini with a shaving of lemon peel in it. She didn't offer him one.

She knew why he had come. The divorce hearing was scheduled for tomorrow. Their lives were about to have a sea change.

She felt high from starting off a love affair with Josh Mahoney. Not that exhilarating high you'd get back in high school or college when you got a crush on a boy. But more mellow. Sure, she still lived on the same street with evil relatives. She was not relieved of financial worries. But there was a recompense lying somewhere out there. She felt certain of it.

"I'm willing to try counseling," Collier began carefully. "I want to reclaim my identity."

Dale looked at his sweat-stained uniform, his fake beard. "I guess you have to be from out of town to really appreciate these ironies."

Collier blinked. "What?"

"I don't know what I mean. I'm saying you're the genuine article. Or something."

"How many drinks have you had?"

Dale looked him straight in the eye, deliberately downed some of her martini. She thought, jerk.

Collier toed the carpet. "Well, tomorrow it happens. If you don't want to reconcile, then all the years just get flushed down the toilet. I can take it, I guess. I'm no stranger to adversity. Life's not all cocktails and laughter."

"Yes, the whoop and holler has truly died out of your life. To use an upstate expression. I know my origins have always been an embarrassment."

"Only because you were so self-conscious about them."

Dale pursed her lips, thinking about throwing the drink in his face, maybe breaking the stem of the glass over his head, just to release the tension. "I tried to run my end of the marriage on the principle that if you reward a man, love him, be the general factotum, he'll give you a good return in effort. In your case though, I can't give you a good report card."

"I haven't always been faithful to you," he conceded glumly.

"Always?" Dale laughed. "You were *always* kind of economical with the truth. But your shimmering self-awareness comes too late."

"There you have it. Go sharply negative every chance you get. But, hey, the door swings both ways. Rannie intends to bring that out in the hearing."

Dale gave a small laugh. "She's a lover of the dark arts of litigation, our Rannie. But I can't see what she'll achieve for you."

Collier cleared his throat. "About the archives . . . "

"Ah yes," trilled Dale. "The unloved remains of my sucker's bet of a marriage." She was starting to feel a bit giddy. "You're worried I'll let them slip in the hearing. Just kind of blurt them out to the judge and then go, oops, did I say that?"

Collier's face hardened, went into a fixed gaze.

Dale said, "Fear not. I want this little divorce detail behind us with a minimum of hassle. Embrace a new maturity. Whatever I'm supposed to do next."

"Fine. And there's one more thing."

"Yes?"

"Hootch Gibson is making all kinds of idiotic threats. Demanding them."

Dale shrugged. "Hey, great. He can have them. Tell him the door's wide open. Bring a U-haul and cart off the fruits of Collier's madcap hobby."

Collier narrowed his eyes. "Sure, you know the truth about their . . . origins. So you sell them, give them away, touch them at all and you're dealing in stolen goods. But if you just leave them right there . . . get the divorce hearing behind us . . . maybe we sit down and reach a resolution."

"Is that your understanding of the criminal code? I didn't think you ever practiced law very much. And what do you mean threats?"

"Hootch claims to have killed two people. I don't believe it for a second."

"Who are the alleged victims?"

"Who cares?" Collier said irritably. He waved a hand vaguely. "One of them's Debone Wigfall. Remember him? Tamzie's husband. Big ugly animal. Leering at everyone like potential mugging victims."

"Yes."

"Well, just to check, I phoned Tamzie's house. She said he had been gone a couple of days. She sounded funny though."

"Funny how?"

"I don't know. Like maybe he was gone, and she wanted to forget she ever knew him."

47.

One of the uniformed cops lounging around the police station coffee maker said, "She say the swimming pool attendant—the one in charge of the youth program—take her into a shed and rape her. Then when she come back to the pool the next day she say dam' if he don't take her in the shed and rape her again."

He and his buddy both laughed and went out of the room leaving Tamzie there with a pair of plainclothes detectives. These two had picked her up early that morning and driven her down to the Lockwood Avenue station, sat her down at a desk, pulled up chairs close by. They told her Debone Wigfall had been shot to death and how come the body came to be found near her Chevette. Tamzie looked from one to the other. Asked if there was any damage to the car.

The detectives, one white, one black, stared straight at her deadpan.

The white one had mustard color hair and chewed nicotine gum. The black one wore a vest with his suit and looked like he was uncomfortable in it. Didn't like that it was too short and showed his belt buckle. Kept tugging at it. They wanted to know all about her relationship with Debone and what she had been doing both in general and at the time of his death.

Tamzie said that while it was a bad beginning for the week, she had no trouble saying Debone's loss would not be mourned. They had been married and divorced and were in a transient pattern.

"Meaning what?" said the white cop, looking puzzled like maybe this was street talk he didn't understand.

"Meaning he was gone be passing through whenever I could manage to jam his sorry ass out of the house. Which incidentally is titled in my name alone. And I made the mortgage payment this month. With money I earned legitimate."

The black cop had a voice like maybe he had been to a white college. Thaddeus had almost the same voice. The cop said, "So you two fell out of love. That murder conviction finally mark him down as a loser?"

Tamzie said Debone had not exactly been coming off the dream season of his career. She had picked him up from prison and let him move in because he would have done it anyhow and probably beat the tar out of her just to set the ground rules.

In answer to other questions, Tamzie didn't know anybody with a fancy target pistol, and she didn't know anybody mean enough to take Debone from the front the way he had been shot. She said she guessed the easy life behind bars had stripped him of the skills that had once made him such a deadly shooter. The white cop must have been new at detective work because he lost the stone face and broke out into nervous laughter.

The black cop looked at Tamzie real serious and solemn. "Sometimes I think my life's like shucking oysters. Trying to pry open that hard stuck-together shell with a nasty little knife that can slip off and gash me to the bone. But leastways an oyster dies without any big fuss. When it comes to human victims, the ones I investigate have gone off with major screaming and pain. Twitchy violence kind of thing. No fun at all for them. But a lot of jollies for the victimizer."

Tamzie said, "Is that a fact?"

The cops said they'd guarantee her immunity if she wanted to confide some secrets in them. She said she had been around long enough to know nothing was guaranteed in life. But anyhow she had no secrets. The cops kind of deflated. Tamzie got up to leave.

"One more thing," said the black cop.

"Shore."

"You work for the Ralstons?"

"That's the truth."

He rolled his jaw, thinking how to word the question. "Is Rannie Ralston having a . . . like, an affair with a young fella named Hootch Gibson?"

That sure stopped her. She stared at him. Finally said, "Her sex life is not what you'd call . . . a busy intersection. She's got her own laws of chemistry. Like on most things."

Tamzie came out of the police station into blistering brilliant sunshine. She thought, stupid mutha. Debone figured to audition for a big time gangsta part. He always looked a lot tougher behind the wire screen at the prison than he was in real life. Now he had been taken down permanently.

Still, the in-many-ways-fortunate event did not let her rest easy.

267

Debone's sudden demise did not make it Hallelujah time. That white boy Hootch wanted her diary and must have been real pissed when Debone didn't deliver. Or he wanted it without paying and smoked Debone before he found out Debone didn't have it. Both of them out-dumbed each other.

Rain had fallen all night, and big puddles stood in the road where Tamzie waited for the bus. She had to keep stepping back when cars splashed through. The cops would keep her car impounded, but she had expected that. Seagulls gathered in a big flock in the little strip of park along the Ashley River.

Growing up, her momma would say things like, "When you die you join a river of souls rolling to the sea of all that gone before." Her momma had scrubbed her face and dressed her out of the Goodwill store. Told her to stay away from T-bird and Boone's Farm and not let the boys feel on her. And Tamzie had ignored that wise advice and ended up with Debone. Now that chapter was behind her. But she wondered about the rest of the wisdom. Time moves like a river and we are all part of a chain of our ancestor's souls. She'd have to seriously study on that.

*

Around ten in the morning, the bus let Tamzie off at the corner of King and Broad next to Berlin's clothing store. She walked down King among the old houses of the rich folks, then took a right on Tradd over to Legendre. She figured she had time to go by and see Dale before she would have to drive Miz Ralston over to the Yacht Club.

Miz Ralston would yell at her about not being there in the morning, but she'd say she had been with the cops because Debone got killed. Not that she'd get any sympathy. But white women like Miz Ralston expected things like that out of the coloreds. And Tamzie's tardiness would allow her to complain to everybody in the Club about her particular servant problem.

The movie folks were out of town in the woods doing a battle scene, so Dale's house was quiet. Dale was polite enough, invited her into the kitchen and made iced tea. White women always made iced tea. It gave them something to do while they thought about things. Like how come Tamzie kept turning up. And why Debone was dead. The newspaper was lying right there with the Region section open, little right column headline, *"Area Man Found Dead."*

Tamzie realized that she and Dale had never really had an ordinary conversation except one time when they talked about delicatessen food in New York. How they both liked those kosher pickles that were so crisp it sound like you're eating potato chips. Otherwise nothing. You couldn't talk across the races.

With her tea in hand, Tamzie said she imagined Dale was trying to think of what to say about Debone's death. "You're figuring I'm in the highly emotional period of grief right after learning the news."

What Dale actually said surprised her. "Do you have a boyfriend? The reason I ask . . . well, Debone didn't seem to be your style."

"As a matter of fact," said Tamzie, "I endure a peck of abuse from the man and won't miss him a bit. In his youth, he had the power to cloud a girl's mind. But it was a no-frills life with him. Get beat around. That's something of a physical challenge which I never 'pacifically care for."

Dale asked if the police knew who had killed him. Tamzie said, "Party or parties unknown done take away my future with Debone. I could speculate on it, but don't believe I will."

Dale said she thought women spent too much time waiting for a man to transform them, make their lives something special. They waited on a man's vision of things, got into a marriage trying to follow along with him. And suddenly they realized women had a timeless vision of how things should be. Your vision was there all along.

Tamzie said she had not come over to grieve or talk philosophy. She was one of the sponsors of Collier Ralston's collection. She had lent him something that she wanted back before it got sold off.

Dale looked at her like she knew Tamzie was lying but didn't particularly care. She said the collection was more trouble than she knew how to handle. Dale tapped the map of the Mason-Dixon line, said it was $360,000. Showed her a Gen. Beauregard letter—$12,000.

Tamzie said in utter astonishment, "I ain't believing it."

"I can show you the entries in *Book Prices Current*. But what I guess I'd like to ask you is who was Tremba Jerome who kept a diary back in 1835? An ancestor of yours?"

Tamzie thought, You're like one of us. You see everything and miss nothing.

Dale took the diary down off the shelf, asked Tamzie if she had read it. Tamzie said she had never really looked at it. And yes she could read. Then realized that sounded nasty and said she was sorry. The pressure of events was getting to her.

Tamzie opened it at random and read, *"Christmas lasted the three days. Gingerbread, ham, turkey, goose. On Sundays we give our folk tickets to visit friends and go courting on the plantations along the rivers."*

Tamzie said Thaddeus Wyndham, a professor-type man, had explained it to her. Her ancestors had owned slaves. The tickets were passes for the slaves to go off the plantation. The overseer on the plantation you visited would sign it before you came back.

Together Dale and Tamzie read on about giving men, women, and children red flannel underwear. By custom, tools were inspected on Christmas day, each woman received a handkerchief, each man a woolen cap. Also extra peas, rice, molasses, and meat. Tobacco. Rum or whisky.

Then Tamzie read to the last of the Christmas entry. Tremba kept a constant fire in the hearth. She had lit it with coals brought from the slave cabin where she had been born. The fire had never gone out since first started by her grandmother who had been brought in chains from Africa. It ended with a single line set apart from the rest:

"Like the fire, I will triumph through endurance."

Tamzie suddenly started talking about her momma Mozelle, how she had an extra proper voice she used around the preacher and with white folks. "Momma had her superstitions and quaint habits. She'd paint the windowsills blue when somebody died to keep the spirit from returning. She paid up her burial insurance so she'd have folks at the funeral say 'That sure is a fine box she's gone go down in the earth in'."

Tamzie started crying and couldn't stop.

48.

Down in Florida, two tropical storms back-to-back were slamming into the Atlantic coast. Up in South Carolina, Jazz-bo Productions started filming at sun-up to try to beat the heat and the coming rain the storms would bring. The reenactors stood around looking authentic drinking coffee out of their tin cups. Hootch had a good hit of Goldschlager cinnamon schnapps in his. To anyone who'd listen, he'd say, "My grandaddy allus used to say there are damn few times when a man should take a drink in the morning . . . but this is one of them. Wuh-huh-yuck-yuck."

After he tired of amusing everybody with his wit, he went back to his jeep, took a large swallow off the schnapps bottle and loaded his Springfield. To be out of sight, he sat down on the running board of the jeep. If anyone asked, he'd say he was putting a grease rag down the barrel to get at those hard to eliminate rust patches.

First count to three while he poured powder from his brass powder flask. Then the paper wad. Ram it down carefully. Now a genuine minié ball all greased up to slide down the barrel. Thing was a bitch of a tight fit even so, and he had real trouble getting it rammed down.

He stood up to see Collier Ralston walking towards him. Double-breasted blouse tailored like the Wade Hampton one stolen from the State Museum. Big white gauntlets. Sword belt and blue infantry sash. Hootch snatched up a newspaper from the back of the jeep, acting real interested in the morning news. Even as cool as he was, his heart beat a little fast.

Another senator had pled guilty to bribery charges growing out of Operation Chump Change. Standing on the steps of the courthouse, he said he wished he had an escape clause in his new contract with the state of South Carolina. That drew a laugh from the reporters.

"Did you catch this action?" Hootch said, slapping the paper. "They're going down one at a time. Pretty soon you'll be in the cross-hairs."

Collier angrily snatched the paper and started tearing it into bits, stomping them on the ground. His divorce hearing was set for that afternoon, and he looked haggard from a sleepless night. He drew his saber half out of the scabbard and slammed it back in. "I'll never go to prison. Dubiel is terrified of my sister."

Hootch chuckled. "Well, bless'd be the family ties that bind. Yeah, in a world of screwed-up masterpieces, Rannie's a rare fucking gem. Creature from hell one minute, desperate bitch in heat the next."

Collier gave him a skeptical look. "What? You're telling me you've . . . *slept* with my sister Rannie."

Hootch rubbed his crotch. "I gotta admit, I got some bragging rights in that area."

Collier shook his head in wide wonder. "She's right. You really are an asshole."

"Sticks and stones may break my bones. But listen here. All this locker room chit-chat aside, lemme interject we could end much of your financial disability by you ponying up the archives. Last chance now. Just eliminate the risk of violent confrontation at one stroke. Whattya say?"

Collier didn't get to answer.

"Okay, good people," Jason Traub boomed over his bullhorn. The crane was hoisting him up where he could look down on the field. "We're ready to get rolling here. Let's get into position. Chop-chop!"

The drummer boy poised his sticks and clashed them down, beating the recall. Uniformed men scrambled up with their rifles, slung haversacks and cartridge boxes over their shoulders tossed out their coffee. Hustled a double time to form up in the field so the filming could start. Hootch went out with them, his rifle loaded and ready to deal the death blow.

Big thunder clouds shaped to the east, fat as whipped cream. An artist might call it a dramatic sky, but the movie makers had to shake a leg or they'd be rained out.

With the ranks formed, the director said, "Awright, people, let's see if we can do this professionally! I'm trying to run a circus-free proceeding here!"

They had practiced it several times before; advance across the field loading and firing. A mess of them fall down and play dead. The battle played only a minor place in the movie which mostly consisted of sight gags of women in elaborate crinolines revealing they had no underpants.

One hundred men rammed down a charge of powder. Slid the rod back under the barrel. Raised the rifle to port arms and half-cock. Capped the nipple with the little copper cap. All set.

Ramrods are normally forbidden on reenactment battlefields. In all the excitement, a lot of guys would forget to take them out of the barrel. Fire the rifle and a great long metal rod would go winging its way towards the enemy ranks. But for movie realism, they loaded using the ramrods.

Collier rode out in front of the line on a white horse which Hootch figured was excellent. Get him up high and prominent. Hootch smiled real big, slid his ramrod into the rifle barrel and tapped the charge just to make sure it was in place. He knew he'd only get one shot. But it would be enough. Ol' Collier'd be beat in every phase of the game.

"Okay, good people, listen up! No one be a deliberate asshole! I want dead, dead and still more dead! Okay now, action here! We're rolling, people!"

Hootch thought, asshole? What is this asshole business? That word is so overused.

They began the advance, loading and firing. Bam bam ba-dam bam. Really loud. Smoke swirling.

Time to go into full production, thought Hootch. He took aim at

Collier's head. Then thought better of it. A damn minié ball would tear a hole bigger than a barn door at that range wherever it hit him. May as well take an easier shot. He lowered it to Collier's back.

Dang, hold still now. Collier bouncing around waving his sword. Horse wheeling. Hold still, hoss. Now . . .

BAM ka-whang!

Collier fell off his horse, thrashing around on the ground. His blood-curdling screams stopped the action dead still. The smoke drifted skyward.

Hootch thought, whang? What was that noise?

"What is this? What is this?" the director shouted through his bull-horn. "Is something out of order? Do we have a set-back?"

"Sunny-bitch!" a bearded rebel yelled and pointed upwards.

A hundred head turned to look. They saw the ramrod flying end over end through the air.

Ohhh, shit, Hootch thought. Didn't I take out the rod?

Whunk! Right into Jason Traub's chest. He let out a squawk like a chicken.

The first big fat drops of rain started to fall.

*

The streets flooded in the pouring rain, and Dale's feet were soaked. She stood in the doorway to the crowded waiting room of the Family Court shaking off her umbrella. What the news called a weak, but drenching hurricane had hit Florida. Heavy rain fell along the east coast as far as Virginia.

Dale had never been in the Family Court building before. It

resembled a social services office with every seat taken and trashy people standing around the walls. The tiny cubicles of courtrooms could have been welfare in-take offices. You waited for your case to be called and wedged into one of them with the judge and as many witnesses as would fit. Bailiffs lounged around with guns on their hips.

Dale asked if the parties ever got into fights, jammed up here waiting, the air charged with tension. Her lawyer Jack Camden said all the time. Some of the judges wore Kevlar soft body armor now. Once Jack had his car vandalized in the parking garage, so he made certain to always allow time to walk over from his Broad Street office.

They stood there in the big mob, Jack perusing a sport fishing magazine he had brought and talking to her about off-the-wall stuff. A baby started screaming, and the mother took it out into the stairwell. Jack Camden said he worried that all this fresh water pouring down was liable to harm the shrimp crop. They'd head out to sea looking for more salinity. Too early to tell because the full effects of the run-off would take a couple days. Some unusual high tides operated in their favor. They might drive more salt water inshore. Counter the adverse effects.

"Am I supposed to understand this?" Dale asked. "Did you just buy a shrimp boat or something?" She was nervous as a cat, a whole phase of her life coming to a final end.

"Hey, be cool," he said. "You don't have to do anything big. Just testify to when you got married and where. That's all. The evidence speaks for itself. Then Rannie and I'll squabble over the house and furniture. We'll probably have a pretty good shrimp season anyhow despite the rain. That's my best guess."

Two of the bailiffs talked about South Carolina now offering condemned killers a choice between electrocution and lethal injection.

"Pretty much time to upgrade to the new technology," one said.

"Yeah," the other agreed, "it's kind of like a realignment. Makes it more of a clinical process. Give him three shots. He's asleep by the time the third one jams his heart up. Stops it cold."

Outside, lightning streaked the sky above the roof of the Mills Hotel.

A bailiff came up and mumbled in Jack's ear. He kept his voice low, but Dale heard him say that Collier Ralston had been shot dead in a movie set accident. She closed her eyes and counted up to twenty-five. Then opened them again. She felt like a fish bone was stuck in her throat.

"Howly vargins," breathed Jack Camden. "The pre-nuptial agreement. You won't be divorced. It doesn't kick in. You're his sole heir. So you get the house. Everything really. Rannie will be so pissed."

Dale sat down in one of the chairs. She remembered Collier standing in St. Michael's on their wedding day waiting for her to come down the aisle. All her friends and relatives said she was so lucky. Money, good looks, and social position. "You know I was once in love with him," she said to Jack. "Have I ever told you that?"

"No, most people don't." He saw the tears that were forming at the corners of her eyes.

Dale had never imagined herself at Collier's funeral. She wasn't old enough to picture such things. That probably came when you hit forty. She said she had to think about this. Shook her head feeling really tired.

Then Rannie came in wearing a slate blue power suit and carrying a briefcase and dripping umbrella. With an icy smile, she said, "Collier's not dead. He must have some little angel sitting on his shoulder."

"What happened?" said Dale, meaning how was he shot.

"When I left him, he seemed to be trying to reenact the hospital scene from *Gone With the Wind*. Screaming and carrying on. So they put him under the ether. As he started to go under, he called out various girl's names, none of them yours."

Dale said deadpan, "You sure have a knack for knowing just the right thing to say in any social situation."

49.

Tumescence, Moira thought. Her hand trembled. She forced it to move across the page.

Slowly she embraced his growing tumescence, her fingertips moving by blind instinct.

'You white beast,' Latanzie groaned.

His breath stinking of cheap brandy, Hunter Gilson laughed cruelly. The black wench stirred his blood. He was priapic. His manhood assumed its formidable presence, indeed stood like a heraldic beast.

With rough vehemence he pinioned her arms above her head. Her breasts flattened out in consortium, but the nipples gathered scrupulously with desire. Eyes closed in rapture, she seemed to be praying. "You must enter me," she said in unsteady voice, black lashes wet with tears.

The vast erection found her wetness. He felt the faint stab of her hip bones, the tension of her muscles. Her ebony body was slick with sweat.

"Perfect sublime truth," he murmured in her ear.

She accepted the stiffness like an article of faith. Following the general impetus, she moved her unconstrained body. Legs clenching and releasing in a spontaneity of attitude. Her head surrounded by a misty radiance, she demonstrated the slow, secret rhythm of the earth.

He sucked the moral beauty of each breast in turn, and a current of sensibility seemed to pass from her body to his. Her response became even more sure. Full of enlightened self-interest, her hips moved in wondrous harmony, taking what her very core being required.

"Oh yes!" she moaned in unmistakable notes. The pleasure was flooding her.

Moira moaned deep down in her own throat. Stood up abruptly, knocking her chair over backwards. She fidgeted, paced frantically up and down the room, hugging her elbows. Her breath came hot and panting as with a deep desperation. God, how could she write this filth? And what was it doing to her? Her anxiety center was running wild. These words, these emotions, were alien to . . . well, to the totality of her life experience. She had stage fright, that was all. She'd conquer this.

Hot flashes went through her like electric jolts. The trashiness of it all. Not knowing where to begin, she had sought Dale's advice—who told her to go out and buy those disgusting books and magazines. Even gave her a list of titles.

The horrible leers of that nasty man in the bookstore when he saw her purchases. Blue Moon Press books by anonymous authors. And the *Penthouse* with those drooling letters to the editor. God she thought she'd die of mortification!

Tears started from her eyes. She needed help. Dale could guide her through this. Dale had gotten her the contract. She would know how to handle this.

No. No, she'd stand on her own two feet. She had shot a man. How many writers could claim that? The fact that she had limited knowledge of . . . of the more sordid aspects of life, well her vivid imagination would triumph over that.

She couldn't keep doing this in her room. This was her sanctum where her author's odyssey had begun. But her mother was always snooping. What if she found the magazines?

The idea arose of taking over Rannie's old bedroom for an office. Not that there weren't plenty of rooms in the house, but it had a pretty view and no one went in there. Rannie wouldn't like it, but Moira had become a more assertive person. She gathered up the dirty books and magazines and her manuscript and went down the hall.

The musty smell in the room could be aired out. Moira flung open the windows to breathe the floating scents of the sea air with the rain pelting down. A flower arrangement would brighten things up. Sunflowers. Johnsongrass. Cattails. Fennel. A nice golden blaze like the late sun of a September day. And September was not far off. It would be perfect.

Such a surprise for Moira to find a great big green plastic garbage bag in the old wardrobe and even more of a surprise to open it and find it full of money. And a gun too.

Moira stroked her pointed little chin and stood there pondering this new development. She needed a nice dress for the cover photo. Rannie had plenty of money and wouldn't miss a little bit. She just left it lying around any old way she pleased. Seemed to Moira like she wanted someone to take it.

It was no fun to shop alone. She'd take Tamzie with her and buy her something as well. Mother paid the poor girl next to nothing. Tamzie deserved a treat.

Without really thinking, Moira left her dirty books and the revised manuscript to *Southern Gale* lying on top of the money.

*

While Dale had her day in court, Tamzie stayed in the house at No. 14 Legendre Street with the rain whipping all around. Once Dale's divorce business settled down, they planned to figure on what to do with all the old books and such.

Around ten when she had brewed a cup of Blue Mountain coffee, Thaddeus appeared wearing a big raincoat with a cape around the shoulders and carrying a dozen roses. She wondered how he had tracked her down, but the man seemed to be a regular bloodhound. And he knew the houses of the rich white folks because he pestered them to donate their stuff to the library.

"I'm real sorry about your husband getting killed," he said, handing her the roses. The blossoms sparkled with water drops.

"The news didn't even make me go lie down," said Tamzie. Then she skipped a beat. "How'd you know I was married?"

"A man in my line of work, it's not hard to look up records. A good-looking woman like yourself was bound to have been married. You didn't seem like the unwed mother type."

"Plus I ain't no mother. I guess you checked that too."

"For true."

"You either a real serious busy-body or else you taking a major interest in little Tamzie."

He said the second one for sure, and before he dripped all over, could he hang up his coat somewhere? She put the coat on a hook in the hall closet and said, "Having an involvement with you is changing things for me. Like that Stevie Wonder song where he says he never had 'a sit-down thought about where the river flows.' It's like I'm thinking about stuff for the first time in my life."

Thaddeus said he could buy into that. If that was the one about having a one-track mind when it comes to thinking 'bout my baby.

She took him into Dale's study with the books and pictures, said he may as well see it since it was probably what he was after anyhow. He took a few books off the shelves, gave her a look like he knew where they belonged and knew she had stolen them every one. The map of the Mason-Dixon line really gave him pause.

Tamzie said, "Collier said nobody cared a hoot about it. They just sat there forgotten on a shelf growing old. He'd give me twenty bucks apiece."

Thaddeus shook his head sadly. "These things are real and they are important. They tell us our heritage. Where we came from. What we once were. You can't treat them like attic rubbish to just toss around."

"Fine. Okay. You bet. I'll give it all back. Except it ain't mine to give back. Even stolen it ain't mine. The only thing I got a claim to is the diary, and I don't give a big damn if somebody say I sold it to them. It's mine."

He looked at her right intent. "What diary?"

She said the one he been snooping around for. The one everybody seem to want. He said show it to him. She did. He held it in a very peculiar way like he was afraid to break the spine. Turned the pages extra careful. Read bits of it to himself.

Tamzie asked what he figured it was worth street value.

He pursed his lips, said, "Three, maybe four. It's hard to say."

"Three-four what?"

"Three or four million dollars."

Tamzie opened and closed her mouth several times. Finally some words came out. "You crazy, you lying, or you shittin' me? Which is it?"

He touched the pages very carefully. "This is quite possibly the most important document of African-American history in existence." His eyes actually teared up. "It should tour the country. Black school children should be able to see it, to read her words. To know that we have a heritage."

"Nunh-uh," said Tamzie.

"Nunh-uh what?"

"Nunh-uh meaning no way. Nunh-uh to what's coming next. Nunh-uh to how I should give it to the Avery Institute because they could never afford such a thing on they own. Nunh-uh to how that Getty Museum got so much truck they'll never display it and it'll just go in a dehumidity room forever all locked up in the dark."

"It would be a tax deduction."

"Against what income? My little piddly pay? Everybody in the world inherits stuff and what do I get? A run-down house on Cannon Street that the red bitch take off me first chance she got. This is mine. It's the rest of my life which ain't been no bed of roses up to this present instant. It's a five-bedroom house and a new Lexus and season tickets to NBA games. What are you grinning at?"

"I think we're having our first fight."

"Well you ain't winning."

50.

Dale wheeled Blake Huston into Rannie's inner law office, the one with the nude painting on the wall. Stood there behind him. Outside, rain poured down, dashing in ferocious gusts against the windows. They were both drenched. Blake's gray hair with its flecks of red lay limp as spaghetti strands across his head.

Rannie put down a newspaper but remained seated in her chair behind the big leather-topped desk with the nude painting behind her. Her voice was reflective. "I've been thinking about maybe doing some advertising. 'Disability denied? No fee unless we win.' That kind of thing. If it brings in business, maybe move to TV."

Dale sat down in a chair. She and Blake sat looking at Rannie. Both solemn. No malign grins. But a time bomb was ticking. Dale was certain of it.

Rannie crossed her legs beneath the big desk. "I know something's up. Some long-buried secret is about to emerge. You're Blake Huston, terror of all decent people of good society. I drove down to your place one time to take you a check from one of my few gentry clients. We were deep-sixing a sensitive matter. Remember that? I had just started practice. My hair was longer then." She combed her fingers through her red hair.

Dale smiled. The little tough-love session for her sister-in-law was developing nicely.

Rannie looked from Blake to Dale and back to Blake again. She seemed on the edge of being agitated. "So what do you have on me?" she asked Blake. "Most of my skeletons don't need closets. Welcome to the wacky world of the Ralston family. You seem to have met my sister-in-law Dale. She doesn't do much with her life except have a body to die for. I've also got a sister Moira. You want to pick a defect in her? Delusional romanticism? You really can't settle on just one. She lives so far up in the stratosphere you need a Hubble space telescope to see her. Then there's my mother. She can spend ten percent of my annual income in a day. She's such a joy. It just takes the drudgery out of work."

"I may be your father," Blake Huston croaked.

Rannie glared at him. "Well this is refreshing candor. I've heard the rumors for years. Rannie's parents are not really her own. That's why she's so aggressive. Rannie is of a syncretic nature that used to be called a bastard. I used to love all that whispering that was designed for me to overhear. Charleston society is such a snake pit delight. Almost on a par with my clients. And they're a choice lot of charmers with the dead eyes of zombies. They're—help me out here. I'm searching for another serpent metaphor."

Blake made a kind of snorting, hacking noise. Dale couldn't read his emotions. It might have been a smile on his twisted face.

"What they don't fully realize . . ." said Rannie. She stopped and knitted her brows. Then leaned forward and pointed a letter opener at Blake. "You dried up old persimmon. We've got by over the years without knowing each other. You think you can just hover here like Banquo's ghost? Be some catalyst in my life? Or do you expect me to nestle your grizzled head on my lap and regret the lost years between us?"

Blake's smile took on a strange edge. His watery old eyes focused on the nude painting. Dale wondered if it reminded him of Mary Canty in her youth. He cackled as though enjoying a salacious memory and rubbed his bad hand with his good one.

Rannie threw herself back in her chair. "Did I mention my brother? Yeah, Collier's a great American. Never serves a day in his life in the U.S. Armed Forces, gets shot in a battle reenactment. I was thinking if he had died I could have given a eulogy at his funeral. Talked about his disbarment as a new beginning. Say he could have had a whole new life but for that bullet.

"Daddy used to say Collier was destined for politics so he didn't fully concentrate in law school. Rannie was more bookish. What he was telling everyone was the kid Rannie had style and grit and determination. Let her alone. Don't try to coach her. She's a natural. An accelerant lit by a match." She threw her hands up in the air. "Whoosh."

She started to laugh, shrill and on the edge of out of control. "I'm lying. That's it. I'm lying. Pure and simple." She laughed some more. "You see, I've been lying all my life. I'm not tainted by love and affection. Collier the Apollo moon shot got all of that. Daddy never paid a lick of attention to me. That's why I'm such a striver. I don't need an analyst to figure that. I was supposed to be modest and sweet. Like Moira. It was something that, you know, was never said. But then nothing was ever said about me. Or to me. Somehow being the responsible one devolved. Or evolved. Whatever. I became little mother-father breadwinner. No boyfriends. No notable liaisons to speak of. This is just part of my baggage."

Dale knew Rannie was sliding to the brink. Her face glowed red as her hair. And Dale didn't care. She had taken all the shit she intended to take off her sister-in-law. It was now pay-back time.

Something was about to explode in Rannie. She was hyperventilating. "What was Collier exactly? I'll tell you. He was one endless disappointed expectation. Or arrested development or something. Collier typed with two fingers. Collier would eat tangerines. He'd take them apart section by section and carefully peel off the white stringy stuff. Stack the seeds in a little pile. What's wrong? Did I wreck your digestion?"

Dale gripped the arms of her chair tensing for a major eruption. A telephone call brought Rannie out of whatever path to madness she had been going down. Rannie listened briefly.

"Do I need this?" she shouted into the receiver. "Do I need this on top of everything else?"

*

Rannie hit the panic button.

The phone interruption came from a King Street dress shop telling Rannie that Moira was spending enormous amounts of money on more clothes and shoes than any six people could wear. And she had that, well, colored girl with her. The one who worked for Mary Canty. Tamzie Jerome. Moira was outfitting her as well. And the store owner just felt that since they were paying in cash—big rubber banded wads of cash—something might be wrong.

As if Rannie didn't have enough to make her life a hell on earth, her lamebrain sister had slipped her leash. She ran out of her office leaving Dale and that desiccated old spider Blake Huston. Ran all the way home through the rain and was soaked by the time she got there. Home meaning her mother's house, No. 1 Legendre.

Shivering and shaking and gasping, she climbed the stairs. Threw open the door to her old bedroom. Big flower arrangements everywhere. Went across the room and whipped open the door to the wardrobe. The green garbage bag was sitting wide open.

A big chunk of the money was missing. On top rested a thick stack of paper. "What is this?" she shouted, coming up with *Southern Gale*.

Naked in the hot night, Randolphia Reston crawled on her hands and knees to the low brute Hunter Gilson. Begging for the intimidating authority of his manhood. Wanting him to enter her and spread pleasure like a downpour marching across a parched landscape. Her heavy breasts hung down, saturated with whorish need. She wept in weak despair, knowing no other way to keep him from going down to the slave cabins. 'I am soaked with desperate desire,' she pleaded. 'I want to breed with you, feel my belly grow with new life.'

Drunk on brandy as was his custom, unshaven and reeking of sweat, Hunter laughed cruelly. 'You bastard strumpet. Born on the wrong side of the blanket. I'll take a dog whip to your fat rump. Give it the pink warmth of a summer rose.'

For a brief moment, Rannie stared dumbly at this macabre passage. Then, "What is this shit? What is this goddam shit?" She flung the manuscript, its pages fluttering like a snow storm of paper. She felt like going downstairs and breaking every piece of Baccarat and Steuben in the house.

"I'll kill you, you diminutive pea-brain! I swear on a stack of Bibles I'll kill you!"

*

In the shop, the owner summoned Moira to the phone while Tamzie tried on dresses in the changing room. A big pile of skirts and blouses the pair had selected lay on the counter next to the cash register.

Her sister Rannie was calling from home. The conversation was one-sided. Moira listened as her sister said, "I've got a client who sat there in the Dorchester Road Howard Johnson motel eating potato chips so the clerk could get a good look at him just before he robbed the place. Wearing red shorts and a white t-shirt. Cops picked him out of the dark with no problem. Real genius that boy.

"I know. You're going, 'Why is she telling me this?' You're thinking, 'Yes, Rannie works for a living. She has to work. It's a world of dramatic revenue swings. She never tires of reminding us.' But what I'd like to remind you of, Moira, is back when I was sixteen and mother decided I was getting over-weight. That threw her into a fever of activity. What would people think if I got really fat? She had to go get me appetite suppressors that were nothing more than amphetamines. Green amphs we called them. Doctors used to dish them out like candy. I had an after school job in a clothing store. Let me tell you, my eyes were open real wide and I had every zipper zipped up, every skirt lined up *just so* on the rack. Then I quit taking them. I realized I had quite enough energy on my own. And anyhow, moderation is in the eye of the beholder.

"Am I making sense? No? I should have remembered. You've got your brain on muscle relaxers. But I am taking time out of my busy-bee workday to talk to you. I talk to you daily. I talk to you like no one else ever does. I talk the hell out of you. I wheedle, I cajole, I plead with you to develop some semblance of lucidity, but to no avail. You don't seem to understand what you're dealing with. All day, every day, in the course of my work I get to contemplate random hyper-violence—social pathologies—stupidity—bestial behavior—a kind of hell broth that conveys the underbelly of gun-culture America today. It has seeped into me and become part of my nature. Like a psychic shaping of Rannie Ralston."

Rannie's voice turned real sweet and patient. "Now Moira, what you are going to do is put that money in my law office. You bring it in a brown paper bag. You don't leave it with the secretary. You tell her it's to be left in my desk by you special. And you put it in the bottom drawer of my desk. Little leap of faith here on my part, believing you can follow those simple instructions. But, Moira, if you fail to abide by my wishes --- if you dispute me on this in any way—I'm going to have a lengthy interview with you, Moira, and at the end make damn certain you die a virgin."

Well. Offensive language. Rudeness. Moira hung up the phone with her ears burning. She thought, And they say I need lithium.

She didn't have a brown paper bag, and she wasn't about to further embarrass herself by asking a store clerk for one. Besides it was raining to beat the band outside. Rannie's old briefcase would do just fine. They had brought the money in it; they could use it to take it back. Of course they had to pay for all these clothes. They had put the poor store clerks to so much trouble.

And then there was the gun. Rannie had been so wound up that Moira had forgotten to ask her what to do with that.

51.

Hootch was not pleased to have botched such an easy shot at Collier. It had broken his winning streak. But sticking the director with the ramrod, putting him in the hospital with a sucking chest wound, had been a real laugh. Now both Traubs had some scars to show for their brush with Charleston.

The cops had been no problem. By the time they got there, the Confederate ranks were broken and everybody milling around under canvas in the downpour. Couldn't remember who had been standing where. The cops tried to confiscate all the rifles and tag them, but Hootch had substituted a rifle from his jeep—1854 Harpers Ferry for the 1862 Springfield.

A hot rain blew through the open door of *Julep*. Outside, the market area was knee deep in water. Florida was getting a Category 1 hurricane with winds around eighty mph. Seas were running fourteen feet in the Bahamas.

Hootch got into his third rum and coke and told Travis he had been reading about prairie dog safaris in the magazine of the Varmint Hunters Association. He tapped the folded magazine that lay on the bar and said that was just what the doctor ordered for unwinding after the business was wrapped. With that ferocious eyesight the dogs got, you got to nail the little rodents from four football fields away. Need to get yourself a $5,000 target rifle and a Roto-Bench style portable shooting table that'll rotate 360 degrees. Got a built-in seat and umbrella stand. Explode the little bastards to smithereens. Red mist.

He figured he'd take some honey along with him who wanted to sit out there and watch him kill shit. Mix the drinks. Wear a camo bikini. Work on her tan. Five days in a motel. Yeah, it'd be a good week.

Travis asked him why he drank like a fish. Sure, Travis liked a drink same as the next man. Many a night he spent shit-faced. But the morning and noon boozing seemed over the edge.

Hootch said he called his habits a managed substance-abuse program. Which was a fancy way of saying if it feels good do it.

"Aside from my pathologies," said Hootch, "what I'm gonna do, good buddy, is break the bank at Monte Carlo. I got my sights on a nigrah diary that will bring long lines of collectors. Party of the first part takes it by force from party of the second part. Party of the first part will meet with third parties for the big score." He made a pistol of his thumb and forefinger. "Collect the cash. Cap the boy. Move on to the next bidder. I figure I can work through four-five collectors before word gets out it's poison. Got a curse on it like the Hope Diamond."

Travis pulled his sunglasses down his nose and looked over the rims. "You gonna screw this one up bigger than that other job."

"Spectacularly wrong," said Hootch.

Travis snorted. "Yore weaving drunk is what you are. Next you'll be knee-walking. Then comes hugging the commode."

Hootch said, "I don't feel like a quaternary patient. That's a new word I learned. It means, like, complicated. All racked up bad."

"No, not you," said Travis. "You ain't the one dumb-ass enough to go ahead and dump that body at Miss Ralston's house right after I told you not to." He waited for Hootch's reaction. Hootch didn't give him any. "Yeah, you wondering why I'm riding you about it. You're thinking ain't the statcher of lim'tations run on that one yet? But what I'm thinking. You wanna know what it is? It's maybe you're about ready for nursery school. Or a head-start program. Get you a Lion King lunch box. A Barbie book bag."

Hootch kind of waved Travis away with his hand. "As offensive as this may sound, you and Mister Willie T. are nothing but managerial chaos."

"Don't nobody call Mister Spainhour 'Willie T.,'" said Travis real slow, deliberate and mean. "Leastways not some booze-a-holic collich kid." Travis reached over for the little lemon slicing knife on the bar, picked it up like he meant to stick it up Hooch's nose.

Hootch pulled his piece out of the folded copy of the varmint hunter's magazine snapped it up under Travis' jaw and held it there. Long blue steel barrel right behind the point of his chin. Enjoyed the sudden look of fear in the man's eyes at this onslaught of firepower. The dumb hick. Trying to play tough guy. Hootch had co-opted that role.

"I've got no image clarity problem at all," Hootch said. "And as for Willie T. with his greed and complacency, well, we all have trouble accepting change."

Hootch stood up and looked around the room. The bartender was frozen, his hands half raised to his shoulders like he thought it was a stick-up. Customers were looking on with expressions that ranged from horrified to scared shit-less.

"It's just a toy," said Hootch. "Stage prop for a movie. Didn't mean to cause controversy." He wagged the pistol around. "Unflagging energy," he said to Travis. "That's me. Party 'til dawn night after night. But I mean, hey, if I don't have a positive attitude, who will?"

*

In mid-afternoon Rannie sat in her office drinking a scotch with her shoes off and feet on her desk reading the *Post & Courier*. In a Chump Change guilty plea, a state senator said, "I've functioned well in society up 'til now. It's important that this fact be taken into account."

His wife Sundi was quoted as saying, "I was afraid of this happening."

In other news, recreational boating deaths achieved a record low according to a Coast Guard Report. Capsizing and falling overboard still caused most fatalities.

The phone rang. Rannie had shut up the office for the day, sent the secretary home early because of the flooding. She shouldn't bother to answer it. It kept ringing. Rannie picked it up to hear Bubba Spainhour's gravel voice on the other end.

"Yore boy's outta control."

She dipped an index finger in her drink and stirred the ice. Sucked her finger off. The sorry swine had the nerve to call her after all that shit with Lenny's body. She had fired his ass. And she wasn't taking him back as a client without him fronting some seriously big bucks. "I'm having a single malt scotch," she said. "No more bourbon. It's all part of contemplating my new paternity."

Bubba said he didn't get that, but did she hear what he said. Rannie asked just exactly who "her boy" was. She said she had close to twenty "boys" at the moment all facing various terms in correctional institutions. Scumbags. Dirtballs. General degenerates. All categories. And all of them, as far as she could tell, out of control to one degree or another.

Bubba said, "Hootchie-kootchie. The college boy Wonderbread kid. The one you said would shine in my organization. Eager young subcontractor or whatever in hell you once called him. Now he's waving handguns in the face of my staff. I ain't got insurance to cover that sort of thing."

"Well that's a striking motif." Her voice was sarcastic.

Bubba had to pause at that one, not sure what she meant. He said, "I got my share of skewed results at the moment. Cops popping their heads in the door every half hour or so asking about Lenny Womble. Some other stuff I won't go into. In light of our attorney-client relationship, I need you to pull in the boy's leash. Sideline him. That's all."

Rannie wasn't half listening. She had just barely missed being in an auto accident in a pelting down rainstorm. Trying to cross two lanes of traffic, make a left turn. Some cunt in a green something or other flying at her with a big dog actually sitting on her lap. When she saw Rannie in the way she didn't even attempt to brake. Just tried to slip into the other lane and found that blocked with a car. Then she was so busy giving Rannie the finger that she could barely control her car, weaving and careening around. Face contorted with hatred.

Rannie had spun her own car around and chased her for two blocks blowing her horn. Water slicing to either side like the wake of a motorboat. The fool pulled over. Rannie jumped out. The bitch actually had the gall to run her window down and spew out a four-letter vocabulary. Rannie grabbed her by the hair, jerked her up through the window and banged her head against the door about five or six times. Black mongrel dog whining over in the passenger seat afraid to come at her. Like he could smell her animal wrath. It had felt good to do it, but she got soaked again. Now she had frigging Bubba on the phone.

She gritted her teeth and talked slowly. With supreme control. "Completely aside . . . and I'm being generous to put it aside on the shelf . . . but completely aside from Lenny Womble's stiff and lifeless body being found in my house, there is the matter of outstanding arrears on his bill. If we can't adjust that to my satisfaction, then *you* will be dealing with your personal problem, Mister Willie T."

Bubba let out his breath like he was tired. "You know, little lady, I like to be friendly with my staff. Anybody can first-name me, call me Bubba, whatever. But even my close friends don't call me 'Willie T.' Now how about saying you understand that?"

Rannie clutched up. "Little lady" her, would he? Repeat after me like she was some school kid lamebrain. She held it. It was hard, but she held it. Didn't just rip loose with profanity. Instead, she said, "If you were here, you could read my lips. But listen closely instead. If Hootch is a problem, get on with the process of closure. On the other issue, apology is not a word in my vocabulary."

Bubba sighed again. "Well, maybe this is no big thing, but ol' Hootch seems to be telling pretty much anybody who'll listen that he's been in your pants."

*

The roof gutters gurgled with rainwater. The late afternoon sunlight was green colored and thin. Dale sat in her living room while Tamzie showed off her new clothes that Moira had bought her.

"Well they certainly look expensive," said Dale.

Tamzie said she read magazines like *Essence* that tried to justify black people squandering money on clothes as an African trait. "They say Africans are into body adornment. What I say is the red bitch Rannie paid for them in a roundabout way. Money she left laying around. If she got that much, it ain't exactly stealing to spend a little of it. Also I'm on the edge of coming into a legacy of my own."

Dale asked was the diary worth a lot of money? Tamzie said it was.

Dale said, "A whole bunch lot?" Tamzie said, "We talking riches of King Solomon."

At that moment Hootch telephoned and said he wanted the diary. He didn't sound particularly menacing. He sounded drunk. "This is like our one free phone call. You know. Before you get some cute idea to go to the cops. See if you can set me up with a recorder running on the phone. So we need a wide-ranging discussion of issues. Or maybe it's narrow. I want the coon thing of Tamzie's." He laughed. "It's a coon-thang. But if there's other topics you want out on the table, feel free."

Dale scanned the street. People with car phones made her uneasy. The way they might be right outside. She didn't see his jeep. "I'm afraid I have to express some reservations about just giving you anything."

"You're cute as a newborn kitten. I know. You're thinking who can prove ownership? There's no title document. Just something lying around your house. And nobody to say it wasn't Collier's like some other stuff. Am I close?"

"Close."

"So you're figuring you'll go public with it. Tell the press about your big discovery. Get those Smithsonian people back down here. Think I'll be paralyzed. Problem is, you'll never be safe. Spend the rest of your life jumping at small noises at night. How long do you think you can take that kind of pressure? Always looking over your shoulder. Think you see me in a crowd, wonder if I'm following you. I don't see you getting complacent under those circumstances. One day you'll just have to say, oh yeah, that was Hootch's diary wasn't it. I guess I just forgot he left it here one day.

"No, what you're going to do instead is put the diary in a Ziploc refrigerator bag. Gallon size. Two gallon. Whatever gets the job done. Keep the rain off it. Then you get in your car right now and drive straight on up to the place on Daniel Island that was in the news. Yeah, where the gate came from that gave everybody a screaming orgasm. You hand it over, I say thanks, see you around. Give you a farewell squeeze if you want. We both drive off."

"And that's it?"

"Yeah, I'll still speak if we see each other on the street. Nothing's happened between us. And don't think about cops. I know. It sounds like a line in a movie. But consider it. What are you going to tell them? I gave you a lewd phone call. I go 'Who me?' Or maybe you get them up to Dan Island. I'm just a goofball guy up there four-wheeling in the mud with my jeep. I won't even be armed so they got nothing on me."

Dale hung up and told Tamzie what had been said. Asked her if she thought they could just ignore it. Bet he wouldn't do anything.

"No," said Tamzie. "I figure we can't rightly ignore it." Tamzie thought hard on the subject. Shook her head in despair. "After we sell the diary, I'll . . . I'll split the money with you. Right down the middle."

"Why's that?"

"I sold it to Collier. Some lawyer would say I have no claim to it at all. And anyhow, there's other stuff I'm figuring on."

"Such as?"

"I figure we're gone have to kill that white boy."

"I was afraid you'd say that," said Dale.

52.

Rannie walked down Broad Street in the rain, really pissed when a gust of wind turned her umbrella inside-out. She threw the broken mess down in the gutter and walked on getting soaked. As she passed the federal courthouse, the fed Dubiel gave a wolf whistle from the doorway where he was standing.

"Wooo-doggies. You never disappoint. I tell you what." He gave a low rippling laugh. Hands in his pockets jangling change and car keys.

Rannie stopped, hunched against the wet, and stared up at him on the steps. Rain spattered on her head. "Is there something you want to say to me?"

Dubiel flashed a cannibal smile. "Gotcher self a boy toy, huh? What a waste. A dam' show-piece gal like you taking old Hootch by the middle laig, huh?"

She visibly flinched. "What?"

"That's his name, ain't it? Hootch Gibson? Hanger-on to that two-bit gangster Bubba Spainhour. Yeah, they're quoting him all over the cop station. 'She longs for the dong' is one of the more colorful ones. Man, there's some personalized home truths there, ain't they?"

Rannie stared in disbelief. He was virtually dancing with vulgar delight.

The edge of Rannie's face twitched. Her mind spun in a fevered web. Longs for the dong. All over the cop station. Somehow her eyes lacked the old malediction, seemed glazed and empty. "I think I'll get my hair cut," she mumbled almost to herself. "I hear those new multi-length layering techniques are great. Really reduce upkeep."

Fighting to repress the maladies of her soul, Rannie walked on to Legendre Street, then down its familiar length to where it met the Battery. She led a life rich in persecution where Fate cursed her in solemn ritual.

"Everything to do with the male animal is awful," she said aloud. "He farts. He pisses standing up and won't put the toilet seat down afterwards. He smokes cigars. He ruts without love, sympathy, or kindness."

Went up the broad steps of No. 1. The sound of her mother snoring carried out into the front hall where Rannie shook herself off like a wet dog.

Mary Canty Ralston sat slumped down in a chair in the drawing room, legs sprawled apart, arms hanging slack. Turned over whisky glass staining the carpet. The rain must have kept her from the Yacht Club and she hadn't paced her drinks. Passed out early.

Rannie poured a Jim Beam straight in a glass and sat down opposite her mother. She lifted a fat family photo album from a table. Pictures fluttered out from between the pages, lay scattered on the floor like fallen gray leaves. After Rannie was a teenager, her mother had given up the project of sticking them on the pages.

She started at the beginning. Rannie the newborn babe. The old colored woman Mozelle holding her all proud showing off the first Ralston baby. Her mother never changed a diaper. Mozelle did it all. A family tale had her mother holding her out at arm's length, a load in her diapers, screaming for Mozelle. "Something's wrong at the rear end!"

Now here she was in a baby carriage wearing a little bonnet. Then in a stroller with a pink ribbon tied into her hair. On a tricycle scowling at the camera. They'd always make you face into the sun, which made you frown and look angry. Then Collier began to come into the pictures and finally Moira. Collier was crying in one. Wearing little short pants with suspenders. Rannie had just bonked him with a big spoon. Family history had her tormenting Collier a lot. Tried to drop him on his head. Push him under water in the tub.

Rannie turned the page. Each year they all lined up on the steps dressed in new clothes for Easter. She wore white socks turned down and patent leather shoes for her fifth birthday party at a table under a magnolia tree in the garden. Neighbor kids in party hats had been dragged over. Rannie had thrown cake at that one, turned it into a fiasco. Beaten up one of the boys.

Her father in hunting clothes with a bird dog. Her father. Right. Collier Ralston, Sr. Callous, unfeeling sonofabitch. He had never loved her. Never carried her on his shoulders. Never kissed her goodnight in bed. He lived distant and aloof. Always at work. Or always tired and going to bed early. Sleeping in a bedroom separate from his wife. Rannie had created a fantasy of his affection which had taken on a false reality of its own.

Sure Mary Canty lived the life of a selfish bitch. Thought of no one but herself. But why would she rack out with Blake Huston? The only thing Rannie could figure was payoff for blackmail. Something she wanted covered up but didn't have the money for.

Mary Canty never tired of telling everyone she had been a great beauty in her day. Blake probably bought her like a high-priced whore. Stories circulated of South-of-Broad women who did that. Desperately needed money for some frivolity they deemed a necessity. Just happen to drop the news to a man that her husband would be out of town. A man who had been openly lusting after her. Flash a little bedroom-eyed look. Honestly, she was just so forgetful about locking up things. Always leaving back doors open. But she had this little nagging problem. The smallest little teensy-weensy matter of a li'l old bill that needed clearing up.

The old woman snored on. They say you snore like that when you've had a bad stroke. Maybe her mother was dying. Rannie knew she'd never be so lucky. She wondered how hard it would be to press a pillow down over her face and keep it there. If she'd buck and fight it. Wake up and struggle for her life.

Rannie turned some more pages. There she was dressed up for

Cotillion, learning to dance at age eleven. Once a boy deliberately spilled punch on her. She had wanted to be pretty. Wanted to be liked by the boys. Be more than carrot-head Rannie the little shame of the Ralstons. She took him by the hair and shoved his face down in the punch. She wanted to drown him, nearly succeeded in crushing his larynx against the cut glass edge. That had certainly caused a stink.

Despite all the big talk about why hadn't Rannie come out at St. Cecilia's, the Ralstons didn't have the money for it. Her father could barely pay the basic bills. Private schools and liquor bills and maintenance on a mausoleum of a house. Her father. Shit, she kept saying it.

The thing was, Rannie had known the truth growing up. Too many people let her overhear the acid-dripping remarks. Her parents fought about it too many times. Collier Sr. shouting loudly behind closed doors that's no daughter of mine. But she could never figure what was so terrible about her. If her father had to choose between a little tow-headed kid who adored him and a pluperfect frigid spendthrift drunken cunt of a wife—I mean where was the choice really?

There. She had said it again. Her father. She couldn't get rid of the habit. She had been valedictorian of her law class. Gave the graduation speech and talked about how her daddy had been the sole inspiration in her life. Her hero. Her role model. Her *ab initio* inspiration for believing the South Carolina bar the noblest calling among all the professions.

But he didn't deserve the respect. He missed it anyway, being in the men's room drinking out of a pocket flask. Died four years later. Just keeled over of a heart attack in his office. Collier had just confessed a little pregnancy matter with an underage girl that had to be cleared up. The girl wanting a whopping big sum of money to not just get an abortion but restore her sense of virginity as well.

Rannie had wept shamelessly at his funeral. The minister hadn't wanted her to talk, but she just stood up and did an oration. Told about viewing a lawyer daddy through a little girl's eyes. Going down on Broad Street to walk home with him at the end of the day. The part she left out was how she'd reach for his big hand, try to hold it with her little fingers. And he'd always pull away. Say don't chatter so much. Daddy has to think about a jury trial he's going to do.

Rannie scrubbed the heels of her hands in her eyes and started to cry. "Fuck you!" she sobbed. "Fuck all of you. Sure, I'll keep being your meal ticket. No one else will. But Rannie Ralston is an island complete and unto her self."

Right after hanging up with Dale, Hootch checked the TV weather report, watched film of wind and waves lashing the Florida coast. The eye of the storm had come ashore in the Vero Beach area and evacuation warnings were in effect all along the Atlantic coast of the state. Lower South Carolina would continue to get heavy rains.

Hootch switched off the TV in his little carriage house on Dubose Street and sorted through his mail. For some reason he had received the Anheuser-Busch "Family Talk About Drinking" video. The flyer along with it said more than two million copies had been distributed in both English and Spanish language. Its objective was to promote responsible drinking among adults. Hootch threw it in the trash and poured orange juice and vodka into his flask. Yeah right, thought Hootch. Knowing when to say when. That's the trick.

Hootch put on his British army flak vest, body armor made with ballistic nylon. One fine piece of workmanship. Sides overlap so no gaps. Snap down shoulder pouch. Eight-by-five bellows pockets with Velcro closure. Rubber recoil bumpers on shoulders for comfortable rifle shooting. Front flap Velcro closure for split-second removal if he got set on fire or something. He looked at himself in the bathroom mirror, tilted his Boonie hat rakishly. Said to his reflection, "Sure I can always benefit from improvement. But I'm highly focused. Proud of my record in high-quality."

He loaded his Ruger, packed extra ammo clips in his vest, Winchester .22 Power Points. It was a fine weapon. Balanced weight. Not butt-heavy. Ordnance steel color. Micro-click adjustable rear sight in a nice brushed satin-blue finish. He had done Debone at twenty-five yards. Grouped his shots just a hair above center of the dude's heart, but still in a nice tight pattern.

Hootch stepped out of his house. What really jerked him up short and almost made him abort the Dan Island mission was Rannie Ralston sitting in his jeep. She had no rain gear. Just sat there soaked to the skin, red hair plastered to her head.

"Nice day for ducks," she said, face perfectly straight.

Hootch looked up and down Dubose Street, wondering what was going on in his life. Palmettos whipped in the wind and fronds littered the street.

Rannie said, "You know it's weird, I've never in my life ridden in a jeep before. You'd think I would have. All that duck hunting with Daddy. But jeeps weren't really around then. You used an old beat-up station wagon. It did just fine."

Rannie said what she wanted was to actually drive one. Hootch thinking, why not? He'd dump her out just before he got on the interstate. Make her walk home in the rain. Maybe get gang raped by boogers.

Hootch tossed her the keys, climbed in and let her crank the engine. Feeling his buzz evaporating, he took a hit off the flask. Asked Rannie if she wanted a pick-me-up. She said no, she was okay. She clashed the gears and drove off.

Then she said, "You know it's funny, you get a kid who turns violent. Got his parents terrorized so they sleep with a baseball bat. One day he's all filled with ill-directed rage and shoots the father with a .22 rifle. The mother comes in, he drills her. The father's lying there still breathing so the kid puts the gun to his head and finishes him off. Then he takes his younger brother and drowns him in the bathtub. And you know what the relatives and neighbors say? He was a quiet kid, an average student."

Hootch chuckled. "Yeah, they always say that. Everybody's an average student. Or at least never below average. Education has gone all to hell in this country."

"And you know what else? He fell in with the wrong crowd."

"Yeah, they always say that." Hootch drank from the flask again. The juice tasted good while it was still cold. And he liked to chew the orange pulp.

That was when she asked to hold his gun. He looked at her, went say what? She drove with her left hand, had her right one out palm up. Said, you're packing aren't you? He said what's it to you? She said well let me hold that bad boy. An imperative statement. Getting that nasty edge. Your basic Rannie. He said no she couldn't hold it. It was his. She said the fuck you talking about? She was his attorney. He better do what she said. At that moment he decided to pop her along with the other two.

The tide was up and flooding the streets, turning the city into a big overflowing toilet like it always did. Cars were stalled out everywhere. No problem for the Wrangler though with its big tires. Just plough on through leaving a wake behind like a motor boat. They went down

Beaufain and turned at Market onto Meeting Street. Follow it straight, it'd take you up to the I-26 ramp.

Right there in front of Aaron's Deli, a little café with nobody at the outside tables because of the rain, Rannie hit the pedestrian. Man in a suit trying to get across the street up to his thighs in swirling water. Smacked right into him, bounced him on the hood and rolled him off. For one second, his face loomed up against the windshield, his eyes and mouth wide open more in surprise than pain. Just dropped him behind leaving him splashing in the waist deep water. People came out of the Deli, pointing at the jeep. The pedestrian screamed in agony. Rannie kept driving.

"Holy shit!" said Hootch twisted around in the seat looking back. "Did you see him?"

"Yeah, I saw him. And recognized him."

"Who was it?"

"A low-level federal prosecutor. His name's Dubiel."

"Jeezus," said Hootch, still looking back. "Did you mean to hit him?"

"Sure."

"You're a real hard-on," said Hootch, just utterly awed.

"You ever kill a man?" Tamzie asked, both hands on the steering wheel.

The windshield wipers on her blue Chevette squeaked as they fought the heavy rain on the Interstate. They needed new rubber strips on them.

"No. No, I haven't," said Dale. "I've led a sheltered life."

"Me too. I know. You white folks think coloreds all cut and shoot. Some do. Sunday morning papers usually got a story on one. But fact is, they're not too good at it. Only guns on the streets of Charleston are Saturday night specials. Piece'a shit. You can't take one of them to a range and practice up, even if you could afford the ammo. Blow up after you let off a few rounds."

A big truck threw up a tidal wave of water. Tamzie fought the wheel, peering through the foggy windshield, wiping it with the heel of her hand. "One weekend night there's a shoot-out right in the middle of Cannon Street. 'Bout six teenagers firing off guns at each other like a cowboy movie. Empty all they guns. Nobody hit. One dude got a slug in the sole of his tennis shoe. That's it. Big badass gangstas."

"What you're saying is you'd have to be up close to hit someone."

Tamzie said, "Uh-huh. And this white boy can take you from a distance. He done Debone like that."

Dale had phoned Josh Mahoney's room, but no one answered. She had his gun. He had never asked for it back.

Daniel Island was a swirl of mist and muddy road. The car struggled, bouncing in deep holes, scraping the bottom. The abandoned house where Tamzie had spent her summers looked more forlorn than ever.

They sat in the car fogging the glass with their breath, listening for the sound of a car engine. Then they heard the jeep. Dale rolled down her window to see it drive up spraying a rooster tail of mud.

The jeep stopped right beside Dale's door. Rannie and Hootch were in it arguing, Rannie in the driver's seat. Dale thought, What on earth? The rain pelted down. Their voices were loud and angry. Rannie wanted to hold his gun, and Hootch said she couldn't. When he leaned forward a little waterfall of rain came off his hat brim.

Dale saw Hootch reach over and take a handful of red hair, yank Rannie out of the jeep behind him. She wasn't pleased and let him know. "You kotex! You douche bag!" She kicked and hit at him but he forced her head down, tightening his hand still more in her hair.

Hootch brandished a long-barreled pistol.

Dale stepped out of her car. "So much for you coming unarmed," she said. She was trying to be cool, but a big knot held her stomach.

He looked around at an imaginary audience, did a double-take. "Did I say that? I must have lied."

"It's not a good habit to get into."

"Yeah, it's a crying shame. I'm surprised the government don't get involved. Impose regulatory reform and some such shit. But don't worry about insulting me, I still got a residue of good will towards you."

Now Rannie yelled some more, fighting his wrist that held her hair. Hootch did a little dance to keep away from her reach. He grinned at Dale and said okay where's the diary? Dale said she hadn't brought it. She kept her voice casual even though fear was eating right through her.

"You know," said Hootch, "I'm sticking my finger in my ear kind of jiggling it around. I'm wondering if I'm hearing things right. I thought I said I'd be requiring the diary."

Dale shrugged. "I don't have it."

The long barrel of the pistol pointed right at her. "You got a learning disability or something? Or you just don't believe in death?"

Dale said impassively, "Some say dying's just a way to escape unhappiness. How 'bout you, Hootch? You unhappy? Or you have a pretty good life? Trust fund and all that?"

Hootch looked over at the driver's side of the car. Tamzie had gotten out. It diverted his attention momentarily. He looked back at Dale. She held up a fat zip-lock bag with two hands. She said she hadn't brought the diary, but something better. An original Margaret Mitchell manuscript.

Hootch looked confused. If he took hold of it, he'd have to let go of Rannie. He solved the problem by smacking her to the ground with the barrel of his pistol. Viciously. Whack, whack. Two good blows on the back of her skull. She let out a yelp and fell to her knees in the mud.

"Have you ever thought of male modeling?" asked Dale, holding out the bag. "Or maybe acting? I like the way you're playing this scene. Economy of movement, yet very expressive. 'Less is more' kind of technique. Get an agent who does vigorous marketing. Can never tell how far you'd go."

Hootch took the bag warily, cocked his head to study her. He said he had his life in order. Had a bit part in a film now. Maybe he would take a swing through Hollywood. He had heard you could shoot wild pig on Catalina Island. He opened the bag, trying to see what was inside but keep an eye on Dale, check on where Tamzie was moving.

Rannie struggled to her feet. Splashed with yellow mud. And kicked Hootch right square in the balls with her closed-toe pumps. He yelled, doubled up holding his groin. But the pistol pointed up in their faces. He slowly straightened up. It seemed to take two, maybe three seconds.

Tamzie shot him.

It punched him back into the mud right on his ass. He looked dazed sitting there. "Sum-va-bitch," he muttered. The gun still pointed at them.

"He's wearing body armor," Rannie warned.

Tamzie stepped close and shot him just above the eyes, blowing a spray of blood all over the tire of the jeep. His head snapped back like whiplash, then he crumpled over onto his side.

The sound seemed to drift away on the air.

53.

THE BACK OF RANNIE'S HEAD STILL HURT FROM WHERE HOOTCH HAD
SMACKED HER WITH THE GUN. SHE PLANNED ON SUING HIS ESTATE FOR THE
BATTERY. FIND OUT HOW BIG HIS TRUST FUND WAS.

Hootch the outlaw had provided a convenient alibi for running
Dubiel down in the rain. She told the cops Hootch had a gun on her,
wouldn't let her stop. It had given her the only laugh she'd had for the
last week. Hard to tell them with a straight face. Dubiel lying in the
hospital with both knees busted, finally realizing that when you tried
the Ralstons on for size, you better be ready to play hard ball.

Sitting behind her big office desk, she turned to the Region section
of the *Post & Courier*. Old dowager Frannie McAlpin had died, and
a cat hospital in Asheville, N.C. was overjoyed at the ungodly legacy
she had willed it. Some people had more money than good sense. A cat
hospital. Then she saw the color picture of Dale, Moira, and Tamzie
with their arms around each other under the caption *Historical Pay
Dirt*.

The article read, *"It's long been a Charleston custom to value kith
and kin and claim even the most distant relations as cousins. The strong
family ties lend an air of permanence and stability to the chain of human
existence. For a trio of local ladies, this recognition of kinship has been a
long time coming."*

Yes, the Jeromes and the Ralstons were related by blood and Moira was telling the whole world about it. But that was the least of the shock.

The article went on to say that Tamzie Jerome and Dale Ralston had uncovered a diary written by a freed slave named Tremba Jerome. While Tamzie and Dale claimed joint title to the book, it would be touring the public schools of the nation over a five-year period under the auspices of the Smithsonian and the Avery Institutes. The diary's unique quality had experts valuing it at a minimum of $4,000,000. The Getty Museum had already made an offer in that amount, but bidding was expected to drive the price even higher.

And that wasn't all!

Drawing on her young lifetime of historical research, Moira Ralston had joined the illustrious ranks of Charleston authors with a $500,000 hardback, paper, film-rights package. *Macumba Love Slave* was largely the story of blockade running, but a strong subplot detailed the brutality of slavery and the forced intermingling of African and Caucasian blood.

"The story is crisp and hot," Moira said. "It blows the lid off Charleston gentility."

The quote had to have been written by the marketing department of her publisher.

Rannie slapped down the paper. Her sister was a frigging lunatic! She needed to be committed right now today.

Mary Canty Ralston came in wearing an Escada suit from Elza's with earrings that matched the buttons on the suit. She brushed past the secretary and seated herself in the office. She had never been there before to Rannie's recollection. The nude painting momentarily threw her off her stride, but only momentarily.

"I've neglected you I know over the years," she said firmly. "You were always so independent. Couldn't tell you a thing. Would argue with a post. So I vowed to be a modern Dr. Spock parent and let you go your own way. Make your own mistakes. Of which there have been more than a few. All the same, it's high time we did things a little differently."

"You've seen the article," said Rannie.

Mary Canty said she hadn't heard about frontal lobotomies for a long time, but she was sure they still did them. She said either way—lobotomized or not—Moira was pretty much finished with the Junior League.

Mary Canty looked at the painting again, shook her head as though trying to exclude it from her world view. She said, "I think it's time you began thinking about marriage and a family."

Moira's hand moved across the page with fluid ease.

The slim Yemassee Indian girl was naked save for a tiny shaman's charm worn on a cord about her neck. It was carved of a bear canine and represented a fetal human. As she waded through the night-dark stream, her breasts hung in a dynamic equilibrium, pulsing with life.

Her flesh was coppery red in the torch flare. There were no flat color tones in her body, and through this effect, she achieved total brilliance. Watching her, Rhett felt as though he were part of her world and could believe the red man's myths of creation.

When she waded out of the misty wilderness of water, she faced him front-on, the pose that symbolizes the numinous, the sacred object. He stared at her navel set in the belly vessel, the generative center. She came out on the bank. They stood face to face. She looked at him through the lashes of half closed eyelids until he cast down his eyes to stare at the supreme distinction of her breasts and wonder what emotions were imprisoned there.

He wanted to fasten his mouth vehemently against those breasts, mark them with the poetry of a new order. His manhood throbbed with the fierce torture of his need. Longed to penetrate her cleft through its somber guise of curly black hair. Pass down the deep defile through the foliage. And have his heart profoundly touched by the wet magnanimity he would find there.

His eyes encountered her wondrous glance like a silent blessing. Would she receive his manhood with all due form and ceremony? Lawfully indulge it in conjugal rights?

Restless birds called from their nests. A snake splashed from a branch into the water.

She stared off into the night with a dreamy, amused smile. Rhett held his palms toward her breasts as though warming them at a fire.

"Ummmm," Moira went with a deep undertone of sound. She squeezed her thighs together tightly, rubbed them against each other. Her eyes closed, mouth slightly slack in dreamy exaltation. So delicious to press two characters together in meaningful intimacy. It sent a warm *frisson* all through her body. Left her shuddering in lingering throes of quintessential pleasure.

Predictably, her snooping mother had found the dirty magazines. And predictably it had excited her indignation. Moira had simply tossed her head with contempt.

"Are you shocked by their openly sensual poses?" Moira had asked. "The . . . lavish spreads of their limbs? I'm told you once had a . . . a tryst with someone not my father. A tryst of no-holds-barred spontaneity, if you catch my allusion."

"This is a cry for help," Mary Canty had said grimly. "I won't turn a deaf ear to your entreaty."

Moira easily dismissed her mother with a light, trilling laugh. Told her she was irrelevant to the pressing concerns of life.

The old Moira was dead. Now she no longer groveled. She moved with ease, grace, and eloquence. Heads turned when she entered the yacht club. "That's Moira Ralston," voices whispered. "She has a major book contract with a mid-six-figure advance."

Her overbearing sister Rannie certainly couldn't swallow Moira's new sense of self-esteem. The poor thing was extremely tense and irritable lately. Moira had been concerned enough that she had found a new hiding place for the plastic garbage bag of money that had been in the old wardrobe. Rannie's business sense was extremely dubious. She had long had a difficult time making her law business profitable. True, the disappearance of the money would provoke Rannie into some attack of vitriolic rhetoric, but Moira was a provocative person. It's virtually the duty of a writer to engender outbursts from the common masses.

Dear sister Rannie seemed so irrationally violent. Perhaps that blow on the head from the murderous Hunter Gibson had loosened a screw or two. Although Rannie had been unstable since childhood. That Huston blood in her. And as they say, blood will always tell.

Moira gazed about her room with serene pleasure. This was her world in all its ennobling influence. A secure place of Old Chelsea china, Queen Ann silver, a vase with Jacqueminot roses. She returned to her writing. It seemed so easy now.

As he lay strong hands on her shoulders, her throat tapped with the pulse of blood in sultry flesh. She was an unearthly shape full of power and sentiment of high art. An untamed body in a world of enchantment. Flaunting tawny breasts and dun-colored nipples like trappings of fame.

54.

"AT THE POINT IN TIME OF MY APPROACH TO THE SUSPECT, I OBSERVED HIM ATTEMPT TO DISCARD A GLASSINE BAG," DRONED THE UNIFORMED FEMALE COP TESTIFYING IN FRONT OF THE JURY. SHE TALKED WITH THE SAME DEADPAN DELIVERY OF MALE COPS, NO INFLECTION AT ALL.

Outside, the weather remained dismal. The hurricane, reduced to a tropical storm, had cut across Florida and become a hurricane again as it soaked up power from the Gulf and set off roaring towards Mississippi and Louisiana. Power went out for a million Florida residents, and a big gambling ship sank off the coast of Cape Canaveral. Thunderstorms hit throughout the Southeast and rain continued to fall in Charleston.

Rain and late August had brought out the mushroom crop and with it had come a client for Rannie. The dunce was charged with possession of hallucinogenic drugs, to wit mushrooms, for distribution, possession of marijuana for distribution, and three counts of possession of a controlled substance in proximity of a school. What a reject from life. Employment history of about two weeks at McDonald's.

The cop was saying, "At that point in time, I took the suspect into custody and . . ."

Rannie's mind wandered. Just that morning, she had been in another little auto altercation. Some vacuous college boy with his tennis shoes untied had stepped off the pavement right in front of her when she had the light. Flitting around the edge of his drooling mouth lurked the hint of a smirk. He had spent his life testing the limits. Now figured he could just cross whenever and wherever he pleased and because she was a middle class wimp and worried about her insurance premiums, she'd stop for him. So she smacked him. Flipped him right up onto the hood of her Cadillac Seville where he bounced a couple of times before falling onto the pavement. There had been the usual mess with the cops, which had almost made her late to court.

It was funny these little sudden outbursts, turning into pure energy and lashing out at smug idiots. When it was over, she felt cleansed, marvelously coherent and alert. Her hellish sister was driving her up the wall. Moira walking around trying to do an imitation of Edna St. Vincent Millay or Elinor Glyn or somebody. Lisping "I find the creative act deeply fulfilling." Little cunt. She had hidden Lenny Womble's bag of money just to piss Rannie off. When this trial was over, Rannie contemplated binding her to a chair and then tying her teeth one by one to a doorknob. Slam the door until she revealed the hiding place. Then maybe lash her to a board and cast it out into the harbor when the tide was racing out.

The woman cop was still talking about something she thought germane. Rannie sighed wearily. Cops. What did they know? She knew she'd have to get up and do a cross-examination in a minute, but her mind wasn't on it.

Just then her client said loud enough for everybody in the courtroom to hear, "That's just a cop's version of what happened. The other witness ain't able to stand up and relate his side of the story."

Rannie hissed at him to shut his fat mouth before he talked his way into prison.

It didn't faze him. "I'd really like to just kind of interject something here. The fact is, I was, like, present but not really like directly involved, if you read me."

"Will you shut up?" she said louder now. The judge rapped his gavel.

"I can no longer hold my silence. The consequences of this trial are something I'm going to have to deal with for the rest of my life. Nobody really cares about my rights. Where's some public interest watchdog group to investigate how I been railroaded?"

"You're fired," Rannie said abruptly.

Her client looked startled. "I'm fired?"

"You heard me."

"You can't fire me."

She drilled him with a hard glare. "Malarkey. Just watch me. I will never again represent you or your damn persecution complex, you ignorant jerk-off."

The judge banged his gavel. He couldn't believe what was unfolding.

Rannie stopped and looked around at the court, an expression of mock innocence on her face. "Am I being offensive? Well then you must excuse me. I've got a ding-bat, plastic-haired sister with no life experience who now condescends to me. I am the sole support of my avaricious, vindictive mother. She complains and carps in high-decibels like she's dying of exposure in winter. Lives in chronic overdraft status."

She stood up, pushing her chair back. Her voice grew shriller. "Sure lots of people come from haunted pasts. But why do I have to subsidize them? I live in a world of federally subsidized this and that. The political élite tells me I don't pay enough in taxes. Is this rewarding? Or is it distressing? You make the call."

"You on the rag or something?" said her client. "Got PMS?" He meant it seriously.

Rannie was absolutely shimmering with hatred. She tossed red hair out of her eyes. "Am I on the *rag* you ask? No, I am making a business decision to cut my losses and leave. Pay real close attention. It might be an informative introduction to the rest of your life. I know. You're unhappy. You want me to play a tearful violin? You want melodic music? Try Gershwin. Try Rogers and Hammerstein."

The courtroom seemed to have gone into a trance. Even the judge was paralyzed.

"You think you're a badass?" she asked her client. "I think your reputation's exaggerated. To me, you're just one more dickhead. But do I care? Do I ask your political and sexual history? Your depravity-laden lifestyle? No, I just ask you to keep your goddamn mouth shut and let me do my thing. Rannie Ralston puts on one hell of a jury trial. She pulls in the crowds. However, your shrewdly selected attorney is firing you."

She waved her arms in a shooing motion to the jury box. "Suspects, witnesses. You can all go home. Take a powder. Vamoose. Skedaddle." She turned back to her client. "You're saying 'Just like that?' What about my file? Every client is entitled to his file. And just so there will be no disciplinary bar shit on the issue, I am returning your file."

Rannie snapped over her old leather briefcase, lifted it up and dumped the contents out on the table. Money showered down like autumn leaves. A gun clunked onto the table. A Smith & Wesson with a four-inch barrel.

For one horrific second the meaning of the gun sunk in for her. The gun that killed Calvin Whitesides.

Rannie snatched it up and flung it with all her force through the tall window of the courthouse.

55

"IT'S AMERICA," SAID JOSH MAHONEY. "NO SOONER DID THE GUN HIT THE SIDEWALK THAN SOME TEENAGE KID SCOFFED IT UP AND RAN WITH IT."

Dale asked, "What did Rannie have to say on the subject?"

"Fifth Amendment. Nobody knows what to charge her with. Throwing a gun through the court house window?"

They sat up at the bar of *Juleps* with tall glasses of amber beer and a platter with a dozen oysters on a bed of ice, lemon and hot sauce. It was early September and oysters were in.

Dale had just come from the hospital where Collier shared a room with Dubiel, the federal prosecutor, both of them sucker-punched by gratuitous violence. Jazz-Bo Productions had caught Collier being shot from a dozen different camera angles. It was perfect for what they were doing—a Civil War sex spoof. Now they had a rebel officer being blasted by his own men. Although it was more verisimilitude than they were accustomed to, they refused to pay Collier extra. They said he was under contract.

Collier asked if she had any plans. Dale said her biological clock was running and she thought it was time to have a baby. A little creature to cuddle and love. Play peek-a-boo, I see you. Collier said he wanted to put their marriage back together. Dale said she couldn't picture him in the equation.

Dale had learned that Josh had told her something fairly close to the truth about his insurance background. Frequently, art was stolen for the purpose of selling it back to insurance companies at less than the amount they would pay on the theft claim. Josh ran an investigative company—he refused to call them private detectives—kept on retainer by most of the property insurance companies in the U.S. They had more expertise on the subject area of stolen art and artifacts than the FBI. His coming to Charleston was accidental really, sparked by an off-the-wall phone call from Moira Ralston to a rare book dealer in New York steering him to Dale's house.

Dale said, "I guess among other amazements, I'm wondering why you never asked for your gun back."

"I saw it as a link between us. Would always give me an excuse to call you one day."

Dale asked, "But everything we did together was kind of an entrapment?"

Josh slurped an oyster off its shell, nodded. "Ethically, it was right confusing. There are a lot of big gaps in my report. And of course I'm not a cop. Most of their rules don't apply to me. For example, there's no criminal law in South Carolina against secretly taping a conversation you have with someone. You could sue me for invasion of privacy, but that's a civil matter."

"You were wearing a wire that day on the beach? Taping what I said?"

"Yeah. In my swim trunks. I couldn't go in the water. Remember?"

"And that night at my house?"

"No. I was on my own time then. Although it would be nice to have a record of it to play our grandchildren."

Dale gave him a look, head cocked to one side.

Josh Mahoney said he was taking a brief vacation and had rented a beach cottage on Edisto Island. He wanted her to go with him. There was no particular obligation on her part, and he would personally clean any fish she caught.

She looked at him with a thoughtful expression on her face, pretending to be turning it over in her mind, yet knowing she'd go off with him and find where it took her. "Maybe we could give it a try for one weekend," she told him. The rest went unspoken.

"For starters," he said. He smiled like he had known her answer in advance.

Dale smiled back. Men always tried to act in control.

Her life was really straightened out in its own way. When she and Tamzie sold the diary they'd be on easy street. While she was waiting on that, the mortgage on her house on Legendre Street was taken care of by an unexpected infusion of cash.

What she wasn't going to tell Josh was she had found a familiar big green plastic garbage bag in her house that morning and a little note from Moira. Inside the bag was close to $300,000 in wads of hundred dollar bills bound in rubber bands. The note said Moira was purchasing the map of the Mason-Dixon Line—from Dale—as a surprise for Collier when he got out of the hospital. Moira thought he needed cheering up. Anyway, Moira said, the money wasn't from her it was from Rannie. Just some she had left lying around and obviously did not need.

Dale lifted her beer in a kind of salute. "You could be on the money."

Tamzie told the police, "Principally we was all shocked."

They asked what happened exactly, and she said she couldn't

remember much although it had been difficult holding the pistol steady. She said the first slug she give Hootch make him sit down with a bunch to think about. When he determine to keep acting up, being bad with his gun and what all, she give him the second one which made him extremely well behaved.

The cops said the first shot would have been critical except for the body armor. But the second one to the head made it kind of a moot point.

On other fronts, Tamzie got a Saturday phone call from Thaddeus Wyndham saying he had a big surprise for her and to reserve the following day. She knew for sure diamond ring time had arrived.

On a hot Sunday morning, Thaddeus pulled up his dark blue BMW in front of her house and got out wearing a Yankee Civil War uniform with a big brass belt buckle that said US on it. The uniform coat was blue like the car. The pants were lighter. The cap had a little brass 54 on the crown inside a round horn.

Tamzie said, "What the . . .?"

Thaddeus explained he was a member of a reenactment group that played the 54th Massachusetts, one of the colored regiments during the war. It got chopped to mincemeat attacking Battery Wagner over on Morris Island during the siege of Charleston. The movie *Glory* was made about it. Thaddeus wanted her to go with him to a Civil War encampment over on James Island at the site of the battle of Secessionville.

Tamzie nearly said I ain't believing this shit, playing dress-up soldier like the white folks, but kept her mouth shut. She needed to clean up her act now that she was stepping out with a man of culture. But playing dress-up soldier . . . well . . . Tamzie said, okay, but she hoped he had packed plenty of deviled eggs and chicken. He said he had. She allowed she was not into army rations, Civil War or otherwise. He said not to worry. She said how about a folding chair? He had that too. She said she wasn't spending the night in a tent with a bunch of men drinking liquor and carrying on about the Civil War, a subject about which she knew damn-all. He said none of that. He was bringing her back early. He had some special plans for later. Tamzie said okay, she'd go.

When she got in the car, she thought here I am sitting with a stranger. Figuring he could smooth talk her into giving away her half of the diary to the Avery Institute. Or did he figure she'd sell to the Getty and he'd marry her two million dollar share? But then she thought, no, Thaddeus wasn't like that. He had liked her pre-diary. Still, every man had his down-side. Some sat glued to TV watching the Chicago Bulls or the Raiders. Others drank or gambled or shot dope. Tom-cat around with the ladies of the night. A woman always had to reserve a part of herself separate from the man because of the part of him she couldn't understand. Which Tamzie was glad she had done.

What Tamzie didn't tell the cops about was some things she did remember vividly. Right after the shooting, Dale had seemed a little awed. Just stood there staring at the dead white boy with the hole in his head. Rannie had looked in the plastic bag and found it was a book Moira had written. Even with her head half split open, Rannie dumped the pages out of the bag and kicked them all over the muddy ground screaming and cursing like she needed a drink of something alcoholic to calm her down.

While Rannie kept busy with this activity, Tamzie had looked in the back of the jeep and found a fat plastic tube with a screw-on lid. She unscrewed it. Inside was so much money that she closed it again real quick.

When Tamzie was a little girl and used to fidget about in church, her momma Mozelle would always tell her to sit up and act like she had good sense. Ever after, whenever she had a problem, she'd always hear that voice and ask herself what would I do if I had good sense? The answer was pretty plain in this instance.

It was not exactly stealing to take it.